DIAMOND SKY

BY

KEN DOUGLAS & JACK STEWART

A BOOTLEG BOOK

A BOOTLEG BOOK
Published by
Bootleg Press
2431A NE Halsey
Portland, Oregon 97232

Bootleg Books may be purchased for educational, business, or sales promotional use. For information please e-mail, Kelly Irish at: kellyirish@bootlegpress.com.

Bootleg Press is a registered trademark.

ISBN: 0974524697

Cover by Compass Graphics

Printed in the United States of America

November 2003

II

For darling Gina Lynn,
Who sadly left us before her time.

DIAMOND SKY

PROLOGUE

Arlie shivered as he slipped the lower half of his body over the side. The river was cold, flowing with mud, swilling with pollution, as the villagers used the river to take away their refuse. He hung on to the side of a boat hewn out of a thick log and looked over at his older brother, Kennedy, named after the U.S. President slain many years before he was born. Like Arlie, Kennedy was hanging onto the side of a log hewn boat, black air hose in his mouth. And like Arlie, Kennedy was shivering.

Arlie was nine, Kennedy was older by less than a year. Today they became diamond hunters. Times were hard. The regular army had taken everything and left their father dead in the dirt the village called a road. They had a mother and three younger sisters to feed. Many of the villagers said they were too young to claw diamonds from the muddy river bottom, but nobody stepped forward to support them, so it was up to Arlie and Kennedy. They were men now, or would be if they were still alive when the sun came down.

Arlie flashed the thumbs up sign to his brother and received it back. Kennedy tried to give him a brave smile, but Arlie saw the look in his wide brown eyes. Despite the fact that he'd worn his lucky red T-shirt, Kennedy was scared. Then, he slipped below the surface.

CHAPTER ONE

BETH SHANNON BRUSHED ash blonde hair off her forehead, shielding her eyes from the morning sun with a hand. Frank was swimming too far from shore.

She was about to call out to him, to tell him to come in closer, when she heard his daughter screaming.

"What?" Beth looked up.

"I just saw a dead body!" Noelle was bounding down the overgrown stone stairway that went up the island's only hill, then on down to the leeward side. She'd been over there, waiting for Victor, her very married boyfriend.

"What did you say?" Beth felt her heart lurch as Noelle charged toward her.

"A dead woman!" Noelle grabbed Beth's hand, pulled her to her feet. She was panting, out of breath. She was a runner, a swimmer. One look at her told Beth the shortness of breath was caused by fear.

"Where?"

"The beach on the other side."

"I'll call Frank."

"No time, come on!" Noelle started back up the stone stairway, blue-black hair swaying in the wind, and Beth took off after her, pushing branches out of the way as she raced up the steps. At the top, by the first of the two long ago abandoned houses, the only buildings on the small island, Noelle stopped so that Beth could catch up.

"Where is it?"

"Down there." Noelle pointed down the other side of the hill. The sun, high above, beat down through a cloudless sky, but Noelle was shivering in the heat. Her face had lost its tan. She was scared.

"Come on, let's go." Beth started down the stairway through the lush overgrowth.

"It's over there," Noelle said when they reached the bottom. "Careful, it's slippery."

"Over where?"

"Under the pirogue." Noelle pointed to an overturned boat. "When the tide started going out, the body started to slide out from under it. Whoever killed her must have split just before we got here."

"I didn't see anyone leaving," Beth said. They were out at the Five Islands, a small island group about two miles off Trinidad's eastern coast in the Gulf of Paria.

"He could've gone to one of the other islands," Noelle said. "Then beat it toward shore as soon as we pulled the dinghy up on the other side."

"How do you know she was murdered?"

"When you see her, you'll know." Sweat glistened in Noelle's hair.

The pirogue was painted white. It was upside down, bow on the beach, stern in the water. Beth saw the arms, head and torso of a woman floating face up. The body from the waist down was under the pirogue's stern. She was nude. She had been shot between the eyes.

"She was murdered," Noelle said.

"Her face," Beth said. The woman was West Indian and young. Her café-au-lait face was the same shade as the girl Beth had seen Frank with the other day, but if this girl had been beautiful, she wasn't now. She had been severely beaten. The left side of her face was swollen and busted up as if it had been hit with a two-by-four. There were burns on her breasts. Cigarette burns, Beth thought. "And her hands." Several of the girl's fingernails had been pulled out.

"The poor thing." Beth crossed her arms in front of herself to keep from shivering.

"So what do we do?" Noelle said.

"We have to pull her up onto the beach, otherwise the tide's going to take her out to sea," Beth said.

"Let's get to it." Noelle started for the body. The gentle splashing sound her bare feet made as she stepped into the water was like a rifle shot to Beth's soul.

"I don't know if I can." Beth's stomach lurched. She gagged.

"Me either, but I think we have to." Noelle sloshed through the water, grabbed a floating arm. She started dragging it toward the beach. "Come on."

Beth steeled herself and they dragged the body out from under the pirogue and up onto the beach. She dropped a dead arm and studied the corpse.

"My guess, she was raped." Noelle seemed more curious than scared now as she bent over the body. "They raped her, tortured her, then shot her. I didn't think people had guns in Trinidad."

"They're against the law, but people have them," Beth said.

"It didn't matter in her case. She was beyond caring way before they shot her. If she saw the gun, she probably thought it was a blessing." Noelle ran a hand through the dead woman's hair. A gesture that tugged at Beth's heart. Maybe she and Noelle had their problems, but the girl was a caring person, she'd make a good doctor.

"I think I know her," Beth said.

"What?" Noelle turned away from the body.

"Well, I don't exactly know her, or even who she is, but she looks like a woman I saw your father with the other day. I was doing laundry at the Yacht Club and I saw her drive by in a new Mercedes. Frank was riding shotgun."

"That doesn't prove anything," Noelle said.

"Noelle, I'm not trying to prove anything."

"We don't like each other, do we?" Noelle stood up, looked Beth in the eyes.

"We don't have to have this conversation now. Not with her there." Beth looked again at the battered woman.

"We've never talked, you and I. Now might just be the time, before it's too late."

"No, now's not the time. I don't think there will ever be a time."

"I guess I resented you," Noelle said, ignoring Beth's objection, "because I was only thirteen when you married Dad. I thought if you hadn't come along, they might have gotten back together."

"They were divorced," Beth said. "And it's none of your business." She backed away from both the dead woman and Noelle.

"Maybe if you could talk Dad into adopting—"

"Noelle, stop it!" Beth was furious.

"I know Dad doesn't want to raise someone else's child, but if you talked to him—"

"I'd rather not talk about this." Beth balled her fists. "It's private." What could she know? Maybe she had graduated from medical school, but she wasn't the one who had the miscarriage, had her insides ripped out. She wasn't treated like damaged goods by her husband.

"Okay." Noelle raised her hands as if in defeat. "I was just trying to help."

"Then help that poor girl over there and leave me alone." She felt like crying. Christmas season, the holiest time of the year, but all Beth wanted to do was to crawl into a hole somewhere and die. Then she looked up, saw the dead girl and immediately took back the thought.

"Beth, Noelle!"

"Down here, Dad!" Noelle shouted.

Beth turned to see her husband coming down the stone stairway. He looked gorgeous, like a country and western singer, silver hair and beard glistening in the sun. He had a towel over his shoulders.

"Dead woman. Murdered," Noelle said.

Frank stepped past Beth. "Oh, Lord!" He dropped to his knees in the sand, grabbed his chest.

"What's wrong?" Beth said.

"Don't know." He gasped the words. He was in pain, struggling for air.

"Dad!" Noelle went to her father.

"Chest hurts." Frank was still gasping.

"Lie down," Noelle said. His face was red. He was fighting for air.

"No, I'm okay." He started to get up.

"No, Dad!" Noelle held him down. "Something's wrong. We're gonna get you looked at."

"Nonsense, I'm fine. We've got guests coming and I've got a barbeque to set up."

"That can wait," Noelle said.

"I'll get the dinghy," Beth said.

"You better hurry," Noelle said.

Beth bolted up the steps, all thought of the dead woman washed from her mind, all caution gone as her bare feet sought purchase. She pushed a low hanging branch out of the way, another hit her in the face as she flew past. She stumbled, caught herself before she went down. God, please let him be okay.

At the top, she turned. She couldn't see the beach below through the thick growth. She caught a quick breath, turned back and started down toward the pier and the Zodiac tied to it.

A step crumbled under her heel. She grabbed onto a branch, kept her balance, continued on. At the bottom, she ran onto the small pier, jumped into the dinghy, untied the painter, jerked on the starter cord. The fifteen horsepower Evinrude sputtered. She yanked on it again. More sputter.

She pulled the choke, then yanked on the starter cord again. The outboard sprang to life and she pushed in the choke, pulled the shift lever into forward, cranked the throttle wide open.

Water sprayed from the sides as the dinghy went up on a plane. Corbeau birds circled above. The buzzards nested on the next island and were a constant presence at all of the Five Islands, but now their presence chilled Beth.

She hoped Frank was all right. She shuddered, why today, of all days? It was Boxing Day, a holiday inherited from the British. Traditionally, the wealthy gave boxes of foodstuffs or gifts to the hired help the day after Christmas. It was still celebrated in Trinidad and some of the wealthy Trinidadians, who had boats in the yacht club, and the yachties who had been in Trinidad for a long time, celebrated the day by putting their dinghies in the water and coming out to Five Islands for what had become Frank's Traditional Boxing Day Barbecue.

Frank's Flaming Hot Sauce, the awful stuff he soaked his ribs in before putting them on the fire, was becoming quite a legend in Trinidad. Beth hated it, but apparently it delighted the local palette. Trinidadians loved it, and they loved Frank.

She braced herself as she rounded the island. All of a sudden she was bucking a sudden wind reversal and a short chop, water sprayed over the side, but Beth didn't let off the throttle. She tasted salt, as water splashed her face, till she turned again and was headed toward the beach.

Frank was sitting now, Noelle at his side. Beth cut the engine and coasted to shore. Then she was out of the dinghy, splashing in two feet of water. She had a hand on the painter and pulled the Zodiac up on the beach.

"He's a lot better," Noelle said. "But we should get him to a doctor."

"I'm fine," Frank said. "It was just heat stroke."

"What about that?" Beth pointed toward the body.

"We'll call the Coast Guard," Noelle said. "They can deal with it. It's what they get paid for."

Beth grabbed a look at the body. Whoever she was, she wasn't going to get any better. Besides, Frank was a more immediate problem now.

"Come on," Noelle said. "We gotta go."

Beth went to her husband, but he waved her away and got up by himself. She offered a smile, but the look she got back shook her more than the body on the beach. Something was wrong and it had nothing to do with heat stroke. He was obviously in shock, otherwise, why would he have even mentioned the barbecue with that poor woman dead over there. Surely she was more important than Frank's Flaming Hot Sauce. Shock. It had to be.

"Are you okay?" Beth said.

"I'm fine." He took the dinghy painter from her, pulled the front of the Zodiac around toward the sea, dragged it back into the water. Noelle climbed in, Frank jumped in, offered Beth his hand. She took it in a Viking grip and she saw the pain in his eyes as he pulled her aboard.

Beth wanted to drive, but Frank took the seat by the engine, started it and in seconds they were headed toward the Yacht Club. The brisk wind and choppy seas kept their speed slow.

"You sure you're okay?" Beth said.

"I said I was fine!" Frank snapped the words and that didn't make sense, because he never lost his temper.

There were a couple men working on the dock as they approached *Shogun*, the sailing sloop Beth and Frank owned and lived on. One of the men, dark as oil with sweat beading on his forehead, was hammering in new planks. About time, Beth thought, she'd been after the Yacht Club for over a month to replace a couple of rotten boards. The last thing she needed was a broken leg because they gave way on some night when she wasn't paying attention.

The dinghy jerked forward.

"Look out," Noelle yelled.

They were charging toward a finger pier. Beth grabbed onto the safety line as the dinghy ricocheted off a pylon. She saw Noelle, face white, hanging onto the safety line on the other side of the Zodiac.

"Frank!" Beth jerked her eyes toward her husband. He was slumped over the gas tank. The dinghy was spinning out of control. She lunged for the throttle, grabbed it, wound it down, punched the shifter into neutral. In seconds the dinghy was floating in calm water.

Beth grabbed Frank's shoulder, pulled him off the gas tank and rolled him onto his back on the floor of the dinghy.

"He's not breathing!"

"Mouth to mouth," Noelle said.

Beth covered his mouth with her own and blew in. She felt his chest rise.

"Okay, One, two, three, let up," Noelle said. Beth removed her mouth as Noelle pushed on his chest. "Now again." Beth covered her husband's mouth again as Noelle counted.

It seemed to go on forever and it seemed like it was over so fast. Hands at her shoulders pulled her away from her husband. Dark men in white coats went to work on him. Somehow, someone had tied the dinghy to the dock. One of the dock workers was dripping wet. He'd gone in the water, probably to grab the dinghy painter and secure it to the dock so the paramedics could get to Frank.

Noelle helped her from the dinghy. The dock was crowded with yachties, concern covered their faces. Noelle was crying.

Several men helped the paramedics raise Frank to the dock and put him on a stretcher. One of the paramedics was pumping Frank's chest. His face was hidden by an oxygen mask. He was so still. They continued working on him as they wheeled the stretcher down the dock, but Beth knew it was over.

"Come on, I'll take you to the hospital," Alice, a friend who lived on a boat called *Song Bird,* said.

"They won't be taking him to the hospital," Beth said. "He's gone."

"You can't know for sure."

"She's right." Noelle took Beth's hand. "He's gone."

"What are you going to do?" someone said.

"I don't know. I guess I'll have to figure out how to get his body home and plan a funeral."

"I know what to do." Alice gripped Beth's shoulder. She was seventy-something, had been in Trinidad with her husband, Hal, forever and knew how the system worked.

"Thanks, Alice. I don't think I could handle it."

"I'll take care of everything," Alice said.

"He'd want to be buried in California beside his parents," Beth said.

"I thought he was Irish," Alice said.

"He was fifteen when his parents came to America. He never lost the accent. He was proud if it." Beth felt her lower lip quivering, fought to stop it.

Later the police came by the boat and made it official. Noelle sobbed as Beth held her hand. Beth held her own tears.

"I have to call Mom," Noelle said after the policemen left.

"Sure." Beth took a phone card out of her purse.

"Could you come up to the phones with me?"

"Yeah." Beth followed Noelle out of the boat. It was three in the afternoon and hot. She felt eyes on her as they made their way down the pier. Living in a marina was like living in the smallest of towns. Everybody knew everybody and in the boating community, everybody cared about everybody. These people were her friends. They wanted to comfort her, but they didn't know how. Death did that.

At the clubhouse, Noelle put the card into the pay phone and punched buttons. She hung up after a few seconds. "Answer machine," she said. "I can't leave a message."

"Try Mark."

"Yeah, Uncle Mark." Noelle punched out the number. "Machine again." She hung up.

"We'll try later."

"Beth." It was Alice coming up the dock toward the clubhouse. "I've talked to the police. They say since there wasn't any foul play, they don't have to do an autopsy. They're going to release the body to the Ramsaran Funeral Home and Mr. Ramsaran says he'll have Frank ready to transport by tomorrow afternoon. I've got you all booked on the early morning flight to Miami, day after tomorrow, connecting through to L.A."

"Thanks, Alice." All of a sudden Beth was shaking. A few hours ago Frank was alive and she'd silently wished him dead. Now he was dead and she wished with every fiber of her being that he wasn't. In her mind she knew it wasn't her fault. In her heart she wondered if she'd ever be able to forgive herself.

"I still can't believe it," Noelle said.

"We should leave a message on your uncle's machine. He needs to know as soon as possible. I'll do it if you want."

"No, I'll do it." Noelle punched out the number.

Chapter Two

Billy Wolfe jogged toward the pier, the Southern California sun not yet up. He was running in the long narrow park that ran between Ocean Boulevard and the long beach below. He stopped to catch his breath. He'd been running hard, chasing away the demons. Panting, he wiped at the sweat that ringed his brow and was seeping down from around the baseball cap. He licked some from his lip, salty as the sea flavoring the early morning mist.

A car sped by and he turned toward it. A '55 Chevy Nomad, a classic. He sighed. He was at the stairway across from his apartment on the other side of Ocean Boulevard. For a second he thought about taking it down to the beach, but decided against it. It was ten to six, soon it would be light. The Five Fifty-

Niners would be lining up now, waiting for the Lounge to open and that first drink.

A kid was running along the beach with a collie barking on his heels. The kid stopped and threw a tennis ball. The dog took off like a dart. Wolfe smiled as it dove for the ball, catching it on the fly. The collie tumbled onto the sand, lost its footing and rolled, but it came up with the ball. Caught it by the light of the early morning moon.

"The Dodgers could use you, girl." Wolfe fingered the bill of his cap. The dog barked, the kid laughed, then started down the beach with the collie running circles around him. Life, that's what the kid had ahead of him. Wolfe sighed.

"Hey, you!" Wolfe turned to the voice and was bathed in light. He put a hand to his eyes as the spot raked over him. "Hands away from your body."

"Sure, officer." Wolfe spread his arms wide. "Can you lower the spot?"

"Step over to the car." The cop sounded young. He didn't lower the light.

"Anything you say." Wolfe approached the car as the cop got out.

"You wanna move over here and put your hands on the hood."

"I know the drill." Wolfe slapped the car with his hands, spread his legs. It had come to this. The cop frisked him, quick, professional. Cold sweat dripped from Wolfe's armpits. He hadn't shaved in two days, his beard itched, his sweats hadn't been washed in weeks. He understood why the cops were hassling him.

"Got some ID?"

"Back at the apartment."

"What're you doing out?"

"Early morning run."

"And you live where?"

"White apartment building across the street." Wolfe pointed. "You can walk me over and have all the ID you want."

"Leave him. We gotta go," a gravel voice from behind the wheel said. The kid cop jumped into the car and the black-and-white peeled away.

"To protect and to serve." Wolfe shook his head, then jogged across the street. Shoulda known better, but if he hurried, he'd make the first round at the Lounge. He stepped into his apartment and to a ringing telephone.

"Wolfe," he said into the receiver.

"You up?" It was Richards calling from the station. He heard someone yelling something in the background.

"Yeah." Wolfe was sober. His hands weren't shaking yet.

"Dressed?"

"Yeah."

"Look, Billy, I know it's the day after Christmas and you don't officially come back till after the first, but I need you on this one."

"You need me, I'm there," Wolfe said. Richards had stood up for him when he needed the extended leave, had stood by him when he needed a friend and had never said a word about his drinking, like some of the others that had come around hinting about maybe he should think about AA. AA fuck, he wasn't a drunk, something only Richards seemed able to grasp.

"Got two for you at the Ocean View Towers."

"Shit, the Towers," Wolfe said. It was where his son had fallen to his death, where his estranged wife had taken her life.

"Yeah, I know the place has bad memories for you, if you can't handle it, I'll understand," Richards said. "But this is the kind of thing that cries out for you."

"I'm on my way." Wolfe hung up. The homicide, it was all Richards could think of. The location, what it might do to Wolfe, didn't enter into it, couldn't enter into it.

Wolfe pulled off the sweats, climbed into a faded pair of Levi's, slipped on a faded Hawaiian shirt, grabbed a corduroy sportcoat from under a pile of CDs on the sofa, put it on. He reached under a cushion, pulled out his shield, hung it from the breast pocket. Outside he went to the curb and got into his car, a twenty-year-old Chevy Impala. The driver's window was open. The key was in the ignition. Lucky the car was still there.

He glanced at the dashboard clock. Five fifty-seven, three minutes till the Lounge opened her doors. He didn't drink in the apartment. He wasn't a drunk. But he was a regular at the Menopause Lounge, standing in line with a few others every morning at six when she sucked 'em in. He'd become a Five Fifty-Niner, an early morning drinker.

The car started with a rumble. Wolfe made a wide U-turn, stepped on the gas. He pulled off the baseball cap and let the breeze coming in the open window cool his shaved head. A tremor rippled through him, hands shaking on the wheel. The imaginary smell of Dewar's canceled out the real smell of the ocean carried on the wind.

He parked behind a black-and-white, put the cap back on, got out of the car. There was another unit across the street, in front of the Towers, overhead lights flashing. A paramedic rig, a Ford van, was parked in front of the cruiser. Past the cruiser, standing in the circular driveway that lead to the Tower's secured entrance, was a uniform and the doorman. Another uniform was leaning against the hood of the cruiser with the flashing lights.

"What do you have?" Wolfe said as he walked up to the black-and-white at the curb.

"Who wants to know?" It was the kid cop who'd frisked him earlier.

Wolfe tapped his shield with two fingers.

"Why didn't you say something earlier?" the kid said.

"You didn't ask, Quinlan." Wolfe read the name off the tag above the kid cop's pocket.

"You shoulda said something," Quinlan said.

"You wanna cut the lights?"

"Yeah, right." Quinlan reached into the car and the flashing lights went out.

"Lt. Wolfe, Sgt. Washington." The big cop was black, the size of a fullback. He had a hand out. "I didn't recognize you earlier. Sorry."

"It's okay." Wolfe took the hand. "What's the deal?"

"Three dead, nineteenth floor penthouse. Two women and a man. Alvarez and Norton, some uniforms, and the paramedics are up there. It's all I know."

"Been following your exploits on television," Wolfe said.

"I guess I shoulda had a warrant before I knocked that door down."

"You took seven kilos off the street."

"Judge chewed my ass, but it's a consolation."

"You ever thought about homicide?"

"I'm thinking about retirement."

"I know what you mean." Wolfe shook his head. He saw the elevator doors open through the entrance to the Towers. Holly Turner stepped out of the elevator. She looked like she was going to be sick.

That wasn't like her. She was a good paramedic and a friend. They'd dated years ago. It ended amicably, way before he'd met Kerry.

She gave him a nod as he passed her on the way to the elevator. They didn't speak. He preferred to view the site as a virgin and she knew it. He punched the button for the nineteenth floor and closed his eyes. He hadn't worked in a year, if he wasn't ready now, he never would be. The elevator doors opened and he stepped out onto a plush orange carpet and too much activity for six o'clock on a Monday morning.

"I didn't touch a thing," Mike Meredith, Holly's partner said. "Just checked for signs of life. None found." The uniforms and suits were out in the hall.

"Got the word you were on the way, Lieutenant," Sgt. Jesse Alvarez said. He was partnered with the albino, Able Norton. Alvarez wore his black, shoulder length hair in a ponytail. Norton's shocking white hair was almost as long and unbound. They didn't look like cops.

"The apartment with the bodies, that the one with the open door?"

"Yeah," Alvarez said.

"Any of the neighbors hear anything?"

"No sir," one of the uniforms said. "But everybody on the floor's up now."

"Okay, keep checking," Wolfe said.

"Yes, sir."

"Give me a few minutes." Wolfe didn't have to say it. Every cop in Long Beach knew about his need to spend time alone with the dead. To give them respect, Wolfe claimed. To talk to them, others said. Whatever, Wolfe cleared an uncanny amount of homicides, so he got his way.

He inhaled the coppery scent of blood.

The state of the apartment and the two dead women told Wolfe the killers were after something very important to them. He didn't think they found it. Nothing was left untouched, every drawer had been emptied, the contents of cabinets were strewn throughout the apartment. Cushions and pillows had been slit and searched. Nothing had been left to chance.

But it was the women that angered Wolfe. They were nude on the bloody carpet, head to head, arms bound together with gray duct tape so that they looked like some kind of ritual sacrifice. Razor slices under the breasts, disemboweled, throats cut. He saw the knife on the floor next to the women.

He dropped to his knees, took the hand of one of the women with his left, touched the leg of the other with his right. Prayer had been alien to him for a long time, but the many hours he'd spent at his grandfather's side took over and Wolfe recited Kaddish, first in Hebrew, then in English. It took less than a minute and it was painful, but these women deserved the respect.

He spent another silent minute with the dead, eyes closed, touching them and silently promising them that he'd find their killer, that he'd avenge them.

"Bastards," he muttered of the evil ones that had done this. The women had suffered badly before their throats had been cut, his heart cried out to them.

Finished with his prayer and respect, he got off his knees and quickly went through the apartment. It was a two bedroom penthouse. The view of the ocean was breathtaking, even at this hour. The living room was furnished with an expensive white leather sofa, love seat and arm chair. The coffee and end tables were oak and glass. The bedroom was the same, white, oak and glass.

The other bedroom had been converted into an office and it was here that most of the destruction and the searching had taken place. Wolfe went to the phone on a desk, saw the answering machine and the blinking light. He checked for caller ID, didn't find it, then he played the messages. There were several hangups, followed by a woman's voice. She was crying.

"Uncle Mark, you're not home, obviously, so I'm going to have to say this to the machine. Dad had a heart attack. He's dead." He heard crying. "I can't reach Mom." More crying, then, " I'm so sorry to have to say it like this, but Beth and I have got a lot of stuff to do, so I can't keep calling. We're gonna leave for the airport at six in the morning, day after tomorrow. We lay over for a couple of hours in Miami, then we have a direct flight on American to L.A . Bye, I can't talk anymore. So sorry."

If the girl was calling her uncle, then one of the women out there was probably her aunt. Was the other her mother? All of a sudden Wolfe wanted to meet that plane. The girl was catching a flight at six am from somewhere that landed in Miami. Southern Mexico? South America? The Caribbean? Where? What time did it arrive in Miami? Los Angeles? Who was she? Who was Beth? Who were the dead out in the living room?

He picked up the phone and punched Captain Richards' number.

"Homicide, Richards."

"This is Wolfe."

"Is it as bad as I've been told?"

"Yeah. There's gonna be a lot of press over this. These people lived in a penthouse."

"You gonna clear it quick?"

"Probably not."

"Shit."

"You're gonna want to keep Alvarez and Norton on this."

"You work alone. Why now?"

"Alvarez is methodical and Norton's brilliant. Also, I've been away, I'm not a hundred percent. Besides, they caught it."

"You can work with them?"

"I wanna find who did this. I don't need any glory."

"Okay, you got 'em. Just remember, don't let Norton get behind the wheel, especially if you have to go fast. He'll scare the shit out of you."

"I'll remember," Wolfe said.

"Anything else you want?"

"I'll let you know."

"Clear this quick, Wolfe, and I'll love you forever."

"You already love me." Wolfe hung up.

"It's a mess." Wolfe recognized Norton's voice. Apparently he figured Wolfe had been alone in the apartment long enough.

"What do you have?" Wolfe said.

"Guy who lives in the penthouse across the hall saw the door open when he left for work. He came over to say hello, saw what was inside and called 911. He doesn't know the occupants well, but it turns out his wife does. They're Mark and Katherine Skidmore." Norton read from a small notebook. Wolfe wondered where Mark Skidmore was as Norton continued reading, "Lived here for two years. The other woman is the wife's sister, Ann Marie. Not Ann, you have to say both names. Skidmore is part owner of an offshore drilling company in the Caribbean."

"Offshore, like out there?" Wolfe looked toward the three oil islands inside the breakwater, *Grissom*, *Chaffee* and *White*, named for the astronauts killed in the Apollo fire.

"No, not like that. Deep ocean stuff. Ann Marie's ex, Frank Shannon, manages the operation in Trinidad, but he spends every other month in Long Beach."

"Why?" Wolfe said.

"The Skidmores are into a lot of stuff. Oil, real estate, military hardware."

"What was that last one?"

"Knew that would get you," Norton said. "The guy said it was like used jeeps, stuff like that. Shannon gets a good salary, enough to afford a yacht and a pretty young wife. Shannon and Ann Marie have a kid that just graduated med school at USC. Name's Noelle. She spends her Christmas vacation with her father and his wife in Trinidad. We're gonna have to get a hold of her pretty quick, tell her the bad news."

"You learned a lot in a short time," Wolfe said. So the daughter was calling from Trinidad.

"Like I said, Mrs. Skidmore was close to the lady across the hall."

"Listen to this." Wolfe played the message.

"That's interesting," Norton said.

"You get the other woman's address? Ann Marie."

"Sixty-seven Bayshore Drive."

"Let's go." Wolfe started for the door. Alvarez was in the living room. "I'm gonna take Norton down to the place in the Shore. That okay with you? Can you handle everything here?"

"We working together on this one?" Alvarez said.

"Yeah. I'm not up to doing something like this myself. Besides, you and Norton caught it. It's your case, I'm assisting."

"You don't have to lay it on so thick, we all know who's in charge," Alvarez said, "but I appreciate the effort."

"It's your case," Wolfe said. "Most of the time I'll go my own way, like I do, but I'll report to you, not Richards."

"Can we clean up here?" Holly was back. Her face was ashen, but she was going to do her job.

"Yeah," Alvarez said. Then, "Okay, you guys go, I'll handle this end."

"I see you still got the beat up Chevy," Norton said as they approached Wolfe's car.

"It still runs."

"Yeah, they don't make 'em like they used to." Norton opened the door, eased himself into the shotgun seat.

Wolfe started the car, made a U turn and headed for Belmont Shore. He squinted against the sun easing its way up in the east. For a second the orange, reds and pinks of the sunrise took his mind off the double homicide. He inhaled the misty air. Two blocks from the beach and he could still taste the surf on it. Then he was back at work, all senses aware, the imaginary scent of Scotch banished. He didn't want a drink now.

"Right at the bay," Norton said as they approached the east end of the Shore.

"Yeah." Wolfe didn't need the directions. He'd moved to the Shore right after college. It had been home ever since. The farthest he'd lived away was his apartment on Ocean, a quarter mile from Second Street. But he still considered himself a resident. He took a right on Bayshore, parked in front of a two story house overlooking the bay.

"Why don't I go around back, just in case." The homes in the Shore all had garages in back, accessed by an alley. Most had sidewalks between them from the alley to the street in front. Norton walked a house down, took the walkway to the back.

Wolfe waited to give him time to get in place. He didn't think anybody was inside, the occupant was over at the Ocean View Towers, dead. But if Norton wanted to play it safe, it was fine with him.

Wolfe got out of the car, started up toward the front when all of a sudden a blond weightlifter type was on the walkway between the house and the one next door.

"Where'd you come from?" Wolfe asked as he pointed to his shield.

"I live in the apartment in back." The weightlifter pointed to the house next door. "And I don't think I broke any laws last night." The blond had a thick Russian accent. He was dressed in beige Dockers and a short sleeved white shirt, biceps bulging against the sleeves. He had arms that could lift a tank and the looks of a male model.

"Okay," Wolfe said.

"Is there some kind of trouble?"

"Police business." Wolfe turned away from the man, started toward the front porch.

He tried the door. It was locked. He knocked.

"Just a minute," Norton said from inside.

"How'd you get in?" Wolfe said when he opened the door.

"Window on the back door was broken," Norton said.

"What a mess." Wolfe looked around the living room. The place had been tossed as badly as the penthouse at the Towers.

Wolfe went to the phone, careful not to disturb anything and checked the answer machine. Three hangups, no messages and no caller ID. He pushed redial to see who she'd called last, got a recording for the bookstore in the Shore.

"In here," Norton said from a bedroom.

"You got something?" Wolfe followed the sound of his voice to a back bedroom. The wall opposite the double bed was lined with bookcases. The books, mostly medical and textbooks, were strewn all over the bed and floor among countless DVD movies.

"Yeah." Norton handed Wolfe a travel agent's copy of an itinerary and a receipt made out for a round trip ticket to Port of Spain, Trinidad. It was made out in the name Noelle Shannon. "Found this too, I think it slipped out of one of the books. She probably kept it there so Mom wouldn't see it."

He handed Wolfe a three by five photograph. A bronze skinned man with white hair and beard had his arms around two young women, one blonde, one raven-haired. The guy looked like he was in his early fifties, like an aging surfer, a beach bum or a sailor. Wolfe guessed sailor as they were standing in front of a sailboat.

"The girl on the phone, you think," Wolfe said, "with her father and his wife?"

"Be my guess," Norton said.

"Poor kid." Wolfe put the picture in his pocket, then picked up one of the DVDs, 'To Have and Have Not' with Humphery Bogart and Lauren Bacall. He picked up another that looked like she'd made it herself with her computer. She'd designed a nice cover for it, three episodes of the 'Honeymooners,'

Jackie Gleason and Art Carney. She was artistic. He shuffled through the rest of the discs, all black and white movies or TV shows, nothing later than the '50s. "The girl likes the old stuff."

"Who doesn't?" Norton said. Then, "They really did a number here," Norton said. "Think they found what they were looking for?"

"Who knows?" Wolfe sighed. Having had enough of the bedroom, he went to the living room, picked up the phone. He called the station and asked for Captain Richards.

"Got another one for you," Richards said.

"Let me hear it."

"Campus police out at the university found Mark Skidmore."

"Dead?"

"Yeah, in one of the science buildings with his throat cut."

"Anything else?" Wolfe said.

"Isn't that enough? You got anything for me?"

"Maybe. Noelle Shannon, Skidmore's niece and daughter of one of the victims, is bringing her father home from Trinidad in a box." Wolfe looked at the travel agency receipt. "Probably on American Airlines, day after tomorrow. She'll connect through Miami. I need the flight info."

"Think there's a connection?"

"Has to be."

"Give me your number and I'll get right back to you," Richards said. Wolfe read the number off the phone, hung up and told Norton about Skidmore. Ten minutes later the phone rang.

"That was fast," Norton said as Wolfe picked it up.

It was Richards. "There's a Beth and Noelle Shannon gonna be on the American flight from Miami that lands day after tomorrow at 1:00 pm. They're bringing back a coffin."

"Thanks," Wolfe said.

"I'll give you whatever you need on this one, Billy. There's no limit. I just want it cleared."

"What happened?" Wolfe's hand tightened on the receiver.

"The dead guy, Mark Skidmore, was pals with Senator Sterling. He called right after I got the flight info you wanted."

"How'd he find out so quick?"

"He forgot to tell me."

"I'd sure like to know."

"You wanna call him up?"

"Not right now," Wolfe said. "But I'll get around to it."

"Tread lightly, Billy. The man's a ball buster."

"I'll be careful."

"Good, now get over to the university."

"On our way." Wolfe hung up.

A car creeping down the block stopped in the middle of the street as Wolfe and Norton were leaving through the front door. The driver cut into Wolfe with his dark blue eyes.

"What do ya think?" Norton said.

"That guy was coming out from the apartment in back of the house next door when I came up to the front," Wolfe said.

"There is no apartment in back."

The driver smiled at Wolfe, then laid rubber all over the road. In seconds the car was around the corner and gone.

CHAPTER THREE

THE ALARM ON BETH'S WATCH WENT OFF at five in the morning, jarring her from a fitful sleep and a bad dream. She reached over to nudge Frank in the back. Then she realized it had been no dream. He wasn't there. He wasn't ever going to be there again.

She sighed and thought about that dead woman out at the Five Islands. She was West Indian and had the same skin coloring as the woman she'd seen with Frank. Was she the same woman? And if so, what did that mean? Beth closed her eyes, tried to put herself back in the laundry room and tried to picture the woman as Frank got out of the car. She couldn't do it. It couldn't be the same woman. It just couldn't be.

She stared through the overhead hatch and studied the heavens. Someone had brutally tortured and killed that woman. Why? And why did Frank collapse when he saw her? Was it like Noelle said, the shock of seeing the body of a woman tortured to death? Or was it more?

"Oh, Frank," she quietly sobbed, "did you know her? Did you have women here too, right under my nose?" She couldn't help herself, she started to cry.

She closed her eyes over the mist and fought to push all thought from her mind. All was quiet, save for the sound of her beating heart. Then she heard a quiet noise. Wood sliding against wood. She popped her eyes open, but kept still, staring at the heavens. A satellite moved overhead, going from west to east, as bright as any star. She took shallow breaths, heard the sound again.

A drawer being eased open. Someone was on the boat. Not on the boat. In the boat. She strained her ears, searching for another sound, proof it wasn't her imagination. She heard another drawer being opened with a quiet, burglar's touch. A faint tingle of silverware. He was in the galley. She listened for another noise.

Silence.

She didn't move. Didn't breathe.

How could he have gotten on board without her hearing? It was a boat. The floors creaked. A cat would be hard pressed to move through the boat silently, and that was no cat out there looking in her drawers.

She closed her eyes, tried to control her breathing. She mentally counted backwards from ten to one, forcing her mind to clear and it came to her, like lightning from a dark sky. All she had to do was to make a normal getting up sound and whoever was out there would quietly slip away.

She stretched, yawned aloud, hoping it sounded more normal to whoever was out there in the galley than it did to her. She didn't hear any movement from the back of the boat as she stepped out of the double berth. She turned on the light, took steady, even breaths, but she heard nothing.

"Want coffee, Noelle?" she said for the benefit of the man in the galley, because she knew Noelle, asleep in the side cabin, wasn't going to hear, not the way she slept. Time to take the plunge. She opened the cabin door, stepped out, started toward the galley, turning on an overhead light on the way.

There was no one there. Not a sign anyone had been. Probably just a kid looking for money or something to sell. Or maybe no one at all. She'd been jumpy, she had a shock yesterday, maybe she'd imagined the whole thing.

Calm, she told herself. She had more important things to think about. Like what was she going to do now that Frank was gone? She didn't have much money. She'd have to sell the boat.

She'd willingly moved to the Caribbean when Mark had gone into business with his cousins. Frank had been Mark's right hand, after all. But Kathy had stayed in California, refusing to move to the tropics. Besides, she'd said, Mark had business in California and would have to divide his time between the two places. What Beth hadn't counted on was that Frank, too, would be dividing his time. Had she known, she might have stayed in California as well.

The boat had been Frank's dream. To sail the world. But as time passed, he seemed to lose interest in the dream even as she had been making it hers. Now the dream was going up in smoke, she thought, but then she corrected herself. The dream was dead.

She went back to bed, closed her eyes, not to wake again till sunlight streamed in the hatch. She sat up, yawned, stretched, the intruder seemed like a dream now. She was sure the whole thing had been nothing more than an overactive imagination.

In the galley she put on the coffee. She was still wearing the same clothes she'd had on yesterday. She slipped out of them and took a shower while the coffee brewed. The enjoyment she usually felt when the hot water cascaded along her body was absent.

Out of the shower, she slipped on clean shorts and a halter top and went back to the galley. She sipped the strong coffee with closed eyes, picturing Frank and the way he sighed every morning after his first long sip of the hot liquid. Maybe lately they hadn't been getting along, but there had been a time, before the miscarriage, when she'd thought the sun rose and fell in his smile.

She climbed up into the cockpit, leaned back in the seat, inhaled the sea air and sighed as she heard Noelle showering below. Then she turned her attention toward two frigate birds riding the thermals above the swiftly moving clouds.

"It's really something, isn't it? The way the clouds move like that?" Noelle said a few minutes later as she came up into the cockpit with her own cup of coffee. Her blue-black hair was glistening.

"Yeah." Beth took another sip of her coffee and looked up. The air was moving overhead, but it was quiet and still below, waiting on the sun to heat the land and start the early morning breeze. The beginning of the day. Beth's favorite time.

"It's like film sped up," Noelle said.

"I guess you're right."

Something thudded into the side of the boat.

"What was that?" Noelle said.

"Don't know." The image of the dead woman from yesterday flashed across Beth's mind.

Noelle stepped out of the cockpit and looked over the side. "It's a waterlogged coconut."

"You know what I was thinking?" Beth said as Noelle sat back down beside her.

"Yeah," Noelle said. "You were thinking about that girl out at Five Islands. You know we never told anybody about her."

"We're gonna have to tell the police."

"I've been thinking about that, Beth, and I don't think that's a very good idea. I think we should forget all about her. Tomorrow we should get on that plane with Dad's body and fly out of Trinidad." The fierce look in Noelle's green eyes startled Beth.

"What about responsibility?" Beth said.

"Being a witness here can be a fatal disease."

"What are you talking about?"

"Witnesses here turn up dead," Noelle said. "Don't you read the local papers?"

"No."

"Well I do. There was a case just last week where a killer was let go. Two people saw him stab somebody to death over a drug deal, but they had to drop the charges before it came to trial, because both witnesses had been murdered. The killer was on television the other day saying justice was served. His attorney said the state never had a case and they knew it. There is no justice here. If you get involved, you could wind up as dead as that woman with the beat up face."

"Not for just reporting it."

"You wanna take that chance? Besides, if we go to the cops, there's no way we're gonna be allowed to leave the country tomorrow. We'll have to stay forever."

"If everybody felt like that, the criminals would rule the world."

"Wake up, Beth. They do."

"That's not a very pretty picture you're painting."

"The truth is often ugly." Noelle took her hand, squeezed. "Believe me, this is something you don't want to get involved in. I've only been here a little over a week and I know that. You've been here for three years, you know it, too. You just don't want to admit it."

"All right, you win. We mind our business and we let the police do their job." Beth didn't like it, but she had to admit Noelle made sense. "But I wanna go back out there one more time."

"What?"

"Something about that woman startled your father. Remember, he had that attack on the beach as soon as he saw the body."

"That was just because he was shocked at seeing a dead woman with a hole in her head."

"I'm going out there and look around. I can't just sit here all day and wait for tomorrow." Beth didn't know for sure if that was the woman she'd seen with Frank, probably shouldn't know, not now, but she couldn't let it rest.

"We gotta pack."

"I'm going." Beth set her cup down and stood up.

"Now?"

"Now." Beth climbed down into the dinghy, squeezed the priming bulge in the fuel hose.

"You're really going back out there?" Noelle looked down at Beth in the Zodiac.

"The water's flat calm. I can be there and back in less than an hour," Beth said.

"Then I'm going too." Noelle stepped over the lifelines, climbed down. "You know the buzzards have probably been at the body. It was pretty bad yesterday, it'll be worse today."

Beth shivered when she thought of the corbeau birds ripping at the dead flesh. Then she jerked on the starter cord. The engine roared to life and she backed off the gas.

With flat seas the fifteen horsepower Evinrude had the Zodiac up on a plane, sizzling over the ocean, like a magic carpet flying over Arabia. Ten minutes later Beth cut the engine as they approached the brick dinghy dock. It was covered in green and easily missed. The rubber boat brushed the dock. Noelle jumped out with the painter in hand. She tied it to a low hanging branch, then Beth stepped out of the dinghy.

"This way." Noelle led Beth up the steps, pushing bush and branch aside, clearing the way.

A few corbeau birds took to the air without protest as the women moved up the hill, letting the thermals carry them skyward until most were dots circling below the huge, fast moving clouds. Beth looked up at the vultures, so beautiful and graceful in flight, so awkward and ugly on foot.

They reached the top of the island and passed the first abandoned house. Beth stopped to catch her breath. Noelle walked over to the building that had been beaten down by years of neglect, wind and rain.

"Careful," Beth said as Noelle stepped up on the concrete porch.

"I was inside yesterday," she said. Then she screamed and jumped back as several bats flew out of the dark living room, most of them missing her face by inches.

"You can go in now." Beth fought back a laugh.

"They weren't here yesterday," Noelle said.

Beth turned away from the abandoned house, glanced at the water tank, cracked and overgrown, and the other house, then started down the hill, making her way on the path to the beach below. The beach was small, but it would have been an excellent place for children to play.

"Move over, slowpoke." Noelle scooted by Beth, moving so fast she tripped and slipped off the steps, sliding part way down the hill before she caught herself, laughing. Then she stopped. "It seems wrong," she said, getting her footing and getting back to her feet, "laughing so soon after Dad—" She let the sentence dangle.

"It's okay," Beth said. "He wouldn't have minded. He'd want you to keep laughing." Beth started down the hill, heading toward the small beach. She wiped sweat off her forehead, hair out of her eyes.

"Oh my God." Noelle stopped her descent down the stone steps, grabbed onto Beth's arm. "It's horrible."

"Oh no." Beth fought the vomit. Black corbeau birds were swarming around the body, ripping and pulling at the flesh.

"There's hundreds of them," Noelle said.

"Yeah." Beth thought of the first time, three years ago, when she and Frank had come out here on *Shogun* for a few days of peace and quiet. She remembered the pelicans coming in from the sea, arriving only minutes ahead of the corbeaus that came from the mainland. Hundreds of birds, vultures and pelicans, circling the island in graceful flight. The birds settled on the trees as the sun went down, the corbeaus and pelicans sharing the same branches. She remembered Frank saying the world would be a lot better place if only people got along as well as birds.

"Guess I should have left her under that boat," Noelle said.

"Guess so." Beth turned away from the sight below and started back up the steps.

"Why'd you really want to come out here?" Noelle grabbed onto Beth's shoulder from behind, gently squeezed.

Beth stopped, turned. They were just out of sight of the corbeau birds feasting on the body below. "I didn't get a good look at her before. I mean, not so that I'd know her. I was afraid I might have, now I guess I'll never know."

"Surely if you knew her, you would've recognized her."

"Not if I'd only seen here once and from a distance." Beth looked away from Noelle.

"You mean like if she was with Dad? That's what you mean, isn't it?"

"Yeah."

"You knew about Long Beach? About Janey?"

"I knew he had somebody there, not who. That I could live with, at least I told myself I could, but he was starting to run around here. It was too much. I was thinking about leaving him."

"Really?"

"I know, it sounds pretty bad, me saying that, under the circumstances, but it was like he was rubbing my nose in it. I felt like if I didn't do something, people would be laughing at me behind my back. That's a hard thing to live with."

"Dad loved you." Noelle put her hands on Beth's shoulders, looked her in the eyes.

"I know."

"It's just that in some ways he never grew up. He was Peter Pan with a roving eye, but he loved you. You have to believe that."

"I do. He was a bastard, but he was my bastard. I loved him, but I couldn't have gone on living with him much longer."

"You should have confronted him. He'd've cut it out if he thought he'd lose you."

"So is she going to miss him, this Janey in California?"

"She loved him."

"I don't think I want to hear anymore." Beth reached up, took Noelle's hands off her shoulders and started back up the steps.

"Wait," Noelle said. "Someone turned that boat over, tied it to that tree, then stuffed that woman under it so the tide wouldn't wash her away. It doesn't make any sense unless they wanted someone to find her. And if she was somebody Dad was seeing, then I think maybe that someone is us."

"Us?"

"A lot of people knew we were coming out here. If she was a friend of Dad's, well, that's pretty scary when you think about it. Maybe that's why he had that attack, because he knew her, because it was one of his girlfriends."

"You're right, that's pretty scary." Beth didn't like the way Noelle said it, like he had lots of girls on the side. She didn't want to think that and she didn't want to think that Frank knew the girl down on that beach. "Listen, dinghy coming."

Noelle started back down toward the small beach, the corbeau birds and the dead girl.

"Stop!" Beth called out.

Noelle stopped. "Why? I just want to see who it is."

"We might not want them to see us."

"Oh."

"Hurry. Quick. And keep down." Beth bent low and started back up the hill, moving fast. Noelle scurried after her, keeping low too. They were in the foliage and closing on the two abandoned houses when the dinghy rounded the bend.

"Do you think it's the killer?" Noelle asked, panting.

"Don't know. Let's wait and see."

They moved behind the house closest to the beach and waited as the sound of the dinghy grew louder, till the chugging motor seemed like a jackhammer thundering along Beth's spine. She wiped sweat from her forehead. They huddled out of sight as the motor slowed, then went into neutral and finally died when its operator hit the kill switch.

"They're at the beach," Noelle whispered.

"Jesus Christ," a man yelled out. "Get them outta here."

"He must mean the vultures," Noelle said.

"Yeah," Beth said.

"Get away, get away," a man below screamed. The thickly accented voice traveled well in the still morning air.

"Brody," Beth whispered. "He runs Corbeau Yacht Services for Sammy Skidmore, where we got most of the work done on the boat. You know, the guy you see every morning on the windsurfer outside the breakwater."

"The one who hisses your name?" Noelle said.

"Yeah." Beth hated the reptilian way Brody called her Lizzy with the sibilant sounds hissing through the gap between his front teeth.

"Let's get the fuck out of here." The second voice carried an American accent up the hill.

"Harris," Beth whispered, quieter than before. "He's Brody's shadow, the guy with the military haircut."

"I don't know him."

"The guy that's always wearing army fatigues and telling stories about Vietnam."

"Oh yeah, the guy with the knife."

"That's him," Beth said. Harris wore a Bowie knife in a scabbard tied to his leg, the way gunslingers used to tie down their holsters.

Noelle nodded, then she coughed.

"I heard something up there," Brody said from below.

Beth clenched Noelle's hand, pulled her into the abandoned house.

They went into the musty darkness, through a small living room full of decaying furniture, into a dark windowless hall and on into a bedroom with boarded windows. The bedroom was almost as dark as the hallway, but a few faint slivers of light snuck in through the cracks in the boards.

Noelle pointed up and Beth followed her finger with her eyes, saw that a part of the ceiling across the room had fallen down over the years. Light peeked in through a crack in the roof. She heard the rustling sound of small animals in the rafters above. Noelle tugged on her shoulder, pointed to the floor on the other side of the room. It was covered in guano.

"Bats," she whispered.

"Quiet," Beth whispered back.

"I don't like bats."

"They'll hear you."

"The bats or the men?"

"Both."

The men were getting closer, coming up the hill. Beth wondered what Brody would do if they searched the house and they were discovered.

"This whole thing's a waste of effort," Harris said. "He wasn't a thief."

"He had some diamonds in Long Beach," Brody said. Beth didn't have a clue as to what they were talking about.

"Says who?" Harris said. "That Jeweler? My money says Sammy Skidmore took 'em. He ripped 'em off and paid the jeweler to fix it so someone else got the blame." Harris sounded like he was right outside the door now.

Noelle took Beth's hand again, squeezed it as they heard the two men outside. Beth squeezed back as one of the bats dropped from the ceiling and fluttered toward the door. Another, then another dropped and followed the first toward the light.

"Shit!" she heard Harris scream. He had been as startled by the bats as Noelle had been earlier.

"Just bats. Harmless," Brody said. "So now we know what you heard, let's go."

Beth heard them making their way back down toward the beach. She sighed.

"It's a good thing they didn't come up on the same side of the island we did or they'd have seen the dinghy."

"A darn good thing, I think," Noelle said. Then, "What was that talk about diamonds?"

"I don't know, their business not ours. Your father's gone now and we've got our own problems."

"Yeah," Noelle said. "Besides, it's good they've got something else to worry about besides us."

They stayed in the dark house till they heard the sound of Brody's dinghy speeding toward Chaguaramas Bay and Corbeau Yacht Services.

"We should go now," Noelle said.

"You don't have to say that again." Beth led Noelle out of the house. They made their way down the other side of the hill, to where their own dinghy was waiting.

Beth, in the lead, clambered over the dinghy dock. She hopped in the Zodiac. Noelle jumped in after her and landed badly. She slipped and started to go down, but Beth caught her.

"Easy," she said.

"Thanks." Noelle untied the painter as Beth pulled the starter cord.

"That was close," Beth said as they motored into the Yacht Club. A shudder ran through her. A woman was dead, murdered, and it looked like Brody had something to do with it, or at the very least, knew about it. What kind of man was he? What kind of man had Frank invited to their table on numerous occasions?

"Dad was wrong about him," Noelle said.

"He sure was."

"What are we going to do now?" Noelle wiped sweat off her brow with the back of her hand, then ran the hand through her hair.

"We're going to do just what you said. We're going to get on that plane tomorrow and take your father home as if none of this ever happened."

CHAPTER FOUR

THE SMELL OF MUSTARD and onions attacked Wolfe as he entered the airport. He stopped. The hot dog vendor was wearing a candy cane striped shirt. He was black, maybe old enough to drive, and he was making hot dogs for a group of nuns faster than a human should be able to.

Wolfe got in line.

"We got time for this?" Norton checked his watch.

"Way the Flash there makes the dogs, no problem."

"Plane's already on the ground."

"Chill out," the kid said to Norton. "You gonna be on time."

"Yeah, chill out." Wolfe laughed, but he cut it short when he thought about why he was at the airport.

"He the man?" The kid said as soon as the nuns were leaving.

"Him?" Wolfe looked toward Norton. "Yeah, how can you tell?"

"I got a nose for guns. He's wearing a piece clipped to the belt under the shirt."

"Yeah, we're the heat," Norton said. "So why don't you fix my buddy up so we can get on our way."

"Nobody says heat anymore," Wolfe said.

"Yeah?"

"Not for about twenty or thirty years."

"Shit, and I thought I was cool."

"So, you a witness or something?" the kid said to Wolfe. "He taking you somewhere for a trial?"

"No. Give me one with mustard and onions."

"Mustard and onions." The kid grabbed a bun. "So why you hanging out with the man, you don't have to?"

"I'm a cop, too."

"Get outta here." The kid grabbed some tongs, fished a dog out of a well of hot water. He dropped it on the bun, squirted on the mustard, added the onions. "If you the man, how come you don't carry a piece?" He handed Wolfe the dog.

"Keep the change." Wolfe handed him a five.

"S'posed to carry a gun if you're a cop."

"That's what they say." Wolfe nodded, turned and started toward the airport concourse and the x-ray machines.

"So, how come you're not carrying?" Norton showed his shield and stepped around the scanner.

"Just don't feel like it anymore." Wolfe walked on through.

"Captain Richards know you don't carry?"

"Yeah."

"Who else?"

"You. That kid back there."

"You're a cop."

"Not that kind, not anymore." Wolfe stopped. The concourse was stuffed with people in motion. "I didn't want to come back. They kept after me. I told Richards if he wants me, he gets me without a gun. If it bothers you, I'll take a walk. You and Alvarez can have the case."

"Alvarez is gonna be tied up for a couple of days. His wife's having a kid."

"I didn't know."

"You've been away."

"Yeah, I have."

"So I guess it's you and me till she delivers," Norton said. "Then we'll see where we go from there."

"Fair enough, we'll see how it goes."

"Deal." Norton offered his hand Wolfe shook it.

"Okay." Wolfe started back up the concourse. He loved the way emotion ran through the airport. The joy of meeting. The sadness of departure. The wonder of discovery. The fear of the unknown. It was all here, dancing on the faces, shivering through the hustling bodies.

"Nervous?" Wolfe said.

"Yeah. I've done this a couple of times. Once a kid shot during a liquor store robbery. The other time I had to tell a wife her husband was killed on the freeway. He was going too fast. Tire blew and he rolled. End of Story. They were hard, but not like this."

"It's gonna be tough." Wolfe watched a long legged blonde as she left the gate. For a second he thought it might be the woman in the picture, but it wasn't.

"Darling," she said as she fell into the arms of a man in Levi Dockers and a sweat shirt with cut off sleeves.

The man turned as if he felt Wolfe's eyes on him. "Hey, Lt. Wolfe. It's been awhile."

"I didn't recognize you at first, Nick. The pretty woman stole my eyes away." Wolfe smiled at the woman.

"You two know each other?" Norton said.

"Yeah, this is Nick Nesbitt."

"From KYTV, that Nick Nesbitt?" Norton said.

"None other," Nick said. "So what brings you to the airport? Coming, going, or meeting someone?"

"Working on a case. You gonna introduce me?"

"Connie Jakome, this is Billy Wolfe, the real Colombo."

"Thanks for the compliment, Nick." Then to the woman. "You're gonna have to watch this man. It's hard to keep a secret when he's around."

"That's because he's the best newsman this town has ever seen," Connie said.

"It's good to see you back, Billy," Nick said.

"It's good to be back."

"You need anything you let me know."

"I will," Wolfe said. Nesbitt linked his arm around Connie's waist and they left.

"He's the guy that used to be married to, you know, the dead woman they found in that alley a year back," Norton said as soon as they were out of earshot. "Seems he got over his tragedy quicker than you did yours."

"He's not a bad guy. Besides, a year is a long time."

"He rakes us over the coals every chance he gets."

"Yeah, well we're cops and he's a liberal reporter, what do you expect?"

"A little fairness."

"Get real." Wolfe laughed.

"There they are," Norton said.

Wolfe turned as the two women came out the gate. "Mrs. Shannon," he said as they approached.

"You know me?" The blonde stopped, pierced him with blue eyes that were alert, inquisitive.

"No, we haven't met."

"Are you from the funeral home?" She tried a smile.

"No. I'm a police officer. My name's William Wolfe. This is my partner, Able Norton. I've got some bad news for you and I don't know any other way to say it, except straight out."

"What?" She said and Wolfe saw the two women link hands in a tight hold.

"Maybe you should sit down."

"Just say it officer." No smile now.

"Day before yesterday, at the Ocean View Towers, there was a double homicide."

"Oh, God." The color faded from Noelle Shannon's face.

"Don't say it." Beth Shannon clenched her free hand into a fist.

"Katherine Skidmore and Ann Marie Shannon were found murdered. Mark Skidmore was found later that morning out at the university, dead. I'm sorry. I know how you feel."

"How could you?" Beth Shannon's eyes turned cold. The tears froze.

"Anger's okay," Wolfe said. "But try not to blame us. It's our job to find the men that did it."

"I'm not angry." Beth cut him with a look. "And there's no way you can know how I feel. So don't pretend you do."

"Other people have lost loved ones," Wolfe said.

"He's right, Beth," Noelle said. "Look at that girl over by the telephones. Her name's Nina. I met her when we changed planes in Miami. She just lost her child."

"Jesus." Wolfe felt the depression surround him like a shroud.

"You okay, Billy?" Norton said.

"Yeah." He looked at the girl. She looked Latin. She was so young. His heart went out to her.

"I want to go home," Noelle Shannon said, bringing Wolfe's mind back to the matter at hand.

"I'm sorry, but you can't," Norton said. "Ann Marie Shannon's home, your home, was ransacked. We believe by whoever killed your mother."

"Beth!" Noelle looked like she was about to burst into tears. "What are we gonna do? Where are we gonna go?"

"We'll get a hotel, but first we have to take care of your father."

"That's being taken care of," Wolfe said. "The medical examiner is picking up your husband's body."

"What for?" If she wasn't angry before, she was now. Her eyes glazed poison.

"We have to perform an autopsy."

"No, you have no right. Frank died of natural causes in a foreign country."

"I'm sorry. His body's here now. He died on the same day his ex-wife and in-laws were murdered. That defies coincidence."

"It was a heart attack. I was there."

"Again, I'm sorry."

"You can't cut him up."

"It's out of my hands, ma'am. Yours too."

"But—"

"He's right, Beth," Noelle said. "He's just doing his job. Dad would want them to find whoever did these things. And if he was murdered, he'd want them to catch his killer."

"But he wasn't murdered."

"You can't know that for sure, ma'am," Wolfe said.

"He might be right," Noelle brushed some tears away.

"They want to cut him," Beth said.

"Dad doesn't care anymore," Noelle said. "We have to let them do this."

"What do you want us to do?" Beth's shoulder sagged. The anger seemed to melt away.

"Officers are going through Mark Skidmore's business records. Others are questioning friends and neighbors. So far we haven't come up with a reason for someone to do this horrible thing." Wolfe looked into Beth's eyes. "We were hoping you could help."

"Excuse me," Beth said. "But can we talk about this later?"

"Later's okay," Wolfe said. Then, "Look, you've no place to stay. I've got a friend who lives on Ocean Boulevard, close to the Shore. He's on vacation. You can stay there." Wolfe saw Norton's eyes open wide, but he ignored them. "The place has everything you'd need."

"I think we'd feel more comfortable at a hotel," Beth said.

"No, you wouldn't. You'd be crammed into a small room, bumping into tourists and businessmen every time you turned around. I'm the one responsible for closing off the house on Bayshore Drive, so let me make it up to you."

"You're sure your friend won't mind?"

"Positive." Wolfe tried a smile. "Now, let's get your bags."

"You think that's wise, them staying with you?" Norton said as the women were collecting their suitcases.

"I'll get a hotel."

"Forget it, you can stay with me. I got plenty of room."

"Thanks."

"Wait till you've tried my cooking before you thank me." Norton laughed. Then, "So you really think there's a connection between this guy's heart attack and these murders?"

"Has to be. I don't believe in coincidence when it comes to homicide."

"What if they don't find anything at the autopsy?"

"She said she was there when her husband had the heart attack, so I'm guessing they probably won't, but it's still connected. We gotta find out how."

"I don't get it."

"I don't either, not yet."

Forty minutes later Wolfe pulled up to the curb in front of his apartment.

"We'll get the bags." He said as Norton hopped out of the car.

He got out and opened the trunk, was about to grab a bag when he felt Beth Shannon grip his shoulder. He stepped back, let Norton get the bags.

"I can help," Noelle Shannon pulled the carry-on bags out.

"The door's not locked," Wolfe said.

"Frank and I have a condo in Huntington Beach," Beth Shannon said as soon as Norton and Noelle were out of earshot. "He uses it on his trips back to

California. I haven't been back in three years, but it was where I'd planned on staying. You might want to check it out."

"So how come you're not staying there now?"

"Noelle can't go home."

"She couldn't stay at your condo?"

"I don't know if she would have. It was mine before I married her father. We're not close, Noelle and I, but under the circumstances I can't leave her alone."

"You got an address for this condo?"

"Seven Eleven Pacific Coast Highway. It's those places on the sand, by the Huntington Beach Pier."

"I know where it is."

"Number 113, next to the pool, you can't miss it." She fished a key out of her purse and handed it to him.

"What's taking you, Beth?" Noelle had the door open and Norton was hauling the bags inside.

"Just a second," Beth said. Then to Wolfe, "Like I said, I haven't been back in a long time. I don't know who knows about the condo, but if Mark's and Ann Marie's apartments were searched, then maybe the Huntington Beach place was too."

"What makes you think so?"

"I live on a boat in Trinidad. Someone came aboard yesterday. I heard him looking through my drawers when I woke up."

"Who?"

"I don't know. I made some noise and he left."

"Did you tell anyone, like the police?"

"No, I thought it was kids."

"I'll check out the condo for you."

"Thanks."

Norton got in the car as Wolfe started it. "They seem like nice people."

"We're going out Pacific Coast Highway to Huntington Beach. Frank Shannon had a place at the Ocean Front Condos."

Wolfe turned into the flow of traffic, heading east on Ocean, toward Second Street and then the Pacific Coast Highway. Fifteen minutes later they pulled up in front of the security gate at Ocean Front. Wolfe parked in the red.

"Can't park there." A security guard scowled as they got out of the car. He was a military looking man in his late twenties. He wore a starched white guard uniform with a forty-five automatic holstered on a spit shined black leather belt. A pair of handcuffs and a night stick dangled from the belt. A cop wanna be.

"Police." Wolfe flashed his shield. The scowl turned to a smile. Wolfe knew how to handle men like this. "We need your help." That got them every time.

"Sure, anything." The guard beamed.

"You got an occupant here, a Frank Shannon. You noticed anything unusual about him?"

"One thirteen? Nice guy, older, not much trouble, but like all the rest, he thinks I work for him. Wants me to keep an eye out for his place, because he's gone a lot."

"Why do you think that is?" Wolfe knew the answer, but he wanted to know if the guard did.

"Dunno."

"Think he might be using it as a hidy hole? In case we get too close, or in case one of his drug deals goes bad?"

"I knew there was something funny about him," the guard said.

"You know, Larry, can I call you Larry?" Wolfe read the name tag over the guard's breast pocket.

"Sure."

"The problem with people like him is the American Civil Liberties Union."

"I hate them," the guard said.

"They want to undo every bust we make."

"They're all socialists," the guard said.

"And they cause us nothing but problems. No matter how dirty someone is, we can never get a warrant."

"I couldn't let you in even if I wanted, I don't have the key."

"I do." Wolfe held up a key. "All I have to do now is get by you."

"What are we waiting for?" The guard grabbed the key. "This way." Wolfe and Norton followed him around a walkway that led down to the beach and around to the ocean-front side of the apartments. "There it is. Next to the pool," the guard shouted back over his shoulder. In his enthusiasm he was almost running. He was ten yards ahead of the detectives.

"You coulda told him the truth," Norton said.

"If I'd said murder, he might have called his boss, you know, done things by the book. We woulda had to wait. This way we get in right away and we don't need a warrant."

"I get your drift," Norton said. Then, "What a deal, the ocean in front and the pool on the side."

The guard was waiting at the door to the condo. "How do you want to do this?" Sweat poured off his forehead.

"How about you unlock the door and we go in," Wolfe said.

"I can go in, too?"

"Sure," Wolfe said.

The guard's hands were shaking as he opened the door.

A 767 roared overhead, taking off from John Wayne Airport, but even the noise from its two oversized jet engines couldn't drown out the sound of the huge noise that exploded from the center of Frank Shannon's apartment. The sound took the security guard's face apart as it lifted him up and threw him back, away from the door.

A wave crashed, masking the sound of the second round as it smashed into Norton, spinning him around like a ballerina and sending him crashing into Wolfe. Their heads collided, skin and skulls smashed together as they fell to the sidewalk, their struggles drowned out by the jet and the sea.

Wolfe was conscious of Norton's body on top of him. He had a massive pain in his ribs where Norton's holstered pistol dug into his side, more pain in his shoulder where his left arm was wrenched behind his back, still more pain in the right side of his face where the back of Norton's head had smashed into him, and he had a pain in his heart, because he hadn't been ready for this. He had been so stupid.

He tried to push Norton off, halfway succeeded as he saw the blue barrel of a forty-five automatic come slicing through the bright sky and then everything went dark.

CHAPTER FIVE

BETH STOOD IN THE DOORWAY and watched as Noelle got in Robbie's old VW Beetle. Wolfe not ten minutes gone and she'd called her cousin. Beth couldn't blame her, Robbie had lost both his parents too. What a cruel coincidence. And what a sad way to see Robbie after so long. A silent handshake. A solemn nod of the head. Dark eyes full of suffering. He was a handsome boy and grief seemed to make him better looking, as if that were possible.

Robbie was the same age as Noelle. They'd been like brother and sister growing up, inseparable. So it was only natural that she'd call him when she got back, but still Beth wondered why she hadn't called Mike Cole, her fiancé. For her first two days in Trinidad he was all she could talk about. But then she met Victor and all of a sudden it was Victor this and

Victor that. Now that Noelle was back home, would she forget him?

Beth eased the door closed. Still holding the doorknob, she leaned her head against the wall. She thought about asking Noelle to introduce her to Janey. Someone had to tell her about Frank. Would it be wrong for the wife to tell the mistress about her lover's death? "Yeah, it would," Beth muttered. She'd leave it to Noelle.

She moved away from the door, padded over the carpet to a couch and sat. She never wore shoes in a house if she could help it. There was a remote on a chrome and glass coffee table. She picked it up, clicked on the television. CNN came on, a woman in a starchy looking suit. Her lips were moving, but there was no sound. The volume was off. Beth studied the control, was about to turn up the sound, but punched the off button instead. There was nothing in the world she cared about right now. The planet could rotate without her, the country would survive if Beth Shannon wasn't tuned into the latest developments.

She put the remote back where she'd found it, sighed and was about to close her eyes when she noticed the blank walls. Bare white, no pictures. She looked around the living room. New furniture, but inexpensive, kind of a dull plaid on the sofa and matching chairs. She felt the fabric, it smelled new. She rubbed a hand over it, bland furniture.

The front window was open, the curtains were moving in the breeze. She hadn't opened it. Lt. Wolfe hadn't either. Whoever lived here didn't keep the place locked up. The apartment fronted onto Ocean Boulevard and the beach beyond, maybe the owner felt the traffic and the beachgoers across the street were enough security. She shook her head. She'd been away three years, not a lifetime. The owner was careless, anybody could walk in and ransack the place and nobody would notice.

The sofa sat back against the wall, facing the flapping curtain. The end tables were made of maple in an early American design that didn't go with the rest of the furniture. The sofa and chairs looked like refuges from a dentist's office.

There were no knickknacks or bric-a-brac. No trophies, no Hummels. The place didn't look like an apartment, more like a hotel room. No, not even that. Hotels put some kind of art on the walls, they tried to look homey, tried to imitate someplace someone might live. This place made no effort to look homey or lived in. It was antiseptic.

She pushed herself to her feet, picked up the suitcases and lugged them to the bedroom. She'd never learned to travel light and Noelle's bag was even heavier than hers. She hefted Noelle's up onto the bed on the left, then hers onto the other one. Twin beds? It was a one bedroom apartment. Did two people live here? Roommates sharing the same bedroom. What kind of roommates?

She flopped down on the bed, sitting with her back to the suitcase, feet on the floor and stared into the floor to ceiling mirrors that covered the sliding closet doors. She avoided looking at herself, instead taking in the bare walls reflected back at her.

The bedspreads were white chenille. Very old, very plain, but nice, like might be found in a kid's bedroom thirty years ago. The carpet was white, walls too. There were no headboards on the beds, nothing in the room with color, save her and the suitcases. It was a ghost room. White on white. Creepy.

Curious, she pushed herself up from the bed and opened sliding doors to reveal an empty closet. No clothes, no shoes, no nothing. She stepped into the closet, ran a finger on the top shelf. Not even any dust.

Nobody lived here.

But Lt. Wolfe had said it was a friend's apartment, that his friend was out of town. She left the closet and looked around the bedroom. There was no bureau or chest of drawers, no nightstands, no lamps by the bedside to read by. No hint that anybody lived here or ever had.

In the bathroom she found towels hanging from the towel rack opposite the sink. Two towels, one blue, one pink. A washcloth was draped over each towel, one green, one white. Not a matching set. She felt one of the towels, clean, but well used, as if they'd come from a thrift store and were hung in the ghost white bathroom as an afterthought.

There was an unused bar of soap in the stainless soap dish that hung above the sink. Beth pulled the shower curtain aside. Again she found an unused bar of soap in a soap dish, but no shampoo or cream rinse. She flashed on Lt. Wolfe's shaved head. Was this his place? No, the policeman had said it belonged to a friend. But what kind of person took everything he owned with him when he traveled?

More curious, Beth padded into the kitchen. Another white room where she found plastic dishes, cheap flatware, frozen dinners and lots of canned stew. It was scary, this apartment.

A ringing sound. Beth jumped, then sighed. It was the doorbell. She went to the door and opened it.

"Billy, oh excuse me, I didn't know he had company." The speaker was a woman with more gray in her hair than black, flashing green eyes and perfect teeth, fleshy lips with red lipstick, heavy in the bust, waist struggling against belted jeans and winning the battle. She was wearing a bright orange blouse, tucked into the jeans and sandals that showed off her painted toenails.

"Who's Billy?"

"Billy Wolfe, you mean you don't know?"

"Lt. Wolfe?" Beth said. "You mean the policeman?"

"You don't know? What are you doing here?" The woman's lips turned into kind of a pouty frown, but she was holding something in her left hand that smelled heavenly. Beth hadn't eaten since Trinidad. She'd been too caught up in grief to touch any of the food on the planes or during the layover in Miami.

"I'm hungry," Beth said.

"What?"

"I'm sorry. I haven't eaten in a while, that smells good. What is it?"

"Just tuna casserole. What are you doing here?"

"You already asked that. Lt. Wolfe told me the place belonged to a friend. My husband just died. I brought his body back for burial."

"What?" The woman's free hand went to her breast. For a second Beth thought she was in pain. "Say again."

"I'm hungry," Beth said.

"Not that, the other."

"I'm sorry, how stupid. My husband died. But I really am hungry. I haven't eaten since yesterday morning."

"You poor thing." The woman brushed past Beth and headed for the kitchen. "You sure can't eat anything Billy left lying around. I swear if I didn't feed him, he'd starve himself to death. You know, sometimes I think that's his plan." She pulled two of the plastic plates from the cupboard, set them on the table and started dumping the casserole out on them.

"So how do you know Billy?" She pulled forks out of a drawer, dropped them next to the plates.

"I don't." Beth sat, took a bite of the casserole.

"My name's Anita. Yours?"

"Beth." She took another bite.

"You want something to drink with that?" Anita went to the fridge and pulled out a couple Cokes. "Billy doesn't drink at home, so this is as strong as it gets around here."

"That's fine," Beth said.

"So what's the deal? You gonna tell me about it?" Anita had a full smile and Beth thought she'd be a woman easy to like.

"What deal?"

"You know, why you're here."

"I told you, my husband died." Then she opened up and told her the whole story. How she'd come back with Frank's body only to find his ex-wife, her sister and his brother-in-law all murdered and Lt. Billy Wolfe the investigating officer.

"And you mean you're all alone? Your step-daughter just left you here?"

"I don't really think of her as my step-daughter. I'm not that much older than she is."

"She just left you?"

"We don't get along all that well."

"So."

"I don't mind, really."

"But to be alone in this place. Brrr." Anita crossed her arms in front of herself and pretended to shiver.

"It is kind of spooky."

"Tell me about it," Anita said. "Billy's been living here for about a year. He hasn't brought a thing from his house in the Shore. Just walked away. Rented this place and furnished it with stuff from an office supply house."

"I thought it looked like a dentist's office."

"They use the same stuff, but somehow Billy's made it look even more sterile. Sometimes I wonder if he did it on purpose, but I know he didn't. He just made some phone calls and some people moved the junk in. I guess you've seen those twin beds. It's like he's making a statement, like he's saying he's never gonna sleep with anyone ever again."

"What are you talking about?"

"Billy and his wife Kerry had some problems. She moved out, to the Ocean View Towers down the street. She hadn't even been there long enough to get her stuff out of the house when my grandson climbed up on the balcony and fell to his death. Kerry took her own life before the police arrived."

"Your grandson?"

"I'm Billy's mother."

"I'm so sorry."

"Thank God Billy didn't discover Kerry's body. At least he was spared that. She shot herself. He never went back to their home in the Shore. Maybe I could understand that if she died there, but she didn't."

"It's where they lived their lives together," Beth said. "He must have loved her very much."

"He did."

"He tried to sympathize with me at the airport. I told him he couldn't know how I feel. He knows." Beth remembered the ashen look on his face when Noelle pointed out Nina at the airport, the girl that had lost her child.

"He knows, but he won't hold what you said against you. He's not like that."

"All of a sudden I feel like I need a little air."

"Yeah, this place can get to you. Come on, we'll take a walk on the beach." Anita got up from the table.

In the living room, Beth dumped her backpack out on the coffee table, took out an empty plastic bottle and went back to the kitchen to fill it. Then she slung the pack over her shoulder. "Okay, I'm ready."

"There's drinking fountains at the beach," Anita said.

"It's a habit. I walk a lot in Trinidad. The tropical sun can lay you out pretty quick if you don't have plenty of water. I always carry it."

Anita went to the door. "I don't have a key, he never locks it, nothing to steal."

"He gave me one." Beth locked the door on the way out. Maybe Lt. Wolfe didn't have anything to steal, but she did.

Outside a cool breeze tossed her hair around. The sun was straight overhead and bright as it ever was in the Caribbean. Beth shielded her eyes against it and almost went back into the apartment for her sunglasses, would have, but Anita had already started toward the street. On the other side of the road a group of kids were playing soccer on a grassy park. Beyond the park Beth squinted and saw the sea. Cars whizzed by, but Anita held up her hand and as if by magic, they stopped.

"Come on." Anita led the way across. It had been three years since Beth had been in California. How nice it was, cars stopping for pedestrians. They went around the soccer game, crossed through the parkway and came to the rail by the steps down to the beach.

Beth sighed as she took in the panorama. The beach that had given Long Beach it's name stretched from downtown on her right, all the way to Seal Beach, almost past her line of sight. Holiday makers were out and having fun, there was an air of festivity in the atmosphere.

"Let's go walk the bike trail for a bit," Anita said.

"Okay." Beth started down the steps to the trail that ran along the beach sand, keeping to the ocean side of the two lane concrete path. It was Saturday and unseasonably hot for December, which explained why the beach was so crowded. Children frolicked in the waves, small because of the breakwater. Older kids tossed Frisbees or basked in the sun. Families had picnic lunches out.

"So," Anita said, "do you think your husband's heart attack had anything to do with his family here getting killed?" The question surprised Beth.

"No, not for an instant."

"It's an awful coincidence."

"That's what your son said, but it's not possible."

"The more you know my son, the more you'll know anything is possible."

"We were on a small island off of Trinidad, four thousand miles away. There can't be a connection."

"I thought Trinidad was an island," Anita said.

"It is, but it's a big one, over a million people live there. We were at these small islands about a mile off the east coast."

"How small?"

"The one we were on had two abandoned houses on it. Maybe there might have been room for a third, but no more."

"That's small."

"Yeah."

"So what caused the attack?"

"What do you mean?" Beth said.

"What was he doing when it happened?"

"That's what I thought you meant. It's kind of sticky, because we didn't tell the police on account of what happened to Frank."

"Didn't tell them what?"

"We'd just found a dead body. Frank saw it, grabbed his chest and keeled over. But after a bit he seemed all right. He even drove the dinghy back to the Yacht Club. We were almost at our boat when he had the attack that killed him. We tried CPR, but it was no use."

"You found a dead body? Like a dead person?"

"Yeah."

"And you don't think something a little more than coincidence it going on?"

"No. It was the shock of seeing the murdered girl that caused Frank's heart attack."

"Murdered. Like, somebody killed her?"

"Yeah, someone beat her, raped her, then shot her between the eyes."

"And you didn't tell the cops?" Anita grabbed her breasts again and again it looked to Beth as if she were in pain. "What are you, crazy?"

"I wanted to, but Noelle convinced me not to."

"My God, why not?"

"Trinidad's a third world country. Witnesses have a way of disappearing, or getting themselves killed. Besides, even if the police were able to protect us, we'd have been stuck in Trinidad forever."

"You wouldn't have been a witness. You'd just be the people that found the body."

"There's more. We went back out to the island the next day. Other people came and we hid. They had something to do with the murder. I'm sure of it."

"Then you have to tell Billy. You're here now. You're safe."

"But I'm going back."

"Billy will keep you out of it."

"He's a policeman."

"I'm going to tell you about my boy. When you think there's nobody you can go to for help, you'd be wrong, because Billy will be there. He won't let any harm come to you and he'll find out who killed that girl that caused your husband's heart attack as sure as he'll find whoever killed your family. You can count on it."

"Trinidad's a little out of his jurisdiction."

"Doesn't make any difference. He let you stay in his house. That means he's taken you on. Nothing stops Billy when he's after a killer. When it comes to murder he's a law unto himself."

"You make him sound a little frightening."

"I don't mean to. Billy's been down himself lately, as I've said. The fact that he's let you and your step-daughter into his life is a good thing. He's been dead too long, it'll be good to have him back."

"He doesn't even know me."

"Maybe you just came along at the right time, I don't know, but I do know that if you let Billy help you, you'll be helping him."

"Okay, you've convinced me. I'll tell him."

"Hey look out!" someone behind Beth said.

"Outta the way!" Another voice, hard sounding.

Something slammed into her back. Beth grabbed onto Anita to keep from falling. Pain bolted up her arm as the backpack was ripped from her shoulder. She grabbed out for it, but all of a sudden a kid on Rollerblades smashed into Anita and now they were both falling, hands grabbing air, but there was nothing for them to hold onto and they went down with the Rollerblader on top of them.

"Sorry." The kid was up in an instant, balancing on the Rollerblades as if he'd been born with them on his feet. He held a hand out for Beth. She grabbed it and the kid pulled her to her feet. Then he helped Anita up. "Are you okay?" The kid couldn't be more than fourteen or fifteen. A worried frown seemed out of place on what seemed a normally happy face.

"Yeah." Beth dusted sand off herself.

"Lucky I ran into you, otherwise you'd have fallen on the concrete and maybe hurt yourself." Now the kid was smiling.

"Lucky my ass." Anita shook sand off as she talked. "If you'd have watched where you were going, we wouldn't have fallen at all."

"Someone grabbed my backpack," Beth said.

"What?" Anita said.

"Someone grabbed my backpack. That's why I fell."

"See it's not my fault," the kid said.

"Who? Where is he?" Anita said.

There was a crowd gathering now. People were looking, but no one seemed to be running away.

"I didn't see," Beth said. "But he didn't get anything, there was only the water in it."

"It'd piss me off, someone stole my pack," the kid said.

"Wash your mouth out," Anita said.

"That's what my mom says." The kid smiled larger.

"Come on, we should get back," Anita said. "This is another one of those coincidences you should tell Billy about." Anita grabbed her hand and pulled her away from the crowd and the bike trail. Beth felt like a child as Anita towed her over the sand toward the steps up to the street, but she didn't protest.

"Okay, I can keep up." She tugged her hand away from Anita, but she didn't slow down. Something was going on.

Mark's and Ann Marie's places had been searched after they'd been murdered. Someone had been on the boat, going through the drawers. Now this.

CHAPTER SIX

WOLFE CAME AWAKE as if from a floating dream. Eyes open for a fraction of a second, then closed again. The light hurt. His mouth felt like it was stuffed with steel wool. His throat was raw, his lips dry. His ribs ached. It was better to be unconscious and that's where he tried to go.

"Can you hear me, Wolfe?"

It was a voice he recognized. He tried to will it away, tried to close his mind against it. But in his heart he knew it was no use. He knew the man. He wasn't going away, not until he got what he wanted.

"I know you're awake. Don't try and shit me."

"Why would I do that?" Wolfe forced his eyes open, only to squint against the light.

"You might think I'd leave if I thought you were asleep. I won't."

"Head hurts." Wolfe raised a hand to his forehead. "What are you doing here, Captain?" Dwight Mitchell wasn't a Captain of Detectives. Not anymore. Now he was a California State Senator.

"Nasty bump where you were clobbered." Mitchell was wearing a dark three piece suit, with the jacket unbuttoned, a watch chain hanging out of the vest pocket. Give him a black hat and he'd look like Wyatt Earp. He looked more like a cop now than he ever did when he was a cop.

"Where am I?" Wolfe whispered through a sore throat.

"You're in the hospital, where'd you think?" Mitchell had an edge to his voice, hard and sharp.

"What's got your goat?"

"You."

"Need water," Wolfe rasped.

"Are you okay?" Mitchell's voice softened. A note of concern?

"Need water."

"Can you talk?"

"Not without water."

"What did you think you were doing?" Not so concerned now.

"Come on Captain," Wolfe said. "No water, no talk."

"Can you sit up by yourself?" Mitchell picked up a glass and filled it from a picture.

"I think so." Wolfe struggled into a sitting position. His head screamed. He took the offered water, gulped it down.

"How long have I been here?" he said after he'd emptied the glass.

"Almost twenty-four hours."

"That long?" The room was blurred. He shifted around so he could face Mitchell.

"Easy, you'll hurt yourself," Mitchell said.

"Yeah." Wolfe hadn't noticed the needle in his left hand, nor the IV drip.

"You wanna tell me what you were up to at Shannon's apartment?"

"Just following up a lead."

"When I assigned you to a case I always forgot about it." Dwight Mitchell brushed baby-fine hair out of his eyes. "You're like a bulldog, once you get your teeth into something you worry it until it gives up what you want."

Wolfe grunted. Dwight Mitchell had always been an enigma. With his long hair, blue eyes and baby face he looked more like a twenty-five year old college student than the California State Senator that he was. He jogged five miles a day, but he smoked. He scorned religion, but believed in God. He loathed politicians, but was one himself. He wore his views, about everything from government to sport, on his sleeve, but nobody could get into his head.

"Why don't you just tell me what you want?" Wolfe said.

"You got a security guard killed and your partner shot up." That edge was back in Mitchell's voice, cutting, even sharper than before.

"How is he?"

"He'll live, no thanks to you. What in the world did you think you were doing?"

Wolfe didn't answer.

"You went to Shannon's without a warrant, without backup, without even wearing a piece and you got an innocent man killed, your partner shot and put yourself out of commission."

"I didn't expect anyone to be there." Wolfe knew it was lame as soon as he said it.

"Tell it to the dead guard's family."

"What's your interest in this?" Wolfe said.

"What?" Mitchell pulled a pack of Marlboros out of an inside coat pocket.

"You heard me. Why do you care? You're not a cop anymore."

"I was asked to take a look into it as a favor, because of my expertise."

"Who asked?"

"What?"

"Who asked you?"

"Not everything is your business, Wolfe."

"What's Senator Sterling's interest in this?"

"Who said anything about Senator Sterling?" Mitchell tapped a cigarette out of the pack, stuck it between his lips.

"I did, and everything's my business when it involves a homicide I'm working."

"Okay, Sterling called me." Now Mitchell was about to flick his Bic.

"No smoking," Wolfe said. "Hospital."

"Fuck you." Mitchell fired up the Marlboro.

"Yeah, fuck me. You want Sterling's backing for Congress? You wanna go to Washington, that the deal, meet the president, what?"

"Watch your mouth, Wolfe."

"You do a favor for Sterling and he campaigns for you. Is that what you're doing here?"

"Why would you even ask something like that?"

"Because I can't think of any other reason you'd stick your nose into an active homicide investigation."

"All right, no need to get hot under the collar. Sterling was tight with the Skidmores. He wants their killers caught and asked me to help."

"There's nothing you can do, except maybe read him my reports."

"I'd like to do more than that. I'd like to be in on the investigation."

"Sorry, Dwight. That's not the way I work. I can't have someone breathing down my neck. You know that."

"That's what I thought you'd say, but as long as I'm here I'd like your take on this thing."

"I don't have a take on it. I haven't even started."

The room was quiet as they stared at each other, then Mitchell said, "I don't believe you. You're holding back."

"I don't know anything, Dwight. Not yet."

"That's your final word?"

"It is."

"Well, I have a final word for you. When you check out of here go straight to your captain. I have a feeling he'll want your badge. And you better find your piece, cuz he's gonna want that too."

"I don't think you got that kind of pull anymore, Dwight."

"I think you'll find I do." Mitchell spun around and in an instant was out the door.

"Hey, no smoking. It's a hospital," a male voice said from outside Wolfe's room.

"Fuck you," Mitchell answered back. He may have gone to the state senate, but he hadn't changed.

Wolfe, still sitting, put Mitchell out of his mind and studied the room. Two beds, a nightstand next to each one. The second bed was vacant. Television mounted on the wall, two chairs for visitors, two dinner trays on wheels, one bathroom and one closet. A bare bones hospital room.

He found the buzzer, was about to push it when Norton wheeled himself into the room. "Hey, partner, how ya doing?" His right leg was in a cast below the knee.

"I've been better. You?"

Norton thumped the cast. He was wearing a white hospital robe and his complexion was whiter than usual, if that was possible. "Bullet nicked the tibia, I'll be right as rain in a few weeks. They offered me paid leave, like you, but I turned 'em down. Alvarez' wife had the kid last night. Eight pound, four ounce baby boy. He's pleased like his shit don't stink, but he'll back at work tomorrow. We'll clear this, don't you worry."

"What leave?"

"You know, like a paid vacation."

"I'm not taking it."

"Either way, you're off the case. Orders from on high."

"I'll talk to Richards."

"Way on high, higher than Richards. You're off the case and on paid leave."

"I've been on leave for the last year."

"Ah, but it wasn't paid. Richards said to stay low for a few days and he'd see what he could do."

"Like hell."

"Why'd I think that's what you were going to say?"

"Because that's what you'd say. So tell me, what do you got?"

"Shannon had a girlfriend."

"No kidding."

"Alvarez knocked on some doors over at the Ocean Front Condos. Neighbor said a tall redhead stays with him whenever he's in town."

"You got a name for this girlfriend?"

"Yeah, I do, Janey Seward."

"The Weather Girl?"

"Big eyes, big hair, big tits and no brains. Janey Seward the KYTV Weather Girl. I called the station, used your name to get through to your buddy, Nick Nesbitt. He said she's on vacation, visiting her folks in Montana."

"You get an address?"

"Of course, 3712 El Jardin."

Wolfe pushed the call button. Seconds later a young nurse with a wide smile, showing plenty of teeth, entered the room. She looked Vietnamese, but she sounded American when she said, "Who said you could sit up?"

"Can you take this thing out?" Wolfe held up the hand with the IV needle in it.

"No way, doctor's orders." She tried a frown, but even a frown on her pretty face looked like a smile. The name tag on her blouse said Darlene Theo.

"I'm checking out." Wolfe wondered what kind of name Theo was.

"But you can't."

"Sure I can. It's a hospital, not a jail. Now, can you take it out?" He was still holding up his hand.

"Sure, but I won't. I'm gonna call a doctor."

"Come on, Darlene, either you take it out or I will."

She turned and started for the door as Wolfe pulled off the tape holding the needle. "All right, stop, I'll do it." She came back to his bedside and took it out. "Now, I'm getting a doctor."

"And I'm getting dressed." Wolfe lowered the safety bar, started to climb out of the bed. His head throbbed, the room started churning, like he was inside a spinning dryer, looking out. He steadied himself, turned his gaze back to Norton, took a deep breath, and lay back down.

"What?" Darlene said.

"Nothing, just a slight dizzy spell," Wolfe lied. He'd been concussed before, he knew the symptoms. He also knew he should stay in the hospital for a couple days. He turned his head to the right. Nothing. He turned left and the spinning started. He faced back to Norton.

"I'm getting a doctor," Darlene said.

"I'm fine."

"You're not fooling me." She left, presumably to get the doctor.

Wolfe sat up. He looked left again. The room started to spin. He faced forward. It stopped.

"Give it a couple of hours," Norton said. "It'll give Alvarez time to get your car out of Impound. He can pick you up and take you over to Seward's."

"What's my car doing in Impound?"

"You parked in the red in front of Shannon's apartment, remember? Huntington Beach towed it to Orange County Impound."

"For parking in the red?"

"Not exactly."

"What?"

"Someone busted the light on Main, plowed into it in the middle of the night. Witness said it was a pickup, but he didn't see who was driving. Impound says it should drive okay, but the whole left side's never gonna be the same."

"Swell." Wolfe slumped back on the bed. "I've had that car since I was eighteen years old."

"You're kidding?" Norton said. "Nobody keeps a car that long."

"Twenty years, my mother gave it to me for graduating high school. Then she packed me off to college in Hawaii and drove it herself for four years." He laughed.

"Sorry."

"Yeah," Wolfe said. The car was the only thing he'd kept. Now he was truly cut off from the past. "I'll live without it. Maybe I'll get something sporty. One of those Miatas or a vintage 'Vette."

"Maybe it's not that bad."

Wolfe closed his eyes.

"The Shannon funeral is at three. Alvarez will take you. You'll have time to stop by the Weather Girl's on the way."

Norton spun the chair around and wheeled away.

Wolfe kept his eyes closed. He'd lied to Norton. If the Chevy still drove, he'd get it fixed, no matter what the cost. A shiver shimmied through him. He couldn't imagine life without it. He'd eschewed everything except that. It was his one link to Kerry. He never drove without imagining her beside him, dirty blonde hair blowing in the breeze, Christmas green eyes sparkling in the sun.

Stupid, he told himself, that old Chevy was just a thing.

He shivered again. No it wasn't. It was his youth, his life, his marriage, everything. He was nobody without it. It was dumb. It belied common sense. But it was true. Nobody. Nothing.

He slept.

"Hey, Wolfe." A hand on his shoulder. A quick shake. It was Alvarez.

Wolfe opened his eyes. Everything was blurred.

"You okay?"

"Yeah." The fog cleared.

"You see my car?" It was on his mind when he drifted off. It was still there.

"I saw it."

"Well?"

"They were wrong when they said you could drive it. It's totaled."

"Aw fuck." Now he was truly alone. Nothing left to hold the memories. He was a blank.

"I brought you some clothes." Alvarez held up a grip.

"What was wrong with the ones I had?"

"Covered in blood. Norton's."

"Check the drawer for my wallet," Wolfe said.

Alvarez opened the drawer on the stand next to the bed. "Yeah, it's here." He took it out. "Your shield too."

Wolfe turned his head to the left. The room blurred, but it wasn't spinning. If he had a concussion, it wasn't a big deal, at least he didn't think so. He lowered the safety bar and got out of bed. He was wearing a hospital gown and nothing else. He took it off. He'd never been shy. Alvarez handed him a pair of faded Levi's and he put them on. It was all he owned now, faded Levi's and worn Hawaiian shirts. Dressed, he started for the door.

"What about the bill?"

"Let 'em give it to the department." Wolfe took his wallet and shield. "We're outta here."

"It's true, you know," Alvarez said. "You're off the case."

"In a pig's ass," Wolfe said.

Outside Wolfe followed Alvarez to an aging Toyota.

"I know it looks shot, but the tires are good and mechanically she's sound. I could drive her to Miami and back and my only expense would be the gas." Alvarez got in the driver's side. The door wasn't locked. "And the way she looks, I don't have to worry about it getting stolen."

"It sounds like you're trying to sell it to me," Wolfe said as he got in.

"I am. You need a car and this one's for sale," Alvarez said. "I bought a brand new Ford Explorer, you know, cuz of the kid. I take delivery day after tomorrow."

"How much?" Wolfe said.

"Did I pay for the Explorer or am I willing to sell you the Toyota for?

"The Toyota."

"Thousand bucks."

"Done." Wolfe didn't really want a sports car. The Toyota would serve him well.

A half hour later they turned off PCH and onto Anaheim and then onto El Jardin.

"Nice area," Alvarez said as they approached the house.

"How you want to do this?" Wolfe said.

"I'd pull up front like we belong." Alvarez turned the Toyota into a circular driveway, bringing it to a stop by the front door. "Then I'd go inside and have a look." Alvarez reached into his jacket pocket and pulled out a set of keys. He turned to Wolfe, held them out and jiggled them. "Information isn't the only thing Norton got out of your friend Nesbitt. She keeps a spare set at the TV station, cuz she's a scatterbrain and is always losing 'em. Nesbitt's words, not mine." Alvarez slid out of the car.

"Nesbitt would know," Wolfe said.

"Come on we don't got all day. Besides, we sit here too long and some nosy neighbor's gonna call the cops. They got a neighborhood watch here."

Wolfe got out of the car and followed Alvarez to the porch. Alvarez rang the bell. "Looks like nobody's home."

"We already knew that," Wolfe said. "She's in Montana."

"What if she doesn't live alone?"

"She does."

"How do you know?"

"You'd have checked." Wolfe winced as he laughed. "It's why I get the big bucks."

Alvarez keyed the door and walked in. Wolfe followed, closing the door after himself.

"Christ, are you ready for this?" Alvarez said. The place had been searched and trashed.

"Like the Skidmore place." Wolfe crossed a tiled entry way and entered the living room.

They went through the house, quiet and quick. Books had pages torn out and were thrown on the floor. Every drawer in the house was open and broken. Clothes were ripped and strewn everywhere. Broken glasses and China covered the kitchen floor.

"Looks like they didn't find what they were looking for," Wolfe said, "and it made 'em angry."

"Look what I found." Alvarez handed Wolfe a photo album open to a photo of Frank Shannon and Janey Seward. The picture had been taken at a restaurant. They were full of smiles, holding up wine glasses, like they were toasting the photographer.

"Okay, let's get out of here," Wolfe said.

"Do we call this in?"

"I'm off the case," Wolfe said, "remember? Therefore we were never here, so how can we?"

"Yeah, yeah, I wasn't thinking." Alvarez headed for the door. By the time Wolfe was on the porch Alvarez was in the car with the engine running. He'd be a good man for a bank job, Wolfe thought.

"I almost forgot," Alvarez said as he pulled it into drive, "Beth Shannon's got a ticket to Miami on American, leaving LAX at nine in the AM. She's going back to Trinidad. So if you want to get anything out of her, you're gonna have to do it at the funeral, or right after."

"Where's the event?"

"Forest Lawn on San Antonio and Cherry."

"Take me to one of the rental car places at the Long Beach Airport."

Fifteen minutes later Alvarez turned off Lakewood Boulevard and into the airport. He parked in front of the terminal.

"I'm gonna rent a car and go to the funeral." Wolfe pulled his wallet out of his hip pocket and handed Alvarez his VISA card. "See if you can get me a ticket on that flight. Then forget all about it."

"Trinidad's a little out of our jurisdiction."

"Yeah, I know, but this case is getting to me. Besides, if I'm out of the country, I'll be out of Richard's hair."

"I can't argue with that."

"You and Norton do what you can here. I'll let you know how it goes from there."

"It's been a pleasure working with you." Alvarez held out his hand and Wolfe shook it.

"We're still working together. I'll be in touch, you can count on it." Wolfe got out of the car and headed for the rental car counter as Alvarez headed for the American Airlines desk.

At the cemetery Wolfe started toward a crowd of people he saw in the distance, then stopped when he saw Elizabeth Shannon. Something about the way the sun lit up her hair tugged at him.

Chapter Seven

Beth stood between Mark Skidmore's brother and his two cousins, who'd flown in from Trinidad, and stared at the four caskets. A quadruple funeral. Rare. And so unjust. Frank should be laid to rest across the street in consecrated ground, with his parents. Maybe the Skidmore's weren't Catholic, but Frank had been. How could the family overrule her like this? She was his wife. She should have fought harder. But Noelle wanted her parents buried together and the families wanted the sisters buried side by side.

She looked at her feet and fought tears. She was surrounded by a sea of Skidmores. She would not cry. She'd thought she'd been alone earlier, but not like this. Her husband was being buried and she was the alien at the funeral. The outcast while Frank was laid to rest beside his first wife.

She felt shunned.

She lifted her eyes. Noelle, dressed in sleek black, with a wide brimmed hat and veil, was biting her lip, knuckles white as she clutched Robbie's hand. Beth barely heard as the Methodist minister read from the Bible. But she heard well enough when he said, "Would you like to say something, Senator?"

"Mark Skidmore and Frank Shannon were my friends. It tears at my heart, this horrible thing." The senator was handsome and charismatic. But Frank had never liked him, she had never met him and somehow she'd gotten the idea that he didn't get on that well with Mark. It didn't make sense him being here. Besides, if he was such a friend, why hadn't he spoken at the service?

"I swear by all I hold holy that we will find the ones who did this and we will put them away." He paused. Away where? How could he say that?

"I know my words offer little comfort to family and friends. I wish I could say more, but sometimes we just have to have faith in God and his infinite wisdom." Infinite wisdom, Beth fought anger. God wasn't here. The Methodist man, the minister, he didn't belong. He wasn't holy, not this youth barely out of pimples.

She wanted to scream.

Noelle did scream. "Mom!" A mournful wail, like a wounded hound. She started for her mother's grave, but Robbie held her back. "Let me go!" She pulled against his hold, but Robbie was stronger. She collapsed in his arms.

Someone tapped her shoulder.

She turned.

It was him. The policeman. Anita's son. "Thank you for coming." She offered her hand.

He moved next to her as Edward Skidmore, Mark's younger brother, went to the first of the graves, Frank's. He bent and picked up a fistful of sod. His face was impassive as he sprinkled dirt down the holes in the ground. Frank, Ann Marie, Katherine, Mark. He was followed by the Trinidad cousins Sam and Stewart. Then a procession of Skidmores tossed dirt over the coffins. Beth felt ill. Frank was at the bottom of a pit. So cold. She started to shake.

Another woman cried out. Beth couldn't see who. Her stomach tightened. She was going to be sick.

"Come on." Lt. Wolfe tugged at her hand, leading her away from the mourners. "It's over."

Beth fought down the vomit as he led her between the headstones. Sprinklers hissed in the distance. She saw an artificial rainbow among them. She used to play in sprinklers when she was a girl. Cool water slapping hot skin, tingling her. God, she wished she could go back to being a child and start over.

"Where are we going?"

"Nowhere. We're just getting some air." Sweat trickled off his shaved head.

"I need it." All of a sudden she remembered what Anita had told her about him. A lump welled up in her throat. She started to shake again. Then she cried, great racking sobs. It was so unfair. Her life. Frank's. The policeman's. Everything.

"It's okay." He pulled her into a hug. She wrapped her arms around him, buried her face in his chest and drenched his Hawaiian shirt with tears.

"I know a place in the Shore. Kind of a Mexican restaurant slash bar. The lunch would be over now.

It'd be quiet, least till the evening crowd starts to wander in."

"A bar?" She sniffed. "I could use a drink before I have to face them." Truth be told, she never wanted to face them. If Noelle knew about Frank's girlfriend, Janey, then the whole family knew. She turned to get one last look at the mourners as they left the grave site. There were a lot of people. Was Janey one of them? Would she have come to the funeral? Would the family have said anything? She shivered. Come on Beth, get a hold of yourself, Frank's dead, put it out of your mind.

* * *

Twenty minutes later they entered the Lounge. Wolfe stopped her at the door with a hand to her elbow. It was habit, he kept a light grip on her arm until his eyes adjusted to the low light. He liked to see who was in the bar. Two Five Fifty-Niners he knew, a retired aircraft executive, named Sam and Jack Priest, an aging writer. Wolfe had read his stuff and liked it, horror stories mostly.

Skinny Dick was behind the bar, wiry and bald. He made good drinks and he made them fast.

"Hey, Billy, the usual?" Dick said.

"No, I'll have a Coke, no ice."

"And the Lady?" Dick's smile was as wide as ever. It didn't faze him that Wolfe had been coming in day after day for a year, drinking Dewar's and water. Dick minded his own business. You wanted to talk, he listened. You wanted quiet, you got it. He was the best bartender Wolfe had ever seen.

"I'll have a Scotch and Coke, Dewar's, if you got it," Beth said.

"We got it," Dick said.

Wolfe winced.

"What?" She'd felt his hand tighten on her arm.

"Nothing." Wolfe led her to a booth away from the bar.

"This place is nice." She scooted into the booth.

"Yeah, It used to be called Taco Town. Dick and his partner bought it to convert to a pickup place and it is that, after dark."

"But during the day it's a Mexican Restaurant?"

"Kind of. They open in the morning at six, to get the early morning crowd, you know, the guy that needs a belt before he goes to work or someone who likes a Bloody Mary with his eggs, but when they bought this place they inherited Juanita Juarez, the best Mexican cook on the planet. People come a long way to have lunch here. A while back they had a lady from Japan. Said she heard about the place in Tokyo."

"Sounds like you come here a lot."

"Yeah, I guess it does." He tried to see into her eyes through the dim light, couldn't. "I hate to change the subject, but there are some things I have to ask."

"Now's not the time." She brushed her hair out of her eyes.

"There's never a good time."

"I know. But not now."

When? He wanted to ask.

"How about tomorrow or better, the day after," she said, answering the unasked question.

But she was leaving in the morning, going back to Trinidad, he wanted to say, but didn't. The autopsy on her husband failed to show anything untoward. Heart attack. But still she was dodging the questions. Something wasn't right. He studied the lines of her face, her chin. She was still wearing her wedding ring. She caught him looking at it and took it off.

"I was upset at the funeral because they didn't bury Frank in a Catholic cemetery."

"Does religion mean that much to you?" he said.

"I suppose not. You?"

"It used too, not anymore."

"You want to tell me why?"

He paused, looked at her hands. They were shaking. She started playing with the ring. Some people were uncomfortable talking to policemen, but he didn't think it was that. She seemed like she was coming apart. She was vulnerable, about to break. Maybe now wasn't the right time to question her.

"I don't usually talk about myself."

"Please. I need to hear about someone else's problems. I need to know I'm not the only one who hurts."

"You're not."

"I know, but I need to hear it. Does that make sense?"

"Yeah, it does." He took a sip of his Coke. It got warm quickly without the ice. "My dad was a cantor as was his father before him, and his before that." He was quiet for a few seconds. This wasn't what he wanted. She was supposed to be the one talking, but he'd started and he couldn't stop.

"My grandfather on my mother's side was a Rabbi. Grandpa Zimmerman, a kinder man you'd never want to meet. He had this number tattooed on his arm. I asked about it on my ninth birthday. We were at the Griffith Park Zoo, just me and him, by the elephants. It was noon straight up, I know the time, because I was hungry and had just looked at the new Timex he'd given me.

"'It's your curse, Billy,' he said, 'this need to know.' Then he told me, right there in front of the elephants. He told it slow. He left nothing out. It was almost dark by the time he'd finished and he'd picked up an audience. There must have been a hundred people, maybe more. Several were crying, none talking. The crowd blocked the view of the elephants. No one asked us to move, such was the power of my grandfather.

"And I told you about my dad, Cantor Wolfe. He taught Physics at UCLA and studied the Torah. My mother loved him with all her heart.

"A week after that birthday, my grandfather the rabbi, and my father the cantor were coming home from a synagogue in Los Angeles. They stopped at an Arco Station, you know, the kind that have those convenience stores. A couple of kids came in with sawed offs. They got eighty-nine dollars and left the rabbi and the cantor in a pool of blood.

"My mother and I lost our faith that day." He sighed, almost felt like crying. "I haven't told anyone about that in a long time. I brought you here to hear your story and instead I wind up telling you mine." He took a sip of his coke. "Then there was the cancer. It's in remission."

"That's why you shave your head."

"I took some time off a few years ago, had chemo. I keep the head shaved in case it comes back. If I have to do the chemo again, I'd be able to keep working, no one would know."

"Then there's what happened to your wife and son. Your mother told me."

"Leave it to Mom."

"She's a nice lady."

"Okay, enough about me. It's your turn."

"Where do I start so you'll understand?" She closed her eyes and stopped playing with the ring. She didn't need it now. Her hands weren't shaking anymore.

"Start at the beginning and the end will take care of itself," Wolfe said.

"The beginning, okay. I was a normal kid, raised in Long Beach. I went to Wilson. After high school I went to Cal State. I lived in the dorms and threw myself into school life."

"How come you lived on campus if you grew up here?" Wolfe said. "Why not stay at home?"

"My parents married young and had always wanted to travel, but they couldn't because of me, so the day after my graduation, they put the house up for sale and left for Europe." She must have seen the look on his face, because she said. "No, I didn't feel abandoned. My folks were great. I grew up knowing they were going to take off when I went to college. I was happy for them and it worked out good for me, because I was a sport brat, I pitched on the girl's baseball team and ran cross country, so I would have been on campus at all hours even if I'd lived at home."

"So, how'd you come by the place in Huntington Beach?"

"My parents bought it for me during my senior year. What a wonderful surprise that was. I loved it there. The sound of the surf. It was my very own place." She sighed. "I missed the dorms, but loved the bus ride up Pacific Coast Highway five days a week to school." She stopped, took a sip of her drink. "I met Frank in my senior year, too. He was a blustery, part time actor, roustabout, pilot and smuggler with a million and one stories, all funny. He stole my heart. He was forty-five, just divorced and swore he'd never marry again. We were married two weeks later.

"Mom was horrified. Dad was barely tolerant. They didn't like him. He was forty-six, I was twenty-two, plus he had an eighteen-year-old daughter. Still I loved him and my parents loved me, so they held their tongues and we had a great Irish wedding. We had a wonderful six years." She stopped talking, took a breath, then a sip of her drink. Scotch and Coke, a crime, but one he could overlook.

He wanted to bring up the girlfriend, but he didn't. Eventually he was going to have to ask her about it. But it could wait. She didn't need that now.

Then she surprised him.

"But the last year wasn't so good. Frank was in the States and I had a friend from another boat haul me up the mast to change the anchor light. I was about six months pregnant. It was stupid, I know, but I liked going up and it was perfectly safe. All I had to do was sit in the bosun's chair while he winched me up, change the bulb, then ride down."

"But?" Wolfe didn't know what a bosun's chair was, but what she was talking about seemed a lot more dangerous than she was letting on. He'd seen sailboats. The top of a mast was way up there. He wouldn't be so eager to climb one.

"But a bee stung him in the hand when I was about ten feet from the deck. He let go of the line. I fell and lost the baby."

"Oh, Lord."

"It gets worse. I can't have kids now. What are the odds? But it happened. Frank never forgave me."

"What do you mean, he never forgave you?"

"Oh, he said he didn't blame me. But it was just under a year ago. Since then he's spent more time than ever in California, with his girlfriend—someone named Janey. And when he was in Trinidad he slept in the salon. That bee sting killed our married life."

"What are you saying?"

"We stopped having sex when I was about four months along. We never started again."

"I'm sorry." Wolfe was embarrassed. Part of him didn't want to hear this, part of him had to. He thought of his son, dead in a fall. She'd lost her child in a fall, too. Even though she'd never got to know the baby, as he had his son, it had to hurt. It did hurt. She was still wearing the scars.

"You're thinking about your boy?"

"Not just him. Before I met my wife I worked with the Big Brother program. I got pretty involved with an African American kid named Randy. At first we just kinda hung out on Saturdays, but in no time we were close. Randy was seven when we met, fifteen when he died of leukemia. Then I got sick right after."

"I'm sorry."

"But I got better. Things were ticking along okay at work and I thought things were going great with me and Kerry, but I guess they weren't, because she moved out. Then somehow Justin climbed over that balcony. That, coming six months after Randy's death, sent me into a year long depression that I'm just now crawling out of. I'm telling you this, because I want you to know I understand where your husband was coming from. I went into depression. Your husband went into denial. I got over it. Your husband would have gotten over the denial. In time things might've worked out for you."

"You're saying I should try and see things from his point of view?"

"Yeah."

She was quiet for a minute or so, then, "I could have been more attentive, I suppose, but I was so caught up in my own feelings. I lost a baby."

"If I'd've paid more attention to my marriage, maybe my wife wouldn't have left. Maybe she'd still be alive, my boy too."

"You're making me feel guilty," she said. "I don't know if I like that."

"I'm sorry." He felt terrible, the last thing he wanted was to make her feel worse than she already did. He took a sip of his Coke.

"So, what are you going to do now?" She asked. "Now that you're over your depression."

"You know, right up until this very instant I hadn't given it any thought, but if I could do whatever I wanted, I think I'd buy some land out in the desert and make a home for a bunch of ghetto kids." He laughed. "But that's not ever gonna happen, not on the money I make. So I guess I'll just have to be content with putting killers behind bars so they can't ever hurt anyone again." He was baring his soul to her and he couldn't stop it.

"That's a good dream, I could buy into that." She sighed, then asked him to take her by the apartment. She needed to change from the black and gray she was wearing into something lighter, before she went over to Edward Skidmores house for the get together. "Strange the way people gather after someone dies," she said.

"I understand why you want to change, but I'd pass on the gathering if I were you."

"You really are perceptive. Maybe I will. God knows, I don't want to go. They all know about this Janey person."

"Janey Seward, she does the weather on the KYTV News."

"Oh, God, you too? Is there anybody who doesn't know?" She laughed.

"Oh, I don't know, let's ask the bartender." He laughed too.

"That was funny," she said.

At first he thought she was being sarcastic, but she was still laughing. So he decided to take a shot.

"You wanna get dinner or something?" Wolfe said.

"Are you asking me out? Like on a date?"

"Just dinner." Wolfe felt his insides churn. What was it with this woman? Why her? Why now? "Not a date. I wouldn't know how to ask someone out. It's been so long, I've forgotten how."

"Where?"

"The steak house down the street's good."

"The place with the fake snow on the roof?" Belmont Shore was a beach town. The steak house was like a beacon in the Shore with it's log cabin exterior and the fake snow. But inside they had the best steaks money could buy.

"Yeah." Wolfe laughed. It was going to be all right. She was going to go with him.

"Then I don't have to change. Let's—."

"My wallet!" Jack Priest screamed out.

Wolfe saw a young man streaking for the door as Beth grabbed her glass, kicked her chair back as she stood and let it fly. The pitch caught the man in the shoulder and stunned him, giving Skinny Dick enough time to leap over the bar and collar the thief.

Wolfe stood, surveyed the situation. "You're not going to make me work are you?"

Dick met his eyes, took in Beth. "Naw." He took the wallet from the thief. "Get out and don't come back." He booted the man out the door. "Everything's fine now." He dropped Priest's wallet by the author's drink, then went back behind the bar. "Lady's got an arm like Kofax used to have."

"Played ball in college." Beth bowed to the smattering of applause, then sat down.

"Remind me never to run away from you," Wolfe said.

"Lucky pitch," Beth said.

* * *

She felt the adrenaline spark through her body. It was incredible how fast she'd reacted. It was almost like the man had been running in slow motion. She felt so proud of herself. And she'd hit him. She hadn't lost the old college touch.

The glow stayed with her all through dinner and into dessert, when he told her Janey Seward's house had been searched and trashed, the same as the Skidmore places.

"Was she hurt?"

"No, she's visiting her parents in Montana."

"They were looking for something?"

"Yes."

"Do you know what?"

"No."

"But you'll find out?"

"I will." He seemed so confident. She reached for her wine. The glass was empty. She thought about ordering another, but didn't. Wolfe had ordered a Coke at the bar and had drunk only water during dinner. What was that about? She'd got the impression from Anita that he was a drinker, and he knew that bartender so well.

"Don't you drink?"

"Not anymore," he said.

"Did you have a problem?"

"Some thought so. I didn't."

"When did you quit?"

"This morning."

"And I'm drinking in front of you."

"It's not a problem." He signaled for the check. "I better get you back."

"There's nobody waiting for me." She looked at her watch. Five-thirty. "But you're right. I've got some calls to make, and a lot to think about." She almost told him she was going back to Trinidad in the morning, but something held her back, maybe she was afraid if he knew she was leaving, he'd find a way to keep her in California. They could do that, cops.

He parked in front of the apartment, got out and opened the door for her. An old fashioned gentleman. Frank had never done that. He walked her up the walkway and waited while she keyed the door.

She turned toward him and was caught in his pale blue eyes. For an instant she felt like a school girl on a date. She wanted to kiss him, but she fought the impulse.

"I believe you've charmed me and for that, I'm grateful. I needed a little time off from my grief." She opened the door. The apartment had been torn apart, trashed. "They wrecked your place, Lieutenant."

He eased her aside and entered the apartment like a cat. She stayed behind him as he went to the bedroom. It was destruction for destruction's sake. Someone had taken a sharp knife from the kitchen and sliced through the blankets and mattresses of both beds.

She gasped when she saw the glass covering the floor. The mirrors on the closet doors had been shattered. Then she saw the bags, hers and Noelle's. They'd been opened and their clothes were strewn all over the bed.

"Can you think of any reason someone would want to search your baggage?" he said.

"No." Beth understood that it was her things the vandals were interested in. Did that make her responsible for what they'd done to Wolfe's apartment?

"Don't worry," he said. "It's not your fault."

"Are you a mind reader?"

"Sometimes."

They heard someone in the living room and she followed Wolfe out of the bedroom.

"What happened?" Noelle was standing in the doorway, staring at the sofa. The cushions had been sliced open, the stuffing was all over the floor.

"It looks like I better get you two into a hotel." He bent down and picked something up.

"What is it?" Beth said.

"It's the rearview mirror from my car."

"I don't understand."

"Somebody thinks you have something they want and they're upset with me for interfering." He went back to the bedroom with her and Noelle right behind.

"What do you mean?" Noelle said, but he ignored her.

He went to one of the twin beds, went to his knees, reached under. Beth heard a metallic click and a popping sound. He pulled his hand back. He had money in it. Several hundred dollar bills. He stuffed them into a hip pocket. Then his hand was back in the box and out again, this time with a gun in it.

"Where'd that come from?" Beth said.

"Gun safe, bolted to the bed frame." He stood up.

"Not too professional if they missed that," Noelle said.

"That's a good observation." Wolfe turned to her, his pale eyes cold.

"Well, I mean they searched Uncles Mark's place and Mom's real good. From what I heard you couldn't have hidden a stamp without them finding it, but they missed a big old safe under the bed."

"It's not that big, just a small steel box bolted to the underside of the frame," Wolfe said.

"How's it work?" Noelle went to the bed, bent over and looked under.

"Four buttons on the side, you have to punch them in the right order to get it to open."

"Like a combination lock," Beth said.

"So how come you keep your gun locked up?" Noelle stood.

"I can get it quick enough if I need it."

"Not really," she said. "Your weapon's been here, you've been somewhere else."

"It's in my hand now," he said and Beth saw the steel in his eyes.

"Sigma forty caliber plastic automatic," Noelle said. "Real deadly."

"You know guns?" Wolfe asked.

"You put a gun in her hands and she can strip it, clean it and reassemble it faster than you can blink," Beth said. "There's nothing about guns she doesn't know and no gun she can't shoot. Her dad taught her."

"You own one?" he said to Noelle.

"I used to own lots, when I was younger, but I sold them all. I'm a doctor, I don't believe in guns anymore."

"Anymore?" he said.

"No, not anymore." She spun around and left the bedroom as if all of a sudden she wanted to get away from the gun and what it represented. Beth understood, she didn't like the look of it either.

"She's right." Wolfe tossed the gun onto the bed and followed Noelle out of the bedroom.

Chapter Eight

Two days later, after three hours in the Miami Airport, Wolfe boarded the BWIA flight to Port of Spain. Alvarez hadn't been able to get him on Beth Shannon's American flight because it had been full. He was barely able to manage the Delta flight to Miami the following day with a BWIA connection to Trinidad. As it was, Wolfe had to fly first class.

Though he'd never been outside of the States before, he had a passport. He and Kerry had been planning a trip to Europe before she'd moved out.

He spent the Delta flight thinking about why Beth Shannon would fly back to Trinidad without telling him. He'd driven her and Noelle to the Marriott by the Long Beach Airport after they had repacked their bags. Stayed as they checked in, waiting for her to open up and tell him that she was leaving. But she didn't, and that didn't make any sense.

Whoever tore his place apart had made a thorough search of Beth and Noelle's things. And they were still striking out. Whatever they were looking for was still out there waiting to be found. He could understand the search. Somebody wanted something real bad, but why trash his car and the apartment? What sense did that make? Why the pressure from Senator Sterling on his old boss? And why extend his leave and take him off the case? If the senator really wanted it solved, like he claimed, it would seem he'd want as many cops working it as possible, not just Norton and Alvarez. They were good, sure, but he was better.

In the Miami airport he bought a couple magazines, determined to take his mind off the case. He took a seat at the boarding gate, closed his eyes and didn't open them till they called his flight.

On the plane he found his place, an aisle seat on the right hand side of the aircraft. A woman who looked to be in her early twenties with pale white skin that looked like it had never seen the sun was sitting by the window. Thick black hair cascaded around her shoulders. She was green-eyed, thin like a model and reminded him of a willow tree.

"Hi," she said when he sat. "My name's Jenna." Her accent was almost English, he thought, but not. She was wearing kind of a low cut peasant blouse made out of green batik that matched her eyes. Her breasts were full and captured his attention. He forced his eyes away, something he hadn't had to do in a long time.

"Billy Wolfe. People I like call me Wolfe." He offered his hand.

"Then that's what I'll call you." She took the hand in a weak, but not a limp, grip and Wolfe felt a tingle, she was beautiful. Full lips, no lipstick, she didn't need it and the whitest teeth he'd ever seen. She was smiling, but the smile was obviously forced.

"Oh, Lord, we're moving. Can I hold your hand?"

"What?"

"I'm afraid of flying." She clutched onto his hand, hard, not like her handshake.

"Easy," he said.

"Sorry." She let off some of the pressure. "I never should have come to America." Sweat ringed her forehead. Her face paled. She was afraid.

"Why did you?"

"Disneyworld. I know, stupid. My doctor gave me these pills, so I slept on the flight over, but I don't have any left."

"He didn't give you any for the trip back?"

"He did, but I was so scared leaving Trinidad, that I took them all."

"Not so smart."

"I thought I could do it. I've been psyching myself up for over a month. I was going to be so brave, but now I see I'm just a big fat coward."

"Maybe not so fat." Wolfe smiled, caught in her green eyes. Almost Asian eyes, like a sleek cat that always gets its way. Those eyes were windows and he was looking right into her. She really was afraid.

"Not fat, but chicken just the same." She tightened her grip as the plane started down the taxiway under its own power. "You're going to have to help me. Do you mind?"

"How?"

"Tell me it's going to be okay."

"It's going to be okay." Wolfe looked out the window. They were moving like they weren't going to be waiting in line for take off. "We should be in the air pretty quick."

"Oh, Lord." She gripped his hand even tighter as the flight attendants went through their life saving lecture. Then the attendants were seated and the plane was turning onto the runway.

"It's gonna be okay." He grimaced as she squeezed. Her nails dug into his palm.

"I hate this." She was breathing fast.

"Just relax." Wolfe squeezed her hand back. She didn't seem to notice. The front of the plane raised as they were pushed back into their seats.

"I really hate this." Her eyes became wild. She sucked her lower lip between her teeth.

"Don't!" Wolfe was afraid she was going to bite through it.

"Sorry." Then she started hyperventilating.

"Stop it, now!" Wolfe said it loud, a command.

"Yeah, yeah," she said and then they were off the ground. She kept his hand in a tight grip for the next few minutes as she fought to control her breathing. Then, when the fasten seatbelt sign went off, she sighed and relaxed her grip.

"What?" Wolfe said.

"It's going to be okay. Otherwise they wouldn't have turned the sign off." She smiled, eyes dancing as she took her hand back.

"I can't place your accent."

"I'm Trinidadian."

"I thought—"

"What? We have white Trinidadians, you know." She was smiling like an imp.

"No, I didn't."

"You thought we were all African."

"I guess. I didn't give it much thought."

"We're a rainbow country, though the West and the East Indians vastly outnumber the whites, kind of the opposite of America."

"West and East, what's the difference?"

"A West Indian is a Trini with African ancestors, like your African Americans if I were to be politically correct. And an East Indian is a Trini with Indian ancestry, I guess you could say an Indian Trinidadian."

"I thought all black people that lived in the Caribbean were West Indians."

"We don't care about those other islands." She laughed. "That's a typical Trini attitude. We like to say God was a Trini and you know, I believe he was."

"How many people?" Wolfe wasn't just making conversation to keep her talking and her mind off the fact that she was shooting through the sky in an aluminum tube at six hundred miles an hour—he was interested. As far as it was possible, he wanted to be an informed American when he stepped for the first time on foreign soil.

"About a million and a half. We're a small country, but we have a large culture." She reclined her seat. "Even though a million and a half is a lot of people, somehow Trinidad's got kind of a small town atmosphere about it, probably because we like to talk and nobody can keep a secret."

"You ever go to the Yacht Club?" It just came out, he didn't want to bring up the reason he was on the plane, but if what she said was true, she might know Beth Shannon.

"I'm a member." All of a sudden the twin windows closed, though her eyes stayed open. He wasn't asking general questions anymore and she knew it. "Why do you ask?"

"Do you know Frank Shannon?"

"Everybody knows that crazy Irishman."

"Can you tell me anything about him?"

"Why?" Wary now, still the sleek cat, but now like a cat that had cornered something maybe a little too big.

"I have some business with him."

"You're the guy he hired to teach them how to sail." Jenna laughed, at ease again. "Only crazy Frank would buy a big boat like that without knowing how to sail it. We all thought he was in over his head, but he's pulled it off. He and Beth have built something they can be proud of. Now that it's finished, Beth wanted to untie it from the dock and just head out, but Frank put his foot down. That's why he hired you."

"She doesn't know how to sail?"

"They don't have a clue. They spent a year fixing the boat, getting ready to sail her away, then they spent two more years in the Yacht Club, planning the big adventure." Jenna shook her head, almost as if she were going to laugh again, but she didn't. "They have this dream. They want to sail around the world. Actually, more Beth's dream now, than his, I think."

"What do you mean?"

"Frank seems to be growing roots. He dresses in suits and ties, not like the yachting community at all. And he hangs out with government ministers. If you ask me, I think he'd like to stay in Trinidad, but it's hard to tell."

"You seem to know them pretty well."

"I know everybody at the Yacht Club, all the locals anyway, and the foreigners that have been in Trinidad for a long time, like Frank and Beth."

"Do you have a boat?"

"Heavens no. You don't have to have a boat to be a member. It's more a social thing. I go every Friday and Saturday to make contacts. I'm saving up to open my own business and when I do, I'm going to need all the yachtie friends I can get."

"What kind of business?"

"Jenna's Tours. There's so many yachties now, somebody has to show them around. You know, take them out to the western shore to watch the giant turtles lay their eggs, or up to the Asa Wright Bird Sanctuary, or the Caroni Swamp."

"Swamp, like in alligators and crocks?"

"Yeah, like that, every night flocks of scarlet ibis come over from Venezuela to roost, it's quite a sight, the red birds meshed with the yellow of the setting sun. You should go if you get a chance."

"You talk like a poet."

"That's why I'm going to be such a great tour operator."

They made small talk, mostly her talking and him listening. Her voice had a musical quality and she had a way of talking that pulled the listener into her words. She was at ease now, talking as if she were sitting in her own office, trying to sell him a tour to watch the giant turtles lay their eggs. It was as if she'd never been afraid at all.

"I have to go to the toilet," she said after a while. "I'd ask you to come with me and hold my hand, but some things you just have to do yourself." Sweat ringed her forehead. He had been wrong, she was still frightened, but she got up and made her way to the head in the front of the first class cabin.

She seemed to take a long time and he started to worry about her, but finally she came out of the toilet and started back to her seat. He was about to get up to let her in when the plane jerked, cutting off the talk in the cabin. He pulled her into his lap as the plane shook and wrestled her into the window seat. She grabbed behind herself, searching for the seatbelt. She buckled up and Wolfe saw the color fade from her face. Her lips quivered, her eyes went wide.

"Thanks," she said.

"You okay?"

"Yeah." She sucked her lower lip between her teeth again and clamped down on it to stop the quivering. Her dark hair, perfect an instant ago, was now wild. Her flared nostrils gave her a doe-like appearance that startled him. Any second he expected her to bolt.

But then they were through the turbulence and flying in smooth air again.

"That was scary," she said and he laughed. She laughed too and for the rest of the flight they talked and laughed as if they'd know each other all their lives.

Three hours later the captain announced that it was raining in Port of Spain and Wolfe saw Jenna tighten up. Her face went pale.

"They land in the rain all the time," he said. But she grabbed his hand and clutched it as she'd done during the take off. Her face had gone white. She wasn't talking now and she kept silent till they were on the ground.

Inside the terminal passengers gathered around the baggage carousel waiting for their luggage. As they pulled it off, they filed in line to await customs inspection.

Wolfe stretched between two tall black men and grabbed his grip from the carousel.

"That's mine." Jenna pointed to a designer bag that matched her purse.

"I'll get it." Wolfe grabbed the bag. It was heavy.

"There's two more."

Wolfe saw them and pulled them from the carousel.

"Wait here. I'll get a trolley." She trotted off toward a row of baggage carts.

Wolfe sighed. She had a kind of wiggle when she moved that caught most of the male eyes in the terminal.

They waited the next half hour in silence while the Customs officers slowly went about their work. It seemed like an eternity to Wolfe, but finally they were at the Customs counter. The officer opened the grip, rummaged through it, found his shield.

"What's this?" the young Customs officer asked.

"It's a badge."

"You here on business?"

"Vacation."

"Have a nice stay." He waved him on.

"So, you're not a sailing instructor," Jenna said when they were out of the Customs area.

"Not a sailing instructor," he answered.

"Then why did you ask about the Shannons on the plane? The real reason."

"Frank Shannon's ex-wife, her sister and brother-in-law were murdered in California about the same time he was dying of a heart attack in Trinidad. Beth Shannon brought her husband's body to California for the funeral, but left right after for Trinidad. I need to ask her some questions."

"You don't mean it?" She grabbed his arm as if to keep from falling.

"I do."

"Poor Beth."

"I think whoever did the killing might come after her next."

"So you're here to protect her as well."

"That's right."

"Then you can start right now, because that's Beth Shannon over there with Victor Drake."

Wolfe followed her gaze. Beth Shannon was on the other side of the terminal, talking to a man with dark, shoulder length hair. The man wore a loose fitting sport shirt, short sleeved, yellow, open at the collar, and some kind of fancy jeans with a crease. Nobody ironed jeans, even if they weren't Levi's. He followed the crease down to Italian loafers. The man wasn't wearing socks. The kind of guy who thought he was cool.

Beth, on the other hand, was wearing the real deal, faded Levi's, as was Wolfe. She also had on a dark blue Caribbean batik shirt, not Hawaiian, but good for here. And she was wearing Nike running shoes. Wolfe's were New Balance, but so what?

"I gotta go."

"Not just yet." She pulled a pen and a card out of her purse. "It's my dentist's card," she said as she wrote on the back of it. "If you have any problems with your teeth while you're here, give him a call. If you want to get together and have dinner or something, give me a call." She handed him the card. "I waitress at the Normandy Hotel, just till I save enough to open that tour company. I get off at ten. We eat late here."

She gave him a quick kiss on the cheek, then took off toward the taxi rank. She walked by Beth Shannon and Mr. Cool without looking at them. Good for her, Wolfe thought. He was about to approach when he saw the change window. There was nobody in line.

He stepped up to the window, pulled two hundred dollars out of his wallet.

"Can you change this?"

"Certainly." The woman behind the window gave him twelve blue TT hundred dollar bills, a couple of red one dollar bills and some change. Wolfe had never been out of the States before, had never used a foreign currency. He spent a few seconds studying it, before slipping the money into his wallet. Then he started toward Beth Shannon.

"Mrs. Shannon," he said as he approached.

"Lt. Wolfe, what are you doing here?" Her smile was quick, genuine.

"Remember those questions I needed to ask?"

"Oh, Lord, I'm so sorry."

"Is there a problem here?" Mr. Cool said.

"No, Victor, this is Lt. Wolfe. He's investigating the murders of Frank's family. Frank's too."

"But Frank had a heart attack."

"Maybe," Wolfe said. "Maybe not."

"You have jurisdiction here, Lieutenant?"

"Is it any of your business?" He knew he shouldn't be so rude, strange country and all, but he couldn't help himself. There was something about the guy that grated on him.

"Maybe, maybe not." Victor Drake threw Wolfe's words back at him.

"If you had nothing to do with Mr. Shannon's death, it wouldn't be, on the other hand, if you did, I can see where you'd be concerned. Which is it?"

"Okay, boys, let's tone it down," Beth said.

"Would I be a little naive if I thought you were here to meet me?" Wolfe said.

"Yes, Lieutenant, you would. We're here to pick up Noelle."

"You didn't know she was on the flight?" Victor Drake said. "Some cop."

Wolfe ignored the barb, but he wasn't going to forget it. "I thought she was staying in California."

"I did too," Beth said, "but she called Victor yesterday and told him she was coming back."

"Not you? She didn't call you?"

"No, she told Victor to call me. I think she was afraid I might tell her not to come."

"Would you have?"

"Probably," she said.

Mr. Cool laughed.

Wolfe felt like hitting him, but he held his anger in check. Something was definitely going on. His emotions were running away. First his crazy and instant attraction to Beth Shannon, now his instant dislike of Victor Drake. Maybe he shouldn't've quit drinking.

"Beth, Victor." Noelle Shannon came toward them with a duffel bag over her shoulder. It looked heavy.

"Let me take that," Victor said.

"See, Beth, I remembered, no room for a hard suitcase on a boat," Noelle said.

"It only took you five trips down here to get it right." Beth laughed. Wolfe couldn't tell if it was real or forced.

"I was an arrogant little snot," Noelle said. "I'm not that way anymore. Give me a chance, you'll see."

"This way, ladies." Victor pointed to a black Mercedes. It was parked in the passenger loading zone. Wolfe shook his head. In L.A. they'd have it hooked to the tow truck before his foot hit the street.

"You two go on ahead," Beth said. "I have some business to take care of with Lt. Wolfe."

"I saw you get on the plane in Miami," Noelle said, "but they wouldn't let me come up into first to say hello."

"Guess we know who's the real cop here," Victor Drake said and once again Wolfe was forced to choke back his anger.

CHAPTER
NINE

WOLFE FELT HER EYES on him as he raised his hand for a cab. There was a light rain and the cars whizzing by splashed water from their tires. It was a dark night, no moon, no stars.

"What's the local time?" He said.

"Nine-thirty or so," Beth said. Her blonde hair was damp and seemed to glow under the overhead lights. She looked like an angel. He needed to say something, but his tongue was thick in his mouth. He was an awkward kid, she was the homecoming queen. Never before had he been at a loss for words. She was going to think he was an idiot.

A rusty Toyota pulled up to the curb, tires hissing on the wet pavement. The car was old, the brakes squeaked.

Wolfe sighed. Saved.

"You want a taxi?" The driver's rich baritone and ebony skin conspired to hide his age, but the gray hair and wrinkled hands gave it away.

"Yes, to the Yacht Club." Wolfe was a cop again. He half expected Beth to ask how he knew she kept her boat there, but she didn't.

"I'm your man." The driver started to step out of the car.

Wolfe held a hand up. "That's okay, we don't have any baggage."

"Makes it easy on these old bones." The driver pulled his door closed.

Wolfe went around the car, reached a hand in the passenger window, dropped his grip on the front seat. Beth dropped her backpack in after. It looked new. He opened the back door for her and they got in.

"Dependable Ted, at your service." The driver handed Wolfe a card. "You need a taxi, anytime, day or night, you call me, hear? I'm dependable, like my name, the name on the card, Dependable Ted."

"I'll be sure to do that." Wolfe put the card in his shirt pocket.

"Now relax and enjoy the ride. I might not be the fastest taxi in Trinidad, but I'm the most dependable."

Wolfe laughed as the taxi started winding its way along the airport access road.

"We'll be on the highway in ten minutes, then it's about a half hour to Port of Spain. The Yacht Club's just up the road from there."

Wolfe looked out the window as they made their way through the night. They were alone on a dark road. Shadows of giant palms, fronds swaying in the breeze, ran before the car's headlights. Ghosts in the night.

"Spooky," Wolfe said.

Beth laughed.

"Everything seems so alien," Wolfe said.

"Night of the soucouyant," Ted said.

"What's that?" Wolfe wanted to know.

"Local vampire type legend," Beth said.

"Not a legend," Ted said. "When the bats replace the birds on the trees. When the night is dark, like this one, that's when she comes out. But you're okay, long as you're with me."

"What's he talking about?"

"The soucouyant is an old woman that sheds her skin," Beth said. "She flies out of her house and looks for human blood. When she finds it, she changes into an animal of some kind and sucks the blood away."

"You're kidding?" Wolfe said.

"No she's not," Ted said.

"It's almost always a child or a young woman," Beth said. "The soucouyant likes innocent fear, it seems."

"That's a good one," Ted said. "I didn't know that."

"Some people put rice in front of their doors to keep her away," Beth said.

"It works," Ted said.

"Like garlic?" Wolfe was getting into it.

"Not the same," Ted said. "Vampire's supposed to be afraid of garlic. The soucouyant's not afraid of anything. She's just lazy."

"I don't get it."

"She has to count the grains of rice before she can enter," Beth said.

"That's right," Ted said. "So if you put the rice out, she passes you by and goes to another house, because she's too lazy to count it."

"You do that?" Wolfe said. "Put rice out?"

"Every night."

Beth made a sucking sound.

"You don't kid about the soucouyant," Ted said. Wolfe couldn't tell if he was serious.

"No you don't." Beth poked him in the side. Wolfe suppressed a laugh.

"Highway coming up." Ted made a left onto it. He kept to the slow lane. Cars and trucks of all ages and sizes flew by them. Junkyard fugitives racing along with cars fresh off the showroom floor. Speed tempered by chaos seemed to be the order of the day. Everybody was in a hurry to get somewhere. Everybody wanted to pass the car in front, but nobody wanted to be passed.

"Do they always drive like this?" Wolfe said.

"Mostly, except me and a few others that have lived long enough to develop common sense."

"I appreciate you taking your time," Beth said.

Wolfe leaned back, watching the night as they moved through it. Billboards told them they were approaching the city. Coca Cola, Pepsi, Breeze, Jesus Saves, Tiny's Tyres. Wolfe thought Tiny was hanging around with some pretty impressive company as they started to slow down. Ted had been driving like a turtle, now he was a snail.

"Uh oh, traffic. Must be an accident." A few minutes later he said. "The wreck must be on the main road. We could be awhile before they clear it, you know, being Old Year's Night and all."

"Old Year's Night?" Wolfe said.

"What they call New Years Eve," Beth said.

"How long do you think?" Wolfe heard a siren off in the distance.

"Nobody wants to work on Old Year's Night."

"Why don't we go to your hotel and have a drink or something?" Beth said. "In an hour or so I'll call a cab. The road should be cleared by then."

"What hotel?" Ted said.

"I didn't book one," Wolfe said.

"Always room at the Hilton." Ted made a right and all of a sudden he was out of the traffic.

Twenty minutes later Wolfe was checked in and moving through the throng in the hotel bar, his grip slung over his shoulder, room key in his pocket.

"I'll have a Coke," he said as he approached the bar.

"Make mine with Scotch," she said. Then, "Whoops, I'm sorry, I forgot about you not drinking."

"Don't worry about it. If I wanted a drink, I'd order one."

"But—"

"Relax, I'm fine." He did his best to make a smile as the bartender dropped the drinks on the bar. He was fast. Wolfe reached a hand for the Coke. Not even a tremble. He was tempted to order something stronger. If she wouldn't have been with him, he would have, but he didn't want her to think he'd climbed up on the wagon and had fallen off so quick.

"Are you all right?" She said. "Because you don't look all right."

"I was just doing mental gymnastics." He laughed and his smile was real this time.

"What do you mean?"

"I was running reasons through my head about why it'd be okay to order a real drink, then decided I couldn't because you might think I was weak."

"I'd never think that."

"But it wasn't the drink that had me twisted in knots. I'm not an alcoholic. My hands are steady."

"But you said you'd been drinking too much."

"And that was the truth. I drank to drown out the world. I was sick with grief for a long time, too long. The grief is still with me, but I can face it now."

"So what had you looking the way you did?"

"You."

"I don't understand."

"I cared what you thought of me."

"I see."

"It's been a long time since I felt that way. I can't explain it, being around you makes me want to check to see if my shirt's tucked in."

"It is." She laughed.

"To a brighter tomorrow." He held his Coke up.

"I'll drink to that." She clinked his glass.

He took a sip. Set the glass on the bar. "You wanna get some air?"

"Sure, we can go out by the pool." She set her drink next to his and wended her way through the crowd toward a door by the back of the bar. She pushed her way through it and he followed her out to the dark night.

Chaise lounges three deep lined the far side of the Olympic sized pool, waiting for the morrow, a hot sun and island visitors seeking the perfect tan to take home and show off. The other side of the pool, where Beth was headed, was lined with round tables, sprouting umbrellas. A giant mushroom patch, making much needed shade for the sunburned tourist who'd spent too long on a lounge chair.

Someone moaned. Wolfe tensed, looked across the pool toward the sound. A couple was stretched out on one of the lounge chairs, kissing, oblivious to all around them, save each other. They seemed young. Must be, Wolfe thought, as sane adults wouldn't grope each other like that with a bar packed full of people, all visible from the pool as if it were high noon and there were no barrier between them.

"Young love," Beth said.

"Yeah." Wolfe looked at the people inside, drinking, celebrating the New Year. He shook his head and looked back toward the young couple. Having just come from inside he knew the revelers couldn't see out. The bar was another world, bright, noisy, festive. Outside it was quiet, dark, somber. The couple was safe from voyeurs and prying eyes.

It started to rain, a drizzle.

The couple on the lounge chair didn't seem to mind.

It started coming down harder.

Still the couple ignored it.

"Let's get under one of those umbrellas." Beth led him to a table, pulled out a chair and sat.

"So, how come you came all the way to Trinidad to question me about who might've killed the Skidmores in California? You could've called."

"I guess I wanted to see you again."

"Really?"

"I don't know why."

"Think about it. I'd like to know."

He studied her to see if she was making fun of him. She wasn't. He turned away, looked to the deep end of the pool. How to answer? He'd already gone too far.

"When I first saw you it was like someone grabbed me in the crotch and twisted me all up inside."

"You really are a romantic aren't you?" She laughed.

"What?"

"Do you always wear you heart on your sleeve like this?" She laughed some more.

"Not always, but you asked."

Lightning flashed, thunder boomed, the sky let loose, rain poured down.

"Let's get out of here," the girl at the other end of the pool squealed.

"We're gone," the man said. They made a sprint for the bar, laughing all the way. Then they were through the door to a round of back slapping applause. Though Wolfe couldn't hear, he saw the hands clapping.

"So what do we do now?" Beth said.

"I don't have any idea."

"Maybe I do." She got up, pulled off her blouse, tossed it on the table. Then she kicked of her Nikes. "Feel like swimming?"

"The people." Wolfe looked toward the bar.

"They can't see." She popped open the button down fly, stepped out of her Levi's, then stood before him clad in bra and panties.

"Come on, hurry up, or are you shy?"

"Shy is something I've never been." He stripped down to his boxer shorts as she watched.

"Nice," she said, then she dove into the pool. She rolled over, once, twice, then came up for air.

* * *

Beth stood in the shallow end. A shiver of anticipation rippled along her bare back. What was she doing? Never had she been so forward with a man. Never had she wanted sex as she did now. It had been a long time, but that wasn't it. There was something about Wolfe. Kind of a cosmic connection between them. She felt it. He did too.

He dove in, slipping into the water with hardly a ripple. The one dive told her he was at home in the water and as if to punctuate the thought, he swam easily across the pool.

Holding her breath she struck out toward him, swimming underwater. Should she wait for him to make the first move? Should she allow any moves to be made at all? Then she chided herself. If taking her clothes off in front of him wasn't a first move, then nothing was. She swam to him, wrapped an arm around him.

"I'm pretty nervous," he said.

"Me too." She let go of him. They were in the deep end. She stopped treading water, slipped below the surface, reached down and pulled off her panties. She came back up with them balled in her fist. She wondered how he'd react if he could see through the dark water, if he knew she was naked from the waist down.

He turned away.

"Relax, I've got a bra on. You can't see any more than you could if I was wearing a bikini."

"But it's not a bikini." He returned his gaze. "And I can see right through it."

"No you can't." She dropped her chin to her chest, looked down. The bra was transparent, her nipples stood out like erasers on number two pencils. "So don't look if it bothers you."

"It doesn't bother me."

"I bet." She dove under, conscious that he got a look at her bare bottom as she did. If that wasn't an invitation, then nothing was. When she came up he was swimming alongside. So he wasn't stupid. She stopped, let go of the panties, started treading water. "It's over my head."

"Yeah." He sunk below the surface. She wasn't stupid either. She knew what he was doing. He popped up with his Boxer's in his hand. "I hope I'm not reading this wrong."

"Stupid man." She flopped onto her back and back stroked her way to where she could touch. To her surprise the rain had stopped, the squall had passed and all of a sudden the sky was clear. She saw the Milky Way overhead, bright as silver gleaming in the sun. A diamond sky. So beautiful. Still on her back, she stopped her swimming, reached behind herself and unclasped the bra. A couple more strokes and it fell away, now she was completely nude, swimming on a dark night with a strange man. She'd never done anything like this before, she felt so wanton. The water was cold, the breeze colder, but warmth coursed through her. She'd never felt so alive. Never, not ever.

She took a breath, sucked it deep into her belly, held it. She'd never made love outside before, never even done it out of bed. All of a sudden she felt his hands under her arm pit. He was lifting her out of the water. No this wasn't what she wanted. She was about to tell him when he pulled her in for a kiss.

Oh, Lord. The tingling started at her lips, went to her breasts and settled like a thunderbolt between her legs. Oh, Lord. Oh, Lord. Oh, Lord. She was having the grandest event of her life, shuddering like she'd been impaled by a prince and he hadn't even entered her yet. How could a kiss set her off like that? It wasn't possible. But she was seeing stars, and not just the bright stars in the sky overhead.

"How?" she mumbled when he broke the kiss.

"What?"

"I had an orgasm." She jerked, she was weak in the knees. "Oh, shit. I'm still having it." She threw her arms around his neck, drew him in for a sweet kiss. "Oh, Lord," she muttered into his throat.

He swallowed her words with her tongue.

"Ah," she breathed into his mouth as he cupped her buttocks, drew her close, stiffed himself into her. She started shuddering immediately as a second orgasm racked through her. She'd never known such pleasure. She wrapped her arms around him and pumped and pumped and pumped, until she felt him shooting into her as she came for a third time, a climax that made the earth move and the stars fall from the sky.

Out of the pool Beth combed her fingers through her hair, twisted the water out. She was nude, starlight glistened from her damp breasts. He was devouring her with his eyes. She curled her toes in the cool breeze.

"We should get dressed before somebody comes out here," he said.

She turned to the bar, saw the crowd inside. How could she have forgotten about them? What if someone had come out while they were doing it in the pool? They would've gotten an eyeful.

"Right." She dried herself off with her Levi's as best she could, then put them on as he did the same. Her bra and panties were lost to the pool. She put on the blouse and giggled.

"What?"

"Your boxers are gone too."

"You're beautiful," he said.

"You're just saying that." She blushed. Then, "We need to talk."

"Later," he said.

"So," she said as they made their way back to the bar, "what are you thinking?"

"I'm thinking I'd like to stop being a detective for a few days and just be a guy in paradise who's found a girl he's nuts about."

"You can do that, just put it aside?"

"I'm going to try. I'm miles away from the job. It can wait a day or two."

She thought about telling him about the dead girl out at the Five Islands and about Brody and his talk of diamonds, but that would bring out the detective in him and he seemed so happy. She couldn't do it, not right now. He'd been so lost for so long. She felt the glow of his joy rippling off of him, like an angel's aura.

She wouldn't give him a few days, but she'd let him have the night. She'd tell him in the morning .

*   *   *

"You wanna eat or what?" Wolfe said as he stepped into the hotel room and tossed his grip on the bed. "We could get something to eat, order room service."

"I don't wanna eat in the room. That seems kind of cheap, you know, coming here for dinner and sex."

"You think?" he said, disappointed. That was exactly what he had in mind. Did she have regrets?

"Definitely cheap." She was playing with the top button of her blouse. She undid it. Then the second. "I don't want to have dinner in a hotel room." She popped another button, then another. "Hotel rooms aren't for eating, restaurants are for that." She undid the last button, pulled the blouse off.

"Right." No time for buttons, he pulled his shirt over his head. "Race you."

"Loser." She kicked her shoes off.

"Bet me." His shoes were off.

The button down flies popped open in stereo and they dove for the bed. Wolfe covered her mouth, went to war with her tongue. He fondled a breast, she grabbed onto his cock, squeezed. He felt like he was going to explode. He'd never known two people could enjoy each other so much.

Afterward they showered together. Hugging, kissing, fondling under the hot spray. He felt like he was back in high school.

"I should call the boat and leave a message for Noelle," she said later.

"You got a phone on board?"

"Radio." She grabbed her backpack, took out a handheld radio. "*Shogun, Shogun, Mobile.*"

"Go *Mobile.*" Wolfe recognized Noelle's voice coming out of the tiny speaker.

"Switch one eight."

"Switching," Noelle said and Beth turned the dial.

"I called her on the hailing frequency," she told Wolfe. "Once you make contact you're supposed to change channels."

"I'm here, Beth, over," Noelle said.

"I'm going to have dinner with Wolfe, so I'll be a little while."

"Okay, thanks for letting me know, *Shogun* out."

"I'd like to stay the night," she said, "but Frank was Noelle's father and she loved him. I can't let her know what happened between us, at least not yet."

"I understand," he said.

Then they took the elevator to the lobby. It was ten o'clock on New Year's Eve, the hotel was full, the lobby crowded. Their hair was still wet from the shower, but it wasn't the wet hair that caused the heads to turn. It was the way they held onto each other, the way they walked, the way they laughed, as if the lobby were empty, save for them. They were acting like teenagers in love and it was infectious. Smiles followed them when they passed.

CHAPTE.
TEA

THE MORNING SUN SPLASHED through the overhead hatch, waking Beth. She knuckled the sleep from her eyes, sat up. She threw her legs over the side of the berth and climbed out as last night came flooding back. The wild sex in the pool. The fantastic sex up in his room.

Then she frowned. She'd expected to find Noelle when she got to the boat, but she'd left before Beth got back. She must've spent the night with Victor. It was none of her business, Noelle was an adult, after all, but the thought of it sent goosebumps running up her arms.

"Hello, *Shogun*." It was Noelle, back at last. "Beth, you up yet?"

"Yeah." Beth popped her head out the hatch. "It's good to have you back."

"Come on, Beth. I'm a big girl." Noelle stepped onto the boat.

"I was just thinking that."

"We didn't do anything." Noelle came down the companionway. "Besides, even if I wanted to, I wouldn't. He's married."

"So where were you?" She knew she shouldn't have asked. It was none of her business, but Beth couldn't help herself.

"We went to the Anchorage and danced the year away, then we talked till dawn."

Beth shook her head.

"I know, I shouldn't have. But his wife's in Europe till next week, so it's not like she was waiting up for him. Besides, nothing happened."

"I'm gonna change." Beth started the coffee machine.

Fifteen minutes later they were on deck drinking steaming coffee.

"Look." Beth pointed to two policemen coming up the dock.

"I didn't think anybody in this country worked before breakfast," Noelle said. "And on a holiday."

"Especially not anyone who works for the government and certainly not the police," Beth finished.

"They must have found about the body somehow."

"Yeah."

They watched as the two West Indian officers walked up the main dock and turned left toward *Shogun*. They were walking out of step, taking their time.

"Looks like they're coming here." Noelle took a sip of her coffee.

"Yeah." Beth did the same.

The policemen squinted into the morning sun. Their uniforms pressed and neat, gray shirts with epaulets, black trousers, black belts, black shoes, black hat brims. One wore sergeant's stripes, the other had no stripes at all. They were tall, angular men, ambling up the dock, enjoying the day, smiling.

The smiles disappeared when they approached the boat and noticed the women watching them.

"Mrs. Shannon?" the one with the stripes said.

"Yes," Beth answered.

"We have some questions."

"Before coffee?"

"We're on important business."

"I have some sweet rolls," Beth said.

The younger officer looked at his superior.

"Another day," the sergeant said.

A frown covered the junior man's face.

"Hello, *Shogun*." A high, squeaky voice interrupted the policeman.

Beth turned toward it and saw a mousy looking little white man, sweating already in a short sleeved, white shirt with a dark blue tie. He had straight dark hair, slicked back into a pony tail, a pointy noise, squinty eyes. He looked up at the two women, like a mongrel dog looking for scraps, no, more like a weasel about to steal a robin's eggs.

"Excuse me," the sergeant said, "we have business here."

"Elizabeth Shannon?" The weasel ignored the policeman.

Beth nodded.

"Your boat's been arrested. You have to leave. I'm to see that you take nothing off but personal possessions."

Beth's eyes narrowed as she took in what the man said.

"It's legal." The weasel reached into a briefcase she hadn't noticed and came out with a fistful of documents. "You have to surrender the ship's papers to me and leave the boat. You can have a few minutes to gather your things."

"I just came back from burying my husband and now you come sniffing around here trying to steal what he might have left behind."

"Your husband owed money to Corbeau Yacht Services and he's not able to repay it."

"They're vultures, just like their name!" Noelle said.

"Our bills are paid," Beth said.

"It says here they're not."

"Get out of here!" Beth was furious.

"I'm here to see that you leave the boat."

"Little man, if you don't stop bothering us, I'll jump down there and kick the shit out of you." Noelle stood and looked down at him.

"Officer." He grabbed the sergeant's arm. The sergeant shrugged him off. The weasel stepped in front of the taller man. "I demand you put these women off this boat. I've got a court order and it's your duty to uphold it." He punctuated his words with pointed fingers, shaking them in the sergeant's face.

"Is it true? Did this woman's husband just pass?" The sergeant asked.

"It's not relevant." The weasel poked the sergeant in the chest with the pointed finger.

"It is to me." The sergeant slapped the weasel's hand away with a crack heard halfway down the dock.

"You can't—"

"Shut up," the sergeant said.

"But—"

"Another word and I'll arrest you and forget where I put you. Do you take my meaning?"

The weasel glared at the policeman.

"Go," the sergeant said.

And the weasel went, walking stiff-legged down the dock toward the club house. The policeman had made an enemy, Beth thought.

"Thank you," Beth said. She saw the policeman in a new light. For him to strike a white man was a big thing, even if nobody in Trinidad would admit it.

"I am truly sorry," he said. "I didn't know about your husband. I should have shown some respect."

"You couldn't have known," Beth said.

"Still, I should have been more circumspect. Anyway, I have to ask you a question that you probably can't answer. It's about your husband."

"Go ahead," Beth said.

"Some fishermen found a body out at the Five Islands and it turns out she was a friend of your husband's. I was hoping to talk to him, but now that isn't possible."

"You were going to ask my husband if he knew this woman?" Beth said, hoping she could come up with a story this man would believe. "He may have. I wouldn't be surprised. I've just learned he was being unfaithful."

"I think I'll have that coffee, after all," the policeman said. "And my name is Lawless, Sgt. Leon Lawless. Please don't make fun of the name. I've heard all the jokes. May I come aboard?"

"Certainly," Beth said. "What about your friend?"

"He'll be going to the bar."

"What for?" The second policeman spoke for the first time. His voice was deep, with a touch of gravel.

"To arrest that little white man for assaulting an officer of the law."

"But he didn't."

"You saw him poke me in the chest," Sgt. Lawless said.

"You want me to put him in handcuffs in front of everybody in the Yacht Club?" A smile lit up the other policeman's face.

"Yes, handcuff him, sit him down in the bar and wait for me. If he utters one word, smack him across the mouth."

"What?" The young officer's eyes widened along with his grin.

"If you want to keep your job, no words will pass that little man's lips, no ears will hear a thing he has to say. Do you understand?"

"Yes, sir. Yes I do, sir."

"Then do it."

"Right away, sir." He made a snappy about face and jogged down the dock toward the bar. He also was no longer the image of the slow moving Trinidadian policeman that Beth had seen so often in the three years she'd been in the country.

"Seems he's going to enjoy arresting a white man." Lawless swung a lanky leg over the lifelines and stepped on board.

"Seems so," Beth said. Then, "How do you like your coffee?"

"Black."

"My husband drank it that way," Beth said, under her breath. She went below to get the man his coffee.

"Yes, your husband." Lawless followed her, uninvited, below. Noelle came down after him and they both watched as Beth pulled a cup from the cupboard above the coffee pot and poured Lawless his coffee.

"Have a seat," Beth said. Lawless sat at the salon table. Beth and Noelle joined him.

"Do you want a sweet roll?" Beth asked.

"No, just coffee."

They sipped in silence for a few moments, with the ticking of the old brass ship's clock counting off the seconds. The man had something to say and Beth had learned that in Trinidad it's best to have patience, especially when dealing with Customs, Immigration or the police.

After a long minute the policeman began to talk.

"Four years ago my wife was taken from me. I loved her very much. We have three children, three girls. I thank the Lord every day that they are easier to raise than boys." There was the beginning of a tear in the policeman's eye. The man was still suffering over a wife he'd lost a long time ago.

"Can you sail this boat out of Trinidad by noon?" He said.

"Not by myself."

"You could with my help," Noelle said. "The two of us could sail her."

"Not really," Beth said. "You've been out with us a couple of times, sure, but we always had the guys from the yard with us, remember?"

"So?"

"I'm not a sailor. You're father wasn't a sailor. We were learning. We bought the boat here and had it refit here and lived on it here, but we've never had it out by ourselves."

"But you were going to sail it up the islands next month."

"We had an instructor coming from the States. He was going to teach us how to sail on the way up."

"But surely the two of you could move the boat in an emergency," Lawless said.

"In an emergency, I suppose so," Beth said.

"You should consider this an emergency, because that little man is going to come back in a few hours with those same papers and take your boat and there won't be anything I can do about it. You should go to Immigration and check out. You should leave Trinidad right away."

"Impossible. I'd have to get Noelle on the crew list. That'll take at least a day. There's no way that obstinate man over in Immigration will do it any quicker. I guess the only thing I can do is hire a lawyer."

"Justice moves very slow in Trinidad," Lawless said.

"There isn't anything else I can do."

"You should go to Immigration about an hour after I leave and check out. The forms will already be filled out and dated two days ago. You will merely have to get your passports stamped. Then come back here straightaway and take your boat away from Trinidad."

"You can do this?" Beth said.

"That obstinate man at Immigration is my son from my first marriage. That's how I know girls are easier. He was never anything but trouble. Into everything and anything. Still, he minds his father."

"And your first wife?"

"She died in childbirth."

"I'm so sorry," Beth said, looking deep into his brown eyes.

"It's not your fault," Lawless said.

"Why are you doing this?" Beth asked, but she knew the answer even as the words left her lips.

"Because you've lost your husband," he said. "That's enough. I won't let you lose your home as well. Make yourself ready to go. Don't spend the night in Scotland Bay. Get out of Trinidad. If possible you should be sailing through the Bocas by noon." Lawless smiled at her as he hefted his lanky frame up from the table.

"What about the man with the papers?" Noelle said.

"That little white man is going to spend a very unhappy couple of hours in jail, but he'll be out by noon. Out, mad and looking for you and your boat, and when he doesn't find them, he'll be after my black skin."

"Will you be okay?" Beth asked.

"Me, I'll be fine. He struck a policeman, after all." Lawless looked very serious now. "But my guess is that those papers are legitimate, I won't be able to help you again."

"I'll be out of Trinidad by noon," Beth said.

"That's best."

Beth followed him topside with her thoughts on that poor dead girl as she watched him walk down the dock. So Frank had been having an affair right under her nose, after all.

"Penny for your thoughts," Noelle said.

"I was thinking that we better start securing this boat for travel.

"I'm baking," Noelle said. It was a only a little before ten and it was already hot.

"Me too," Beth said, as she stepped onto the boat. Her head was still spinning from the royal treatment she'd received from the Immigration officer. True to his word, Lawless had arranged it so that she was checked out in record time. Both the forms and the stamp in her passport were dated two days ago.

The government of Trinidad and Tobago had no authority to seize a boat that was outside their waters. The backdates on the clearance forms made the weasel's papers worthless, unless, of course, he showed up again before she managed to get *Shogun* out of the country.

"And we're gonna get out of Trinidad now?" Noelle said.

"Not exactly."

"What do you mean?"

"Remember me telling Sgt. Lawless that your father and I have never sailed by ourselves?"

"Yeah, but we decided we could handle it, you and me."

"There's something else I neglected to tell you."

"What?"

"Grenada's about twelve hours away and I've never been out after dark."

"Swell."

"And I don't know how to navigate."

"It just keeps getting better."

"On the plus side, it's a big island. We shouldn't have too much trouble finding it."

"It's a bigger ocean."

"You're telling me, but I figure we can get the boat to this deserted island halfway between Trinidad and Venezuela and hide out till tomorrow. We could motor there, then go over the charts and instruments and figure how to get this boat up island."

"You mean the abandoned leper colony Dad told me about?"

"Yeah."

"Do you think we can do that?"

"We're two bright women. How hard could it be?"

"Yeah, if all these other sailors I've met around here can do it, we can."

"That's the spirit, now all we have to do is figure out how to get this old girl out of the Yacht Club."

"You're kidding?"

"I wish I was." Beth moved behind the wheel, put her hands on it. She turned it left, then spun it right. "It drives like a big, sluggish truck unless it's under sail, then she handles like a Corvette." She looked over her shoulder at the line of boats snugged safely in their slips. Could she get *Shogun* past them, make the turn, then get her out past the breakwater without damaging them or without taking out the Yacht Club bar?

"What are you thinking?" Noelle said.

"We have to get out of here without running into any of the other boats."

"I see what you mean." Noelle looked over the boats in the marina.

"Every time the guys took it out they backed up till they were away from the pier, then turned it around and motored out."

"They did a one-eighty in that little space there?" Noelle was looking at the area between two rows of boats. She shook her head. "You can do that?"

"Yeah, everybody does."

"How?"

"They sort of play with the throttle and the gears, going in and out of reverse as they add and back off the power. They make it look so easy, but if I try it, I'm afraid I'll take out half the marina."

"So what are we going to do? If we stay in the Yacht Club that man will come back and take the boat."

"That's not gonna happen. You go down and unplug the phone," Beth said. Noelle went below as Beth disconnected the electricity and the water.

"Okay," Beth said when they were back in the cockpit, "we're ready." She pushed the start button.

Nothing.

"It didn't start," Noelle said.

"I know." Beth studied the gauges. "Oh, yeah, we have to turn on the ignition first. She did it, pushed the start button again, the main engine rumbled to life, the boat lurched forward, but the spring lines kept it from plowing into the dock. Beth punched the stop button.

"What happened?" Noelle said.

"I started it in gear. Dumb, dumb, dumb."

She turned to look around the marina to see if anybody had noticed. They had. Yachties on their boats were staring, Alice among them. Two or three of the dock workers were looking, too. What was the big deal? People started their engines around here all the time. But after she thought about it for a second, she understood. They knew she didn't have a clue. Would one of them come over and ask what she was doing? Offer help?

Maybe they'd think she was doing some work on the engine. No, they knew better, they'd probably think she was just starting it to see of she could. Nobody would suspect she was thinking about motoring out of the Yacht Club.

Beth shifted it into neutral.

"Okay," Noelle said, "are we ready now?"

"I guess we are."

Beth looked around the marina again and saw that Alice had lowered her dinghy into the water. She started the engine as Alice climbed down from her boat and started the dinghy.

"I think she's going to help if we get into trouble." Beth hoped she was right.

"How does she know we're leaving?" Noelle said.

"We started the engines. It doesn't take a genius."

"So what do we do now?"

"I think you should undo the lines, then hop aboard as I ease the boat back."

"Look," Noelle said, "company."

A group of yachties were coming down the dock.

"Going somewhere, Beth?" Ron from *Wind Catcher* said in his Southern accent. He was a short, blustery man with red hair and a beard to match. He came to Trinidad with five other boats from Oriental, South Carolina. The South Carolinians were all in the Yacht Club, had been for the last six months. Beth thought they were all wonderful people.

"Yeah, we gotta go."

"I'll get your bow lines." Ron bent and took the starboard line off a cleat.

"I'll get the spring lines." Bill from *Sail Away* hopped onto the finger pier. He was a tall, thin man from Florida with close set eyes, elephant ears and a pelican nose. Like Ron he carried a Southern accent. He was a true gentleman who had been in the Yacht Club for the whole time she'd been there with Frank. She'd never heard him swear and he was the kind of man who'd spend all day helping you fix something on the boat. He'd been a great help to her and Frank.

Other yachties got her other lines. None of them asked what she was doing or where she was going. They knew she wasn't experienced, shouldn't be doing what she was doing. Somehow they must have found out about the weasel and his papers and they were trying to help.

"Don't try to turn it around," Ron said. "Just back her all the way out and around the breakwater. Keep the power on about a third and she'll handle just like you're backing the station wagon out of the garage."

"I'm here if you get in trouble, girl." Alice revved her fifteen horsepower Yamaha. Beth was glad to see her alongside. "If it looks like you're gonna crash into something, I'll push you off."

"Thanks." Beth gave her a thumbs up sign. Alice returned it.

"We'll walk you out," Ron said. "Add just a touch of power till you clear the pier, then up to a third as soon as we toss the lines on board."

"Okay." Beth felt the sting of sweat in her eyes, wiped her forehead with the back of a hand. "I'm adding the power." There was a subtle change in the engine sound. The boat started to move. She grabbed a glance at Bill. He was leading her out with the spring line, then all of a sudden she was past the finger pier and he threw the line onto the boat. She looked forward, they had already tossed the bow lines aboard.

Beth looked over her shoulder, tried to imagine she was driving a car. She added the power a third of the way, like Ron had said. And all of a sudden she was out of control.

"Left, left, left!" Noelle screamed. "You're gonna hit the boats."

Beth spun the wheel, she hadn't had it centered.

"Too far, come back, come back!" Beth spun the wheel back, too far.

"I'm here!" Alice put her dinghy between *Shogun* and a ketch she was about to bang into. Alice had her Yamaha wound all the way up as she pushed *Shogun* away from it.

"That was close!" Ron shouted. It was his boat.

Now *Shogun* was going too far to the left, but that was all right, Beth had already cleared the breakwater.

CHAPTER ELEVEN

WOLFE SQUINTED AGAINST THE SUNLIGHT streaming in the window. Shielding his eyes with a hand, he looked outside. From the sun he saw it was close to noon. He'd slept late.

Although he'd told Beth he wanted to take a few days away from police work, he couldn't get the case out of his mind. He decided to call Norton, not just to find out about the Skidmore case, but also to find out how his friend was doing. He punched out the phone number. The call was answered on the fourth ring.

"Norton."

"It's Wolfe. How's the leg?"

"Forget about me, boy. You've got trouble."

"What kind of trouble?"

"One of your neighbors called the cops. Your front door was open and your stereo had everyone in the building awake. Even though the place had been trashed, they couldn't help but see the scales and white powder on your coffee table."

"Swell."

"It gets worse," Norton said.

"Go on."

"They searched the apartment and found the strongbox bolted to one of the beds in the bedroom."

"It's a gun safe. I left it open when I took out my weapon."

"It wasn't open when the uniforms found it."

"What'd they find inside?"

"Nude photos of those women up in that penthouse."

"From the murder scene?" Wolfe felt his stomach churn.

"No. They were taken before the women were killed. Whoever took 'em was a sicko."

"And Richards thinks it's me?"

"There was press all over it before it got to him. He didn't have much choice. You're the suspect. They know you've gone to Trinidad, they're onto the local authorities there and they're pulling out all the stops."

"Jesus."

"You're a cop, Billy. You're a suspect, the only suspect I might add, in a multiple homicide, and it looks like you've fled the country. You'd be in custody now if the cops over there knew their mouths from their assholes."

"Thanks for telling me, Able."

"Hey, we go back. I know you didn't do this. Alvarez and I will do what we can here. You need anything, call."

"Thanks, Able."

"Keep your head down."

"Yeah, I gotta go." Wolfe hung up. Then he grabbed his grip and took the elevator to the lobby. He'd checked into his room with a credit card. It wouldn't take the locals too long to figure out where he was staying.

The desk clerk was on the phone when Wolfe approached the reception to check out. There was a newspaper on the counter. Wolfe stared at his picture on the front page and all of a sudden he knew who the clerk was talking to and what he was talking about.

"Put it on my bill." He picked up the newspaper.

The clerk stopped talking, nodded. He looked scared.

Wolfe walked out the door and stepped into the front seat of a waiting taxi.

"Cab's taken," the driver said.

"Thought you were waiting for me." Wolfe handed the driver a blue hundred as he heard the sirens off in the distance.

"Where you wanna go?" The driver slid the bill into a shirt pocket.

"Away from here."

"I'm driving. Don't have to tell me twice." The driver shoved it in gear and tore away from the front of the hotel, slowing only to look at the police cars as they roared by on the other side of the street.

"Looks like a close call for you," the driver said.

"There's another hundred in it for you if you can find the Yacht Club."

"I can find the Yacht Club." The driver slowed as he approached traffic.

Wolfe tried to ignore his picture as he scanned the newspaper while they moved through the crowded streets. It was incredible, they were saying he'd killed Mark Skidmore, his wife and sister-in-law. How could they have it in print that fast? Who called them from California?

He read on and learned that the Skidmores were one of the wealthiest families in Trinidad, Mark being the American cousin to Sam and Stewart and a host of other Trinidadian Skidmores. Mark divided his time between Trinidad and America, Wolfe already knew that, balancing his time between his business interests in the two countries.

Wolfe turned the page and saw a picture of Mark Skidmore with the prime minister. The story went on to say that Mark was well loved in Trinidad, would be missed and that the Trinidad and Tobago Police Department would stop at nothing to find his killer, William Wolfe, and bring him to justice.

Wolfe crumpled the paper. There was no mention that he was a cop, nor any reason given as to why he'd suddenly shown up in Trinidad.

"How can anyone believe this crap?"

"What?" the driver said.

"Nothing."

The driver pulled the cab into the Yacht Club parking lot. "We're here." He held out his hand.

"There's another one of these in it for you if you wait for a few minutes." Wolfe gave the driver a second blue hundred.

"I'm waiting."

At the Yacht Club he learned that Beth and Noelle had left with the boat an hour earlier. Why? It made no sense. Was she running away from him, from what they'd shared together?

"It's good that I had you wait." Wolfe said as he climbed back in the cab. "Can you take me to a cheap hotel?"

"The kind of place where they don't ask too many questions?"

"Yeah, that kind of place," Wolfe said.

Fifteen minutes later he was in a hotel room in the center of the city. He set his grip on the lumpy bed, then used the newspaper as a weapon and swatted at a roach that was sitting bold as brass in the middle of the wall. He missed. He wondered what to do next. He had no car and every cop in the country was looking for him.

He was about to pull his shirt off and step into the small shower, when he heard sirens again and they seemed to be getting closer. The cab driver must have told. He grabbed his grip and left the room.

There was a row of businesses on the opposite side of the street, all closed save for a fabric shop with the banner, "New Year's Day Sale," in the front window. He couldn't see anywhere to go, but he couldn't stay were he was.

He crossed the street, passed between a bakery and a religious book store to an alley behind. He went left, but stopped when he saw a police car drive by at the end of the alley. It had to have been the taxi driver who called the cops, and he'd given him all that money. Was there no honor anymore?

Any second he expected the police to come blasting toward him. One side of the alley bordered on the high back fences of private homes. Razor wire and glass bottles decorated the tops of the fences, there would be no escape that way. The alley was a trap, and the only way out was back the way he'd come. And there were police there now.

He had to hide.

All of the businesses had back doors facing the alley, but of course they'd all be locked, as everything was closed because of the holiday. Then he remembered the fabric store. He saw an open wrought iron door that closed over a wooden one. That had to be it. Sweat trickled down his back. He tried the wooden door. It opened. He slipped in and shuddered with the loud sound the door made when it latched closed, but someone had a stereo cranked up. Rod Stewart was singing loud about a big bosomed girl with a Dutch accent. Wolfe doubted whoever was out front had heard him come in.

He locked the door.

The window in the top part of the door was covered by a blackout shade. He pulled the shade aside and peeked out in time to see a police car race down the alley from the right.

Letting the shade fall he looked around. The room was cluttered with cloth. Colors of all kinds splashed against his eyes. Piles of cotton batiks were heaped along the walls in no particular order. Bolts of solids, checks, and florals were stacked in the center of the room. There was a small bathroom by the back door, a desk by the bathroom. It too, was covered in color. And the room was cold. The air-conditioning was on high.

The music stopped and the silence was loud. Instinct said hide. He turned to the bathroom, stopped. It would be the first place they looked, if they looked.

He heard muffled voices from the store out front. If they were the police, he had only seconds. He clenched his fists again in quick desperation. The sweat under his arms felt like ice in the air-conditioned room.

Time to act, and like a mole, he burrowed into a pile of batik, making sure his legs, feet and grip were fully covered.

"I'm telling you there's no one back here." The voice was young and female.

"He's a dangerous man and he's somewhere close by." Sounded like a cop.

"A murderer?" The female voice.

"That's what we said." The speaker was standing close enough to touch.

"She was right. The door's locked." A second male voice. A second policeman.

"Told you," the girl said. "I come in through the back when I open and I always lock it back up as soon as I get inside."

"Okay, let's go," first male voice said.

Wolfe sighed to himself. Obviously the girl didn't always lock up after herself and it was a good thing he'd done it for her, because if he hadn't, the police would have searched the room and it would all be over. He didn't think they'd be leaving the area anytime soon, which meant he wasn't going anywhere either. In only a few hours he'd been transformed from policeman to criminal.

Who?

Why?

How?

His thoughts were interrupted by Rod Stewart's gravelly voice drifting large into the back room, assaulting him through the pile of cloth. She was cranking it up loud again. The cops must be gone. But they'd still be across the street and they'd still be patrolling the neighborhood. For the time being he was trapped. But he was better off than he'd been just a short while ago. He was keyed up. He took a breath, held it and concentrated on slowing his rapid heart beat. Once that was under control he filled his mind with Beth. Eventually he closed his eyes. A veteran of many stakeouts, he could sleep anywhere.

He woke when the music stopped. He lay still, listened to the sounds of the girl up front closing up the shop. Then it was quiet.

Stretching, he pushed the fabric away, sat up, then stood and stepped out of his bed of batik. In a few seconds his eyes were accustomed to the dark. He checked his watch, seven-thirty. A cool Saturday evening and he had no place to go, but one thing was for certain, he couldn't stay where he was.

It took him less than a minute to realize that he was locked in.

The windows were barred. The back door was latched and the barred door was probably locked behind it. He went out into the front of the shop. Same thing. Barred door, barred windows.

He looked up and saw his way out. No bars above.

When he was younger it would have been easy, but he wasn't younger and it was going to be hard. The cash register would have to go. He unplugged it and set it on the floor.

He pulled the counter under the skylight. Standing on it, he could reach the ceiling. He wondered if he still had enough power in his arms to pull himself out. Before finding out he'd have to break the glass. He picked up a five foot bolt of cotton batik, climbed up on the counter, squeezed his eyes shut, jammed the bolt up through the skylight.

The shattering glass rained on him, but he was more concerned with the wailing burglar alarm.

He tore a large piece of cloth off the bolt, then tossed the roll of cloth aside. The high pitched siren urged him on. He bunched the cloth into a bundle and used it to wipe the glass from around the edges of the skylight. When the sides were free of shards he dropped the cloth, tossed his grip out through the skylight, took a deep breath, held it, thrust his hands through, jumped, and pulled himself out and onto the roof.

Blue lights flashed in the distance, cutting into the hot Caribbean night. They had to be operating well above their usual efficiency level. They really wanted him. He started to move away from the approaching police cars. The asphalt tiled roof was hot with the leftover heat from the day and it warmed his feet through his running shoes as he made his way to the back of the building.

He looked for a ladder or drain pipe, finding none, he dropped his grip to the ground, dropped to his knees, lowered himself over the side and dropped to the alley below. He hit the ground, grabbed his grip and charged toward the end of the alley, determined to make it before the police.

He didn't.

The siren pierced him before he saw the car and he dove behind a row of garbage cans as the police car rounded into the alley, lighting up the night like a strobe light on a dark dance floor.

A second car followed the first and he heard two or more sirens on the street beyond, in front of the fabric shop. They were out in force.

The two police cars braked behind the fabric shop and four cops piled out of four doors, all with guns drawn. Wolfe shivered. The largest of the bunch started shouting into the store and two others began clawing at the barred door.

It looked like the four policemen were giving that door their undivided attention, so Wolfe decided to take a chance. He stood and eased his way out from behind the trash cans. If one of the cops turned, he'd be seen—an easy target. He crossed his fingers as he backed out of the alley, something he hadn't done since he was a kid. Then he turned and started down the street at a brisk walk.

It was a hot night. People were out on their porches. Some said hello, others nodded their heads when he walked by. All would remember him. He was white, out after dark, downtown. He looked up at the crescent moon and saw a shooting star. He thought about Beth. Where was she? Why had she taken the boat to sea? Was she all right? He hoped so.

He took his eyes off of the heavens and saw a sun-faded movie poster advertising a James Bond movie as he passed behind the Strand movie theater. He hadn't been to a movie in a long time.

Around front two young boys were buying tickets at the box office and blue lights were coming down the street. Wolfe groped in his pocket, pulled out some money. He bought a ticket and stepped into the theater as another police car whizzed by.

The lobby was crowded and he felt the press of people as he moved toward the ticket taker. Inside the theater he fumbled forward, waiting for his eyes to adjust to the dark, finding a seat seconds before the screen was hit with bright words on a black backdrop.

PLEASE DON'T SMOKE MARIJUANA
IN THE THEATRE AUDITORIUM.

And most of the first row lit up. Then others amid laughing giggles followed suit. Not everyone, but at least two or three in every row. Wolfe tasted the pungent smoke, repressed a laugh as it wafted through the theater. The Rasta man next to him lit up a cigar-sized joint and a young woman a few seats down was taking a small, tightly rolled one out of her purse. She couldn't be more than sixteen or seventeen, he thought, as she put the joint to her lips and lit it with the flick of a Bic.

Then he did laugh.

This is what his government had been fighting for as long as he could remember. He glanced around the theater. No violence here. Just a theater full of people having a good time on a Saturday night.

He laughed louder.

"Hey man," the Rasta said, smiling. He was holding the cigar between his fingers, offering it.

"Why not?" Wolfe said.

Chapter Twelve

"Take the wheel." Beth kept a hand on the helm as she stepped aside to make room.

"What?"

"Take the wheel. If you're going to help me get this thing up island, you're going to have to know how to steer it."

Noelle moved into place, put her hands on the wheel.

"Keep it pointed toward that island to the right of the Five Islands."

"The prison island?"

"Yeah, we'll slip between it and the mainland, then make a left out to the leper colony." Beth looked over her shoulder. Thank God the Yacht Club was out of sight. She wondered if that weasel man was back with his papers. If he was, at least he wouldn't be able to spot them. He wouldn't know where they'd gone.

"So, how come you're here?" Beth said as soon as she started to feel safe. The question was rude, but she had to know if she could trust Noelle.

"What do you mean?"

"Why did you come back to Trinidad? Certainly not to be with me. Not to help me save a boat I'm going to sell as soon as I get the chance."

"I figured you'd probably sell it," Noelle said. "I was hoping you wouldn't, but I can see you don't have much choice. You don't have any money, do you?"

"I've got the boat and maybe a couple thousand dollars in the bank," Beth said. "Nothing else."

"Dad wasn't much for saving money."

"No, he wasn't," Beth said. "And I still need to know what you're doing here. Is it because of Victor?"

"Maybe, partly, but mostly I guess I wanted some time away from Mike. I don't think I'm ready to get married."

"Come on, tell the truth. You're stuck on Victor, that's why you came back."

"It shows that much?"

"Yeah, it does."

"Do you think he knows?"

"Probably not, he's so used to women falling all over him, he expects it as his due."

"I hope you're right. I don't want him to think I'm chasing him around like a lovesick fool."

"Noelle, I need to know if I can count on you. I have to take this boat at least up to Grenada, probably up to St. Martin or the Virgins if I want to get a good price for it. Are you with me as far as Grenada or should I give up right now?

"I'm not a quitter, I'll stay."

"How about if I can't sell it there, if I have to go on, maybe up to Miami?"

"Beth, I'll stay with you till you get wherever it is you have to go. No matter how long it takes. I'll see it through, you have my word." She held out her hand, "Shake."

Beth took the hand, shook it.

"Oh no!" Noelle said. "Look at the temperature gauge."

"I don't get it, we just changed the impeller."

"What's an impeller?"

"A round rubber, gear type thingy. It's the part of the raw water pump that pulls the seawater up through the heat exchanger to help cool the engine."

"Jeez, I'm impressed," Noelle said.

"Don't be. Brody changed it just before you came for your visit. He sent me to the chandlery to get a couple and I watched him do the job. He lectured me the whole time." Thinking of Brody sent a ripple up her spine. "God, the way that man calls me Lizzy gives me goosebumps. Brrr."

"You think that's what it is, the impeller thing?"

"I don't see how and I can't check it till after we shut the engine down, so for now we're going to have to go slow.

Four hours later they limped into the large bay at Chacachacare Island, home of Trinidad's abandoned leper colony. Noelle had taken to the wheel like a natural, even though they weren't motoring much faster than they could swim.

"We'll have to get fairly close to shore, over there," Beth pointed. "That's the old nun's quarters. It's about thirty feet deep there."

"No problem," Noelle said.

"I'll get the anchor ready." Beth climbed out of the cockpit.

One of Frank's faults was thinking she'd never be able to master driving the boat. The guys had taught her how to drop anchor, because of the belief that when they left the Yacht Club to start their world tour, Frank or the autopilot, would be doing the driving and Beth would handle the windlass. In a way, she supposed, it had worked out. She knew how to work it, how to anchor in close quarters without hitting another boat.

She signaled Noelle to slow down, then to stop the boat. Holding onto the rolled headsail for support, she wiped sweat from her brow with the back of a hand, then stepped on the down button as she pulled up on the chain, allowing the anchor to fall from the bow roller. She played out a hundred and fifty feet, then motioned for Noelle to put it in reverse to set the hook.

"Well, it took a little longer than expected, but we got her here," Beth said as she stepped into the cockpit.

"Are you going to check the impeller now?"

"No, we have to wait till the engine cools. Let's celebrate the successful completion of our first voyage with a drink."

"Good idea." Noelle had a wide smile on her face. Beth laughed, she may have graduated from medical school, but in a lot of ways she was still a kid.

Fifteen minutes later Beth had a rum and Coke in hand and was watching the setting sun as it painted the sky orange behind the deserted leper colony. She spent a minute worrying and wondering about the wretched lives the lepers must have lived, so far from family and friends, and yet so close.

"It's like a miniature city." Noelle was sitting opposite Beth in the cockpit holding her own drink. Her words broke a five minute silence.

"Your father used to like this place. The dormitory where they lived still has all the beds, but they're all rusted out now. The hospital has high ceilings and stained glass windows, it must have been very nice, considering."

Noelle studied the hospital in the fading light and Beth saw her quiver. Three two-story buildings made their way up the hill. They were painted a sort of beige-brown, the roofs were corrugated tin and rust. Trees surrounded the hospital buildings. The patients would have had a perfect view of the bay. It was a hospital, but it was a prison, too.

"Pretty buildings for a not so pretty people," Noelle said.

"Something like that, but they took good care of them. They had a church and a cinema and the ones that weren't too sick had their own little houses. Look." Beth pointed. "Can you see where the old road winds around the island from the doctor's houses to the hospital?"

"It's all crumbling back into the ocean. It's a shame."

"I think everybody just wanted to get away from here."

They listened to the quiet sounds of the evening breeze and the gentle lapping of the small waves as they splashed against the shore. In the advancing shadows, the hospital across the bay looked peaceful and inviting. Beth felt like she'd passed her first test. She got the boat to Chacachacare, despite the overheating engine. That was something.

And tomorrow she was going to get them to Grenada. She didn't know how to navigate, but they had a GPS on board and it would tell them if they strayed off course, if she could figure how to program the position into it. How hard could it be?

A shooting star bolted across the sky and Beth thought of Wolfe. She could kick herself. She should have called him. What was he going to think when he went by the Yacht Club and *Shogun* was gone? She'd have to call him as soon as they got to Grenada.

"Okay, it's been almost an hour, let's check that engine." Beth stood, went below, then into the engine room behind the side cabin. Noelle followed. "There she is, a Perkins 4236. Big, blue and powerful, that's what your father says."

"You gonna check the water?"

"Yeah." Beth did. "It's full." She went to the tool box, took out a screwdriver.

"You know what you're doing?"

"No." She went to the impeller housing, started to unscrew the cover. Water started leaking out before she took out the first screw. "Shit, I forgot to shut off the seawater intake." She reached under the engine for the seacock, shut it off and the water stopped leaking out of the impeller housing.

"You really don't know anything do you?" Noelle laughed.

"Not a thing." Beth laughed with her as she took off the cover. "Look at this." She stopped laughing as she extracted the impeller with a needle nose pliers.

"What?"

"It's the old one, the one Brody changed." Beth moved away from the engine, went to the cabinet where she'd put the spare impeller. It was still there. "I don't understand, I saw Brody change this. Heck, we motored to Scotland Bay and back after you got here and the engine didn't heat up. I don't think I like this."

"Are you saying somebody changed it back?"

"Yeah," Beth said. "Somebody changed it back."

"Brody," Noelle said. "Must have been. He wanted to make sure you didn't get the boat out of Trinidad. But I don't see why he put the old one back."

"He wanted the boat to be able to make it down to Corbeau, but not much farther. It was his guarantee we wouldn't get away, but he screwed up by not taking the spare. Duh!"

"Duh!" Noelle laughed.

"Yeah, duh!" Beth put in the new impeller, tightened the housing, turned on the seacock. "Now let's have another drink while we fire this baby up."

"Do you hear that?" Noelle said as she came through the companionway into the cockpit.

"Yeah, and it's getting closer." Beth recognized the sound of a powerful boat moving fast across the water and in less then a minute a speedboat roared into the darkening bay.

"*Speed Kills*," Beth said, "Victor Drake's boat. How'd he know we were here?"

"Guess we'll have to wait and find out."

Beth suspected she knew. Noelle must have phoned when she went below to disconnect the phone and cable. Beth felt like screaming, but instead she said, "Let's put some fenders out," and went to the forepeak, opened the hatch, reached in, took out two rubber fenders and handed one to Noelle. Noelle watched as Beth hung the first one over the side, securing it to the lifelines. She copied Beth.

"When did you learn how to tie a double half hitch?"

"Just now. I watched you. I'm a fast learner."

"Are you guys okay?" Victor yelled above the sound of his engine. Beth thought his cultivated English accent made him sound a little gay.

"Cut your engine and come aboard," Beth yelled back.

"What?" Victor yelled, louder than before.

She ran a finger in front of her neck, mimicking cutting her throat. Victor got the message and shut off his engine.

"Are you guys okay?" he said again.

"We're fine, Victor." Beth tossed him a line, then tied it off on a cleat. Victor secured the line to the bow of the speedboat. When he finished Beth tossed him a second line, which he tied to the stern. Then, with the small speedboat safely rafted up to the larger sailboat, he grabbed onto the port shrouds, pulled himself up and over the lifelines with the ease of an athlete.

"I came by the Yacht Club and your boat was gone. I got worried and came looking. Are you all right?"

"You came awful fast." Beth nodded her head toward the speedboat.

"I heard Corbeau is trying to take *Shogun*." He sounded angry. "They have no right to Frank's boat. I loved that man like my father, I won't let them get it." Beth started to revise her opinion of him.

She thought of the long arguments he and Frank used to have over the chessboard. She knew they enjoyed the verbal fencing or they wouldn't have kept it up for the last three years. They argued about everything. Politics, religion, technology, everything.

A light wave rocked the boat. Victor steadied himself by grabbing on to a shroud. Then said, "You don't have to go."

"Yes we do. If we stay, we lose the boat. Apparently Frank owed Brody money I didn't know about."

"Maybe he didn't. It would be just like Brody to phony something up. It wouldn't be the first time he took advantage of a situation. You should stay and fight. I'll help. I've got the best attorneys in Trinidad."

"You know how it works," Beth said. "They'll impound the boat. Justice is slow in Trinidad. The boat could be on the hard for over a year, maybe two. I can't take the chance."

"Can the two of you sail it? I could at least help with that."

"It's good of you to offer," Beth said, "but it's something we have to do by ourselves."

"It is not." There was a spark in his voice she'd never heard before. "You aren't very experienced and Noelle has no experience at all."

"We got the boat here," Beth said as the wind started to pick up.

"It's one thing to motor a few miles and set anchor, quite another to sail all night to Grenada. The two of you will never make it, not with this boat."

"What's wrong with this boat?" Beth had to fight to keep from stamping her foot.

"Not a damn thing, but it's too big for someone who's as inexperienced as you. So, let me help. I'll not only see that you get to Grenada safely, I'll teach you guys how to sail this thing in the process. You need my help and I'm offering, so take it."

"We accept," Noelle said.

Beth slapped her with a look, but Noelle ignored her and she finally surrendered. "Okay, you win. And thanks."

"When were you planning on leaving?" he asked.

"We've already checked out. We were going to leave at first light."

"I'll tie *Speed Kills* to the old pier. We'll leave right away."

"Aren't you afraid someone might steal it?" Noelle asked.

"Steal from me?" He laughed.

"I'll follow you to the pier in the Zodiac." Again Beth was struck by the contradictions in the man. So nice and so arrogant.

"I can do it," Noelle said.

Beth caught Noelle's smile and the slight way she was shifting back and forth.

"Okay." She watched as Victor climbed back into his boat, and Noelle slipped over the side into the dinghy. The rumbling of *Speed Kills'* inboard covered the sound of the dinghy's small outboard, but it didn't cover the way Noelle stared at Victor.

Back on the boat, Victor was a whirlwind. He laid the chart out on the nav table and spent a few minutes explaining how to chart a position using lines of longitude and latitude. He showed them how the GPS worked, a wonderful instrument that used satellite information to tell them not only where they where, but what course to steer to get where they were going, and how far away their destination was.

An hour later they hauled anchor by moonlight and Victor had Beth turn *Shogun* into the wind as he raised the main. With the sail up, Beth started to bring them back around. The boat rocked and jumped as Victor unfurled the jib. The sound of the wind in the flogging sails, the big American flag flapping overhead, the waves slapping against the Zodiac as they towed it, the banging halyards all combined to electrify Beth.

"It'll be a little rough for the first half hour or so," Victor said as he steered the boat out through Boca Grande and into the churning sea, "but after we're away from the land it should calm down." And he was right, in no time the halyards stopped clanging, the wind magically filled the sails and the boat slid through the water the way a skater glides over the ice.

"It's wonderful," Noelle said.

"I'm going below to use the facilities," Beth said and she went below.

Coming out of the toilet she saw both bilge pump lights glaring at her from the electric panel. They only glowed red when they were pumping water, and they only pumped water when there was a leak.

"We've got a problem down here!" she yelled.

"What?" Noelle stuck her head down the hatch.

"Get Victor!"

Victor jumped through the companionway. He saw the lights on the panel straightaway.

"We have to find the leak." He started pulling up the floor hatches in the salon. Water was flowing under them, coming from the stern, flowing down into the deepest part of the engine bilge, where the two pumps were pumping it back out into the ocean.

"It's too much water! We have to stop it!" He opened the door to the aft sail locker and crawled in, scooting over the spare sails and under the cockpit. "Hand me a torch."

"How bad is it?" Beth got the flashlight and passed it back to him.

"Water is pouring in around the rudder post," he said. "We can't stop it from above."

"Does that mean we're going to sink?"

"If we don't stop the leak," he said as he crawled back out.

"How can we do that?"

"Do you have any packing material?"

"I don't even know what it is."

"Then you probably don't. We can use rags instead. The rudder post is in a tube that comes up through the boat. The tube is welded onto an aluminum plate that's bolted to the fiberglass hull. Someone has drilled through the plate and water's leaking in. We can cram rags up the tube and slow down or temporarily stop the leak, but first we have to stop the boat."

"Someone did this on purpose?" Beth said.

"Let's stop the boat first, then we'll talk about it."

"Okay," Beth said.

"What we're going to do," Victor said, "is called heaving-to. We're going to sheet in the main as tight as possible, then we're going to backwind the jib."

"Won't that make the boat heel over in the opposite direction and push us around in a circle?" Beth said.

"Not really," Victor said. "The sheeted in main and the keel will try to force the boat to go one way, the backwinded jib will try to force it to go in the opposite direction. The result will be that we won't go anywhere at all. We'll just sit here." And in five minutes time they were sitting calmly, bobbing along in four foot seas. The boat was perfectly balanced. There wasn't a cloud in the star-filled sky.

"How come it waited till we were out here to start leaking?" Beth said. "How come it didn't happen when we motored out of the Yacht Club?"

"I don't know," Victor said. "Maybe they filled the holes with something that would hold fast as long as the boat was in calm water, but it was jarred out when we hit the lumpy seas."

"So what do we do about it?" Beth wanted to ask who would do such a thing, but Victor wouldn't know any more than she would. Besides, stopping the flow of water was the most important thing right now.

"Let's go below and check," Victor said. They followed him below and once again he took the flashlight and crawled into the sail locker under the cockpit.

"Is it still leaking?" Beth called in after him.

"A little," he said, "but not as bad as when we were sailing. We have to stop it and I can't do it from in here." He came back out. "If we were at the dock it would be simple, but we're not. Someone has to go down there and jam some rags up that tube."

"You're not serious?" Noelle said. "We're in the middle of the ocean."

"Yeah, dumb idea," Victor said. "We have to go back. We'll never make it to Grenada."

"Brody really doesn't want this boat to leave Trinidad," Noelle said. "First the impeller, now this."

"What impeller?" Victor said.

Beth told him.

"If that's his game, then he wins, temporarily," Victor said. "Because we really do have to turn back. We don't have any choice. But don't worry, he won't get the boat, that I can guarantee."

"I won't take the chance." Beth fisted her hands. "We're not going back. There is no way we're going to let some creep sink us or make us stay in Trinidad. We'll just have to fix the leak and go on to Grenada."

"We can't go down there," Victor said.

"Sure we can. We have scuba gear on board and full tanks. You could go down and plug the leak."

"Not me," Victor said. "I don't dive. Never have."

"Then I'll do it." For an instant she thought he was afraid, but she abandoned the thought right away.

If he wasn't a diver, he couldn't go into the water, not without scuba training. "Noelle, you and Victor can cut up a towel into rags, then soak them in Vaseline, that might waterproof them and help keep the water out."

Fifteen minutes later Beth tied a line around her waist. Noelle held the other end. Victor lowered the swim ladder.

"All right, I'm ready."

Getting over the lifelines was awkward. She'd never gone down the swim ladder with a tank on her back. And night diving was something she'd never done. And she'd never done it in the open sea, either.

But she made it without stumbling or slipping. She shivered when her foot touched the water. She had the rags in a pouch tied to the weight belt. She checked to make sure they were secure. Then she slipped on the fins.

"Good luck, Beth," Noelle said.

"Back in a flash," Beth said with more bravado than she felt. Then she slipped into the black water and shivered again, but this time not from the cold. She sucked on the regulator, drew a deep breath, held it, then exhaled and dropped below the boat, into the dark.

Chapter Thirteen

THE MOVIE FLEW BY in a haze of cheers and boos. When Trinidadians went to see a film they were absorbed by it, shouting encouragement to the good guys, cat calling during the love scenes, hissing the villains. Before he knew it the movie was over and he was on the street again.

He had nowhere to go, so he started up the road, following a group of young people, two boys and two girls. The teenagers were still talking about the movie, imitating the characters, rehashing the lines, reliving the climax. They'd had a good time at the show and they were still sharing it.

And Wolfe felt the afterglow. He'd smoked marijuana a few times in college, but he'd never enjoyed it, preferring Scotch and water instead.

Tonight, despite the mess he was in, he'd had fun. He'd been carried away by the film. For a few hours all his cares were gone. It was easy to see why a man with a low paying job, several kids, piles of bills and a dead end future would go to the movies and smoke a joint on the weekend.

He stopped and looked at the sky, taking in the stars, like a child seeing the heavens for the first time. The teenagers kept walking and talking away. Their happy voices carried to him on the cool night breeze.

"Can you help us out here?" rasped a not so happy voice. Wolfe was jolted out of his reverie and his attention was riveted on the scene ahead. Two men were confronting the kids, asking for money. The one speaking was spitting his words through a filthy beard and matted dreadlocks.

"We don't got nothing," one of the boys said.

"Bet you do," Dreadlocks said.

"Honest," the boy said.

"You got some money for us or you gonna be fuckin' sorry," Dreadlocks said, and Wolfe had the picture. Two men. Late twenties or early thirties. Unkempt. Street people. He moved closer. The men had their backs to him. The children were too frightened to notice.

"All we had was enough to go to the movies," the boy said.

Dreadlocks grabbed one of the girls by the arm, to keep them from running away, Wolfe thought. The girl was too frightened to scream, but her wide eyes caught Wolfe as he moved up behind the men.

"Listen, boy, you give over what you got or you be sorry." Crack heads, Wolfe thought. The underbelly of the snake.

"Let the girl go," Wolfe said.

Dreadlocks stiffened, but the other man spun around to face Wolfe. He had a knife in his right hand and a glint in his bloodshot eyes. He was tall, six-six, Half a head taller than Wolfe, but he was crack thin. Crack thin and crack crazy.

"You wanna mind your own business?" the man with the knife said.

"No," Wolfe said.

"You gonna pay if you don't," Knifeman said. Brave words, but the knife was shaking in the man's bony hand.

"One way or another, everybody has to pay." Wolfe tossed his grip aside and moved closer, keeping his eyes on the blade. Instinctively he lowered himself into a crouch, turning sideways to the man, making himself a smaller target. He wasn't a natural like others he'd known, but he knew how to fight. If you were one of the few gringo kids in the Barrio, and the only Jewish kid in school, you had to fight just to keep your place in line at the cafeteria, and Wolfe liked to eat.

Knifeman came in quick, leading with the blade, holding it like a sword. The shakes were cocaine induced, like his courage. Wolfe stepped aside, but the man was faster than he anticipated and Wolfe felt the tip of steel slice across his stomach as he brought the back of a hand down on the man's wrist.

First, the snapping sound of breaking bone.

Second, the clattering of the knife on the sidewalk.

Third, the scream.

Wolfe hit him in the mouth, cutting off the scream and cutting his fist on breaking teeth. Knifeman left the ground, arms flaying, bleeding, and landed on his back, his head making a sickening thud when it hit the concrete.

"You can't do that," Dreadlocks said.

"Let the girl go," Wolfe said.

"I don't think so."

"Let her go and you can walk away."

Dreadlocks was silent for a few seconds, weighing Wolfe's words. The girl looked frightened, but she wasn't struggling and the other three teenagers, to their credit, hadn't run off. The four kids all looked to Wolfe with hope in their eyes.

"You a bad ass?" Dreadlocks asked.

"Yeah." Wolfe kept his eyes locked on the man as he ran a hand through the slice in his shirt and touched tender skin. He studied the blood on his fingers and winced. The cut was starting to hurt.

"You want me, come through her."

"Then you die," Wolfe said.

"What about my friend?" Dreadlocks cut into Wolfe's eyes with a hard stare.

"You don't really care, do you?"

"No." He relaxed his grip on the girl, let her go and backed away. One step, two, three. He turned and ran.

"Is he dead?" one of the boys said, looking at Knifeman laid out on the sidewalk.

"No, he'll be okay." Wolfe didn't know or care if he was telling the truth.

"You hit him hard. That was cool," the other boy said.

"We should move away from here, before the police come," Wolfe said.

"But you're the good guy." This from the girl that had been held captive.

"I'm afraid the police don't think so," Wolfe said and the four youngsters followed his gaze to the flashing blue light coming toward them.

"Look away so they don't see your white face," one of the boys said. Wolfe did as instructed. The two girls linked arms around him, one on each side. The boys moved in front and they walked away from the man laid out on the sidewalk.

The police car sped by ignoring what appeared to be a group of kids leaving the movies and a passed out drunk. Neither unusual for Port of Spain on a Saturday night.

"Are you hurt bad?" one of the girls said. He hadn't realized it till she asked, but he was holding on to them for support.

"Don't know," he said, economizing both words and strength.

"Can you walk?"

"Think so."

"What do you want us to do?" one of the boys said. Wolfe wasn't sure which one.

"I need to go to the Normandy Hotel. I have a friend. Waitress in the restaurant."

"Kind of far," the same boy said.

'Shut up, Leon. We're gonna help him," the girl that had been held by Dreadlocks said.

"Bleeding," Wolfe said.

"Matthew, take off your shirt. Julia give me that little knife you always got in your purse."

"Since when you the boss, Wendy?" Leon said.

"Since now, because I know what to do and you don't."

"I got it." Julia pulled a Swiss Army knife out of her purse.

"I said I need your T-shirt, Matthew," Wendy said.

Wolfe winced as the boy nodded and pulled it off.

"What are you doing?" Leon wanted to know.

"I'm making a compress to push against the cut. It will stop the bleeding," she said as she cut the cotton shirt in two. Half she folded. "Here," she said, handing it to Wolfe. "Hold it tight against the wound. Not so much that it hurts, just enough to stop the flow of blood."

"Leon, go back and get his bag. Matthew, take this and go over there and get it wet." She handed the other half of the shirt to the boy and pointed to a water tap in front of a bakery. The bakery was closed, but the tap was dripping. She wiped Wolfe's brow with the damp cloth, then ran the cool rag around his neck, under his shirt and along his shoulders. It gave him a quick chill.

"Take a few easy breaths," she said, "and try to calm down." She couldn't have been any older than fourteen, but he obeyed, bringing the air in slowly and letting it out the same way, while she held his hand, giving him a gentle squeeze with each breath.

"It's quite a ways, think you can manage?" Wendy asked.

"I'll make it."

"Okay, you can lean on me."

Wolfe wrapped his arm around her and they made their way through the dark streets. Every step cut into the fire in his belly, like smoldering steel through ice. He bit into his lower lip to divert the pain and tightened his arm around Wendy's waist. She didn't seem to mind. He counted the driveways they passed, then he counted parked cars, then he counted every step he took, but no amount of counting countered the pain and finally he gave into it, closed his eyes and passed out.

"Wake up." He felt the slap on his face. "We're almost there." It was Leon speaking, "Don't quit now."

He opened his eyes. He was still on his feet.

"Only a few more blocks. You can do it," Leon said. "We're gonna get you to your girl, but you gotta hold on just a little more."

"I can do it," Wolfe grunted.

"Sure you can," Wendy said. They started up again. Step after step. Wendy's arm was wrapped all the way around his waist. She was holding the compress tightly against his stomach. He must've dropped it when he passed out. "I know it hurts," she said, "but it's not bleeding so bad now, you're going to be okay." Her sweet voice soaked into him and gave him strength.

He matched her small strides, eyes closed, faith open, the fire in his belly consuming him. Two blocks, five minutes, an eternity. Then they were in the restaurant.

"Back table," Wolfe said.

He saw her making her way through the tables toward the bar. He watched as she took a bottle of wine to a party on the balcony. She saw him too, kept her eyes on him as the two girls helped him into a seat with his back to the wall. He smiled at her, nodded. She nodded back, met his eyes, held them, then returned the smile.

Wolfe raised his hand, attempted a wave, then passed out, his head thudding against the table.

"Wolfe, are you all right?" He opened his eyes. It was Jenna, but obviously he wasn't still in the restaurant.

"Am I in a hospital?"

"No, you're at Wendy's."

"I'm thirsty." He felt like he did when he was in the hospital in California. He started to get up.

"Whoa there, get back down." She pushed him back against the pillows. "The doctor said you're to stay put for the night."

"Doctor?" He started to get up again.

"No." Her voice was as firm as the hand pressing against his chest. "You've been asleep for the last two hours." She moved from the bed and brought a glass of water from the bathroom. "Here." She helped him sit up.

He took the offered glass and drank. When he was finished, she helped ease him back onto the pillow.

"I'm in trouble," he said.

"No kidding."

Gingerly he felt his wound.

"Wendy's father is a doctor. Twenty stitches, it's gonna be a great scar."

"Twenty," he whispered. "It hurts like hell."

"Lots of blood. Your clothes are ruined."

He looked around the room, taking in the expensive furnishings. Two book lined walls, teak bookcases, a large rolltop desk, teak also, facing a large window. The curtains were drawn. It was a man's room, covered in wood grain and browns. The bed seemed out of place.

"How's the patient?" The voice was deep, baritone and reassuring. A doctor's voice.

"Better than before," Wolfe said.

"That's what a doctor needs to hear."

"You're Wendy's father?"

"Dr. Powers at your service. And would you be the young man everybody is looking for?"

"I didn't do it," Wolfe whispered, "and they know it."

"Oh, I believe you. You stood against two strangers just to see that a fourteen-year-old girl was safe. A man that did the things they claim you did would have minded his own business and turned away, leaving my daughter and her friends to whatever fate awaited them."

"I have to get out of Trinidad."

"That is being arranged," the doctor said. "In the morning you'll leave on a sailboat bound for St. Martin. Normally, for a wound such as yours, I would prescribe bed rest for at least a week, but in your case it would be very bad for your health. There is talk of a reward and once the figure is announced, and I'm sure it will be quite large, we can expect Wendy's friends to start talking. Nothing stays secret in Trinidad for very long."

"I can't let them check my passport," Wolfe said. "It's gotta be on every list there is."

"Don't worry. You won't be on the crew list. None of the islands board boats as policy. The captain takes the ship's papers and crew's passports to Customs and Immigration. The papers are inspected, the passports are stamped."

"How do they control illegal immigration, drugs, cocaine, marijuana?"

"Simple," the doctor said. "They don't."

"That's crazy," Wolfe said. "What about the US Coast Guard?"

"Ah, yes, there is always them. This boat will take about two months getting to St. Martin, stopping at all the popular anchorages along the way. It will very much look like a normal cruising sailboat, enjoying the ever popular Caribbean. It will do its utmost to avoid your Coast Guard."

"Why?"

"It's carrying an awful lot of marijuana."

"A drug boat?"

"What can I say, it's my brother's boat. He smuggles marijuana into the British Virgins. Not a lot, but he does all right. He won't make millions, however he likes his work and the sense of adventure that goes with it."

"I can't go on a drug boat," Wolfe said.

"And you can't stay here. How long do you think it will take even our inept police to figure out where you are? Now if you will excuse me, I have to be at the hospital in half an hour. Jenna will see to everything."

"Saying thank you hardly seems like enough."

"No, Mr. Wolfe, it is I who should thank you. You came to my daughter's aid when most would have turned their backs," he said. Then he was through the door and gone.

"And you?" Wolfe turned to Jenna. "Why'd you help me?"

"I owe you for what you did on the plane, remember? I never would have made it through that flight without you. Besides, I've always had a space in my heart for the underdog and that's you right now."

"How soon before I leave?"

"In the morning, you set sail just before dawn." She got up from the side of the bed and started for the door. "Get as much rest as you can."

It was ten to midnight when Jenna woke him. He rubbed his eyes, ran his tongue over his teeth. He needed a toothbrush, a shower and a lot more rest.

"The police have been to Leon's. We have to go."

He sat up. He was naked under the covers.

"Put these on." She handed him a pair of his Levi's. He pulled off the covers and slipped into the jeans without underwear. She didn't avert her gaze and he didn't care. "Now this." She was holding one of his Hawaiian shirts, the pink one with the yellow hibiscus flowers. He put it on.

"My shoes."

"No socks." She handed him his running shoes.

"It's okay." He put them on. A dull fire burned in his abdomen. He felt nauseous.

"Where's the doctor?"

"He's gone. He decided to take the family up to the Asa Wright Nature Center for a few days."

"Good time to see the birds," Wolfe said.

"He didn't want them here."

"I guess I can understand that." Wolfe steadied himself on his feet, feeling light headed. He took a deep breath, winced as he felt his stomach muscles expand against the stitches. He took a step forward, stumbled, caught himself, grabbed onto the desk, rattling the roll top.

"Quiet," she whispered.

He followed her out of the house. They stopped on the front porch, where he inhaled the cool night, tasting the air. It smelled like a storm was coming soon, but it wasn't the electricity in the air that set his arm hairs tingling. Something wasn't right. Why did he have to be quiet?

"I forgot my bag."

"No time," she whispered. Then, "That's my car, there." She pointed to a white van, parked under a giant weeping willow. The street lights were out, the neighborhood was dark. All the better to kill someone, he thought.

"Nice," he said as they made their way down the walk toward the van.

"Brand new. I'm going to use it in my business."

"I thought you were a waitress."

"Not forever. I've got plans."

"And ambition."

"Right," she said. "I'm going to do day tours for the yachties, you know, Caroni Swamp, the vegetable market, stuff like that."

"And up to the Asa Wright Nature Center," he said. "You told me."

"Yes, that, too."

She unlocked and opened the passenger door for him. He felt a chill run up his back as climbed in the van. He reached over and unlocked the driver's door while she walked around the front of the vehicle. He watched while she put the key in the ignition, but he reached out and grabbed her hand with a squeeze and stopped her from starting the engine.

"What?" she said, startled.

"I'm not getting very far tonight, am I?"

"How did you know?"

"You were whispering in the house. If nobody was home, why whisper?"

"Ah."

"Why?" he asked.

"For the money," She said and he tightened his grip. She gasped, then he relaxed and let her have her hand back.

"Where is it going to happen?"

"At the traffic light before the highway."

"Do they know about the Yacht Club?"

"No."

"Where do they think you're taking me?"

"To the Hilton. I didn't want to involve the doctor's brother."

"Why not?"

"Because I have some money invested in the cargo."

"Small country," he said.

"What are you going to do now?"

"Go a different way." He saw the car parked up the block. It was a hot night and they gave themselves away by having the windows down. He hadn't been very long in Trinidad, but he'd been long enough to know that nobody left their cars with the windows down, not unless they were policemen and they were sitting in it.

"Okay," he said. "The damage is done. I can't go back inside, because they know about the doctor and I can't go with you because they're waiting for me up the road. I guess my only option is to run for it."

"You don't have a chance," she said.

"Not much of one, you're right, but better than if I let you drive me into their waiting arms."

"It was a business deal. They offered a lot of money. Nothing personal." She was cool, not the least ruffled that he caught her out.

"They offered Judas money, too."

"You're not Christ," she said.

"I'm going to step out of the van and start running. Maybe I can get myself lost before you get to that traffic light." He didn't know what else to do. If he took off at an angle, away from the van, keeping it between himself and the policemen down the street, and if she took off a few seconds later for the traffic light, maybe the police would follow her thinking he was still in the car.

But he needed that few seconds. He took the key out of the ignition, tossed it into the back. She was scrabbling after it even as he went out the door. He tried to run, but didn't get far. He was woozy from the loss of blood. The stitches in his stomach felt like he was being beaten with a whip. Every step another lash.

The heat of the blast slammed into him before the sound of the explosion that blew up the van and woke up the night. He threw his arms out to break his fall, but landed on his stomach anyway. Fighting for air, he rolled across the cool grass till his body thudded into the doctor's front porch. He kept low and crawled around to the side of the house.

In seconds the neighborhood was up and the street was crawling with police cars, their blue lights flashing.

"You okay, Mister?" It was Wendy, tugging on his sleeve.

"I think so"

"Come back inside," she said and he followed her up onto the porch and back into the house.

Chapter Fourteen

Beth slid into the water and ripples of chilling current ran from her skin to her core. This was the deep, home of the great white and the hammerhead. She was in their territory now. She spent a few seconds floating on the surface, relaxing her nerves and gathering her courage. It was dark down there, and cold.

She took a deep breath from the regulator and exhaled, the sound of her own breathing offered small reassurance. She was not an experienced diver, but she wasn't a novice either. She'd been diving for the last few years, but never at night and never alone and always in calm conditions.

She took another breath and held it this time, listening to the silence and seeing the dark. She was stalling. She couldn't do it forever. She was going to have to go down there.

They could lose the boat if she didn't. Worse, they could lose their lives. It was up to her, all up to her. She exhaled and bit into the regulator, took another breath and dropped a few feet under the surface, into the black water.

She was alone with only the sound of her breath and her beating heart for company. She held her hand up in front of her face. She couldn't see it. She brought it closer, till she was touching the face mask and still she couldn't see it. She looked toward the surface, but it was gone. There was no up, no down. She was trapped in the vertigo.

She chewed into the regulator with clenched teeth and tasted saltwater. Mucus dribbled from her nose. She wanted to blow it out, but not in the dark. She didn't want the snot inside the face mask for even a second, but moving the mask away from her face to clear her nose was out of the question.

She felt the pressure building in her ears and she reached up and pinched her nostrils closed through the mask, forcing air into her blocked nasal passages, clearing herself. And then it hit her, something was wrong. Why should she have to clear herself? And then she understood. She was going down. She had too much weight on and she was going down.

She cleared herself again and fought the impulse to lash out toward the surface. If she was down far enough a rapid assent could be dangerous. Then she thought she felt something move by her in the dark and all she wanted was out of the water. She sucked on the regulator, filling her lungs, straightened her arms above her head, and brought them back to her sides. She moved through the water, but was she going north, south, up or down? She couldn't tell.

All she saw was more dark and she was hyperventilating, using up the air. She wanted out. Now. She was getting too much oxygen and she wasn't thinking. Then she remembered the button to add air to her BC. She pushed it, making the vest more buoyant, counteracting the lead in the weight belt. She started to float upward. But she couldn't wait. She lashed out with a great kick toward the surface, pulling the regulator from her mouth and gasping for air as she broke through.

And then she was back under and gagging on seawater. A rolling wave pushed her against the boat and she pushed off, feeling the ablating bottom paint, slimy and slippery, as she shoved against it. A second wave rode under her and this time there was a loud thunk when the scuba tank banged into the fiberglass hull and she swallowed more water.

She was right under the boat. Safety so close and she was going to drown. She tried to call out, but only gagged on more water. She had to do something. What? The flapping regulator banged into her head. In her panic she tried to push it away, but it wouldn't go. She finally figured out what it was and stuffed it back into her mouth, took a long pull on the sweet air.

She tried to swim away from the boat, but she was no match for the current and the rolling waves. It was like trying to walk up a steep hill with roller skates on, no matter how hard she tried, she just slid back on the rolling wheels.

A second breath and she started to calm down. She allowed herself to float just below the surface. She was there now. No more vertigo. Her head was clearing and she was starting to think straight. The thought of going back down there sent shivers slicing through her, but she couldn't give up, and she couldn't believe that she hadn't used the flashlight, how stupid.

She didn't want to be in the water any longer than she had to, but she didn't want to panic again, either. She closed her eyes, opened them, it made no difference. She reached for the flashlight, turned it on and watched the dark eat up the light. She turned it toward the boat and smiled when she saw the red bottom paint.

She swam under, guiding her way with the flashlight shining on the keel. The boat seemed huge, like swimming under a great whale.

She made her way to the stern with short strokes and rapid breaths. She shifted the light to the rudder. She knew Victor was in the sail locker above with the trouble light, waiting to see if she was able to stop the leak.

The black water seemed to swallow up the small amount of light coming from her flashlight. She had to keep it pointed at the underbelly of the boat or she couldn't see anything at all. She studied the rudder. It was swaying back and forth as the boat rocked with the waves. She grabbed onto it and looked up. She saw light flickering around the stainless steel rudder post.

She fished in the bag tied to the weight belt, pulled out a fistful of rags and jammed them up toward the light above. After she stuffed all the rags up the tube and around the post, she let go of the rudder and kicked toward the surface.

She broke through and floundered against the waves for a few seconds, then swam toward the swim ladder. The scuba tank pulled against her as she pulled off the fins, but she didn't want to take it off in the water, so she fought its weight and struggled up the ladder, reaching the top without any breath to spare.

"Did you do it?" Noelle asked.

"Yeah," Beth said, smiling. "I did."

"Atta girl." Noelle helped her out of the BC and Beth felt like she was walking on top of the world.

"You did it!" Victor said, coming up from below. His grin was about eight miles wide. Beth felt a glow of excitement and satisfaction spark through her. She couldn't imagine any better praise out of him than that smile. "You really did it," he said again. "I'm proud of you." God, she was being killed with his praise.

"Then we can head on to Grenada?" Beth said.

"I still don't think that's a good idea," he said. "Those rags aren't going to keep the water out for very long. We should head back."

"I shoved them up in there good. We'll be okay," Beth said. "I want to go for it."

"You're the captain," Victor said. "If you don't mind I'll take the first watch. Noelle can spell me and you can get some sleep. You've earned it."

"How long are the watches?" Noelle asked.

"Two hours should be about right," Victor said.

Beth thought that he was making an awful lot of decisions, but it was clear to her that even though she was the captain, she was going to have to rely on him a lot, at least until she knew what she was doing.

"I'm not the least tired," Noelle said. "So I think I'll stay on deck if that's okay."

"Fine with me," Victor said.

"Make sure you clip on," Beth said.

"I'm clipped on now." Noelle lifted up her tether, showing Beth that it was both clipped to her inflatable life vest and the binnacle. If she fell overboard, she'd be tied to the boat.

"Okay." Beth went below and crashed in the salon. She heard Victor and Noelle talking and laughing as she drifted off to sleep. She slept poorly, waking often, and always she heard the two above. They seemed to talk the night away and finally, after what seemed an endless time, Beth fell into a deep sleep.

"Your watch in fifteen minutes, Beth." Noelle gently shook her awake. "We let you sleep an extra two hours."

"Okay, I'm awake." Beth sat up and stretched her arms above her head. It seemed like she'd only been asleep for a few seconds, but if she'd had an extra two hours, that meant that six hours had gone by.

"You're gonna love it up there," Noelle said. "Not a cloud in the sky. The water's almost flat and the wind is perfect. A gentle beam reach."

"You're learning the lingo," Beth said on her way to the thermos in the galley.

"Victor's teaching me. There's really a lot to this stuff. You can't just get in a boat and sail away."

"Don't I know it." Beth sipped at her coffee.

"Bring it up with you," Noelle said.

Beth followed her up to the cockpit and gasped. Noelle was right. The stars were wrapped around the sky. She felt like she was in a fairytale.

"All right," Victor said. "Everything is all set. The wind is out of the southeast and the current is with us. The autopilot is set. All you have to do is sit back and enjoy yourself."

"I can do that," Beth said, "but what if the wind direction changes?"

"It won't, but don't worry, I only take catnaps at sea. I'll pop up every fifteen minutes or so and see how you're doing."

"Great," Beth said and that's the way she felt. She took a deep breath of the ocean air and held it. Victor was on his way below before she let it out. "You can get some rest, too," Beth said. "I'll be okay."

"I'll have a cup of coffee with you, before I go to sleep." Noelle went below, returning with a cup for herself.

The two women drank the hot coffee under the stars and enjoyed the quiet evening as the boat sliced through the calm sea.

"Victor's asleep on the starboard settee," Noelle said. "And he looks like he's sleeping pretty solid. I don't think he's going to be popping up every fifteen minutes."

"That's okay," Beth said. "I'll be fine. You go below and get some sleep."

"Sure?"

"I'm sure."

"Okay, Beth, but you call if anything happens or if you get lonely."

"I will," Beth said as Noelle went below.

Then she was alone.

"What?" she jumped. Something had splashed by the side of the boat, scaring her. It came up again and she smiled. It was a lone dolphin. He paced the boat for awhile, sometimes going under, sometimes riding the surface. For an instant she imagined it was Wolfe, trying to tell her something, but then she let go of the fantasy and the dolphin went under one last time and was gone.

Then the wind started to pick up. She glanced at the compass, on course and the sails were full. Everything seemed fine.

And then it started to blow a little harder. She thought about waking Victor, but didn't. She didn't want him to think she was a complete washout.

Then she saw clouds and rain off the starboard side and realized that the increase in wind speed was due to a squall. It was going to cross their path. She felt a few drops of rain as it approached, but the boat was on autopilot. She thought everything would be okay.

Then she was in it. *Shogun* heeled over with the wind and she was in trouble. The autopilot was being overpowered by the wind and she couldn't see through the rain. She scooted behind the wheel as Victor burst into the cockpit.

"What's going on?" he yelled to be heard above the wind.

"Squall," Beth said as Noelle came up into the cockpit.

"Too late to reef the main," he said as he cranked in some of the headsail. "We have to ride it out." He grabbed the wheel and clicked off the autopilot. And for the next twenty minutes Beth and Noelle watched as Victor handled the boat. Even though they took a lot of water over the side as the boat slammed through the swells, Beth wasn't worried, because he seemed to be enjoying himself.

Then, as quickly as it was upon them, they were through it and the night was clear again. The sea flattened out, the wind was back from the southeast.

"That was fun," Victor said. Then, "If you don't mind, Beth, I'll steer awhile and give the autopilot a break."

"I'll stay up, too," Noelle said. "There's no way I can get back to sleep. Not a chance."

"Then I'm going below," Beth felt like she'd screwed up, but that didn't stop her from falling straight to sleep and dreaming about shooting stars and dolphins.

"Beth, we're almost there." Noelle's voice rang down from above.

Beth opened her eyes. Five minutes later she was on deck. Victor and Noelle looked as fresh as if they'd slept the night away. Beth felt as if she hadn't slept at all. She stretched and gave in to a yawn.

"That's Grenada, dead ahead." Victor turned the wheel a little to port.

"Coffee?" Noelle passed her the thermos.

An hour later they laid anchor in Prickly Bay. The water was clear, the sun was hot and Beth was aching for a swim.

"I have an idea," Victor said.

"Yes?" she said.

He rubbed the back of his neck, then ran a hand through his thick hair. "We could patch those holes in the rudder plate with underwater epoxy. That stuff gets hard in water. It won't be a perfect fix, but it'll stop the leak for awhile."

"How long?" Beth asked.

"I've heard of underwater epoxy repairs that lasted years."

"Well, Victor, I guess you've saved the day again."

Victor and Noelle took a taxi to St. George's to buy supplies, something they hadn't had time to do in Trinidad, and Beth called the small shipyard in the bay on the radio and told them her problem with the rudder leak. In less than ten minutes she heard a dinghy approaching. She stuck her head out the companionway as it came alongside. A big man, dark skin, dark eyes, darker mustache, was driving the dinghy. A young white kid was standing in the bow, painter in hand. Beth had to stifle a laugh when she saw his flaming red hair, freckled face and tiny ears. His head was egg shaped, eyes wide, nose too small for his face, mouth too small, too. Like Mr. Potato Head, only the potato was too big for the rest of the parts. He couldn't be more than seventeen.

"So you got a rudder leak?" The big West Indian said.

"That's what she said on the radio, Harvey." The kid sounded like he was from Georgia.

"Okay, Wally, cleat her off."

"Yeah, boss." Wally wound the painter around the starboard deck cleat. Maybe the ears, nose and mouth were too small, but he had the most beautiful green eyes Beth had ever seen.

"Bad thing, that," Harvey said two hours later, after the leak was fixed. He wiped sweat from his forehead with an oily rag. His skin was about the same color as the oil, so Beth hardly noticed.

"Whoever did it should be hung," Wally agreed. "But you were wrong about one thing, ma'am. Those itty bitty holes wouldn't have sunk the boat."

"Really?" Beth stared into the kid's emerald eyes.

"True," Harvey said. "I seen a lot a things on a lot of boats, but never deliberate sabotage. You're lucky, though. Either the bastard didn't know what he was doing, or he didn't want to sink you. I think he just wanted to scare you."

"What do you mean?" Beth said.

"Not enough water coming in to sink the boat," Wally said.

"Kid's right," Harvey said.

"But the bilge pumps were going off."

"Well they would, wouldn't they?" Wally said. "Soon as enough water came in to set off the switches, but they're set real low. You could've sailed to Miami and back and been okay with them tiny holes."

"Mind you," Harvey said, "it's always better to fix a leak. It's never good when the ocean comes in from the bottom of the boat."

"Or any other way when you think about it," Wally said.

She had the men go over the boat, checking everything she could think of, the lines, blocks, sails, and thru-hulls. They couldn't find anything else wrong, but Harvey warned her saying, "There's lots someone can do to mess up a sailboat that you can't see right off, so you best be careful."

After they left she thought about Victor's insistence that they either fix the leak immediately or head back to Trinidad, and she concluded that maybe the great Victor Drake might have panicked a little himself.

She didn't like the holier than thou attitude he sometimes got, but she knew she needed somebody and he was a competent sailor. When they returned she asked him if he wouldn't mind staying on for a few days and show them how to handle the boat.

"I'll stay with you for as long as it takes," Victor said. "And this is a perfect place to learn. The wind is always blowing."

"Not here." Beth squinted against the sun as Noelle was sweeping the marina with the binoculars.

"Why not?" Victor sounded disappointed.

"We're too close to Trinidad. The farther away we get, the better I'll feel."

"Grenada is a separate country. Nobody's going to take your boat away here."

"I just don't feel safe this close to Trinidad." She picked her sunglasses up from a cockpit cushion and put them on.

"Okay, when do you want to leave?" he asked.

"How quick can we set sail?"

"As soon as we get the rudder fixed," he said.

"Already taken care of. Two guys from the local yard came by and fixed it."

"They put a diver in the water and used underwater epoxy?" he asked.

"Yes they did."

"Then we can go now. We can spend the night somewhere in the Grenadines if that's what you want."

"Boat coming in under sail," Noelle said.

"Black schooner," Beth said. "It looks like Alek's boat." Alek worked for Brody and Corbeau. She didn't like him, never had. He had a cruel streak.

"It's not *Viper*, same kind of Taiwanese built boat." Victor held his hand out and Noelle gave him the binoculars. "But this one's flying an American flag. Nice paint job, better than Alek's." He handed the binoculars back to Noelle.

An hour later they weighed anchor. Beth saw the name, *Snake Eyes*, on the back of the schooner as they sailed past her, making their way out of the bay. It was almost identical to Alek's, but she supposed it was a production boat. There were probably a lot of them around. Still, it was painted black, like Alek's boat, and it reminded her of Brody, Corbeau and why she wanted to be as far away from Trinidad as possible.

CHAPTER FIFTEEN

THE SECURITY GUARD WAVED them through and Dr. Powers drove between two long rows of covered speedboats and into the parking lot. Bright stars glowed through the scattered clouds. It was sprinkling lightly. Powers parked behind the bar, but he left the engine running, with the wipers going. "The boat's name is *Cayenne*. You'll find it on the west wall. Go down the jetty till it ends, turn right and keep going, it'll be the last boat, you can't miss it. It's a forty-five foot sloop, white and fast looking."

"I'll find it."

"Then this is goodbye." The doctor held out his hand. Wolfe shook it and met his crooked grin with one of his own. He liked the man, there weren't many like him.

"Will you be okay?" Wolfe didn't want Powers suffering because of what he'd done for him.

"I don't think anyone will bother me. They might come around, but it's nothing I can't take care of. In Trinidad it's who you know and who knows you. I know a few people and everybody knows me."

"I thought she was such a nice lady," Wendy said from the back seat.

"She was, Wendy." Wolfe turned to face the girl. "But they offered her a lot of money. It was just too tempting." Wolfe's mind went back to the night before. He and Dr. Powers peeked out the front window as the van blazed. The fire department and police arrived, the whole neighborhood was outside and they stayed up till they finally towed the burnt out hulk away at three in the morning. He wondered how long it would take before whoever blew it up learned that he hadn't been in it.

"I would never tell on a friend, not for a million dollars." Wendy leaned forward, with her elbows on the back of the front seat. She was holding up a silver crucifix on a gold chain. "This is for you. For luck. I think you might need it."

"Thank you, Wendy." He lowered his head. She slipped the crucifix over it and he felt the warm chain on his neck. What would his mother say?

"Keep it on," she said. "It works."

"Catholic?" Powers asked.

"Jewish." Wolfe fingered the cross.

"We'll say a mass for you come Sunday, can't hurt," Powers said.

"It'll help," Wendy said. "We'll pray that nothing bad happens to you."

Wolfe smiled as Wendy held out her hand, copying her father. He shook it, feeling the warmth in her grip.

"It's time," Powers said.

Wolfe opened the door, stepped out into the early morning. He smiled as Wendy climbed into the front seat and waved to him. He waved back and watched till the car was past the speedboats and going through the security gate. Then he turned away and walked around the outside bar toward the pier.

The yellow lights along the dock cast an otherworldly glow on the sailboats and their tall masts, bobbing back and forth with the gentle morning swell. As he walked between them, Wolfe couldn't help thinking about the people living aboard. Older retirees, middle aged couples that had sold everything for the dream, and younger people just starting out, the hippies of the new millennium. Gypsies all.

He stopped at the end of the dock and stared at a sleek looking sailboat with the name *Cayenne* on the bow.

"You looking for me?" The baritone voice startled him, but he got a bigger surprise when the man with Dr. Powers' voice popped out of the companionway. His reaction didn't go unnoticed. "I get that a lot when people knowing Jimbo first meet me," the man with Dr. Powers' voice said.

"I wasn't expecting—"

"What, a white man? You can say it, we're in Trinidad. You don't have to be politically correct here." The man stepped over the lifelines, hopped onto the dock.

"Spitting image." Wolfe blinked away his surprise. "I'd've thought you were twins."

"Good one." The man laughed. "Name's T-Bone. Glad to have you. I was beginning to think I was gonna have to sail up island alone. I hate that."

"I'm Wolfe." He offered his hand. T-Bone took it in a firm grip.

"Wolfe? That a first name or a last? I don't like last names."

"First name's Bill."

"Okay, Billy Boy, mine's T-Bone, not Tee, and not Bone, can't shorten it." He pushed his shoulder length hair out of his eyes.

"T-Bone," Wolfe said. He hated being called Billy Boy, hated it all his life, but somehow coming from a man named T-Bone, with a natural twinkle in his eye, it wasn't so bad.

"Like the steak," T-Bone said. He reminded Wolfe of a fugitive from a Grateful Dead concert, beard, tie-dyed shirt, faded Levi's and bare feet.

"You're really his brother?"

"Daddy was a sailor, a girl in every port." T-Bone jumped down into a dinghy that was tied to the back of the boat and went to the outboard engine. Wolfe watched as he undid the mounting screws, then hefted the outboard up to the dock. "Some cruisers tow their dinghies with the engine on it. I do too, for short hops sometimes, but usually I mount it on the stern of the big boat. Less weight back there that way." Back on the dock he climbed back onto the boat. "Hand her up to me."

Wolfe picked up the engine, handed it up and T-Bone mounted it on the back of the boat.

"We're ready to go," he said. "I'll start the engine, then you take it off the cleats and hop aboard."

"Right." Wolfe looked down at the stern lines.

T-Bone looked at Wolfe the way a high school principal frowns down at a wayward student.

"What?" Wolfe said.

"You ever been sailing before?"

"No."

"Christ," T-Bone muttered through his beard.

Twenty minutes later they were sailing in calm water with T-Bone steering.

"Okay, take the wheel," he said, "while I pull the dinghy closer."

"Want me to stay on your same course?"

"If you can."

"Piece of cake." Wolfe moved behind the wheel.

"Just hold her steady," T-Bone said. Then he went to the cleat the dinghy painter was tied to and pulled the dinghy closer to the boat. "I usually like her about a wave length behind, but I got a long painter in case of bad weather, then I can let it way out." With the dinghy secured back on the cleat, T-Bone took the wheel again.

"Different than a car," Wolfe said.

"You'll get used to it," T-Bone said. Then, "Just look at this. The sun coming up, shimmering seas, makes one glad to be alive."

Wolfe saw something off the bow and pointed.

"Good eye," T-Bone said, "but the right thing to do would have been to say, 'Sailboat at eleven o'clock.' Then you don't have to use your hands. It's always better to keep them free for the boat."

Wolfe nodded.

"Say, you wanna learn to sail like a pro, or are you just along for the ride?"

Wolfe saw the way his face lit up and knew there was only one answer he could give. "I'd like to learn."

"That's great. I used to teach, but what I'm doing now is easier. Besides, I like living on the edge." T-Bone smiled at Wolfe with crystal blue eyes you could almost see through. "You know anything about boats?"

"A friend at work has a sportfisher. I've helped him tear apart his diesels."

"You put them back together again?"

"I'm a good mechanic," Wolfe laughed. T-Bone was a wiseass. He'd always had a soft spot for wiseasses. "I can rip apart a diesel and have it running better than when it was new."

"So if I give you the ten minute tour, you'd understand what makes a boat tick?"

"I think so."

"Let's go." T-Bone, flicked a switch by the start button. "She's on autopilot now." He led Wolfe below, took him through the engine room. "A boat's gotta be one with the sea." He pointed to a valve. "That's the raw water intake. We use seawater to cool the main engine, generator and refrigerator motors. We pump it through the watermaker to make the water we drink. We use it to flush the toilets, hose down the deck and wash the dishes. If there's ever a leak aboard, chances are it'll be in this room, most likely a hose clamp or something I forgot to check. I'm pretty good at keeping everything shipshape, but nobody's perfect, that's why we got three bilge pumps. Unless we hit something really big, those babies will pump the water out faster than it's coming in."

"That's comforting to know."

"Tell me about it."

Back on deck, T-Bone explained how the sails worked, took Wolfe through a tour of the winches, furling system, blocks, steering, GPS and autopilot.

"Okay, you've got the basics, by the time we get to Grenada, I'll have you pretty much on your way, and in a week you'll be acting like you were born on a boat. Now let's go sailing."

T-Bone clicked off the autopilot and they spent the day dodging squalls, jibing, tacking and even practicing several man overboard drills. At first the stitches in his belly screamed, but Wolfe ignored them. There was something to being on the water, in the middle of nowhere, steering a small boat, that charged him to the core. After awhile the thrill of the sea seemed to stomp out the pain of the knife wound.

Wolfe sighed, inhaled the sea air. At the end of the day they were sailing under a reefed main in twenty-five knots of wind, the jib rolled in halfway. They were headed for the narrow opening into Hog Island, on Grenada's south coast. The waves were cresting at ten feet and it didn't look like they were going to reach the protection of the bay before the squall was upon them, but it wasn't the storm that had them worried. It was the white and orange Coast Guard cutter off their stern.

"Won't be long before they're on us," Wolfe said.

"Grab the main sheet. We'll jibe and see what's what."

Wolfe started hauling on the main sheet until the boom was centered, then he cleated it off. "Ready when you are," he said.

"Okay, jibe ho," T-bone yelled and Wolfe released the starboard jib sheet and started hauling hand over hand on the port sheet as T-Bone swung the boat around. "All right," he yelled when the jib came over and Wolfe released the mainsheet. "You're the fastest learner I ever saw. You don't need me anymore," T-Bone said as the boom slipped over the top and they were on the opposite tack.

T-Bone grabbed a glance over his shoulder. "They changed course," he said. "Let's jibe back." They repeated the maneuver and were back on course for Hog Island.

"What's the plan, Captain?" Wolfe knew if they were boarded, T-Bone would lose the boat and they would wind up in jail, probably in Grenada.

"We can't let them board," T-Bone said. "That would be very bad."

"They might not find it," Wolfe said.

"Oh, they'll find it. They'll take one look at this old hippy and they'll tear the boat apart. Now, if I looked like you, I could probably bluff it out, but I don't, so let's pretend we don't see them and let out the rest of the headsail."

"In this weather?" Wolfe said.

"Speed, we want speed," T-Bone said.

"You're crazy. We'll never out run them, they have four times our speed."

"We'd never let out the jib if we knew they were back there, would we?" T-bone said.

"No."

"So let's pretend we haven't seen them and act like all of a sudden we're in a hurry to get back."

"What have we got to lose?" Wolfe took the jib sheet off the winch and watched as the big foresail unfurled. The boat leaned over and picked up speed.

And the Coast Guard cutter added power and started closing fast.

"Be sure to keep the Porpoises to starboard."

"What porpoises?"

"Rocks, that's their name." T-Bone pointed.

"I don't see anything."

"Keep looking, they're kind of hard to see in weather like this."

"I have 'em." Wolfe saw a group of rocks that stuck about three feet above the water.

"Good, don't hit 'em." T-Bone laughed.

"Will the white sloop ahead heave-to and prepare to be boarded." The voice crackling over the cockpit speakers sounded young and inexperienced.

"Shit," T-Bone said and it started to rain. "Good omen," he said, then he slipped the winch handle into a winch and started to crank on the jib sheet, tightening it, increasing their speed. No match for the cutter, but it would get them into the bay five minutes earlier.

"Are you going to answer?" Wolfe asked.

"Not just yet."

"When?"

"When we get a little closer to land." He moved away from the wheel. "She's yours, I'm going below."

"What?" Wolfe took the wheel.

"If they get a good look at me, we're gonna be boarded. We don't want that," T-Bone said. Then he slipped down the companionway, out of sight. "I'll talk to them, all you have to do is wave."

"I repeat, will the sloop heave-to and prepare to be boarded." The young voice on the radio was more insistent.

T-Bone waited a few seconds with the mike in hand, then he clicked the talk button, "Negative." He released the talk button. "Let's see how they like that."

"This is not a request. Heave-to and prepare to be boarded."

"Guess they didn't like it," T-Bone said. "And they're not going to like this even more." He clicked the talk button. "This is the sailing vessel *Cayenne*, bound for Hog Island. I repeat, I will not heave-to. Can you put on someone a little older. Someone that understands radio etiquette. Oh yeah, and begin your next transmission by identifying yourselves. *Cayenne*, standing by." T-Bone laughed.

"Shit," Wolfe said.

The wind picked up to thirty knots, their speed picked up half a knot and it continued to rain. Wolfe wasn't wearing foul weather gear, but the electric situation kept his mind off the wet and the cold.

"This is Captain Andrews on the United States Coast Guard cutter *Puerto Rico*, operating in concert with the Grenadian Government. We are ordering you to heave-to and standby to be boarded." This voice was older and from the timbre of its delivery, Wolfe knew it was a voice used to being obeyed.

"Well, Captain Andrews, if you don't steer to port real quick, you're gonna run aground on the Porpoises."

The cutter turned to port. A few seconds later the radio cracked to life again. "This is the United States Coast Guard cutter *Puerto Rico*, once again I am ordering you to heave-to and standby to be boarded."

"The bastard didn't even thank us," T-Bone said.

"American tax dollars at work," Wolfe said.

T-Bone thumbed the talk button. "This is the sailing vessel *Cayenne*, out of Hog Island. Captain Powers speaking. I am a sailing instructor and I have a sixteen-year-old student on board. Presently said student is below heaving his guts out all over the salon. I would love to accommodate you, but as captain of this vessel, I have to put the safety of the crew and the vessel first. However I will gladly accept your boarding party in about thirty minutes, after we are safely at anchor in the bay."

"Negative. We will send a launch alongside and board you under way if need be."

"If you send a boarding party over in these conditions, you will be putting your young men at risk. If I was on this boat alone, I'd follow your orders and heave-to, but I will not put the life of my student at risk. Surely the safety of your men is as important to you?"

"I will evaluate the risk."

"Now I have to give him a face saving way not to board us," T-Bone said up to Wolfe, then he clicked the talk button. "I'll tell you what. I'll alter course to Prickly Bay. The water is deeper there, you should be able to motor in right behind me. By the time I get the anchor down, you can have your launch in the water, and by the time I snub the hook your men can be safely alongside."

"You say you're out of Grenada?"

"Registered in the BVI, but operating out of Grenada. I teach sailing. A lot of the charter customers that come down here need a refresher course before they're qualified to take a boat out by themselves. If there were more people like me down here, then there would be a heck of a lot less work for you guys."

"I hear that, Mister." Captain Andrews seemed to be warming to T-Bone. "Too many people come down here, charter a boat, get in trouble and yell for help. The charter companies should be more responsible."

"If they were, then I'd be out of a job." T-Bone laughed into the mike.

"All right, Captain Powers, continue on your course for Hog Island. We won't molest you any further today," Captain Andrews said as the cutter motored alongside the sailboat.

"Put your hand to your mouth, like you have a mike in it," T-Bone said to Wolfe and Wolfe put his right hand up to his face as T-Bone clicked the talk button. "Thanks very much, Captain Andrews. Fair winds to you and if we meet somewhere down the line I'll buy you a beer."

"And fair winds to you, Captain Powers. Maybe I'll drink that beer someday."

"Wave," T-Bone said to Wolfe, who turned toward the cutter and waved. Several crew members on board waved back. It was impossible for Wolfe to single out the captain through the rain. Then the cutter veered off.

"Okay, Billy Boy, let's get her in before that storm catches us." T-Bone came back up on deck.

"I don't know where you've been, my friend," Wolfe said, "but it's caught us."

"Yeah, it is a little too windy out here, let's roll in some of that jib."

Wolfe grabbed a winch handle and started cranking in on the jib, but after a couple of turns it started getting harder to crank and then he couldn't move it at all. He let a little out and then tried grinding it in again, but he met the same resistance at the same spot in the line. "I think it's jammed," he said.

"It happens sometimes, the line bunches up on the roller. I need to change the lead, something I've been meaning to do. I'll go up and fix it." Wolfe watched as T-Bone stepped out of the cockpit. He bent low to grab onto the lifelines but a wave crashed into the side of the boat before he got a hand hold and T-Bone went flying over the side and into the water head first.

Wolfe threw over the two life jackets, they should have been wearing, but weren't, then grabbed onto the cockpit cushions and tossed them over, too. He wanted to give T-Bone as much to grab onto as possible, and he wanted the spot good and marked in case he lost sight of him. Then he went back behind the wheel and spun it to the right, away from T-Bone and into the wind, keeping his head turned toward T-Bone as the wind brought the boat to a stop. T-Bone was too far away for him to get a line out to, he was going to have to tack back. Thank God they'd practiced the maneuver on the way up from Trinidad.

He turned the wheel to the left and let the wind fill the headsail. The boat started to come around and Wolfe let out a little of the mainsheet to allow the main to fill and the boat started to move. Wolfe kept his eyes on T-Bone the whole while and shuddered each time a wave rolled under him, and he sighed with relief when T-Bone grabbed on to a floating cockpit cushion.

As he fell off the wind, the boat picked up speed and he was on course for T-Bone's position in the water. But he was going too fast. He had to reduce sail or he'd go right over him. And the headsail was jammed. With no way to bring in the jib, he'd have to drop the main.

He stepped out of the cockpit, holding onto the boom for support, and moved as quickly as he could across the slippery deck up to the mast. Like T-Bone, he wasn't wearing a life jacket. At the mast, he uncleated the main halyard and let the main drop. Even as it was falling, he was making his way back to the cockpit. There was no time to tie the main onto the boom, it was just going to have to flog around on deck till he got T-Bone out of the water.

Back at the wheel, he pointed *Cayenne* toward T-Bone, who now had a cockpit cushion under each arm. The wind was gusting up to thirty knots and he was still going too fast. For a second he thought about calling the cutter, but that was the last thing T-Bone would want.

He kept on course until he was two boat lengths from the man in the water, then he cranked the boat into the wind and lost sight of T-Bone as the headsail started flapping and blocked his vision. He could only hope as the boat slowed to almost a stop, but with the wind and current it wouldn't stay stopped long.

He looked over the port side and saw T-Bone, close enough to throw a line to, and still hugging the cushions. He had both cushions wrapped under his left arm and he was waving his right hand in the air. Wolfe tossed him a line and he almost screamed as his friend tied it around the cushions.

Then he started laughing. He put the line on a winch, and started grinding his friend toward the boat. Once T-Bone was alongside he pulled himself aboard and hauled the cushions up after himself. Then he grabbed Wolfe and planted a wet kiss on his forehead.

"Billy boy, you are the fastest learner I have ever seen and I'll knock the block off anybody who says any different."

"You saved the cushions! What were you thinking?" Wolfe said.

"Hey, I got a hard butt." T-Bone wasn't even breathing hard.

"And a harder head," Wolfe said.

"Guess I better fix that jib." T-Bone went forward and fixed the jam, then raised the main. Then he stood there, holding on to the mast, with his long hair and beard blowing in the wind and yelled back to Wolfe. "You don't really want to go to Grenada, do you?"

Wolfe shook his head.

"Where do you want to go?" he yelled to be heard over the rising storm.

"I'm looking for a girl," Wolfe shouted.

"Shit, aren't we all." T-Bone jumped down into the cockpit.

"This one's on a boat called *Shogun*."

"Hey, I know that boat." T-Bone said. "Owner died of a heart attack."

"I'm looking for his wife and daughter. They might be in some trouble."

"Damsels in distress?"

"Maybe."

"Keep her on course, I'm going below for a minute."

Alone with the squall, Wolfe kept the wind on the beam. Though he was dog tired, every fiber of his being was awake. They took spray over the side. Wolfe tasted the salt in the air. He was a kid with a new toy and he didn't know if he'd ever be able to put it down.

The cockpit speakers crackled to life again and Wolfe heard T-Bone call first the charter company in Secret Harbor and ask about *Shogun*. They didn't know the boat, however his second call to the shipyard in Prickly Bay yielded better results. They told T-Bone that *Shogun* had just this morning headed up island.

"We'll head up to St. Lucia," T-Bone said as he came up from below. "Everybody goes through Rodney Bay. There's this place, Typhoon Willie's. We'll wait there and ask questions. I know everybody in the Caribbean that can be trusted to keep his mouth shut. We'll have a lot of eyes looking, a lot of ears listening."

"Thanks," Wolfe said.

"You wanna go now or you wanna wait for weather?"

Wolfe pointed up island.

"You sure you don't want to wait for better weather?" T-Bone was laughing now.

Wolfe shook his head, no. He was laughing too as he spun the wheel away from Grenada and the protection of the bay and out into the storm.

CHAPTER SIXTEEN

VICTOR CAME UP from the head and took the wheel from Beth as they approached the reefs around Union Island in the Grenadines.

They set the anchor with the sun fading from the horizon.

And the engine died.

"Could be nothing," Victor said, but after several failed attempts to start it back up, he said there was water in the fuel. "Maybe a blown head gasket."

"How can that be? We just had the engine rebuilt."

"It looks like whoever did it, screwed up somewhere."

"Brody," Beth said.

"What are we going to do now?" Noelle asked.

"I'll have the guy that works on *Speed Kills* fly up tomorrow and check it out. He's the best mechanic in the Caribbean, but if it's a head gasket or a cracked block, you're going to be here a while."

"Can your mechanic fix it?"

"Sure, but you might have to wait for the parts."

Three days later Beth was sitting in an outside restaurant overlooking the anchorage, waiting for bacon and eggs. Victor and Noelle had gone over to Palm Island on the ferry for the day and wouldn't be back till just before Victor's 6:30 flight to Trinidad. His mechanic's son had been in an auto accident and he didn't want to leave Trinidad until the boy was well. Victor had some business to take care of that he said would take a couple of days. He promised to return in less than a week with the mechanic in tow.

Beth was beginning to think she was stuck forever.

The waitress brought her breakfast, but Beth didn't notice, because she was watching the black schooner *Snake Eyes* wind its way through the reefs.

"Kesha," she called out to the retreating waitress, "if you wanted a diesel engine fixed, who would you call?"

"I thought you was never gonna ask. Sittin' here waitin' for a lazy mechanic to come up from Trinidad, dumbest thing I ever heard. Call Henry. He be da best. He there, down da way." She pointed a bony finger toward the street. "Green building, yellow door, can' miss it."

"Thank you." Beth put the money for her breakfast, along with a generous tip, on the table.

"Not gonna eat da eggs?" Kesha scooped up the money.

"Not this morning." Beth pushed her chair away from the table, stood and pulled her clammy T-shirt away from her body. It was early and already her clothes were sticking. Down the street she knocked on the yellow door.

"He not home," said a girl about nine or ten. She was selling vegetables by the side of the house.

"When will he be back?" Beth asked.

"Just now," the girl said.

"Does that mean the same here as it does in Trinidad?"

"What it mean in Trinidad?"

"Oh, I don't know, five minutes, a half hour, maybe next week."

"Yeah, it the same." The girl pulled at a braid and asked, "You wanna buy some vegetables while you waitin'?" Her smile was like a quarter moon on a dark night, perfect white teeth, two twinkling stars for eyes.

"How much are the tomatoes?"

"One Eastern Caribbean Dollar a pound?"

"One EC a pound?"

"Yes ma'am and you get to pick your own." Beth looked at the man sitting under a shade tree not too far away and recognized his smile. It matched the girl's.

"Maybe I could use some tomatoes."

"How many you want?" Her smile grew and Beth was hooked.

"How many should I buy?"

"Many as you need."

Beth picked up two tomatoes and put them on the scale. The girl dropped a pound weight on the other end.

"Not enough, you need more, has to make a pound."

Beth put two more on the scale.

"Oh, no! Over a pound!" She picked up the pound weight, replaced it with a two-pounder. "Oh, lady, you need more, has to make two pounds."

"How about if I take one off?"

"You can't do that. Once you put them on you have to buy them."

"Then how about you put a half pound weight on and I pay you a dollar fifty?"

"I only have these two weights."

Beth looked over at the girl's father who was flashing a lot of bright teeth from the inside of the largest smile she'd ever seen.

"I guess I should pick some more tomatoes," she said.

"I guess." He laughed.

"She's quite a salesman." Beth dropped two more on the scale.

"She put me out of business, now I just watch."

"I can see why."

"You come back in a few years, I'm gonna be a rich man. But till she makes me rich, I have to repair diesel engines. My name's Henry and I bet you be lookin' for me."

"Yes, I am. I have a diesel engine that doesn't want to run."

"I can come later today."

Beth thought about Victor and Noelle enjoying themselves at Palm Island. Victor would be back by sundown. She didn't know why, but she felt intimidated by him. He called her the captain, but he made all the decisions, and he'd decided on bringing his mechanic up from Trinidad. He didn't like it when he didn't get his way. He wouldn't want Henry on the boat. There would be an argument and she'd give in for harmony's sake.

"Can you come earlier?"

"Can't, gotta wait till Darla sells her vegetables. It's my morning job."

Beth looked over the vegetables on the small table, tomatoes, cucumbers, white radishes, she loved those, and a few heads of lettuce. "How much for the lot?" Beth asked.

Darla's eyes lit up, but she caught a sharp look from her father and frowned.

"You don't have to buy it all," he said. "That wouldn't be fair to you and it wouldn't be fair to Darla."

"I can't wait till this afternoon," Beth said.

"You want me to look at it before the ferry comes back from Palm Island?"

"Yes." How had he figured that out? "Is it that obvious?"

"I tell you what," he said, "you stay and watch Darla. She be too young to be selling by her lonesome, an' I'll go look at your motor."

"Let me get this straight. You go look at my engine and I take your place under that tree?"

"That's about it."

"My dinghy is at the dinghy dock."

"Here, you might want this. Our sun is powerful hot." He held out his wide brimmed straw hat.

For the next two hours she sat under the wide willow tree, her back against its bark, the passing day shielded from her eyes by the broad brim of Henry's hat. Every time she heard a customer she opened her eyes and made sure Darla was all right, then she dozed back off. Twice Darla woke her with fresh lemonade. Beth was in heaven.

"How much for tomatoes?" Beth opened her eyes at the sound of a Russian accent, and peeked out from under the hat. There were two of them. The one speaking was blond, with his back to her. The other man had black hair and rippling muscles.

"A dollar a pound," Darla said.

The blond man spoke in Russian with his companion. They were laughing.

"My friend is saying a dollar is too much," the blond man said. He waved his hands when he talked and he stood ramrod straight, like he was pushing his shoulders skyward, trying to be taller. Alek did that.

Darla's smile faded to false. There was something about the blond man she didn't like. Beth pushed the hat back, not wanting to miss anything. The dark haired man turned. It was Vassi, one of the Russians who worked at Corbeau. He caught her stare and started babbling in Russian. The blond man glanced over, saw Beth and frowned. Beth bit into her lip to keep from screaming as the Russian stalked away with the muscle man in his wake.

The blond man had Alek's face, without the scar Alek had under his lip. It must be a twin. And that black schooner that looked so much like *Viper*, now she knew why. Twin boats for twin boys.

"I can speak Russian," Darla said on her way over to Beth.

"Really?" Beth pushed herself up, dusted off. She was frightened.

"My father used to be a communist. I grew up in Russia."

"What happened to your island accent?" Beth tried to sound normal, not scared.

"If I don't sound like everybody else, the other kids think I'm stuck up."

"How good is your Russian?"

"I was born there. I'm nine years old. We only came back last year."

"So that's why you lost your smile, because of what those men were saying?"

"They said I was pretty, for a little black girl. Only they didn't say it so nice."

"I see," Beth said.

"But when that big man saw you, he said, 'Look, it's her,' and the man with the white hair said that they should leave, 'right now.' They came on that black boat that came in this morning."

"How can that be? I don't even think they've come ashore yet."

"They've been anchored at Chatham Bay, on the other side of the island, since yesterday. They could have walked easy, or come around in a dinghy and now they don't have to go back, because now their boat is here."

"Really?" Beth said.

"I think you should go away," Darla said. "In the middle of the night, when they're not looking." And Beth thought that Darla was one smart girl.

"How can I? My engine isn't working."

"It will be," Darla said. "My dad can fix anything that runs."

"There's your father now," Beth said. "I hope he has good news for me."

"Of course he does, I told you my Dad can fix anything." Darla waved and her father waved back. "He's got arthritis, it hurts when he walks," Darla said. "He pretends it doesn't, but I know better."

Darla was right. Beth saw the grimace in Henry's eyes as he walked, but he grinned at her and his eyes lit up when Darla ran to him and took him by the hand.

"Got it running," he said.

"What was wrong?" she asked.

"Nothing wrong with the engine, just water in the right fuel tank."

"How'd it get there?"

"Somebody put it in."

"Why would anybody do such a thing?"

"Somebody would do it if he wanted you to think there was something wrong with your motor. All he would have to do was sabotage one tank. When he wanted the engine to quit, he'd go below and switch from one tank to the other and the engine would stop. The danger is that he could cause permanent damage, but he didn't. Your engine seems to be okay."

Beth remembered Victor going down to use the head just before they came to the reefs. "Would you do me a favor and not tell anyone the engine's working?"

"You don't want the White Trinidadian to know?" Henry said.

"It's the Russians on that black schooner I'm worried about." She couldn't imagine Victor doing anything to sabotage the boat, he'd helped them so much, after all. But she didn't want to take any chances. "Victor's going to Trinidad on the 6:30 plane. There's no reason we have to say anything till the plane takes off. We'll leave tonight, if we can get out of here without the Russians seeing us."

"They spent last night at Sophie's bar. If they go there tonight, I'll ask her to let them drink for half price, and I'll ask her to serve them doubles."

"Now all I have to do is get past the reefs after dark," Beth said.

"Very dangerous," Henry said.

There was a steel band playing in the background as Beth brought up the anchor. The sound of the band on shore helped cover the sound of the rattling chain as it clanged over the bow roller. She wanted to leave the bay with as little attention as possible. The black schooner was dark, the crew was ashore. Henry had reported that they were drinking heavily at Sophie's.

Beth looked back at Noelle. At first the girl had wanted to wait till morning to leave, but when Beth told her the engine was working and that the Russians worked for Brody, she agreed that they should leave at once.

There was a breeze and the water was choppy. Boats were bobbing at anchor, their anchor lights, atop the tall masts, weaving patterns in the night.

"See the lights on the south end of Palm Island?" Beth said.

"Sure, that's the hotel," Noelle said and Beth didn't have to wonder how she knew that.

"Try to stay halfway between them and the red light marking the buoy on the left. That should keep us off the reef until we get out of this channel."

"Then what?" Noelle asked.

"Then we're through the most dangerous part."

Noelle steered and Beth kept watch. The wind increased and Beth wished she had gotten a weather report. It was turning into a chilly night. Then the rain came, but not hard, just enough to keep them cold and uncomfortable.

"Beth, we're in sixteen feet of water." Noelle was bobbing on her toes and heels.

"It's okay, as long as we stay between the lights." She tried to sound more confident than she felt.

"Beth, it's twelve feet." Noelle stopped bouncing, but her knuckles were white on the wheel. She was waiting for them to hit bottom.

"We'll be all right," Beth said. "Stay between the lights."

"Twenty feet, twenty-five, thirty. It's getting deeper," Noelle said, reading the depth sounder. Then they were through the reefs.

"Keep your current course. I'm going to run below for a second and look at the chart." She saw the look in Noelle's eyes. "It'll be okay, don't worry."

"I hope you're right," Noelle said.

Beth went below. The boat was rocking more, because they were away from the shelter of the reefs. Beth held onto the hand rails for support, made her way to the chart table. It took her less than a minute to decide what to do. She scooted out from behind the table and went topside.

"Turn left," she said.

"But it's the wrong way."

"We're going out to sea."

"But I thought we were going to hug the islands," Noelle said. "You said it was safer."

"If we head up toward Martinique, we'll have better wind and we won't have to worry about any reefs."

"Martinique, that's at least twenty-four hours away." Noelle pushed the hair from her eyes. The wind blew it right back. It was a constant battle she couldn't win, but she kept trying.

"I know," Beth said, "and it's the last thing *Snake Eyes* will suspect. They'll be looking for us in the Southern Grenadines. Meanwhile we'll be in the French Islands, where they have real law and real police. If they try anything there, they'll go to jail for a long time." The sky was clear behind, but there were clouds ahead, covering the stars, blocking the moon. Beth hoped they wouldn't bring more rain.

"You know what I mean. Twenty-four hours without rest, just the two of us. Do you think we can do it?" Noelle had one hand on the wheel, the other holding her hair back.

"Of course we can. People do it all the time." Beth pulled a band out of her hair, "Here, you need this more than I do."

"But we're so inexperienced." Noelle held the wheel with her foot while she put her hair back with the band.

"We can do it," Beth said. "We just have to believe in ourselves."

"I know, how hard can it be?"

"Right."

Thunder rumbled ahead and Beth shivered as they started to move under the clouds. In a few minutes they'd be far enough from the reefs and they could turn toward a course for Martinique.

Thunder rumbled again, louder, closer.

"Think we'll get more rain?" Noelle asked.

"Maybe," she said. "Turn to zero three zero."

"Turning to thirty degrees." Noelle spun the wheel until the compass needle told her she was on course. Now the dark skies were off to the left and the wind was on the beam.

"I guess it's time we got our feet wet and raised a sail," Beth said.

"You want me to turn into the wind?"

"No, I don't think we'll use the main just yet. Let's see how she does with just the jib." Beth freed the starboard jib sheet, then she freed the furling line from the self-tailing jaws, but she kept four wraps on the winch as she cranked on the port sheet. She stopped cranking when the sail was halfway out and cleated off both the furling line and the jib sheet.

Wind filled the sail and the boat picked up speed. Noelle shut off the engine.

"Wow," she said, "it's like magic." Rain was falling on the left, but the squall wasn't affecting them. It was clear on the right and clear ahead. The waves were coming from behind and Noelle was wearing a smile that would light a Christmas tree.

The winds aloft shifted and the cloud cover moved over them, blanketing their world in darkness, but they were steadily moving away from the squall.

"It's kind of spooky." Noelle scanned the horizon, looked astern. "Hey, I saw a light."

"Where?"

"Behind us."

Beth turned. "There's nothing there now."

"There was." Noelle sounded tense. "It was on for a few seconds, then off."

"It was probably just a star that got blocked by a low cloud back there, we're both a little jumpy. There's no way they could have followed us. We only have the ocean to worry about."

"And the wind and the rain," Noelle said, loosening up.

Six hours later Noelle was back on watch. "Beth, I saw it again."

"What?" Beth was waking from a dreamy sleep on the starboard cockpit seat. She sat up, stretched and yawned.

"The light behind us. It's still there."

Beth turned, this time she saw it, too. Then it winked out. "Could be fishermen," she said.

"It's not," Noelle said. "Not this far out. Not this late."

"You want me to let out more of the jib?" Beth asked.

"Let it all out."

Beth did and they sailed on a perfect beam reach at eight and a half knots, till morning, when the wind shifted to just off their nose.

Noelle saw it first. The white sails against the dawn. About a mile behind. "Sails at six o'clock," she said.

Beth turned to look. "Check with the binoculars." But her words weren't necessary, Noelle already had the long glasses to her eyes.

"It's them," Noelle said. "How could they have followed us?"

"Radar." Beth lowered her hand from her forehead. She looked west and saw the steep green of St. Lucia through the early morning light.

"They've got all their sails up," Noelle said. "What are we going to do?" She turned toward Beth.

"Use the engine and put up more sail," Beth said. She didn't have any illusions about what those men would do if they caught her. At the very least they would take the boat back to Trinidad, dropping them off along the way. She didn't want to think about the worst.

Noelle started the engine. The rumbling of the diesel was music to Beth's ears. Henry knew his business.

"Okay, turn into the wind and I'll go up and hoist the main." Beth had never pulled the sail up by herself before, but she'd seen Brody do it when they took the boat out on her trial runs and she'd watched closely when Victor had done it. She thought she could handle it.

"They'll gain on us when we slow down," Noelle said.

"We're just going to have to be quick about it," Beth said. "Once we have the main up, turn back on course and give it the gas. We're going to use all we have."

Noelle eased the boat into the wind and the headsail started to luff as the wind fell out of it. Then she crawled on hands and knees up to the main.

"You didn't clip on!" Noelle yelled after her.

"No time," Beth called back.

The wind gusted, giving *Snake Eyes* a burst of speed and Beth trouble as the boat rocked with the waves. She uncleated the main halyard and started to haul up the sail. She struggled it about a third of the way up the mast, but she wasn't strong enough to get it any further. She dropped to her buttocks and wrapped the mainsheet around a winch, put in a handle and started grinding.

"I need help here."

Noelle scurried up from the cockpit. "We gotta hurry, they're getting closer!" She dropped to the deck and they both grabbed onto the winch handle and cranked.

"Just a little more," Beth pulled on the handle with an effort she didn't know she possessed. "Got it," she said and the sail was up.

"Okay, let's get back there and get her on course."

They crawled back to the cockpit, fighting the slippery deck and the rocking boat.

Beth took the wheel.

"They're getting closer!" Noelle said. The boat was coming toward them at an alarming rate. Beth turned back on course. Another fifteen or twenty minutes and they would have been on them, but the wind filled *Shogun's* sails and she heeled over onto a starboard tack, gliding through the waves, just off the wind.

"They'll never catch us now," Noelle said.

"We're smoking." Beth was as tight as the jib, muscles rippling, sweat dripping from her brow.

"We're losing them!" Noelle squealed.

Beth grabbed onto her hair to keep it out of her eyes as she turned around. They were steadily pulling away from *Snake Eyes*.

"I'd say we have about a knot, maybe a little more, on them. At this rate it'll be ten or fifteen hours before we're out of radar range." But she didn't think it made any difference, because by then they would be in Martinique. And the first thing she would do would be to notify the *gendarmes* about *Snake Eyes*. She sat back behind the wheel and spent a few seconds enjoying the morning. The sun was glowing yellow-orange on the left. Whitecaps on top of three to four foot swells were quartering them from the right. The wind was fresh on her face and they were leaving *Snake Eyes* in their wake.

"I'll bet they figured they'd just sail alongside and snatch the boat," Noelle said. Then, "But they won't give up, will they?"

"Not if he's like Alek." Beth said. "He'll keep coming and coming, waiting for us to relax, or make a mistake. Then he'll be there and he'll pounce."

"What are we going to do?"

"We'll go into a marina in Martinique and stay put. Alek's brother and his friends can nose around all they want, but they won't be able to do a thing. You can't bribe the French to look the other way like you can a lot of these other island governments. One wrong move and our Russian pals will be learning the language from the inside of a French jail."

Beth looked over her shoulder at *Snake Eyes*. "Damn, it looks like they've picked up some speed."

Then a blast like a gunshot ricocheted across the deck and the jib sheets shot away from the snapping jib.

"Roll it in!" Beth said.

"Got it!" Noelle yelled to be heard above the popping sounds and she started grinding on the furling line. Once the sail was furled in everything quieted down. They were sailing almost straight up. They weren't pointing as close to the wind. They'd lost half their speed. And Beth knew they wouldn't make Martinique before dark and she was afraid they might not make it at all.

"What happened?" Noelle asked.

"The clew blew out."

"What's that?"

"It's the hole at the bottom of the sail that the line is attached to, and I'll bet that if we examine it, we'll find that it's been cut or the stitching was undone, something."

"Can we fix it?"

"No, the line ripped clean through the sail. It'll take a sailmaker to repair it."

"That's not good." Noelle turned and looked behind. "It looks like they're closer already. Can we get to Martinique before them?"

"Maybe we could if the wind was right."

"But it isn't!" Noelle said.

"Then we'll just have to make it right," Beth said.

"How?"

Beth looked at the compass, then she turned her face into the wind. She grabbed a breath of the crisp breeze and pointed. "Go that way."

"But that's away from everything."

"It'll be a beam reach, so we'll go fast, even without the jib. And once we're sure we're out of their radar range, we can turn back toward the islands."

"Okay." Noelle spun the wheel, and in a few seconds they were pointed away from the island of St. Lucia and out toward the Caribbean Sea.

Snake Eyes turned too, but *Shogun* was a light race boat and she had the wind. An hour later *Snake Eyes* was a speck in the distance, two hours and she was out of sight. Now it was just Beth, Noelle, *Shogun* and the open sea.

"All right," Beth said. "Let's put her on autopilot and study the charts."

After looking at the charts, Beth decided on St. Lucia because it was the closest island and they could be there by sunup and because there was a marina in the lagoon at Rodney Bay with a large international community.

"I thought you said Martinique would be safer because it's part of France," Noelle said.

"Yeah, but that was our course when they were following us. If they guess that we turned around, they could be waiting for us. We can sneak into St. Lucia before the sun comes up and hide out in the marina."

The sun was setting off to their right when Beth spun the boat around and headed south. If Brody wanted to get her boat bad enough to send Alek's brother after her, she knew he wasn't going to give up just because *Shogun* was able to out run *Snake Eyes*. That she knew for certain. By morning he could even have a plane in the air. She needed to be in that marina by then.

Chapter Seventeen

Wolfe followed T-Bone to a table in Typhoon Willie's. T-Bone ordered a Red Stripe from a slim-in-all-the-right-places, West Indian waitress. Wolfe ordered a Coke.

"Lotsa young couples," Wolfe said, looking around the restaurant.

"St. Lucia doesn't have any waiting period for marriages. Add that to the fact that it's in the tropics and you get a lot of people coming here to tie the knot, especially Japanese."

"Why?"

"Weddings and receptions can cost upwards of fifty grand there. It's cheaper to elope, plus you don't offend anyone by not inviting them to the shindig."

Wolfe looked across the restaurant to a young Japanese couple holding hands. They looked happy, in love. He thought of Beth, wondered where she was.

"So," T-Bone took a sip of his beer, "we haven't talked about you being a cop." Wolfe had explained everything on their sail up from Grenada. "Usually I don't like cops, but I thought about it and I'm gonna make an exception in your case. I shouldn't, but I can't help it, I like you, so here." T-Bone dropped something that looked like a dead rat on the table.

"What is it?"

"Short hair, male wig." T-Bone said. "Matches this." He slapped a blue Trinidadian passport on the table between them. "Now you're Daniel Arthur Steele. Danny Steele."

Wolfe picked up the passport, opened it and looked at the picture of himself staring back. The photo had been copied somehow from his driver's license. Someone had very skillfully added hair.

"How?" He said as he stared at the wig.

"Scanned your license onto a buddy's hard drive, then used Photoshop to add the hair. Wasn't hard."

"You did this? That's why you went ashore by yourself earlier?"

"Yep, well, my friend helped."

"What's your friend do for a living?" Wolfe closed the passport. Whoever T-Bone's friend was, he was good.

"You don't wanna know," T-Bone said. "But you might wanna know this. As of tomorrow, if anybody checks with the government of Trinidad and Tobago, this passport will come up legit. You're in their database, or rather Daniel Arthur Steele is. Also the US visa will be on file at the American Embassy in Port of Spain. You need four thousand bucks in a bank account in Trinidad before they'll give you the visa, here's your bankbook." T-Bone tossed the bankbook on the table.

"Jesus." Wolfe picked it up. "Twenty-four thousand dollars?"

"Relax, it's TT dollars, six-to-one remember? But like I said, you're gonna have to pay me back."

"How'd you do all this so fast? And before you say anything, I do want to know."

"It's not that amazing." T-Bone had a wide grin on his face. "The passport, bank account and other supporting documents were originally set up for someone else. But the other guy didn't need it any more and my friend owed me a large favor. It all fell into place, so to speak."

"What other supporting documents?"

"TT driver's license." T-Bone tossed it on the table. "Had to make the hair a little different for that and we added a mustache. We only had the one photo to work with and we had to make the license look different from the passport."

"I suppose this is legit, too." Wolfe studied the photo. He didn't know how they'd done it, but it didn't look like the same picture.

"The best forged documents are the real thing. They're real hip to that in the States, but it's still the sticks out here." T-Bone was grinning like he'd just won the lottery. "You also might want your Yacht Club membership card." He tossed it on the table. "Your Country Club membership card." He tossed it on the table. And the coup de gras, your Visa Card. Remember that's a credit card, you charge anything on it, I'm not responsible for paying it back. The bills will go to this address in Trinidad." He tossed a slip of paper on top of the card. "From there, they're posted to one of those mail drops in Miami. You can change the address to any place you want."

"I don't believe it." Wolfe gathered up the cards. "What happened to the other guy?"

"What other guy?"

"The original Danny Steele."

"He was arrested in Venezuela and sent back to Trinidad. You might've heard about it. Escaped drug lord. Paid the cops in Trinidad to look the other way, then skipped to Venezuela. He was hiding out there till all this was ready, but he partied a little too hardy, talked a little too much and the DEA popped him and arranged for him to be taken home. Bad for him. Good for you."

"Thanks, buddy, you're amazing. You really are."

"You can thank me, Danny boy, by picking up the check tonight."

"I didn't like Billy Boy, I hate Danny Boy."

"Sorry, you're stuck with it."

"I don't believe it." Wolfe said as he saw a pair of dinghies approaching the beach in front of the restaurant.

"What?"

"I saw that guy in California." Wolfe was calm as he watched the blond bodybuilder he'd seen at Ann Marie Shannon's house get out of one of the dinghies. "How about that, there's two of 'em," he said as the blond's double got out of the second dinghy.

"Alek and Fredek Petrov," T-Bone said.

"What?"

"That's their names. Russian Mafia wanna be type guys. Alek works for Corbeau Yacht Services in Trinidad. You don't usually see them together. Fredek works in St. Martin. Strong arm stuff for one of the casinos."

"You really do know everybody down here."

"Not everybody, but in my line of work, it helps to know about characters like them. How do you want to play it?"

"By ear, I guess."

"Okay, we'll see how it goes."

They sipped at their drinks and watched the men pull their dinghies ashore. They were still sipping when they came into the restaurant. One of the twins asked for a seaside table, louder than he had to. And he was more upset than he had to be when told they were all taken. The waitress said she could put two tables together for the six men, but it would be toward the back. The loud mouthed one didn't stop complaining until the tables were joined and she was taking the drink orders.

"Another round?" Wolfe said.

"You still buying?" T-Bone said.

"You know I am."

"Then I'm still drinking."

Wolfe got up to get the drinks. He saw two yachtie couples on stools at the bar, going over a couple of bags of things you need on a boat. Epoxy, seizing wire, twelve volt light bulbs, other stuff. They must have come straight from the local chandlery to enjoy happy hour and the sunset from the beach bar.

"How much you pay for the seizing wire?" Wolfe asked.

"About five bucks," a portly yachtie said. Wolfe guessed he'd just retired, bought a boat and headed down from the States. His clothes were new, his face bright red.

"I'll give you twenty. I've got kind of a personal emergency and I need it right away."

"Son, I don't know what kind of emergency you could possibly need the wire for," the yachtie said, "but it's yours for a round."

"Deal." Wolfe ordered five Red Stripes and a Coke from the bartender. While he was waiting, he studied the Russians in the mirror behind the bar. One of the twins caught him looking and Wolfe saw the recognition in his eyes. He looked away and took one of the beers, the Coke and the wire back to his table.

"I bought a little something from those yachties." Wolfe took his seat, slid a Red Stripe over to T-Bone, took a sip from his Coke.

"What?"

"This." He showed T-Bone the wire.

"Seizing wire? What the fuck for?"

"Think about it," Wolfe said.

T-Bone was quiet for a few seconds. Then he shivered and for an instant Wolfe thought his whole face kind of twinkled. "Which one?" he said.

"Whoever follows me to the head."

"They're bad men," T-Bone said.

"Yeah, they are." Wolfe leaned back, took another sip of his Coke. "When I get up, you should make some excuse to go out to the boat, make sure the twins think you're coming right back."

T-Bone nodded.

"Ready?" Wolfe said.

"Any time," T-Bone said.

"Going to the head," Wolfe said loud enough to be heard across the room as he slid his chair out from under the table.

"Okay," T-Bone said. "I'm gonna shoot out to the boat and get some more money. If you're not back before me, whatever you did in there was a sin."

Wolfe walked through the restaurant, turned down the corridor to the toilets. He slipped into the women's and waited. He heard someone pass on the other side of the thin swinging door. His instinct told him it was one of the twins. He moved into the corridor, took three quick steps to catch up to the Russian, slipped a loop of the seizing wire over his head and tightened it with a quick jerk.

"You can die now." Wolfe drew back on the wire. "Or we can walk out that door and have a little talk."

The Russian started to speak. Wolfe pulled a little harder on the wire.

"No sound, nod your head, yes or no," Wolfe whispered. "Yes, for we talk. No, for I kill you now."

The Russian nodded yes.

"Which one are you, Alek or Fredek? Nod once for Alek, twice for Fredek."

The Russian nodded twice and with one hand holding the wire loop around his neck, the other in the small of his back, Wolfe pushed him forward, guiding him out the back door and into the dark.

Outside Fredek started to turn, but Wolfe brought a foot behind one of his knees, forcing him to kneel on the damp earth.

"Don't make me have to kill you." Wolfe kneed him in the back, forcing him forward even more, till he was face down on the ground.

Fredek tried to talk, but could only gag with the wire around his neck. Then he squawked as Wolfe's hand went up his shorts and he put a smaller loop of the seizing wire around his testicles.

"Now," Wolfe said, "one wrong move and you spend the rest of your life singing soprano." He stepped off the Russian and stood aside. "You understand what I've done?"

Fredek shook his head.

"The wire around your balls and neck. Seizing wire. Very strong, easy to bend." Fredek started to move.

"Don't." Wolfe leaned forward, reached his hand under the Russian's loose fitting shirt and removed the gun.

"Forty-Five auto, very bad." Wolfe thumbed the release and the clip fell out. He threw it toward the ocean and grinned when he heard the splash. "Played ball in college." Then he pulled the slide back. A round flew up, landing about five feet away. "And one in the chamber. Very dangerous."

He loosened the wire noose around the Russian's neck, then slipped it off.

"Okay, you can get up. Just remember that I've got you on a leash, one wrong move and you can kiss 'em goodbye." Fredek pushed himself from the ground and gave a high pitch little yelp when Wolfe gave a slight tug on the wire looped around his testicles.

"You'll pay," Fredek Petrov said.

"One way or another we all have to pay," Wolfe said. "But right now I'm holding the hand with all the aces, so to speak. And here's how I want to play my cards. You're going to walk to your dinghy with your hand on the gun. You'll get in the dinghy and you'll do your best to convince your friends at the bar that I'm your prisoner. I'll get in after you and I'll drive. Your friends will assume you're taking me out to sea to do away with me."

"You're insane," Fredek said.

"Maybe, but I don't have wire wrapped around my balls. I'll play out about ten feet. One wrong move, if I even suspect you're trying to signal your brother, and I'll jerk off your nuts."

"And they'll kill you."

"I'd rather be dead than the way that'll leave you, but hey, that's just me." For emphasis Wolfe gave a slight pull on the wire. Fredek let out a quick grunt.

"Here," Wolfe said. "Stuff it in your pants, make sure your friends see it when we get in the dinghy." He handed the gun to Fredek, who did as instructed. Wolfe led him to the rubber boat like he was taking a dog for a walk. He risked a glance at the bar as they were pushing the boat into the lazy ocean and fought a grin when he saw the smug look of satisfaction on the face of Fredek's twin.

"Okay, hand it over," Wolfe said after they were out of the sight of the men in the restaurant. The Russian handed over the gun. Wolfe tossed it into the sea.

"Stupid, it was a good gun," Fredek said.

Wolfe motored up to *Snake Eyes* and kissed the side of the black boat with the dinghy.

"Anyone on board?"

"No."

"Okay, get up the boarding ladder." Wolfe followed Fredek up with a hand on the wire leash. On deck he said, "I need some line to tie you with, then I can take the wire off."

"You're not going to kill me?"

"Not if I don't have to. You can walk away from this. Now where's the line?"

"There." Fredek pointed to the cockpit seats.

"Get it," Wolfe ordered.

Fredek lifted up the cushions to get at the storage locker underneath, then pulled off the hatch cover.

Wolfe pulled out some spare line, saw a roll of duct tape and grabbed it too, then, still using the wire leash to coax cooperation, led Fredek up to the mast.

"Hands behind your back," he said and he tied the Russian to the mast.

"Now you will take this thing off?"

"First we talk."

"You promised."

"What do I look like? We talk, if I'm satisfied, we both go back to shore like pals. If I'm not, you'll be squeaking a note or two higher." Wolfe grinned as the blood rushed to Fredek's head. He glared at Wolfe, but Wolfe stayed quiet.

"What do you want to know?" Fredek finally said.

"Why did you kil! Skidmores?"

"I didn't."

Wolfe gave a quick tug on the wire. "Talk to me, let's be friends."

"No," Fredek said and Wolfe pulled harder. "All right, I'll tell you.

"Good, don't make me yank on it again."

"Shannon was skimming off some of the diamonds and substituting fakes."

"Diamonds? What diamonds?"

"Diamonds that are mined in West Africa somewhere, by rebel groups. I don't know which ones, that's Brody's department. He gets guns from Sterling-Skidmore in the States. The diamonds are smuggled into Florida on supply boats that pick up construction equipment for Skidmore Oil, some of the guns go out on them."

"Jesus," Wolfe said. What had he walked into? He needed Fredek's trust. "Tell me about the diamonds, how do you change them into dollars and tell me what I have to do to get a piece of the pie."

"You want to be cut in." Fredek sighed and smiled. Wolfe grinned back. For the first time since his capture Fredek had to be thinking that there was a way out for him, after all.

"I don't want so big a cut that anyone will be too resentful," Wolfe lied. "The way I figure it, there's enough to go around. Think about it. You guys could use me. I'd like to be on the side of the big money for a change."

"You have been resourceful," Fredek said.

"Talk to me," Wolfe said.

"Take off the wire."

"Sorry, talk first, trust later." Wolfe tugged on the wire. "What did Frank Shannon have to do with it?"

"He was going to smuggle the diamonds into Florida for Brody."

"How."

"They're fiberglassed in the hull of his boat, under the refrigerator. Millions of dollars of diamonds. Shannon was supposed to go into the Skidmore yard in Florida and Alek and I were going to get them out of there and deliver them to Brody at his house in Palm Beach."

"So that's why Beth Shannon left Trinidad in such a hurry, because she has the diamonds."

"She doesn't know. Brody made up some phony bills right after Shannon died. Then he went to the government and got a writ attaching the boat. She fled to keep him from getting it."

"So Frank Shannon died of a heart attack before he was able to get the diamonds to the States."

"Brody found out Shannon was skimming, so he wanted to teach him a lesson. He kidnapped Frank's girlfriend, let his men have her, then tortured her to death and arranged for Shannon to find the body. Sort of a message that his wife and daughter would be next if he didn't return the diamonds he skimmed."

"That's what caused his heart attack?"

"Yes, Shannon died before Brody could get his hands on him."

"Sometimes revenge isn't too smart." Wolfe clenched his fist. He could just imagine what Beth had gone through. He should have pushed her, found out about it. Instead he acted like a lovesick kid, telling her he wanted a few days off from being a cop. She must have felt like she had nowhere to turn.

"Brody sent me and Alek to California to find out what we could from Mark Skidmore. It turns out that he was working with Shannon and that they skimmed off ten million dollars worth of the diamonds, way more than Brody had thought, and smuggled them into the States on their own."

"That's a lot of skimming."

"We're talking about a lot of diamonds. This is no small operation."

"Tell me about this guy Brody."

"He's a big man. Tall, like a basketball player, but he's thick in the shoulders, like one of your American football players."

"Not what he looks like, tell me about *him*."

"He owns Corbeau Yacht Services in Trinidad. But his yard also refits the ships the oil companies use. It's much cheaper for US companies to send their ships down to Trinidad than to have the work done in the States."

"Let me guess, that's how he smuggles the rest of the guns into Trinidad."

"Brody's smart."

"But you're smarter, you're after the diamonds for yourselves, you and your brother, aren't you?" Wolfe remembered the way they tore apart the Skidmore penthouse, Ann Marie's place and that weather girl's.

"Are you crazy? You must have heard of the Russian Mafia, that's who Brody is. Nobody goes against them. They want their diamonds back, the one's glassed into Shannon's boat and the ones he stole."

"So, where are they, the diamonds Shannon stole?"

"No more. Let me go, and we talk."

"Sorry?" Wolfe tugged on the wire.

Fredek screamed.

"Stop that!" Wolfe was afraid that the sound would carry across the water to shore.

"Then stop pulling on that damned wire."

"We're not friends yet. Tell me about Shannon's diamonds. Then I'll quit."

"I've told enough."

"Don't make me jerk 'em off."

"Mark Skidmore said they were in a locker at the State University in Long Beach. We forced him to take us there, but when we cut the lock it only had books in it. Turns out Frank didn't trust his brother-in-law, he lied about the locker number."

"How do you know?"

"Mark said he dropped Shannon off and waited in the parking lot across the street. Shannon didn't have the diamonds with him when he came back."

"So you killed Skidmore and left his body out at the university. How come you didn't check the other lockers?"

"It's not possible to break into every locker at the university, not even for ten million dollars. Our only hope of getting them is if Beth Shannon knows about her husband's locker. Brody thinks she does."

"What's his plan?"

"He's on his way here. When we find her, he's going to sweet talk her back to Trinidad. Once the boat's safe in his yard, he'll get the locker number out of her."

Wolfe didn't have to ask how Brody planned on doing that. He moved behind Fredek, picked up the duct tape from the deck where he'd set it when he'd tied the man to the mast.

"What are you doing?" Fredek said.

"Making sure you stay quiet." Wolfe slammed Fredek's head to the mast, then slapped tape to his mouth, muffling him. "Maybe I should to a better job." He wrapped tape around Fredek's head and the mast, around his neck, mouth and forehead, turning him into part of the boat by securing his head to the mast.

"I saw those women you tortured. This is for them." Wolfe jerked the wire, severing Fredek's testicles from his body.

Wolfe left him in muffled agony and went below. He grabbed a serrated knife from the galley and went to the engine room, where he sliced through the hose coming from the raw water intake, he stepped back as the ocean rushed into the boat.

The engine compartment bilge pumps came on. They were designed to take out more than a damaged hose would allow in. Wolfe jerked the wires from the float switches and the pumps shut down.

Satisfied, he went topside and looked out across the bay.

The cockpit cushions were still off, the hatch cover still open. He found two five gallon jerry cans of gasoline. He took one below, where he stripped a sheet off the bed in the aft cabin, tore it in half, then rolled one of the halves up so that it resembled a white snake. He soaked the rolled sheet half with gasoline, then stuffed the snake's tail into the gas can.

Wolfe set the giant Molotov cocktail in the center of the salon, looked around, saw a pack of cigarettes and several matchbooks on a shelf above the settee. He got the smokes, took one out of the pack, lit it, then dropped the pack and a book of matches into his shirt pocket.

Back at the gas can, he broke off the filter, opened a matchbook, stuffed the burning cigarette between the matches and smiled as he set the book under the snake's head. When the cigarette burned down to the matches, they'd ignite, lighting the snake. He hoped it would make about a five minute fuse.

By the time he was back on deck Fredek was weeping. Wolfe had the other half of the rolled sheet around his neck as he lowered the second jerry can into the dinghy and motored over to the other black schooner.

He left the outboard running as he climbed aboard the twin ship, cut through the raw water hose, then set up the gas can cocktail in the center of the salon. He lit another cigarette and made another snake, but this time he broke the cigarette in half, giving himself about two minutes, he thought.

Then he dashed up the hatch, leapt into the dinghy, cranked the throttle full and zoomed away from the boats. When he judged himself a safe distance, he cut the gas and waited. *Snake Eyes* went first, in a blinding, blazing explosion. *Viper* blasted apart a few seconds later.

Wolfe motored over to *Cayenne*.

"I liked the fireworks," T-Bone said, "but I don't think we should stay and watch what comes next."

"You're the captain," Wolfe said.

"I think this is a good night for motoring down to Castries. We'll anchor off the airport, maybe go ashore and watch the honeymoon couples. We can come back in the morning. What do you think?"

"I'll get the anchor," Wolfe said.

CHAPTER EIGHTEEN

NOELLE WAS BEHIND THE WHEEL as they motored into a rising sun and Rodney Bay on the northern end of St. Lucia. Palm trees lined a sandy beach that was home to several three and four story hotels. The beach was deserted, the tourists still asleep, recuperating from yesterday's fun in the sun and last night's beach parties.

Like the hotels, the boats at anchor were quiet too. A lone windsurfer, wearing orange and green, was the only sign of life. Beth watched as he bent and twisted on his board, trying to coax it across the bay. A gust blew through and he gathered speed, but as quickly as it had come, it was gone and the surfer was stalled again.

"That looks like a good spot, behind that yellow boat." Noelle pointed toward a yellow sloop.

"I'll get the anchor ready." Beth stepped out of the cockpit and went forward. The morning air chilled her and she shivered when she saw the masts sticking out of the calm water. She pointed right and Noelle turned the wheel away. Beth made sure they were well away from the two sunken ships before she dropped the anchor. Once she was satisfied the holding was good, she gave Noelle the sign to cut the engine.

"What do you think happened to them?" Noelle asked as Beth came back into the cockpit.

"Don't know." Beth picked up the binoculars and studied the masts sticking out of the water at odd angles. "But we've got our own problems. We have to check in and get into the marina as quickly as possible."

It was a quarter to eight when they got to Customs and Immigration, but the officer was already in and willing to do the paperwork. They were welcomed into his office and he bade them sit across from his desk. He was friendly, smiled large, and when they finished the forms and had their passports stamped, Beth asked about the two sunken boats in the harbor.

"Happened last night. Deliberate."

"For the insurance?" Beth asked.

"Someone didn't like them. Set them afire."

"Who would do such a thing?" Beth said.

"We're looking into that." He leaned forward and lowered his voice in the way West Indians do when they gossip. "They were two brothers, same kind of boat. One got killed, the other is going crazy and I guess I can understand why."

Noelle gasped.

"Are the crew still on the island?" Beth asked.

"Of course," the customs officer said. "Only happened last night, you don't think we let them leave so quick."

"Beth," Noelle said as soon as they were outside the door, "we have to leave right now. Once we're away from here we're safe."

"I think you're right," Beth said.

"You wanna go back in and check out?"

"No, let's just go to the boat and get the Heck out of here."

"That's got my vote, big time," Noelle said.

They went straight to the dinghy dock, climbed in and headed out toward *Shogun*. The windsurfer was gone, but seven or eight small sailboats were making their way across the bay followed by a Boston Whaler. Kids in the tiny sailboats, two adults in the Whaler. A sailing class.

"Mama following the baby ducks," Noelle said.

"You have to learn young if you're going to make a living off the sea," Beth said.

"I think I might come back and work on one of these islands when I finish my residency," Noelle said.

"You wouldn't make much money out here," Beth said. "But you'd be appreciated a thousand percent more than you'd ever be in California."

"Yeah, money isn't everything."

"It sure isn't," Beth said as she motored the Zodiac alongside *Shogun*.

Noelle cleated off the painter, then climbed aboard. Beth cut the engine and followed. She stepped over the lifelines and stopped in her tracks. Alek Petrov was in the cockpit. He had a hand over Noelle's mouth.

"Finally," he said.

"What do you want, Alek?" She tried to sound indignant.

"Give me a break," he said.

"Are you going to try and take the boat? That's piracy, you'll go to jail."

"Shut up!"

"You'll never get away with this."

"I already have."

He was right. She looked to shore. There would be no help from that quarter. Even if she screamed, nobody would hear. *Shogun* was too far out. No one would notice if she just hauled up her anchor and motored out of the bay.

Harris from the Corbeau Shipyard, wearing his signature Army fatigues, came up from below.

"How many men to capture two women?" Beth said, no pretext at surprise now, just indignation.

"We are five. Sasha, Vassi and Serge are below." Beth knew them. Vassi had been with Alek's twin on Union Island, the other two were fair haired Russian look-a-likes from Siberia that worked at Corbeau. They didn't talk much, but were excellent sailors. "We were six last night, but we had some problems."

"Someone sank your boats and killed your brother," Noelle said.

Alek slapped her across the face and she almost fell.

"Hold your tongue or I'll let my men have you, then throw you overboard."

Noelle started to say something.

"Shut up, Noelle!" Beth said.

"Smart, Beth, but then Brody said you were smart. Now tell me about Wolfe."

"What?"

"Tell me!"

"He's a policeman from California. He was investigating the Skidmore murders. He wanted to ask me some questions, but I came back to Trinidad before he had a chance, so he followed me."

"He went all that way just to ask some questions?"

"That's what he said."

"I think he lied to you, but it makes no difference, I'm going to kill him."

"I don't understand," Beth said, but she was beginning to. "It was him," she said, "wasn't it?"

"He killed my brother. He will die horrible and slow."

"Why tell me?" she said.

"You're connected somehow."

"I'm just trying to save my boat," Beth said. "That's all. Surely you can understand that."

He looked long and hard at her. He started to say something, stopped, then cocked his head. For a moment he looked child-like, lost and hurt. Then his eyes glazed over and he looked away.

"Harris, start the engine and let's get out of here."

A few seconds later Harris shouted from the cockpit, "She won't start!"

"Shit!" Alek hurried to the cockpit, pressed the start button. "Go below and see what's wrong."

After a minute that seemed like eons to Beth, Harris came back on deck. "Starter clicks, but nothing happens."

"Any of you idiots know anything about diesels?" he screamed.

None of his men spoke up.

Beth thought of the childish expression a moment ago and contrasted it with his clenched facial muscles and burning gray eyes and realized that he was as crazy as a mad dog. The only way to deal with him would be to put him down.

"You're all worthless!" Alek's face was red, his right hand clenched into a tight knuckled, pumping fist. "All right, we'll sail off the anchor. Can you at least do that?"

The men scrambled to do his bidding.

"You two, follow me," Alek said and the women obeyed. Alek went to the bow, opened the forepeak hatch. "Get in," he said.

"You're kidding," Beth said. "It's over a hundred degrees in there."

"It'll be uncomfortable, but you won't die."

Beth knew there was no point in arguing, so she climbed down the hatch. Noelle came down after her. Alek closed the hatch on top of them and they looked for a way to get comfortable among the diesel jugs, bundled lengths of line, buckets and tools.

It was hot, but not dark. Plenty of light came in through the Plexiglas hatch. The hatch also had latches on the inside. If it got too hot, she could open it a little and let in some air, but not if they were sailing, because water coming over the deck would flood in and drench them.

"There are no winch handles!" Beth heard Harris shout.

"Yes there are, find them!" Alek was raging and Beth thought that maybe they were better off where they were than up on deck. The crew was silent, save for Harris, who seemed to be bearing the brunt of Alek's verbal abuse.

After a bit, Beth heard Harris say that there were no winch handles anywhere on the boat. She thought that was strange, *Shogun* was a big race boat, sixteen winches and six handles. The handles all had plastic holsters, one on each side of the mast, four in the cockpit. Where could they be?

"All right," Alek screeched. "We'll sail without the handles."

"How can we do that?" Harris tried to reason with him.

"We'll pull up the main and cleat it off. We might not be able to tighten it, but it can get us out of here."

"Why don't I go ashore and buy a couple winch handles?" Harris said.

"Why don't you shut up?" Alek said.

It was quiet above for a few seconds, then Beth heard someone hoisting the main and felt movement as the boat shifted with the wind.

"Cleated off," Harris said.

Beth heard footsteps overhead and saw Alek move over the Plexiglas hatch to step on the windlass button to bring up the anchor. The chain started to fall into the chain locker behind her.

Think, she told herself. The rattling chain echoed throughout the small compartment. Noelle had her hands over her ears. If only she could stop the banging and clanging of the falling chain. Then she grinned, reached overhead and jerked on the DC wires to the windlass, ripping them from their terminals.

Immediately the stuffy compartment went quiet.

"Motherfuck!" Alek screamed from above. He bent low and Beth saw the river of hatred flowing from his eyes through the Plexiglas. He opened the hatch.

"The windlass doesn't work! What's going on with this boat?"

"I don't know," she said.

"Where are the winch handles?"

"I don't know. They're supposed to be at the mast and in the cockpit."

"They're not there!"

"Someone must have stolen them."

He slammed the hatch shut in a rage, still screaming. "Harris, take the men ashore, get winch handles, an electrician and a diesel mechanic."

"We all don't have to go," Harris said.

"Yes, all of you, go! I want to be alone with the women."

Beth didn't like the sound of that. She looked around her prison for a weapon, then she took some half inch line off a hook and started to uncoil it. She tied a small bowline loop in the end of it and fed the line back through it.

"What are you doing, Beth?" Noelle asked.

"When he sticks his head down here again, I'm gonna loop this around his neck and we're gonna pull for all we're worth."

"That's murder!"

"He wasn't kidding when he said his men would use you. When they get tired of us they'll toss us overboard, probably with our hands tied behind our backs. You heard the man, he's insane."

"But to kill someone?"

"Him or us." Beth heard the sound of the dinghy motoring toward shore. Now they were alone with Alek.

"I'm sorry, I just don't think I can do it."

"Okay, honey, just stay back. I'll do it myself."

Then without warning the hatch opened, but Alek was standing and Beth had no chance to get the noose around his neck.

"Hot down there?" He laughed, then he started squirting them with the saltwater hose.

"Stop it!" Noelle yelled, holding her hands in front of her eyes, but Alek laughed and kept the hose trained on her.

"Fucking cunt!" He blasted her in the face with the water. Then he moved the hard spray to her breasts, soaking the halter top till he could see through it.

Noelle backed away from the center of the compartment till she had her back up against the chain locker and Alek couldn't reach her with the spray, but he was a man possessed. He dropped to his knees, stuck the hose in the hatch and aimed it toward the back of the compartment.

"Missed me, missed me, you fucking pervert!" Noelle shouted.

"You fucking whore!" Alek stuck his head down the hatch after the hose. "You won't get away from me so easy." He saw them cringing against the chain locker and laughed. Like a hyena, Beth thought.

Then she looped the noose around his neck and jerked. Noelle jumped forward, grabbed onto the rope and helped Beth pull. There was a screech out of Alek, then a crack as his neck broke, followed by a stench as his bowels cut loose when his body flopped into the compartment.

"I was wrong, "Noelle said. "I can do it. I just needed the proper motivation."

"We have to get out of here," Beth said. The body was shuddering, doing it's death dance.

Noelle scrambled up and out of the hatch. Beth looked at the body slumped at her feet, finally still. What did Wolfe have to do with all of this? It didn't make any sense. There had to be more to what was going on than just Brody wanting to get her boat so he could sell it and recover a past dept. People didn't kill for that kind of money.

"Better hurry, Beth. Dinghy's coming."

"What now?" Beth climbed through the hatch in time to see her Zodiac come alongside. "Oh, Lord, it's Brody, and he's got a gun."

"Where's Alek?" Brody said. He was wearing orange shorts and a bright green T-shirt. He was the windsurfer she'd seen earlier and he was standing in the dinghy as sure footed in the bobbing Zodiac as he had been on his board. He gripped the painter in his left hand. He had a pistol in his right.

"He's dead." Beth threw the words at him as if she dared him to make something of it.

"Good." Brody handed the gun to Harris. "Put this away."

"Sure, boss." Harris lifted his shirt and stuffed the gun, an automatic, between his belly and his tight fitting fatigue pants.

"Permission to come aboard?" Brody said.

"Help yourself." Beth wondered why he bothered asking. "You're the one with the gun."

"That's no way to talk, Lizzy. The gun was for Alek." He grabbed on to the shrouds, pulled himself on board. "Harris told me what he's been up to. It's my fault and I'm sorry. I knew he had a few screws loose, but I never dreamed he'd harm you. He was just supposed to find you for me so I could explain myself."

"I don't understand," Beth said.

"Me neither," Noelle said. "Those guys have been chasing us all over the Caribbean."

"So Harris said and I'm sorry about that. I don't know what got into them. I blame myself, I never should have sent them, but Alek had been getting on my nerves lately and I saw a chance to get rid of him for a few days. Besides, he had a boat."

"Not anymore," Noelle said.

"No, not anymore."

"If they weren't supposed to grab my boat and take it back to you, what were they supposed to do?" Beth said.

"Like I said, find you. Frank owed the yard fifty-eight thousand, too much for me to write off."

"*Shogun's* worth more than that."

"Three hundred and eighty-five thousand US dollars according to the appraisal Frank had when you were in the yard last month."

"I didn't know about any appraisal."

"He didn't want you to know. We worked on it when you were off the boat."

"I don't understand."

"I don't either, and I don't want to. I just want my money and I believe I've worked it out so that we'll both be happy about it. I've got a buyer for *Shogun.* He won't go the whole three-eighty-five, but he'll do three-fifty. You're losing some money, I know, so in fairness, I'll knock eight thousand off the yard bill and we'll run the sale through my company, so you won't have to pay the usual eight percent commission. The buyer's willing to wire fifty thousand into my account and three hundred into yours as soon as he sees the boat safely back in Trinidad."

"Three hundred thousand dollars, Beth," Noelle said.

"What about Alek, his brother and that." Beth pointed to the masts sticking out of the water.

"Alek and Fredek were a little off. They killed their father when they were sixteen, stabbed him to death because he abused their mother. The courts in the old Soviet Union ruled the homicide justified, so I'd guess the old man was abusing the boys as well, because a lot of men abuse their wives in Russia and nobody seems to care. On top of that, Fredek had a nasty habit of going to prostitutes, then brutally beating them."

"And they worked for you?"

"Not Fredek. I didn't know Alek had enlisted him."

"So what do we do about Alek now?" Noelle said.

"We could call the authorities, of course you two will probably spend years in a St. Lucian jail, or we could dump the body at sea."

"I vote for option number two," Noelle said.

Brody turned to Harris. "The winch handles are under the mattress in the V berth."

"You hid them?" Beth said.

"Right after I disconnected the starter motor. I didn't think about the windlass though. You must have jerked out the wires when Alek was bringing up the chain. That was fast thinking."

Ten minutes later, after Brody had reconnected the starter and the windlass motors, Harris had his heel on the foot button, bringing up the anchor.

"We'll be in Trinidad in two days," Brody said from behind the wheel. "I'll have my bill paid and you'll have almost a third of a million dollars."

Beth nodded. She didn't believe a word of it, but she didn't know what to do. There were five of them and they had a gun.

"All this effort and you only get fifty thousand dollars." She knew she shouldn't say anything, but she couldn't help herself. "It doesn't make any sense."

"Ah, Lizzy," Brody hissed, "you don't trust me."

"It's not that. I just wish I knew what you were up to."

"I wish I could tell you what it was all about," Brody said and she shivered at the cold in his voice. "Perhaps someday, but for now all you have to know is that you're going to get a lot of money."

"What if I told you I could get the money Frank owes you? What if I could give you a check as soon as we got back to Trinidad?"

"Is that what you're saying?" Brody was pure snake now. His voice more than a hiss. She felt the venom. She didn't know why he wanted the boat, but he wanted it. Playing with him could be fatal. She'd been foolish to try.

"I suppose I could get the money," Beth said. "But why would I? It would break me, and I'd still have this white elephant of a boat to keep up." Chills ran up her spine as his dark eyes bore into her. "The boat's yours. I don't know why you want her, and I don't care. Frankly, three hundred thousand is more than I'd planned on getting. If you'd've come to me with that offer, rather than send that squinty little man to try and throw us off the boat, *Shogun* would've been yours from the get go, the Petrov twins would still be alive and I'd be back in my apartment in Huntington Beach enjoying the Southern California weather, instead of this sauna I've been living in for the last three years."

"Sometimes I revert to subterfuge when the direct approach would be more appropriate. I admit I'm not the best at judging people. I thought you'd want to keep the boat. After all, you and your husband spent a lot of time, money and hard work making her what she is. I thought the sentimental value would be priceless."

"Sentiment doesn't put food on the plate."

"We'd already decided to sell it when that man came with the papers," Noelle said.

Good girl, Beth thought.

"I wish you would have said something."

"Come on, Brody, you didn't give us a chance," Beth said.

Brody steered to the right to get out of the path of a boat that was coming into the bay under sail. He shook his head, looked out to sea.

"That policeman, Wolfe. Harris says he killed Fredek and sank the boats. Why would he do that?"

"I guess he likes me." Beth stared into his hard eyes. Noelle put a hand on her shoulder, squeezed.

"What do you mean?"

"Just what she said." Noelle squeezed Beth's shoulder again. "It's obvious Mr. Wolfe thought those men might harm Beth, so he fixed it so they couldn't."

"Not many men can kill. It takes a special sort of man."

"I saw Mr. Wolfe last night," Harris said, stepping into the cockpit. "Fredek had a gun on him, he didn't look very special then. Still, considering how it turned out, you have to give the man credit for a certain flair. I wouldn't want to be on his wrong side." Harris eyed Beth the way no woman likes to be looked at.

"Oh, Mr. Wolfe is very special," Noelle said. "And he's in love with Beth. I imagine he's very upset right now, not being able to find her and all."

"Your husband isn't even cold in his grave." Brody bored into Beth.

"So, what are you, a priest?" Beth angry, stepped out of the cockpit and went to the port shrouds, grabbed onto them and stared out at the boat coming in under sail. There were two men in the cockpit, one of them had binoculars trained on her.

"I got the message that you didn't want me to make him mad." Noelle had followed her. "But I couldn't help myself. He's such a reptile."

"So how long have you known about me and Wolfe?"

"From the start. Victor and I went straight to the boat from the airport, because we thought you'd be right behind us. I didn't want to, but Victor was curious about Wolfe. We hung around for hours. Finally, when you didn't show up, we went to the Anchorage. Dumb me, I didn't expect a thing, but when I saw the look on your face the next morning, it was obvious you did more than talk."

"What do you mean?"

"You used to look like that after you married Dad, but the look went away. It was good to see it back again. I was happy for you."

"You didn't say anything."

"It wasn't my place."

"But your father had just passed away."

"And I loved him, but I knew what kind of man he was. He never hid his girlfriends from me."

"That boat's changing direction," Beth said. "It's almost like they want to intercept us."

"No, they're turning again," Noelle said.

The man with the binoculars lowered them as Beth read the name off the bow, *Cayenne*, then she looked up and gasped. It was Wolfe. She stuck her hand in the air, fingers spread. She hoped Brody thought she was just waving to the boat as they passed and she hoped that Wolfe got her message.

"He must love you," Noelle said. "There is no other explanation."

CHAPTER NINETEEN

"THAT'S *Shogun*." T-Bone took the binoculars away from his eyes.

"What?" Wolfe gripped the wheel tighter.

"White boat there." T-Bone pointed.

"Take the wheel." Wolfe accepted the binoculars as T-Bone replaced him at the helm. He swept the boat with the long glasses. His pulse raced when he saw Beth and Noelle hanging onto the shrouds by the mast. They were all right. He started to put his hand up in a wave.

"Don't!" T-Bone said.

Wolfe dropped the hand, put the binoculars back up to his eyes.

"Told you everybody came through St. Lucia."

"Yeah you did."

"That's Brody behind the wheel."

Wolfe moved the binoculars off Beth to the man at the helm. He was tall, athletic looking with hair so black it seemed dyed.

"The others are the guys off those boats you sank last night." T-Bone turned onto an intercept course.

"Yeah." Wolfe said, still looking. "I see two of 'em."

"I saw two go below."

"What about the other Petrov twin?"

"Didn't see him," T-Bone said. "He could be below, too."

"So there's five we know about for sure, probably six." Wolfe still had the binoculars to his eyes.

"Three to one," T-Bone said. "We got 'em out numbered."

"They're armed," Wolfe said.

"That's just gonna make it more interesting," T-Bone said.

Wolfe took the binoculars away from his eyes, looked at his friend. T-Bone smiled. He wasn't afraid.

"You turn away soon as the women get a look at you. We don't want to take the chance one of those men might recognize you."

"Right."

Close now, Wolfe studied the men in the cockpit. Except for the man at the wheel, the others weren't paying him any attention. He saw recognition in Beth's eyes as they passed. She stuck her hand in the air, fingers stiff, extended. They were only a boat length apart when Wolfe turned away, *Cayenne* heading into the bay *Shogun* heading out.

"She waved, she saw us," Wolfe said.

"Yeah, but that wasn't a wave, she was signaling something with her hand like that. Almost like a crossing guard with a hand up to stop traffic. But her fingers weren't together like she was telling us to stop, it was something else." He ran a hand through his hair. "She was making a five."

"She's telling us there's five men holding them."

"If that's true, then Alek Petrov ain't with 'em. He wasn't one of the one's I saw go below. I wonder what happened to him." He paused, then, "Ah, well, it'll all become clear, meanwhile we gotta look like we're anchoring, in case they're looking," T-Bone said. "Start bringing in the jib."

"That's crazy, we should go after them."

"Relax. We will. As soon as they're outta the bay and round the corner, we'll follow." He finished with the winch.

"We might lose them."

"We won't. Now go drop the main."

"You sure?"

"Just in case they're watching, you'll be bringing it right back up. Don't worry."

Wolfe went to the mast and brought the sail down. T-Bone was right, they couldn't just go charging after them. They had guns. The last thing he wanted was for Beth and Noelle to get hurt. He cleated off the mainsheet.

"How about calling the St. Lucian authorities?" Wolfe said as he stepped into the cockpit.

"What are we gonna say? You wanna tell 'em about those two boats underwater over there?" T-Bone pointed. "Or you wanna tell 'em *Shogun's* stuffed full of diamonds worth more then their annual budget? That's probably not a good idea. Or do you just wanna tell them five Russian guys kidnapped two American women and are taking them back to Trinidad? If those guys are as bad as I think they are, they'll shoot it out with the St. Lucian Coast Guard, and they'll probably win. Then what happens to our damsels?"

"Okay, we don't call for help."

"Right, we gotta do this ourselves, but it's not as bad as you might think. My guess is Brody needs your girl alive, at least until she signs the boat over to him. I know, supposedly the boat's been attached by his boatyard, but I'll bet he's found out by now that the Trinidadian government's not gonna let him just take the boat. They'll impound it, auction it off, pay the yard bill then give what's left over to the owner. That could take years and anytime during that process, if the owner comes up with the money to pay the bills, she gets her boat back."

"So he's gotta keep her alive until he gets her back to Trinidad."

"Yeah, and my guess is he'll treat her okay. So I don't think we gotta worry about that just yet."

But Wolfe was worried about that.

"We wanna put the motor on the dinghy before we go after them," T-Bone said. "Just in case."

In case of what? Was T-Bone thinking they might need it as a life raft?

* * *

"What was that all about?" Noelle had her lips to Beth's ear.

"I was trying to tell him there's five of them."

"Think he figured it out? Two of them are below."

"He's a smart man."

"Seems so," Noelle said. "Think he's got a gun?"

"I don't know."

"Some of these guys got bulges under their clothes where they shouldn't have," Noelle said. "So Harris isn't the only one armed."

Beth looked back at the men in the cockpit. Harris had his Bowie knife hanging from his Sam Brown belt as usual, but Beth saw the bulge under his green army shirt where he'd stuffed the gun Brody had handed him.

"I could try and get one," Noelle said.

"I don't think that's a good idea."

"You know I know how to use one, and I just learned that I can kill."

"Let's wait and see what develops. It's almost two days to Trinidad. Besides, maybe Brody's on the level."

"You don't believe that?"

"No, I don't."

Beth sighed. Brody had gone to a lot of trouble to get *Shogun*. Two boats were sunk, two men were dead, and he seemed willing to forget that. Fifty thousand dollars was insignificant compared to that cost. It didn't make sense.

"He must think we're pretty stupid," Noelle said.

"Let him go on thinking that," Beth said, then she got an idea. "Listen, I'm going to go below and try to call Wolfe on the handheld. I'll have to call on sixteen so that means Brody or one of his men might hear. I'll call from the head and try to disguise my voice, but they could get curious and follow the conversation. Can you stand by the radio and make some kind of distraction as soon as you hear me?"

"I'll slip, fall and scream like I'm in labor. That'll get their attention."

"Good girl."

"I'm going below," Beth said as they made their way across the deck.

"What for?" Brody said.

"I'm gonna use the head," Beth said.

She went to her berth, grabbed her backpack, took out the handheld, then went to the head. She didn't have to worry about being overheard, the engine noise would cover her.

She sat on the toilet, closed her eyes. Please, Lord, let them hear. She turned the radio on. What to call herself so Wolfe would understand? She couldn't say she was calling from *Shogun*. She disguised her voice. "*Cayenne, Cayenne*, this is *Sweetheart*." She heard Noelle scream, then thud to the floor.

"*Sweetheart*, this is *Cayenne*, go." Not Wolfe's voice.

"One-eight and wait." Beth switched channels.

"*Cayenne* here," the man said.

"Who are you? Put Wolfe on."

"My name is T-Bone Powers. I have been engaged by your friend to assist in your rescue."

"Can I speak with Wolfe? Please."

"In a minute. He's too stuck on you to think clearly." He clicked off, came back on a few seconds later. "He tried to take the mike away. I had to promise him just a few more questions. Tell me about Alek Petrov."

"He's dead, over." Stuck on her. What did that mean? Did it mean he was in love with her? Lord, please yes, please have it mean that.

"Yeah, okay. I'm guessing Brody's taking the boat back to Trinidad and needs you alive till he gets there. Am I right?"

"Roger, he says he has a buyer. The deal's very attractive. I'm supposed to get three hundred thousand dollars. Over."

"Are you in any danger?"

"I believe so. Over."

"Can you slow that boat down enough so that she doesn't run away from us?"

"Maybe."

"Do it if you can, but don't get caught at it."

"I'll be careful."

"Okay, now listen up, this is important. You and Noelle put on life vests and keep them on. If we shoot off a flare, I want you guys to go in the water and for Christ's sake, stay together. Do you copy that?"

"Yeah, I copy, flare, jump, stay together, pray you guys get us before the sharks." Beth shivered.

"You don't have to worry about sharks."

"Figure of speech. Over."

"Okay, chances are we won't have to shoot that flare, but it's good to have a back up."

"Do you have a plan? Over."

"No, but we're working on it. Here's Wolfe."

"We're going to get you out of there," Wolfe said. "We don't know how yet, but we will. Just keep your head down and don't do anything to agitate those guys. Pretend you're going along with them."

"I will." She wouldn't have had to pretend if that Harris wasn't along. Brody wanted the boat for whatever reason. He wouldn't do murder if he didn't have to. Harris was something else altogether. He was after more than the boat.

"T-Bone says we'll keep monitoring one eight just in case, but you're not to use the radio anymore unless it's an emergency, it's too dangerous."

"Okay. Over."

"Take care, we're gonna stay right behind you."

"I'll take care. Out." She hugged herself and sighed. He must be in love with her, otherwise why was he here?

Back on deck she heard Brody say, "Harris, you and Vassi get Alek up on deck."

"You don't mean it." Harris looked like he was going to be sick and Beth repressed an urge to laugh.

"Get him up here. I want him off the boat."

Noelle started up after the men as they made their way to the forward hatch.

"Where are you going?" Brody said.

"Your man doesn't look like he's up to the job," Noelle said.

"And you are?" Brody had the kind of smug look on his face that Beth hated.

"Mister, I choked him and dragged him down into that hole, I sure as heck think I can help drag him out of it, and as for tossing him over, it's a pleasure I don't want to miss."

"Me either," Beth said. "Call your men back, we'll do it."

"I don't believe you." Then, "Harris, Vassi, get back here."

Beth grabbed onto Harris' Bowie knife as he stepped back into the cockpit and pulled it from the scabbard.

"What?" Harris had been surprised. He wasn't as quick as he liked people to believe.

"In case we have to bring him up a piece at a time," Beth said.

"Give it back," Harris sputtered.

"Let her have it," Brody said. There was mirth in his eyes. Something else. Disbelief?

"I just wanted to show them I was tough," Noelle said. "I figured if Harris threw up and I didn't, he'd be too embarrassed to fuck with me anymore."

"He's not fucking with you," Beth said.

"He is with his eyes."

Beth stopped at the mast, pulled the main halyard out of the self-tailing jaws, unwrapped it from the winch, then pressed the snap-shackle on the other end of the line, springing it open. "We'll use this to haul the body out."

"Good thinking," Noelle said. "I'll go below and tie the line to him, since it was my idea, then I'll guide him through the hatch as you winch him up."

* * *

Wolfe was anxious as they sailed *Cayenne* out of the bay, afraid *Shogun* would be too far ahead, but he worried for nothing. They rounded the corner and he saw them, not far ahead, still motoring.

"I don't get it, he's got good wind." Wolfe looked at their own main and headsail. They were full and *Cayenne* was moving through the water like a thoroughbred.

"Some people like to motor," T-Bone said. "Never been able to understand it." He clicked on the autopilot, then went below and came right back up. "We're gonna see them a lot better than they're gonna see us." He took a pair of high-tech looking binoculars out of a case.

"They've probably got binoculars, too."

"Not like these. These are Canon, Eighteen, Fifty, Image Stabilizing, top of the line, super fucking binoculars. A steal at fifteen hundred bucks." He handed them to Wolfe.

"Better than those?" Wolfe gestured to the binoculars hanging on the binnacle.

"Can Superman kick the shit out of Batman? Take a look."

Wolfe put the binoculars to his eyes. "I don't believe it. It's like I'm right there with them."

"Okay, stay low in the cockpit, that way they won't know you're looking even if they check you out with their own far away eyes."

"The women are going forward," Wolfe said, watching. "They're at the mast, it looks like they might be going to raise the main."

"Not without turning into the wind, they're not," T-Bone said.

"Well, she's doing something with a winch by the mast."

"Maybe he's gonna turn into the wind," T-Bone said. "That's a fast boat, we might have a hard time keeping up if he decides to sail. Especially if he puts everything out."

"Think he might?" Wolfe said, still looking.

"I would." T-Bone didn't sound like the confident wisecracker Wolfe had come to know. Had he misjudged? Were they going to get so close, only to let *Shogun* slip away?

* * *

"Let's do it," Noelle raised the hatch, climbed in. "It stinks down here."

"I can smell it from up here," Beth said.

"Okay," Noelle said from inside the forepeak, "send down the halyard."

"Halyard coming down." Beth watched as Noelle wrapped it around the body, cinching it tight under the lifeless arms.

"It's a good thing rigor hasn't set in yet," Noelle said, "or we'd play hell getting him out of here."

"Are you ready?"

"Start winching."

"Starting." Beth started grinding, conscious of the men in the cockpit watching. She shot them a quick glance. They were laughing, all of them, Brody too.

That made her mad. Brody never laughed. She put her back into it and wound the handle around the winch.

"He's coming out," Noelle shouted from below.

Beth turned away from the laughing men to the grisly sight of Alek's head. She stopped grinding and his dead head was suspended in the center of the open hatchway, even with the deck, rocking back and forth. The eyes were open, the skin translucent. It gave her the creeps. She bent over the winch and started grinding for all she was worth and the body started to rise out of the hatch, almost like the devil himself was making it float up from below.

* * *

"Holy shit!" Wolfe said.

"What?" T-Bone wanted to know.

"Look for yourself." Wolfe passed him the binoculars.

"Mother of God." T-Bone whistled. "Looks like we know what happened to Alek Petrov. Who do you think did it?"

"Search me."

"Here, I've seen enough." T-Bone handed the glasses back to Wolfe.

"I wonder what they're up to."

"They're gonna dump the body."

"And they're making the women do it," Wolfe said. "Bastards."

* * *

Beth felt the strain as she ground on the winch. Alek was out up to his knees. A grim specter haunting the boat and all who were on her. It didn't matter if they tossed his body over, his soul wasn't leaving the ship. Beth didn't believe in ghosts, an afterlife, heaven or hell, but this she believed. They weren't going to get rid of Alek just because they were dropping him overboard. *Shogun* was a death ship. Beth felt it to the quick, to the bone.

"Hurry up, Beth!" Noelle shouted. "I want to get out of here."

"I'm going as fast as I can!" Beth shouted back. A couple more turns and Alek was almost out of the hole, held in place only by his feet against the rim of the hatch. If she brought him up any higher, his body would come flying toward the mast, toward her, because the halyard came down from the top of the mast to the forepeak hatch at an angle.

"Can you hang onto a foot so he doesn't swing back here?" Beth shouted.

"Gotcha." Noelle grabbed onto one of the body's feet and Beth went back to work at the winch and brought it out of the hatch, till Alek was suspended about a foot above the deck.

"Hang on till I cleat off." Beth snugged the line into the self-tailing jaws. Then went to the body and held it aside as Noelle climbed out of the hatch.

"I feel so icky." Noelle faced the grinning men in the cockpit and did a little bow. "I'm gonna get them, I swear," she muttered.

"They won't be laughing in a few minutes."

"What do you mean?"

"Can you push him over the lifelines?"

"You're not gonna help?"

"When you get him over, I'm gonna cut through the main halyard." Beth followed Noelle's gaze to Harris' Bowie knife resting by the winch. "Yeah," she whispered, "they won't be using the main."

"You get back on the winch and pull him up just a little more." Noelle grabbed onto the body's leg to keep it from swinging away when Beth let go.

"Okay, kiddo, it's you and me." Beth gave Noelle's arm a squeeze.

"You and me," Noelle said.

Beth went back to the winch and struggled the handle around two more times as Noelle walked the body to the starboard side of the boat. As soon as she had it over the lifelines, Beth picked up the knife and sliced through the line. The body plunged into the sea, pulling a hundred and twenty feet of line after it, snapping and whipping back and forth inside the mast with a deafening racket that made Brody scream back in the cockpit.

"Why'd you do that?" Brody was furious.

"It seemed the quickest way to get rid of the body," Beth said.

"You stupid—" Harris said, but Brody grabbed his arm and he shut up.

"Do you know what you just did?" He was out of the cockpit, standing over her as she got up. He was angry enough to kill only an instant ago, but he had his temper back under control in less time than it took to blink. Beth didn't want to make him lose it again.

"I cut the body loose. Just like they cut down a hanging man in a Western movie."

"It was cool," Noelle said.

"Yeah, cool." Brody looked Beth in the eyes, then Noelle.

"I think I'm going to be sick," Beth said. "I'm going to the head." All of a sudden she wanted to be away from them.

"Not so tough, after all." Harris was gloating. He was worse than the Russians.

She bent over, grabbed her stomach and scurried down the hatch to the sound of Harris' laughter. She was every bit as good an actress as Noelle.

CHAPTER TWENTY

BETH CLOSED THE DOOR to the head, then got the radio. Her heart was racing. She was breathing like a sprinter who'd just crossed the finish line. For an instant out there she thought Brody was going to kill her. She pushed the talk button on the handheld.

"*Cayenne, Cayenne, Sweetheart.* How copy?" She crossed her fingers.

"You're not supposed to use the radio," T-Bone said.

"I know, I just wanted to let you know that I disabled the main."

"Okay, we'll be able to keep up. Now hide that radio and get into your life jackets."

"Yes, sir." How did he know they didn't have the life jackets on yet? She hid the radio, opened the door and was face to face with Harris.

"Get out of the way." She tried to push by him.

"That's no way to talk." He grabbed her, put a hand between her legs.

She kneed him in the groin, then grabbed him by the neck as he bent over and shoved him out of the doorway. His head thudded into the bulkhead opposite. She grabbed him by the throat before he had a chance to sink to the floor and banged his head back against the bulkhead again with all her strength. Then she kneed him again as her fingers closed around his windpipe, nails digging into flesh. She was going to ripe it out.

"Enough!" It was Brody.

"Not enough!" She let go of his neck and he dropped. He was unconscious. She stomped on his hand, heard bones crack. She brought her foot up. This time she was going to stomp on his head.

"Stop it!" Brody pulled her away before she could deliver the final blow.

She was stunned, the sound of his shouting voice ringing in her head as he held on to her.

"Calm down!" He said.

"All right," she said and he let her go. She was shaking.

"What happened?"

"He touched me in a place he shouldn't have."

"And for that you were going to kill him?" Brody had a quizzical look on his face, like a school kid trying to understand a math problem. She'd never seen him like that. He almost seemed human.

"Nobody touches me there unless I invite it."

"I'll tell the men. I don't want any more bodies on this trip." He started for the companionway, stopped and turned back. "On second thought, maybe I should have let you kill him. Any man that has to use force to get a woman isn't a man."

"No, you did right. I was out of control. A slap would have been sufficient."

"With Harris, probably not." He looked down at the man on the floor, contempt filled his face now. "You did good, Beth."

"I'll get Noelle to set his hand. Better to do it while he's unconscious. I'm afraid he won't be much use to you for a while."

"Right now, I wonder why I had anything to do with him at all."

"Why did you?" Beth pressed. She had him talking and somehow it seemed important that she keep it up.

"I didn't have any choice. He came with the shipyard. It was thought that I needed someone like him to act as sort of an ombudsman between me and the American yachties. As if I couldn't understand them, or they me. I never needed a snitch to tell me what they want. They want the best possible job done for the lowest possible price." Now he was angry and his anger scared her.

"Frank always said you were fair."

"Have Noelle tend to his hand." He turned away, started toward the companionway.

* * *

"She's on the radio again," T-Bone said. "Didn't I just tell her it was too dangerous?" He grabbed the mike. "Go, *Sweetheart.*"

"I just got done talking to Brody and he let it slip that he's not the boss. He's working for someone. I thought you should know, just in case."

"In case of what?"

"I don't know."

"Okay, info noted. Please don't run the risk of calling again unless it's an absolute emergency. We don't want you hurt."

"All right, *Sweetheart* out."

"You were a little rough on her," Wolfe said.

"Yeah I was, but we can't have her running to the radio every ten minutes. She's bound to get caught."

* * *

Beth felt Harris' hate as sure as she felt the sweat under her arms. She'd broken his thumb and two fingers and he was in pain. He'd been staring fury at her ever since he'd come to.

"Ease out the jib," Brody said and he shut down the engine as Vassi took the furling line off the winch and started to crank on the jib sheet. The big headsail caught the wind and *Shogun* heeled over and picked up speed. Even without the main she was fast. Beth hoped Wolfe would be able to keep up.

Twenty-four hours later Beth opened her eyes, then covered them with a hand against the sunlight streaming through the overhead hatch. It was hot in the forward double birth that she'd shared with Frank up to about a year ago. Now it was his daughter sleeping by her side. She rose, opened the hatch and looked out. They were just passing Point Saline on Grenada's south coast and from the looks of the weather, they were going to have a rough crossing to Trinidad.

She got up, got some coffee in the galley, took a sip as Brody came down the companionway, smiling. She knew it probably wasn't smart, but she had to know what was going on.

"Why the guns, Brody? What's it all about, really?"

"Beth, if you mind your own business, you can walk away from this tomorrow with a fat check. If I thought for a second you knew what we were up to, I'd kill you. If I didn't like you, you'd already be dead. If Harris had his way, he'd have his fun, then kill you. Am I making myself clear?" He wasn't smiling now.

"Perfectly."

"I'm telling you this because I think you're a smart woman. I'll want your signature on a few papers when we get back to Trinidad, I'll hand you a check and a pair of tickets to Miami on the first flight out. I'll expect you on it."

* * *

Wolfe was alone on deck with the rising sun as they sailed south on a beam reach, just off of Grenada's south shore. He looked up at *Shogun* and at the gray squall ahead. Soon *Shogun* would be in it.

He turned west to a long line of flat that extended forever. A world with no borders, boundaries, bosses or businesses. A world shared with nature and all her glory. A world devoid of petty people and petty minds. A world that was never boring. Work was hard, rewards were few, friends were fast, luxury was rare, moments were enjoyed.

Then he thought of Beth and his imagination ran wild. Could he adapt to this lifestyle? Could he sell his home and buy a boat? Would she sail away with him? Was he being stupid even thinking about it?

It started to rain and the wind kicked up, whipping through the mountains on the island. T-Bone was below on the SSB radio, trying to get a weather report. But Wolfe didn't think they needed one. The weather was coming fast.

"We got rain," Wolfe shouted down to T-Bone. "We got wind and we're getting more." Wolfe shouted louder. "And we're gaining fast."

"Why didn't you say so?" T-Bone popped through the companionway, looked at the boat ahead. Now the wind was up to twenty-five knots, sliding off the runway at Point Saline. "I got a weather report. They say it's gonna be bad." He looked at the dark gray squall line ahead as the rain picked up.

"You needed the radio for that?"

"Not really, I was talking to a boat about six miles ahead. They're reporting fifteen knots of wind and five foot seas. Once we get through it, we'll have smooth sailing."

"What are you saying?"

"I got a plan."

"It's about time," Wolfe said.

"We can put everything up and sail through this storm, and be in Trinidad a good hour before them. We'll wait outside of Customs and Immigration and take them when they least expect it, when they think they're home free."

"They're gonna have guns," Wolfe said.

"And we'll have friends."

"What kind of friends?"

"The kind that are gonna be plenty upset when I tell them how some Russian guys made me throw their dope overboard."

"You didn't throw any dope overboard."

"We know that, but they won't."

"I don't know why I asked."

"Don't worry about it. This Brody character is playing right into our hands."

"So you don't believe he's going to let her go?" Wolfe said.

"Not for a second. Once she clears the boat through customs and he gets it into his boatyard, those babes are toast."

* * *

If it weren't for the circumstances, Beth would be enjoying herself. She was at the wheel and *Shogun* was moving through the choppy seas under a reefed headsail. She thought back to when Victor had taken the helm during that squall and the fun he seemed to be having as he drove the boat through the wind. At the time she didn't understand it. She did now.

Then Harris noticed the boat behind them and pointed it out to Brody. "How come they're not reefed up in this weather?"

"Maybe they're crazy," Noelle said.

"Maybe they want to catch up to us." Harris grabbed the binoculars. "It's that boat we passed as we left St. Lucia."

"Are you sure?" Brody said.

"I'm sure."

"It's Wolfe, isn't it?" Brody turned on Beth. "Get away from the wheel." He was mad. Beth thought he was going to explode. "Let out the sail!" he screamed and the Russians jumped to do his bidding.

* * *

"It looks like she's cleared the Porpoises," T-Bone said. Wolfe hadn't slept in over thirty hours and every muscle in his body ached, but he was wide awake. He felt like he could go on forever. Tension and anticipation sparked through him.

"I don't see any rocks." Wolfe looked over the sea, then back at T-Bone. His friend had stuck a flare gun between his belly and his pants and he was grinning, wild hair dancing, like he had been charged by a cartoon electro-shock machine.

"Just off her starboard side."

"What?" Wolfe shouted.

"They're there." T-Bone pointed ahead and to the right. "Take the wheel."

"Sure." Wolfe slipped by to take control of the boat. "What are you going to do?"

"Tighten sail." T-Bone slapped in a winch handle, started grinding in the jib sheet. *Cayenne* heeled over more as the rails slid into the water. "Turn a little to port, off the wind."

Wolfe did.

"I want to gain speed and stay well away from the rocks."

"I still don't see them!" Wolfe spread his legs wide, to keep his balance. The sea was snapping whitecaps, spitting foam over the deck. The wind whistled through the shrouds. He tightened his hands on the wheel, squinting, straining to see the boat ahead through the rain.

"Look between one and two o'clock." T-Bone pointed.

"I see them." Waves broke around the rocks, the white caps shooting higher than the surrounding sea. "How many are there?"

"I don't know," T-Bone said. "Most of them are below the surface."

"Any boats ever been sunk on them?"

"I imagine that's how they were discovered," T-Bone said and Wolfe pictured a tall ship breaking apart, all hands jumping over the side, grabbing at broken pieces of the boat, grabbing at each other, grabbing at crowded life rafts, and being pushed back into the cold sea.

"Frightening," Wolfe said.

"Very," T-Bone said.

"What's he doing?" Wolfe said, eyes again on *Shogun.*

* * *

"What are we going to do?" Harris shouted. Brody was trying to keep the boat going straight as Harris eyed the boat behind.

"Go below and get the guns," Brody shouted at Sasha.

"Yes, sir," Sasha scurried below. In no time he was back with a couple of small pistols in hand. He kept one for himself and handed the other to Vassi.

"Twenty-five caliber? Those are toys," Noelle said.

"This ain't no toy." Harris stuck his good hand between his fatigue shirt and his flesh and came out with the automatic Beth had seen when Brody boarded. It was twice the size of the ones Sasha and Vassi had. It wasn't a gun, it was a cannon.

"No, that's not a toy," Noelle said as Brody snatched the gun from Harris.

"We're going to have to turn around," Brody said. "Serge take the wheel."

"It's too dangerous to jibe," Beth said.

"Not without the main, it isn't." Brody said and Beth had to silently agree. Jibing in bad weather was very chancy, but without a boom to come slamming across the deck when the wind caught it from the rear, a jibe was no more dangerous than a tack.

"All right, you," Brody waved the gun at Noelle. "Get out of the cockpit, go up by the mast, both of you."

"It's not safe up there!" Beth said.

"You got life jackets on. Go!" He was going to shoot if they didn't, Beth crawled up to the mast. Noelle did too.

"When we come abreast of them, we start shooting," Brody shouted. "I want them both dead!"

* * *

"She's jibing," T-Bone said.

"What?" Wolfe said.

"Turning." T-Bone's voice dropped an octave, like he couldn't comprehend what was going on. But then he grabbed hold of the situation and started issuing orders. "Keep on a steady course, I'm going below for a second." T-Bone slipped down through the companionway and in a few seconds was back with two large square pieces of wood.

"What's that?" Wolfe asked.

"Sections of the cockpit sole, the boat's floor. Teak, three quarters of an inch thick. I think we might need it up here."

"Why?"

"Shields."

Wolfe nodded, then turned his attention to the boat in front. *Shogun* had completed her turn and was headed back toward them. Wolfe turned a bit to the left, mindful of the rocks.

"My guess is they'll sail as close to us as they can get, shooting away as they pass," T-Bone said.

Wolfe didn't say anything. He kept his eyes on the boat in front. It looked like they were planning on coming along their left side. His emotions were whirling out of control. Beth was on that boat. He didn't want anything to happen to her.

He turned *Cayenne* a little more to the left. T-Bone met his eyes, but didn't say anything. *Shogun* was charging toward them, jib tight, heeled over, slicing through the waves. *Shogun* turned a little to her right, to avoid the collision course Wolfe had put them on, but he turned a little to the left, keeping the boats nose to nose, racing toward each other, like two great animals about to do battle.

Shogun turned again.

Wolfe matched it as cold shivers rippled over his skin. Beth was on that boat. He would turn aside, but not till the last minute.

"After I set this up, I'll turn on the autopilot and we'll go below." T-Bone was laying the hatches across the cockpit seats.

"We're not going to hide behind your wooden shields?"

"Of course not," T-Bone said, "but they're going to think we are." Then he went below and seconds later returned with a bagged sail. Wolfe watched while he propped it under the teak floor covering. Now instead of lying across the two cockpit seats, the teak shields rested on the port seat and on the sail underneath.

"This way it'll look like we're hiding under the wood and they'll shoot where we're not." He checked out his handy work, appeared satisfied. "Turn on the autopilot."

"No," Wolfe said. "You go below. I've got other plans."

"Hope you know what you're doing." T-Bone slipped down the companionway, but kept watch as Wolfe kept *Cayenne* on a collision course with *Shogun*.

"Any minute!" Wolfe yelled.

"What's going on?" T-Bone said. From his position, looking up and out the companionway, he could see Wolfe behind the wheel, but nothing else.

"Ramming speed," Wolfe said, as *Shogun* bore down on them like a hulking demon.

"Oh, God!" T-Bone said.

A wave altered Wolfe's course, but he corrected, keeping his eyes on the bow of the approaching vessel. *Shogun* was slicing through the water like a sharp razor through soft skin. He gripped the wheel harder. Then *Shogun* broke to his left. They were turning. The amazement zapped him like a cardiac arrest. It worked. He faked them out.

Wolfe turned, not away, but toward *Shogun*. He kept them on a collision course. *Shogun* turned a hair to the left and he corrected, keeping *Cayenne* aimed at the bigger boat's bow. There was no doubt in his mind who'd lose in a collision. The basic laws of physics favored the larger vessel. He moved the wheel slightly to the right when *Shogun* was only a few yards away.

He heard the skin crawling sound of the two boats scrapping hulls, but he didn't see the damage they were causing each other, because he was busy scurrying around the wheel. He dove under T-Bone's teak floorboard shields as the Russians opened up. The first few shots went wild. Then two thunked into the teak. Wolfe crouched low, hugging the sail. Another ricocheted off a winch. Another slammed into the teak. Then the screeching, scraping and shooting stopped and they were temporarily out of danger.

"It's all right," T-Bone said, coming up through the companionway. "They're behind us and out of range."

"Sorry about your floor." Wolfe stood and set the floor hatches on the port cockpit seat.

"Sod the floor," T-Bone said.

"And your boat. It sounded like it was coming apart."

"You're alive. They missed. That's all that counts," T-Bone said.

"The women are up by the mast hanging on for dear life," Wolfe said.

"Then we better save them," T-Bone said.

* * *

"You missed," Brody wailed as if he hadn't been shooting, too. Beth had no problem hearing him above the sound of the choppy sea. "All right," he said. "We'll just have another go at it."

"You're not gonna fool them again!" Noelle shouted. What was wrong with the girl?

"Try not to get him agitated," Beth said.

But Noelle didn't pay her any mind. "They're too smart for you!"

"I'll get them this time!" Brody shouted and Beth didn't understand. He was acting like a kid, engaging in a shouting match with Noelle. How stupid.

"No you won't!" Noelle shouted. And Noelle, she should know better. Brody had a gun.

"We're going to turn around and finish it." He pointed the gun up at Noelle.

But she ignored it and shouted back. "That's what you think, they're gonna finish you!"

"Shut up, Noelle!" Beth said under her breath.

Brody started the engine, then shouted out to Beth and Noelle. "They won't get away now."

"They don't wanna get away!" Noelle shouted.

"I said, shut up!" Beth punched Noelle in the side.

"Yeah maybe I better." She stopped taunting him.

* * *

"They're turning around." Wolfe was back at the wheel. T-Bone had just come back up from below, after having replaced his damaged floor hatches.

"I spend all of my spare time on this boat," he said. He was talking loudly, but Wolfe heard the sigh in his voice.

"I'm sorry about hurting it," Wolfe said.

"It's not your fault," T-Bone said, "but I'm taking over command now. I don't think *Cayenne* can take much more of your methods."

Wolfe nodded, meeting T-Bone's eyes. There was a grim determined set to his jaw, a sturdy, unafraid timbre to his voice. "What do we do now?"

"We let them catch up to us." T-Bone let out some of the mainsheet and the boat slowed from seven to five knots. "Look there!" He pointed. "Those are the Porpoises, right off our starboard side."

They were close to the rocks and Wolfe still had trouble seeing them. If T-Bone hadn't pointed them out, he'd have missed them completely. He looked behind. "They've completed their turn."

"Look ahead," T-Bone said. "We're headed directly for the south coast. When I tell you, turn to starboard. Keep turning till Grenada is off the port side. That'll be a ninety degree turn. Hold that position till I tell you differently."

"But the rocks?"

"We should be past them by then."

"Should be?" Wolfe said.

"Should be," T-Bone answered.

Wolfe checked behind them again. He didn't have to tell T-Bone *Shogun* was getting closer. He turned away and eyed the coastline, looked again toward the rocks, but they'd moved past and he couldn't see them through the rising swell.

"What are you doing?" he asked, as T-Bone let out more of the mainsheet.

"Slowing the boat down even more."

Wolfe looked over his shoulder. *Shogun* wasn't far behind now and she was rapidly closing the distance. "Shit," he said, staring at the stainless steel bow roller. Two heavy anchors rested in it and to his eyes they looked like great steel tipped battering rams, charging up the ass end of their small boat. He gripped the wheel in a fit of panic.

"Don't!" T-Bone yelled. "Not yet."

And Wolfe stayed his hand. He'd been about to turn, but there was something about the authority in T-Bone's voice that screamed out to be obeyed.

"We don't turn till the last possible moment. We want them to think we're running. Otherwise, we could all find ourselves swimming." So Wolfe kept a steady hand on the wheel as T-Bone worked the lines, making ready for the turn.

He grabbed another look over his shoulder. The twin anchors seemed to be aimed right between his eyes.

"Hold steady your course," T-Bone said, as the monstrous form of the boat behind filled his vision. "Eyes front," T-Bone said.

"Holding." Wolfe turned away from *Shogun* and faced Grenada's south shore.

"Steady, steady," T-Bone cautioned.

"I am holding it steady!" Wolfe felt like there were a million eyes shooting laser-like pin pricks up his back, but he held the boat steady as T-Bone commanded.

"Now!" T-Bone screamed.

"About time!" Wolfe spun the wheel to the right as T-Bone played the sheets. The wind from behind filled the jib and the boat heeled and picked up speed. Wolfe risked a quick look back and shivered. *Shogun* slipped by, missing them by less than a yard and T-Bone whipped out the flare and fired it off.

Chapter
Twenty-One

"There's the flare, come on, let's go." Beth was holding fast to the halyards coming down the outside of the mast, with her mouth pressed to Noelle's ear. She was talking loud, but not shouting, to be heard above the noise of the sea. Cold rain ran through her hair, down her back. Goosebumps peppered her arms, icicles churned up her spine, stabbing her at the base of her neck. A wave broke over the deck.

"In this weather!" Noelle pulled away from Beth, eyes wide. "That's crazy talk! We can't!" She grabbed onto Beth's wrist, fear evident as rain washed over her face.

Lightning flashed in the distance. Beth counted, one-one-thousand, two-one-thousands, three-one-thou— . Thunder boomed—about a half mile away.

"It's suicide!" Noelle shouted.

"I'm going!" Beth let go of the lines as another wave washed over, drenching her. "Come on!" She took a step as the boat jerked. She struggled to keep her footing as the boat jerked again. She slipped, felt herself going down, but she grabbed onto the shrouds as if they were the stop sign she used to swing around on her way to school when she was a little girl, and kicked off, swinging herself over the lifelines.

She sucked in a deep breath and squeezed her eyes shut as she flew over the side. Her stomach tightened involuntarily, the icy spasms ripping through her intensified and she clenched her teeth against them as she smacked into the ocean.

The sea punched the breath out of her as if she'd been hit in the stomach with a sledgehammer. She gasped, sucked in water and slid below the surface. She tried to spit it out, gagged, there was no air. She popped her eyes open in panic, saw nothing. She was in the cold dark and this time she had no tank of air on her back.

She was going to die.

* * *

Wolfe saw Beth and Noelle dive into the sea. He tried to keep his eyes on them, to fix their position in the water.

"You see them?" T-Bone shouted.

"They went in over there!" Wolfe pointed to where they'd gone in the water, but the seas were too choppy. He couldn't see them.

"We've gotta bring the boat around! Turn into the wind!"

Wolfe spun the wheel to the right again while T-Bone went to the mainsheet to make ready for the jibe when they came around.

"What about the jib? Wolfe shouted.

"We're gonna backwind it, it'll force the boat to turn faster," T-Bone said. He was the picture of calm while Wolfe felt like he was coming apart. T-Bone started cranking on the mainsheet, preparing for the jibe when the wind would be at their back. And like T-Bone had said, the headsail backwinded and *Cayenne* made a snappy turn to starboard. "Keep her coming," T-Bone said as he let out the mainsheet. The boom came across the deck and then they were pointed back the way they'd started and toward where Wolfe had seen the women go into the water. "See the damsels?" T-Bone said as he made ready to trim the headsail.

"No." Wolfe strained his eyes over the sea.

"Damn." T-Bone said.

* * *

Beth felt as if her lungs were about to burst. Any second and they were going to take over, force her mouth to open, force her to suck in the seawater that would kill her in their quest for oxygen. Then she remembered the life vest. She fumbled for the cord, found it, pulled it. Instantly the CO_2 cartridge filled the vest. She felt like she was being crushed as it blew up around her, constricting her chest, but she shot upward, broke the surface, coughing and spitting.

She gobbled air, then was under again, but only for an instant as the vest brought her back up. She flayed out with her arms, flapping against the sea, in a desperate struggle to keep her head above water. Though the waves were high, she rode over them and quickly got her panic under control. She started treading water, breathing more normally. Without the vest, she'd have drowned.

She saw nothing ahead, turned and saw *Shogun's* stern. Brody was looking aft. He appeared to be shouting, but she couldn't hear. Was he trying to get her attention? The boat was moving rapidly away, but all of a sudden it stopped and lurched to starboard with a soul wrenching sound that drowned out the roar of the sea.

Beth didn't understand. One second *Shogun* was moving away from her, the next she was on her side taking on water. It was as if the boat had been hit by a missile. She watched fascinated, the agonizing groan of *Shogun's* destruction seemed to go on forever, but in reality it was over so fast. *Shogun* was on her side, going down.

"Beth!" Noelle's scream pierced the storm. In her panic, she'd forgotten about her.

"Noelle!" Beth shouted.

"Behind you!"

Beth turned, saw the girl only about twenty feet away. Miles in this kind of weather. She was about to shout out to her, when Noelle tucked her head into the water and swam toward her. The girl was a seal. In seconds she was at Beth's side.

"Are you all right?" Beth shouted out.

"My life vest didn't inflate. Think yours can support both of us?"

"Turn around," Beth shouted. Noelle did. Beth wrapped her arms around the girl, hugged tight and leaned back.

"Are you okay?" Noelle said.

"Yeah," Beth said. Her mouth was at Noelle's ear, she didn't have to shout.

"What happened to *Shogun*?"

"I don't know." Beth said and they watched as *Shogun* went down.

"There's our help!" Noelle pointed.

"Thank God," Beth said as *Cayenne* came toward them out of the rain, but she wasn't slowing down.

"They don't see us!" Noelle said.

"Over here!" Beth screamed.

Cayenne was going to run right over them.

* * *

Wolfe was afraid Beth and Noelle were lost. He kept his eyes on the sea, scanning back and forth, then he saw *Shogun* stopped up ahead, listing and all of a sudden he understood. T-Bone had gambled that they'd be so caught up in the chase that they wouldn't see the rocks. *Shogun* had run aground. She was sinking.

"Keep looking, the damsels will be between us and the boat going down." T-Bone was still the calm man and Wolfe appreciated his friend's steely nerves. "Quick turn to starboard!" T-Bone shouted all of a sudden. "Or you'll run them over!"

"What?" Wolfe turned the wheel, saw the women in the water. They were clinging together, bobbing through a frothy sea as they sailed past. "We have to stop!"

"No, keep going." T-Bone pulled the life ring out of its bracket and tossed it overboard. Wolfe gaped as it flew to the sea, pulling a yellow pole behind it. When the pole hit the water it floated, sticking straight up, with a waving orange flag atop it. "Better than cockpit cushions," T-Bone said.

It was then that Wolfe saw the blood covering T-Bone's thigh.

* * *

"They're not stopping!" Noelle shouted as *Cayenne* sailed past, almost close enough to touch.

"They can't," Beth said, arms still wrapped around Noelle, mouth still to her ear. "By the time they slowed her down they'd be too far away to get us. They have to sail back."

"Look." Noelle pointed to the man overboard pole.

"It's their marker." But knowing they'd marked the spot didn't make it any easier to watch the sailboat move away.

* * *

"You've been shot!" Wolfe said.

"Yeah, someone got off a lucky shot through the companionway." T-Bone's face was ashen, contorted in pain. "But we don't have time to worry about that now. Turn to starboard, bring her up on a beam reach and prepare to tack. We still got damsels to rescue."

"You got it." Wolfe turned the boat. For a flash of a second, seeing the blood turning T-Bone's khaki shorts red, he'd forgotten about the women. T-Bone hadn't. Wolfe stopped the turn when the wind was on the beam.

"Get ready. We're gonna do that figure eight, man overboard recovery that you shoulda done that time I went in the drink." T-Bone wound the starboard jib sheet around its winch. A wave washed over the side, but the rain had slacked some. The squall was moving away. "Okay, now! Tack this motherfucker!"

"Tacking!" Wolfe cranked the wheel to starboard as T-Bone, blood running down his leg, cranked on the jib sheet. By the time Wolfe had *Cayenne* facing into the wind, T-Bone was cranking on the main sheet, centering the boom. "Take her all the way through!" T-Bone unleashed the port jib sheet. Then he jumped to the starboard jib sheet, ripped it out of the self-tailing jaws and started hauling, pulling on the line like a mad man.

"Are you all right?" Wolfe shouted.

"Fine, fine. We're halfway there. Get ready, stay focused!" They were about to come down on their path, about to loop the eight as T-Bone let out some of the main. "Get ready to tack again!" Now T-Bone was snugging the port jib sheet back into the self-tailing jaws. "Okay, come about." T-Bone tried to shout it, but the volume wasn't there.

But Wolfe felt the urgency and spun the wheel to port as he scanned the choppy seas ahead. How could they possibly find them in those waves? "I don't see them."

* * *

"They're turning!" Noelle shouted. "They're turning!"

Beth felt Noelle's excitement, but it was dampened with the knowledge that it was a lot easier for them to see the sailboat with its tall mast and white sails than it was for the men on board to see them, floating in the rough sea. Thank God for the man overboard pole. It wasn't exactly right next to them, but it was in the ballpark. If they sailed to that, Beth felt sure she could get their attention, they'd be looking, after all.

They rode over a wave and *Cayenne* looked awfully close, but when they went down in the trough it looked hopeless. Foam smacked them from the side and Beth felt as if she'd been slapped by a giant child. She was so cold, so tired, it seemed as if each wave were a demon determined to rip Noelle from her arms. Her hands, clamped to her elbows in a desperate effort to keep Noelle in her grip, were numb. How long did you have to be in the water before hypothermia set in? Hours, yes hours. She'd only been in the water minutes, but it seemed like an eternity, it seemed like she was going to die in it.

They rode up another crest. Beth turned to look for *Shogun* and found her mast sticking out of the water, sails thrashing, whipping the mast back and forth in the rough seas. She must have been holed, because she was below the surface and sinking fast. She strained her eyes for survivors, but saw none. That didn't mean Brody, Harris and the others weren't still alive, Beth realized. They'd be as hard for her to spot as she and Noelle would be for Wolfe to find.

Again they sank into another trough and Beth saw only a wall of water ahead. Then again they were up on the swell and Beth felt like she was riding on top of the world. The rain had stopped now, the squall, moving from east to west, was past, but the winds from it were still stirring up white caps and big seas. Clouds still covered the sun, but despite that, she could see all the way into Secret Harbor, see the tall masts in the charter boat marina. Going down into the trough she looked over at *Shogun's* mast again and saw the white foam spuming up from the rocks. *Shogun* had run into rocks? What rocks? Then she remembered the Porpoises. *Cayenne* had set a trap and led *Shogun* into it. That's why that T-Bone person had wanted her and Noelle to wear life vests. He'd planned it, planned on sinking her boat.

Anger rippled through her, chasing away the fear, chasing away the cold, giving her new energy. Damn him. The boat was paid for and she had no insurance. Double damn him.

Something came out of the sea, scurried through her hair like a crab. Beth screamed.

"What?" Noelle had been taken by surprise.

Something wrapped itself up in her hair, and jerked her head back. Beth tried to keep her arms wrapped around Noelle, but couldn't. Instinctively she lashed out at whatever it was that had hold of her. She kicked, jerked herself around and came face to face with Harris, his face a mixture of panic and rage. Fist still in her hair, he tried to push her head under. She struck out with a right fist, bringing it up from her waist with everything she had even as he was dunking her. She connected with his chin, felt bones crunch and teeth rattle as she broke his jaw.

But still he held on with his fist wrapped in her hair. She struck out again, catching him in the chest, but she was fighting against a man crazed with panic. Harris, jerked on her hair, tried to get a leg over her shoulder, attempting to ride her as if she were a flotation device.

She was going under. She thrashed against him, hitting him again and again, anger driving her. But he was too strong and he managed to hold her head under and get a leg up, straddling her. She had to get free, otherwise she was going to die. She couldn't give up, wouldn't give up. She grabbed onto his leg, pulled it into her face even as he was trying to use it to suffocate her and she bit him on the inside of his thigh, chomping into him as if he were prime rib. He jerked like he'd been shark bit and she pushed toward the surface.

He was screaming when she broke through, and though he no longer had a leg around her, his hand was still fisted in her hair. He jerked on it and agony ripped through her body, red pain from her neck to her groin.

"Let her go!" Noelle screamed.

"Aghhhh!" Harris screamed louder, but his hand relaxed and Beth was free.

"Asshole!" Noelle had his bad and bandaged hand in a tight grip with both her hands and she was twisting and wrenching it back and forth and Harris was whacking at her with his good hand, trying to make her let go. Once, twice, three times the man smacked her face with an open palm. He brought his hand back again for another whack, but Beth got hold of it from behind.

"Aghhhh!" Harris let out again as he turned glazed eyes toward Beth. It wasn't pain in his face any longer, nor fear. Harris was beyond that. He was insane.

* * *

"Back a little to starboard," T-Bone said after Wolfe had completed the turn.

"Do you have them?"

"They're over there." He pointed.

"Where?" Wolfe moved the wheel trying to see.

"Easy. Steady as she goes." They're dead ahead, twelve o'clock." T-Bone ripped the jib sheet from the self-tailing jaws, letting it luff and thus slowing them down. Then he was on the mainsheet, trimming the sail. "Keep her steady. In a few seconds I'm gonna luff the main as you turn back into the wind."

Still seeing only foaming seas, Wolfe could only follow T-Bone's directions, trust him. Then he saw the orange flag waving on top of the man overboard pole. He was about to shout as T-Bone luffed the main and they slowed even more.

"Get ready to head up," T-Bone said. Blood was oozing down his leg. Wolfe could only imagine the effort it took for his friend to stand.

"Are you gonna be okay?" Wolfe shouted.

"Get ready. Now!"

Wolfe turned into the wind and they passed the man overboard pole. "I see them!"

"Oh fuck." T-Bone didn't have to say anymore. Wolfe saw what he saw. The woman were struggling with a man in the water.

"We have to speed up."

"We do and we'll pass them by again."

"We don't and he'll kill them."

"Start the engine," T-Bone said.

"Right." Wolfe pushed the start button and the diesel rumbled to life.

"Add power and hand me the gaff."

Wolfe bent low, snaked a hand under the stern seat and pulled out the gaff, a five foot stainless steel pole with a wicked spike at the end of a stainless loop. The hook was a good four inches in diameter, the gaff being designed to bring aboard big fish.

"Maybe you should steer and let me gaff the son of a bitch." Wolfe held the wheel as he stepped away from it.

"Maybe you're right." T-Bone looked down at himself. The whole lower half of his body was covered in blood. He was running on willpower alone. He took the wheel from Wolfe. "Okay, go up to the shrouds and hang on. I'll get you close. Don't be fancy, get him anywhere with the hook, jerk like you mean it and you'll kill him. Don't miss."

Wolfe crawled up to the stanchions, grabbed on, stood and leaned over the side as T-Bone shoved the power forward full.

* * *

"We have to kill him!" Beth shouted.

"Yeah!" Noelle released his hand, fisted her hands in his hair as he'd had his hand in Beth's. "Die, asshole!" Noelle scissor kicked herself out of the water as she pushed Harris under. In a panther-quick move, Noelle had her legs wrapped around his head. She pulled her hands out of his hair, grabbed onto his shoulders as he struggled under her, face below the surface and she twisted as if she were driving a giant corkscrew into the earth.

And despite the sounds of the raging sea, Beth heard his neck snap.

"Die!" Noelle screamed again.

"Let him go." Beth grabbed onto Noelle's arm. "He's dead."

"Good!" Noelle spread her legs apart, pushed him away.

Beth pulled on Noelle's arm, leading the girl away from the body as it popped through to the surface, floating only an arms length away like an obscene log.

* * *

"Get back here, now!" T-Bone shouted. Like Wolfe, his friend had seen the struggle in the water and its outcome. It had seemed to go on forever and it was over so fast.

He started back toward the cockpit. He'd crawled out to the shrouds as the boat was jumping around in the waves, he was going to have to crawl back.

"Lose the gaff, get back here!"

Wolfe tossed the gaff over the side and made the cockpit in three leaps.

"Let out all the line you can on the dinghy," T-Bone said. "I'm gonna circle around 'em so they can catch onto it."

Wolfe jumped to the stern cleat, unwrapped the dinghy painter and played it out till the dinghy was trailing the boat forty feet behind. "She's secure!"

"I'm gonna run the boat between them and the body. Dead guy on the left, damsels on the right.

Once they're in the dinghy, haul it up. I want 'em on board as quick as possible."

"Right!"

"Okay, we're close enough, I'm gonna slam her into reverse, then cut to starboard as soon as they're abeam."

Wolfe felt the boat shudder as T-Bone went from full forward to full reverse and prayed he hadn't torn apart the gear box.

* * *

"Beth, look!" Noelle shouted and for a flash of a second Beth thought there was another one of them, but when she followed Noelle's eyes, she gasped. *Cayenne* was bearing down on them. Once again it looked like she was going to run them over.

But at the last instant she veered to starboard and sliced between them and Harris' body. Beth reached out, clutched Noelle's outstretched hand. What were they up to? Then *Cayenne* made a sharp turn to starboard and Beth saw Wolfe in the cockpit, pointing to the trailing dinghy and now she understood. They meant for her and Noelle to grab onto the line as the boat slowed to a stop. She gave Wolfe a thumbs up signal to let him know she understood, grabbed a quick look into Noelle's eyes, saw that she understood, too, then the line was on her, digging into her waist as the boat turned.

CHAPTER
TWENTY-TWO

"**THEY'VE GOT THE LINE!**" Wolfe shouted.

"Pull the dinghy up. Cleat her off by the shrouds. Let's get 'em aboard." T-Bone backed off the reverse power, the boat was in irons now, main and headsail flapping. The rain was gone. Sunlight was sneaking through the cloud cover, bathing the lighthouse at Prickly Bay in an early morning halo.

Wolfe grabbed the long painter, took it off the stern cleat, jumped out of the cockpit and dragged the dinghy up to the side of the boat. He cleated it off, then went over the side. He hit the water with a shout. Stupid, because he hadn't time to grab a breath before he was under. He came up with a quick stroke, sputtering.

He saw Beth first. She was holding onto the front of the dinghy. He swam toward her, grabbed the line that secured the dinghy to *Cayenne.*

"I can't see Noelle!" Beth shouted.

Wolfe couldn't either.

"One second she was holding onto the line, then she was gone!" Beth looked frantic. Wolfe saw right off that she was worried for Noelle, not afraid for herself.

Wolfe looked up to T-Bone.

"There!" T-Bone was pointing toward the stern.

"Get in the dinghy, then pull yourself up onto the boat! I'll get Noelle!" Wolfe let go of the line and swam toward the direction T-Bone was pointing. He saw Noelle as soon as he got around the dinghy and swam toward her. She was treading water and looked done in, but she was holding her own. "Are you all right?"

"Yeah."

"Can you make it?"

"I think so!" she said. Like Beth, Wolfe sensed no fear. Noelle would keep trying till she had no more to give. These were remarkable women.

Wolfe looked toward the boat. *Cayenne* had turned a bit and the mainsail had picked up wind, she was sailing away. Swimming against the choppy seas would be tough going for Wolfe alone, impossible if he had to do it with an arm wrapped around Noelle.

"We'll wait for him to come back!" Wolfe said. The weather had cleared. With Beth on board to help, T-Bone would be able to get the boat back to them. Then Wolfe remembered T-Bone had been shot.

Smoke bellowed from *Cayenne's* stern. T-Bone had it in full reverse to stop her forward momentum. What was he doing? He couldn't back it up to them.

The best he could do would be to hold her in place. Did he expect them to swim to the boat?

"Look!" Noelle shouted.

Wolfe saw the dinghy plowing through the water. Thank God T-Bone had thought to put the engine on it.

"We're gonna be okay!" Noelle whooped.

Beth cut the throttle, slowed the dinghy and came alongside as if she'd been picking drowning men out of the water all her life. She held an arm out and Noelle grabbed onto it with a Viking grip and Beth pulled her aboard. Wolfe kicked himself over the rubber tube, fell into the center of the dinghy, landing next to Noelle, who was laughing like his dad used to laugh at the *Honeymooners* when he was a child. A giant belly laugh that said everything was all right with the world and it was funny.

Although Wolfe had only been in the water for a few minutes, he was panting. He was exhausted. He needed to close his eyes, sleep. It had been so long, but seeing Beth, water logged and shivering, with that determined look on her face as she steered the dinghy back toward *Cayenne*, shot new strength through him.

Wolfe pulled himself up, grabbed the painter as Beth brought the dinghy alongside *Cayenne*. He secured the painter on a deck cleat, then, standing in the dinghy, held on to *Cayenne's* lifelines while Noelle pulled herself aboard. Beth killed the engine, then she was on board, too. Wolfe sighed, feeling his new strength ebb from his shoulders.

He didn't think he had the energy to pull himself up. He was losing his grip on the lifelines. He closed his eyes, remembered Samson, Cantor Wolfe's favorite Bible story. Okay Dad, he silently prayed, this one's for you. He grabbed onto the shrouds and hauled himself aboard. He stepped over the lifelines, a foot touched the deck, he slipped, then he was down, flat on the deck. Beth went to her knees by his side.

"T-Bone—" Wolfe pointed to the stern, followed his own pointed finger with his gaze. There was nobody behind the wheel. T-Bone was down, too. "My friend's been shot."

"I'll go." Noelle dashed across the deck, jumped into the cockpit.

Wolfe started to pull himself up.

"Take your time. Noelle can help your friend."

"I'm okay." Wolfe sucked in a deep breath. This woman had been on the run. She had been a prisoner and had been in the water a lot longer than he had and she was telling him to take it easy. It was as if she hadn't gone through anything at all. And Noelle—the way she'd run back to the cockpit when only minutes ago she was fighting to stay afloat. These women were tough.

"What are you, super women?"

"Yeah, Wolfe, something like that." Beth laughed, stood, offered her hand and helped pull him to his feet.

"He's lost a lot of blood," Noelle said as they stepped into the cockpit. "We have to get him to a hospital."

T-Bone was sprawled out on his back on the port cockpit seat. Noelle had his shorts off, he was nude from the waist down, but one could hardly tell, because the lower half of his body was covered in red. Sticky red, gooey red, flowing red. His face was bone white. Wolfe balled his hands into fists. How could he possibly survive? He'd bleed out.

"Don't write me off yet," T-Bone croaked.

"Get me something to use for a compress!" Noelle said.

Wolfe shot below, came back up with a clean towel.

"This is gonna hurt," Noelle said to T-Bone. She wadded the towel into a compress. "Ready?"

"Yeah." T-Bone grimaced as she pressed it to the wound. "Yeowouch," he said. Not a scream, more of a growl.

"Okay, guys," Noelle said. "Take this boat to the nearest doctor. I can stop the bleeding, but he's gonna need more blood, and that bullet's gotta come out."

"Grenada," Beth said.

"Prickly Bay's the best," T-Bone moaned. "Can get a car from there to the hospital. It's an easy bay to get into, Wolfe, piece of cake."

"Yeah, buddy. Piece of cake," Wolfe said. "We'll get ya there."

"I know you will." He sighed. Then, "We did it, didn't we? The damsels, we saved 'em."

"Yeah, boy, we saved 'em."

Wolfe turned toward the bay, glanced over to the Porpoises expecting to see *Shogun's* mast, but it was gone. The boat had been broken by the sea, gone down to a watery grave.

* * *

"Only have room for one." The ambulance driver said. A driver and two paramedics had come with the van. The driver was being obstinate. The three of them could not ride with T-Bone, one only. Noelle was the obvious choice. And in seconds the red ambulance was screeching away from the dock, siren wailing.

Cayenne was moored at the Prickly Bay Boatyard and they started back toward the boat. On board Beth said, "You got some dry things I can borrow?"

Below he found her a pair of Levi's and his green Hawaiian Christmas shirt, one of his favorites, he grabbed the yellow shirt with the hula dancers for himself. He went to the head for towels as she was pulling her T-shirt over her head. She wasn't shy, but why should she be, they'd slept together, after all.

"These are Spooner's, very old, collector's items." Wolfe held up the two shirts.

"You collect shirts?"

"No, they're just old." He smiled. She looked so good.

"Let's get changed and get to the hospital."

"Right." He tossed her the Christmas shirt. Then pulled his clothes off. It was as if they'd been changing in front of each other all their lives. He was comfortable with her. What was that all about? He wondered why he wasn't aroused as he'd been that night when they'd made love in the pool. He was dog tired, he told himself. He was worried about T-Bone. As for her, she didn't seem the least interested in him.

"You got shoes?" she said.

"Yeah." He found his Nikes for himself, T-Bone's sandals for her. "These should fit." They did. The Levi's were a couple sizes two large, but cuffed and worn with a belt and the shirt on the outside, they looked fine.

He sighed, everything was moving too fast. It was as if he was on slowmo and she was on fast forward. He'd pulled all nighters in the past when he was working on a case. He'd stayed up all night drinking. Once he'd stayed awake for forty-eight straight preparing for a trial. He'd been tired before. He was no stranger to fatigue, but never had he felt like this. It was as if he were out of his body, watching himself going through the motions. Had it not been for her, he'd've collapsed on the settee. But as it was, he could only follow her off the boat, to the taxi. He slept on the ride to the hospital and was barely awake when she pulled him out of the cab.

* * *

Beth shook her head as she studied Wolfe, struggling to stay awake, but she remembered how dazed he'd seemed when they'd changed into the dry clothes and how he'd slept in the cab. She shivered with a tiny excitement. Taking off her clothes in front of him was daring, exciting and wicked all at the same time, but he'd hardly seemed to notice. True they'd made love that night, both in the pool and up in his room, but making love and being in love are two different things.

She felt something for him. She couldn't deny it. But was it love?

"Can I help you?" a young West Indian woman in a nurse's uniform asked.

"We're here about our friend who was shot. My sister's with him. Noelle Shannon." Beth didn't know why she'd called Noelle her sister. Step-daughter didn't seem right. Nor friend. They were closer than friends now.

"Ah, Mr. Powers. He's in surgery. Your sister has scrubbed and is removing the bullet even as we speak."

Beth gasped, looked around the waiting room to hide her shock. A West Indian couple was attending to a boy with a broken arm. Their son probably. They were getting ready to go home. There was nobody else waiting.

"Please don't be surprised that I know. We're a small hospital, we don't get many gunshot wounds. Especially ones that come in with a white lady doctor."

"She's not—" Beth had been about to say Noelle wasn't a doctor, not yet, but she caught herself. Noelle had finished med school, had started her residency, but she hadn't come close to finishing. She knew better than to pass herself off as a doctor. She wouldn't do that, not without good reason. Beth decided to hold her silence. "I was about to say, 'She's not going to be much longer, is she?' Do you know?"

"No," she said, "but if you'll have a seat, we'll let you know as soon as we find out anything."

Wolfe flopped down on the sofa, picked up an old news magazine, but was asleep in seconds. Beth took the magazine from his lap, scooted next to him, snuggled against his shoulder and closed her eyes. What was Noelle up to? Was Wolfe's friend going to be okay? It must have taken tremendous stamina and will power to keep going with a bullet in his leg like that. He was truly heroic. Wolfe too. Her very own hero. And that was her last thought before she drifted off to sleep.

* * *

Wolfe opened his eyes to a bright overhead light and a West Indian lady smiling through about a thousand wrinkles. If he had to guess her age, he would have put it at two hundred and ten. She had no teeth. Her hair was shocking white, not gray.

"Your friend is out of surgery and asking about you." Her gums smacked when she talked. Wolfe thought she was an angel.

"Is he going to be all right?" He was groggy.

"Yes suh. He goin' be fine." She had a cup of steaming coffee in a cobalt blue cup in an outstretched hand.

"You really are an angel." He took the offered coffee. "An angel of the Lord right here in Grenada."

"Oh, suh!" Her toothless smile lit up her face. She backed away. "If you jus' follow me." Wolfe shook Beth awake and they followed the old woman.

Noelle was on the phone when they entered the hospital room. T-Bone was warded with three West Indian men. They were all smiles and appeared to be laughing at something he had said.

"Can you all hush up." Noelle cupped the phone. "I'm trying to talk here." She smiled at Beth, then went back to the phone.

"She's talking to her boyfriend in Trinidad." T-Bone grinned, despite the blood loss and the pain he had to be in. Wolfe admired him.

Noelle gave T-Bone a look that said to hush up, but that only got him going more. She had a lot to learn about him.

"This guy is married, can you believe it? And almost as old as me." He laughed. "Actually that shouldn't disqualify him. It's good she likes older men, 'cause I just might propose."

"Stop it," Noelle said to T-Bone. Then into the phone, "I'll have to call you later tonight." She turned away from them, mumbled something, then hung up.

"It's a good thing Dr. Shannon came in with me," T-Bone said, "cuz the only doctor they had on call was a guy delivering a baby. I wouldn't a made it if she wouldn't a got me right into surgery, stopped the bleeding and fixed me up." He looked up at the unit of whole blood dripping into his arm through an IV. "I got so much West Indian blood in me now, I'll never be able to pass a pan man without dancing."

"Is it possible to shut him up?" Noelle said.

"Can't be done," Wolfe said.

"Yeah it can," T-Bone said. "I'm gonna rest now. Danny boy, why don't you take the ladies someplace quiet and tell them what's been going on."

"Danny boy?" Beth said. "That's not your name."

"He'll tell you all about it," T-Bone said.

And Wolfe did. He took them out to the lobby and told them about the diamonds, how they were mined by evil men, then traded for guns and drugs, weapons for kid soldiers, cocaine and heroin to give them courage.

"Conflict diamonds," Noelle said.

"What?" Wolfe hadn't heard that expression.

"That's what they're called. Conflict diamonds. I read about them in Newsweek. It's been on CNN, too. It's how these would be dictators finance their child armies."

"There's more." Wolfe told them about the Petrov brothers. About how they were the killers of the Skidmores in Long Beach and about how they'd framed him for the murder by putting photos of the murder scene in the gun safe in his apartment.

"But you couldn't have put the photos there," Noelle said. "I saw you take your gun out of the safe. It was empty then. And it was empty just before I left for the airport and I saw you boarding the plane when I got to the gate at the last minute. Someone had to have put them there after I left, and since I saw you at the airport, it couldn't have been you."

"You went back by the apartment?" Wolfe said.

"I lost an earring, so I stopped on the way to the airport to see if it might be there. It's why I almost missed the plane. I met your mother. She was cleaning the place, remember it'd been trashed? We searched all over for it, but we didn't find it."

"Holy Moses, My mother." Wolfe sighed. "I gotta call her." He stood, went to the bank of phone booths, made a collect call. Anita answered on the first ring. He told her he was okay, everything going to be fine and he'd be home in a few days, not to worry. She said, she'd worry, it was a mother's curse, then she wished him God speed, something she hadn't done in a very long time, and hung up.

Finished with the call he went back to Beth and Noelle and told them about the diamonds Frank Shannon had stolen and how he'd probably squirreled them away in a locker at the university.

"My old locker," Beth said.

"What?" Wolfe said.

"College isn't like high school, you don't get lockers, but they have some in the Language and Art buildings. My major was French, my minor Spanish." Beth laughed. "I was dating one of the Spanish profs, he had a locker he didn't use and I didn't like carrying heavy books in a backpack, so when he offered me the locker, I took it. Then I met Frank. He was fluent in about half a dozen languages and studying two or three more, so hanging around, waiting for me at the language lab was something he enjoyed. In no time he'd won all the profs over, was studying on his own and using the lab as if he were a student. I graduated and never went back to the university, but Frank never quit. He took over my locker, stuffed it with books. The campus became his home away from home. Everybody up there loved him."

"Yeah," Noelle said. "Dad was up at the University every chance he got when he was in town, working on his biggest challenge, Japanese."

"If we go to the police in Long Beach and tell them the whole thing, along with Noelle's story about the gun safe being empty, that should get them off your back," Beth said.

"If they believe us," Wolfe said.

"If we drop ten million dollars worth of diamonds in their laps," Beth said, "they're gonna believe us."

CHAPTER
TWENTY-THREE

BETH JOGGED ACROSS the tarmac to the small Liat
twin-propeller aircraft. The travel agent in St.
Georges wasn't able get them on a direct flight to
Miami as all the flights were full. The best she was
able to do was a quick flight to St. Lucia, where they
had to spend a day before they could make their
Miami flight, connecting through to Los Angeles.

She was nervous with Wolfe, wanted to talk, but
hadn't had the opportunity, and she wasn't going to
get it on the plane as she was sitting in front and he in
the rear. Boarding the plane she smiled, she'd always
hated the hassle of flying, but if you had no baggage
and no carry-on, not even a paperback book, then it
was no hassle at all. In fact, it was kind of fun. She
wondered if that was what it was like for the very rich
who jetted around to a house here, a house there.

They didn't have to travel with bags, because everything was set up for them when they arrived. And if it wasn't, they probably had someone on the payroll to handle their things.

For a brief moment she thought about keeping the diamonds. She could be rich herself. But then she buried the thought in the ash can of her mind. Those diamonds were responsible for a lot of death. She didn't want anything to do with them.

In her seat, she fastened her seatbelt, snugged it up, turned to look back at Wolfe. He was asleep already. The man could sleep anywhere. No, she corrected herself. She had to remember he'd been up for so long, chasing after *Shogun* to rescue her. She almost felt guilty for having slept on that journey.

She sat back when the pilot started the engines and listened to the throbbing sound. The plane vibrated as they taxied to the runway and she closed her own eyes and felt every bump and jolt the small plane made. Still, with closed eyes, she shivered when the pilot revved the engines prior to take off. Then they were shooting down the runway and she felt a tingle at the base of her neck. She opened her eyes, spun her head around and caught him looking.

Blood rushed to his head. He was embarrassed. Was it because of that stupid wig? Or was it something else? He gave her a smile, then a thumbs up sign. She waved, then turned back to the front of the plane. So he wasn't so tired that he'd forgotten about her.

As the plane circled to land at St. Lucia's Vigie Airport, Beth looked out the window and saw Rodney Bay only a few miles to the north. She saw the boats in the bay and those two masts still sticking up out of the water, reminders of how Wolfe had come to her rescue. How long before the government removed them? Would they be there forever, reminders to sailors how dangerous life on the sea could be? She sighed, looked away.

On the ground, she found Wolfe waiting for her as she deplaned. He seemed wide awake now. Finally. He held out a hand. She took it and they followed the other passengers toward the Customs terminal. He let go of her hand, wrapped an arm around her waist and she fell into him and they shuffled along with the crowd like two teenagers in love.

At least that was what she seemed to be feeling. What about him? He hadn't said a word. She wondered what the other passengers must think of them, dressed alike as they were, faded Levi's, Hawaiian shirts, no baggage.

"I'll bet everyone thinks we're coming here to get married," she said.

"What?" His first word since they'd left the airport terminal in Grenada.

"No waiting to get married in St. Lucia. People come from all over the world to get married here." She nodded to a young Japanese couple ahead at the Immigration desk. "Them for instance."

"I knew that, about the no waiting."

Outside, in the encroaching darkness, Wolfe hailed a cab. "Can you take us to a hotel that has rooms for one night?" He said and Beth felt her heart sag. He'd said rooms, plural.

"I know just the place, quiet, on the beach, not too expensive and they always got a place for those who don't have a reservation." The driver was West Indian, about fifty. "No baggage?"

"None." Wolfe opened the door for Beth, scooted in after her.

"Not even a toothbrush?"

Wolfe slid a hand behind himself and pulled a wad of hundreds from his hip pocket. He peeled one off, leaned forward and handed it to the driver. "How about we mind our business and you mind yours?"

"Yes, sir." The driver put the car in gear and in what seemed no time at all, he was parking under the portico of the Honeymoon Hotel at Reduit Beach in Rodney Bay.

"This isn't exactly what we had in mind," Wolfe said.

"Yes it is." The driver pulled the automatic transmission into park. "You said you wanted a place that would take you for the night without reservations. This is it. Unless you want one of those seamen hotels back in Castries. The lady wouldn't like one of those."

Wolfe got out of the car, started toward the lobby, stopped. "This is kind of awkward."

"You're thinking one room or two?"

"Exactly."

"After all that we've been through, I think one and we'll see what happens."

"Right." He pushed open the door to the lobby and rented a room on the beach.

"The Honeymoon Suite," the clerk, a young West Indian girl said.

"I don't think we need anything like that," he said.

"Don't worry." The girl laughed, "They're all the Honeymoon Suite."

"Is there a place nearby where we can buy a couple toothbrushes?" he said.

"Across the lobby, turn right. The hotel shop." The girl smiled wide. "We usually don't get people so anxious." She smiled wider, showing large white teeth.

"What did she mean, anxious?" Wolfe said when they were out of earshot of the girl.

"To get married," Beth said as they passed the hotel restaurant. Then, "You want to eat before checking out the room. I'm kind of hungry." She was nervous, too.

"Yeah, but not here. I know a better place."

"Really?"

"Typhoon Willie's. They make the best hamburger this side of the States."

"Okay, Typhoon Willie's it is."

Beth was surprised ten minutes later when a blustery yachtie-type welcomed them as they entered the restaurant. "Remember me, from the other day?"

"Should I?" Wolfe said. But Beth got the impression that Wolfe knew the man.

"Name's Jack McGreggor off of *Wind Dancer*. You bought me and my friends a round of drinks for a roll of seizing wire a few days back."

"You must have me mistaken for somebody else." Wolfe's wig disguise wasn't doing too well.

"So you wouldn't know about a guy named Petrov that was tied to one of those masts with a roll of seizing wire wrapped around his private parts?"

"Seizing wire, Wolfe?" Beth said. "Ouch."

"That guy ripped me off when I hit a jackpot at a casino in St. Martin," Jack said. "When I called him on it he hit me in the belly. It liked to have killed me. In my day the outcome would've been different, but I'm sixty-six years old."

"I'm sorry about that," Wolfe said.

"Not your fault." Jack punched Wolfe on the shoulder. "We cruisers don't come down here to get robbed and beat up. The way I figure it, you did us all a favor, but me especially. Whatever you're having tonight is on my tab."

"Thanks." Wolfe started toward an empty table, stopped, turned back to the man. "Petrov stole a few bucks from you, and gave you a shot to the stomach. That's hardly a reason to celebrate his death."

"You had to have been there," the man said. "It was in his eyes, he'd've killed me if he could've. I knew it, and he knew I knew it. When you punched his ticket, you did the world a favor. Now, sit yourself down over there with your lady and enjoy your dinner. Start with the Chilean Cabernet, it's the best wine they got here."

"Thank you." Beth took Wolfe by the hand and led him toward the table.

The waitress came as soon as they sat and Beth ordered a bottle of the Cabernet. Wolfe ordered them each a burger, fries and a Coke for himself. She could hardly wait for the food to arrive. She hadn't eaten all day and she was ravenous.

The drinks came first. He clinked glasses with her, but didn't toast anything. She sipped. Jack was right. It was good. She took another sip, then a long swallow. Immediately it went to her head. She should've eaten first.

"I'm not hungry anymore, you?" Wolfe set his Coke on the table. She saw the look in his eyes.

"No." She finished her glass while Wolfe dropped some bills on the table.

They were barely outside the restaurant when he pulled her into his arms and swept her away with a hungry kiss. He opened his mouth and she sighed her breath into him. Her legs were all a quiver, never had she felt like this. Love, lust, she didn't know what to call it. She only knew she never wanted it to stop.

He broke the kiss. "If we don't go now, I'm going to rip your clothes off right here."

"Rip 'em off."

"Come on." He wrapped an arm around her and led her toward the hotel where he fumbled with the room key. He was as nervous as she was, but somehow he got the door open.

The room was dimly lit by the moonlight, sneaking in through wisping curtains that concealed a partially open window. A single ceiling fan whirled above the bed that took up the center of the room. It was hot, there was no air-conditioning, or if there was, it wasn't working.

Wolfe closed the door, then took her in his arms again and enfolded her in another deep kiss that sucked her breath away. She felt shivers running through his body and instantly knew he was experiencing the same emotions as she. Joy, heat, fire.

She pulled away. "I have too many clothes on." She pulled the shirt over her head exposing her breasts, twin globes that shone in the moonlight that filtered through the window. He grabbed her, took a nipple in his mouth. Ecstasy. She'd never known there could be such power in sex. And they were just getting started.

He switched to the other breast as she kicked her shoes off. His lips moved up to hers as she fumbled with the button down fly. She squirmed her waist away from him and the Levi's dropped to the floor. She stepped out of them. Now she was nude. He broke the kiss, stepped back and took in her body.

"Get your clothes off or I'll be the one doing the ripping," she said.

In an instant he had them off and had her back in his arms. She felt his erection, pulsing between his legs and hers. It was hot.

"Let's move to the bed." It sounded like her voice. Was she talking? She couldn't be sure. She must have been, because he lifted her up as if she weighed no more than a teddy bear and carried her over to the bed.

"Better?" He said.

"Much." She pulled off his wig.

"I forgot about that." He moved on top of her, covered her body with his, covered her lips with his and again drank her breath away. He was magnificent.

"Oh, Wolfe," she moaned.

He lowered his mouth to her neck.

"Oh, Lord!" She arched her pelvis. She wanted him inside her. Now.

But he delayed entry, instead, seeming content to drive her wild with that thing he was doing with her neck. So this is what foreplay was all about. He cupped her breast, squeezed, then lowered his hand till it was between her legs. His middle finger found the center of her and she screamed in joy.

"I want you in me," she husked, but he ignored her, kept doing what he was doing with those fingers. "Ooooh." She arched her body, throwing it up against his knowing, probing fingers "Yessss." She was out of control. Her pleasure had taken over and it was marvelous, miraculous, staggering.

"Now, now, now, do it now!" She screamed it as she thrust against that hand. He was holding her in a way that defied all logic, gripping her, fingering her, rubbing her all at the same time. How could this be happening? "Oh my, God," she wailed as wave after wave of wonderful washed over her.

And still he didn't stop. That hand kept working its magic as if it had a mind of its own, feeling, fingering. She humped against it, all the way through the orgasm and building into the next. My God, was he ever going to stop? "I'm coming again!" she shouted. What was happening? She'd never shouted before. He'd turned her into a lusting animal and there was nothing she could do about it.

He eased his hand away.

"Put it back!"

But he put something else there instead and she cried out, wailing into the night, a soul that had been lost, but now was found.

* * *

Sweat dripped off his body, as he stared up at the ceiling fan. She had been wild. He had been wild. Never had he let himself go like that. Never had he received so much pleasure by giving pleasure. It was as if every spasm of her orgasms were his, too. As if they were one. He could never leave her, never let her go.

So much had happened to him in the short time since he'd left California. Could he ever go back to his old life? Certainly not without her. Would he ever feel that satisfaction he used to get when he solved a murder? Would he ever feel the special way he did when the verdict was guilty, the sentence life?

No.

He didn't need to think long to figure that out.

But would he go back? Could he?

"You wanna get married, Wolfe?" Beth said, her voice dreamy with sleep and exhaustion.

"Not till morning," he said.

"You mean it?" She was on her back too. Her hand found his, squeezed.

"Might as well. I can't live without you." He laughed.

"Can we live on a boat?"

"I don't think I'm ready to retire yet. I've been away from the job for a long time. I miss it."

"We could buy a boat and live aboard in the Long Beach Marina. We could sail on the weekends, you know, go to Catalina."

"I'll sell my house."

"Really?"

"Yeah."

"I'll sell the condo."

"We'll get a big old boat and adopt a dozen kids," he said.

"Oh, you." She rolled over, climbed on top, smothered his lips with her own.

Before he knew it, he was hard again. It had never happened this fast before. She'd bewitched him and held him helpless as she lowered herself onto his erection. She leaned forward, offered a nipple to his mouth. He took it, teased it with his teeth as she rocked over him matching the rhythm of the overhead fan. In and out. In and out. He was about to explode when she stopped.

"Not yet." She pulled the breast away, replaced the nipple with her tongue, probing his mouth.

He ached to move, felt himself quivering. Every hair on his body was alive as if electricity was sparking through him, standing them on end. Every pore oozed sweat. He was drenched in it. He was consumed in heat. The fan was doing a lousy job.

Then all of a sudden she started moving with a jackhammer-like frenzy, raising herself and thumping against him as if she were trying to smash coconuts with her buttocks. Slam, slam, slam. She stared into his eyes with hers wide open, waving her arms overhead as if she were a hula dancer worshiping the sun. Slam, slam, slam. Now her blonde hair flew wild, a shimmering halo in the moonlight, as she shook her head back and forth. Her breasts bobbed up and down and she was keening, a long, high pitched wine. Slam, slam, slam.

"We're getting married!" she screamed, loud enough to let everyone in the hotel know. "We're getting married!" She slammed into him a final time, then stopped as if she knew he was ready. "Married," she whispered as release overcame him.

* * *

Beth woke up to a gnawing hunger and Wolfe's prodding. The sun was up, the clock by the side of the bed read 10:05. She never slept that late. She smiled, but she'd never been put to bed before the way she'd been put to bed last night.

"I'm going for a jog." He was dressed and ready to go.

"Mmmm," she said. "Should I change our flight reservations?"

"Yeah, let's stay a few more days." He leaned over, kissed her. "A short honeymoon's better than no honeymoon."

"So you haven't changed your mind? You still wanna go through with it?"

"I'll get those toothbrushes on the way back."

They were married in a simple civil ceremony right after lunch. Someone else might have missed the big wedding, the preacher, the reception. But other than Noelle, there wasn't anyone for Beth to invite, and Wolfe wasn't in a position to invite anyone. He'd asked her if she wanted to wait till they got back to California and got everything cleared up, but she cut him short. She was in love. It was like the movies. She wanted to get married now.

After the ceremony they went back to the hotel and made love. Beth was in heaven, because it just kept getting better. She was the luckiest woman on the face of the earth. She drifted off to blissful sleep.

It had been dark for sometime when Wolfe shook her awake. "I'm famished," he said.

"You wanna do it again?" she mumbled.

"Not right now." He laughed. "I was talking about something to eat."

"Oh, that. I'm never gonna be hungry again."

"Then come along and watch me gobble up one of Willie's steaks." He grabbed her around the wrist and dragged her out of bed.

"Okay, okay." Now she laughed. "I'm coming."

But in the restaurant they didn't get a chance to eat, because Jack McGreggor met them at the door. "Don't go in there." He grabbed onto Wolfe's arm, led him away from the door. "Cops."

"They looking for me?" Wolfe said.

"Her too," McGreggor said. "They know you got married today. They're here because it's a yachtie hangout. They'll start with the hotels when they finish here."

"What are we gonna do?" Beth felt like the world was closing in on her.

"You got anything back at your hotel you absolutely gotta have?"

"Just a couple toothbrushes," Wolfe said.

"Good, let's go."

Wolfe started after him without question.

"Where are we going?" Beth said.

"My boat. I'll have you in Martinique by morning."

"You'd do that for us?" Beth said. "Why?"

"Because I know people," he said. "I retired from the NYPD. Spent thirty-five years on the job. I think I can spot an innocent man."

"Why Martinique?" Beth said.

"Because you don't have to show clearance papers from your last port to enter the French islands," McGreggor said.

"I have a phony passport," Wolfe said. "I'll clear in with that."

"How come you didn't use it here?" McGreggor said.

"I did, but I used my real name when we got married."

"Wolfe you should have said something," Beth said. "I could have waited."

"Dinghy's over there." McGreggor led them to a Zodiac that had been pulled up on the beach. "We'll race the sun to Martinique."

They lost the race, but not by much. They checked in with Customs at 9:00. Saw a travel agent at 9:30 and were on a plane bound for Miami by noon.

CHAPTER
TWENTY-FOUR

WOLFE SCANNED THE CROWDED TERMINAL as he passed through it. Even though it was eleven o'clock in the evening, every gate had passengers boarding or deplaning. Friends and relatives waved loved ones goodbye or hugged them hello. Businessmen carrying briefcases, students wearing backpacks, women dressed in power suits, kids in all manner of dress, so many people. Impossible to spot a stakeout.

"See anyone?" Beth said.

"No." Wolfe scratched the back of his head. He was wearing the wig. It itched.

"You think it's okay?"

"Probably." The odds were good that the St. Lucian authorities had figured out he was traveling under the Dan Steele name as he'd checked into the hotel using that name with Beth, then married her using his real name. If they'd done that, then it was only logical to assume there was a chance the airlines would've been notified, that someone could be waiting to arrest him on arrival.

"What do you mean?"

"Chances are if they knew I was coming in, I'd have been arrested at the gate."

"Yeah," she said, "that makes sense." Then, "My stomach's growling, can we grab a sandwich or something on the way out?"

"Sure." Wolfe spotted the kid in red and white selling hot dogs. "There." He pointed.

"Hey it's the policeman that don't wear a gun." The kid had his tongs in the well as they approached.

"Don't you ever go home?" Wolfe said.

"Man's gotta earn a living," the kid said.

"That's a fact," Wolfe said.

"Lot's of action around here." The kid dropped the dog onto a bun. Picked up the mustard and squirted it on.

"What kind of action?"

"Your ghosty friend. He been around with a Mexican dude. Others too. They be looking for you." The kid sprinkled the onions on, handed the dog to Wolfe. "One for the lady, too?"

"Yeah." Wolfe nodded.

"Your picture was all over the television with that shiny shaved head, that's how I know it's you they're after. Knew it the second I saw the ghost dude. But don' worry, you be cool. No one's gonna spot you with that fake hair." The kid handed over the second hot dog

"You spotted me."

"That's because I'm observant. But just in case any of them cops are too, I'd stay way away from the restaurant across the terminal, you understand?"

"Yeah, thanks."

"So, how come you're helping him instead of calling the cops?" Beth said.

"Hey, lady, I'm no snitch, besides I'm a good judge of character. No way could the Wolfman have done what they say."

"Keep the change." Wolfe handed the kid a hundred.

"It ain't enough." The kid laughed.

"I know." Wolfe led Beth away.

"He can't be more than fourteen or fifteen."

"They grow up fast in L.A."

"I guess." She took a bite of her hot dog, chewed, swallowed. "Hey, this is good. Maybe you didn't over tip after all."

"My wife the comic."

"So how come they didn't arrest you when we got off the plane?"

"The wig maybe. We were almost first off, my guess is they're still waiting at the gate."

"Then we should get out of here."

"You don't have to say that twice. That way." He touched her elbow, directed her toward the long corridor that led down to baggage claim and out into the street. "I want you to take Noelle's deposition." He pulled it out of his hip pocket and handed it to her. "Just in case I don't make it out of here."

"What?" She put the deposition in her own hip pocket.

"Take these too. He handed over his two passports, the American one in his real name and the Danny Steele Trinidadian one that T-Bone had gotten him. She stuffed them in the pocket along with the deposition.

"As soon as they take me away, you call Nick Nesbitt of KYTV. He's got an easy number to remember, four-three-four, sixty-six, sixty-six. He got knocked out of the anchorman's slot on the evening news about six months ago by Gail Sterling."

"Any relation?"

"Yeah, she's the senator's wife. Nick loved that job. He'll crucify the senator if that's what it takes to get it back. You guys get the diamonds, find me a good lawyer, then blow the story wide open."

"Relax, Wolfe, we're gonna get out of here."

"Norton's too good a cop. A wig isn't going to fool him."

"Maybe we should go to a phone and call a lawyer right now." She sounded scared.

"No, I want it on television. The senator's behind this, but I can't prove it. That's a job for the press. They'll find the connection between Sterling-Skidmore's war surplus operation and the weapons they were exchanging for the diamonds. They won't go digging on one cop's word, but you drop ten million dollars' worth of diamonds in their laps and the whole world's gonna sit up and take notice. The president himself couldn't sweep that under the rug."

They were at the end of the concourse. Most of the passengers turned right, toward the baggage claim. Only a few more steps to the street. For a second Wolfe thought they were going to make it. He pushed his way through a set of double doors, inhaled the crisp night air.

"Hey, Billy."

Wolfe turned toward the voice. It was Dwight Mitchel. The baby-faced ex-captain of detectives.

"Senator Sterling's man." Wolfe said to Beth, "Fade away, remember what we said."

"Not so fast." Mitchel grabbed Beth by the arm.

"Let her go, she hasn't done anything," Wolfe said.

"She's with you. That's enough."

"Actually, It's not." Norton came up behind Wolfe. "Take your hands off her."

"She's under arrest." Mitchel's blue eyes flashed under the overhead lights.

"No, she's not," Alvarez said. "And if you don't take your hand off her, I'm gonna break it and charge you with assault."

"I'm in charge here," Mitchel said.

"Now!" Alvarez advanced toward him. Mitchel jumped back, letting go of Beth's arm. "Smart." Then to Beth. "You should go and find Billy a good lawyer."

She looked at Wolfe. He could tell she wanted to say something, but she held her tongue. He nodded and she moved away.

"She doesn't go anywhere," Dwight Mitchel said.

"We came down here to get Wolfe, "Norton said. "We got him."

"We need her, too."

"Why?" Norton said. "Tell me and I'll go after her."

"She's getting away." Mitchel was agitated. He knew about the diamonds. It was the only thing that made sense. He really was Sterling's man.

"State Senate's not good enough for you, Dwight?" Wolfe said. "You gotta get your hands dirty for Sterling, kiss his ass? Did he promise you he'd support you when you ran for his spot or did he just promise you a cut?"

"Watch your mouth." Mitchel's face went red.

"You'll never see the diamonds, Dwight. Tell Sterling that."

Mitchel brought his arm back, but Norton grabbed him in mid-swing. He was favoring his right leg.

"What's with you two?"

"I'll tell you all about it down at the station," Wolfe said. Then, "How's the leg? Is it gonna heal?"

"It's getting better. I made 'em take the cast off, the bone was barely nicked."

"If it's any consolation, the guy that shot you died hard."

"That's good to know."

Wolfe turned to Mitchel, "Did you think you could frame me for the Skidmore murders and walk away clean? Come on, Dwight. It's me. I didn't put those photos in that gun safe and I can prove it. Sterling should've hired more reliable help."

"He's raving. Take him away." Mitchel was trembling now. Gone was the confident man Wolfe had known for so many years.

"Okay." Alvarez took Wolfe by the elbow, steered him toward an unmarked Ford Taurus. He opened the back.

"Cuff him."

"You do your job, Dwight and I'll do mine," Alvarez said.

"He's under arrest!"

"We'll sort it out down at the station," Alvarez said. Then to Wolfe. "You can get yourself out of this?"

"Yeah."

"Okay, how about we call the uniforms." Alvarez pulled Wolfe away from the unmarked. "You can ride along with them and me and Norton will ride on down with Dwight and see what we learn along the way."

"No!" Mitchel started to back away.

"I wouldn't, sir." Norton grabbed him, spun him around and cuffed him. He did it fast.

"Not bad for a man with a bad leg," Alvarez said.

"Take these off!" Mitchel commanded.

"I heard the word frame," Norton said.

"He's lying. Who are you gonna believe, him or me?"

"Actually, him," Norton said.

"I'm a California State Senator."

"Which is why I'm going to be very gentle with you," Alvarez said.

An airport black-and-white cruiser pulled up behind the unmarked. The uniforms got out.

"We need you to transport this man to Long Beach PD." Alvarez showed his shield. "You can follow us on down."

A few minutes later, Wolfe slid into the back seat and one of the uniforms closed the door after him. At least he wasn't wearing handcuffs. But he was a prisoner none the less, as the door had no handles and he was separated from the officers in front by a strong wire mesh.

Alvarez and Norton had put their careers on the line for him, but he'd've done the same if the situation had been reversed. They'd been sent out to arrest him, but after hearing only a few words of his story and seeing Dwight's reaction, they cuffed Mitchel instead.

Wolfe looked out the window at the airport traffic as they pulled away from the curb. Norton was driving the unmarked. Alvarez was in back with Mitchel. Wolfe frowned. Alvarez liked to move in close, in a frightening sort of way. He'd gotten more than one confession before he arrived at the station with a suspect. But Mitchel was no terrified husband who'd killed his wife in a jealous rage. He was as cool as they come. He knew the law, knew police procedure. It would take a lot more than handcuffs and a ride to the station to make him say anything he didn't want to.

He was about to sit back and rest when he saw him. Brody. The man he'd seen on *Shogun* as they passed going in opposite directions in St. Lucia.

"Stop!" Wolfe called out.

"Not till we get to Long Beach," the uniform riding shotgun said.

"That's one of them!" Wolfe said. Then he saw Beth. Brody was following her.

* * *

Beth felt someone looking, turned and saw Wolfe waving from the back of a police car slowly moving through the airport traffic. He was trying to say something, but she couldn't tell what. She wanted to run up to the car, open the door, but all that would accomplish would be to get her a ride to jail, too. He was pointing back the way she'd come. She spread her arms to say she didn't understand as the black-and-white moved away with the traffic.

She turned to the way he'd been pointing.

"Looking for someone?" Brody grabbed her arm just above the elbow.

"What are you doing here?"

"Thought I went down with the ship?" He squeezed. It hurt.

"No, I, I don't know."

"Don't talk. I've got a silenced pistol in my hand. Do you believe me?"

She looked. He was wearing dark slacks and a loose fitting corduroy sport coat with a white shirt, open at the collar. A casually dressed business man. One hand was wrapped around her arm, the other was inside the coat. She had no doubt it was holding a gun.

"So you know where the diamonds are, after all."

"I don't know what you're talking about."

"We'll see." He pulled her into the traffic, weaving between cars, toward the multi level parking structure on the opposite side of the road that circled through the airport.

A car honked. He jerked her past it.

"Watch where you're going!" the driver hollered as he went by. She was about to shout out, but his fingers dug into her arm. He'd shoot her right here, in the middle of the road. She knew he would.

Across the street, he pulled her toward the parking lot. What was he going to do with her? How'd he get here?

"The black van over there." He was still squeezing. She tried to pull away, couldn't.

"Hey!" The scream echoed through the parking lot as a blur of red and white careened into Brody, knocking him over. "Come on, lady." The kid that had sold her the hot dog grabbed her hand, jerked her away. "The stairway!"

Beth ran after him without a thought. The stairway seemed so far away. Then the rear window of a car in front of her shattered. She dropped to the concrete as something slammed into the headlight of another car.

"Stay down!" the kid screamed. "Come to me!"

Beth looked up. The stairway door was open, but she couldn't see the kid. He must be on the ground holding it for her.

"Hurry lady!"

Beth started crawling.

Another car window shattered. Brody said the gun had a silencer on it. That's why she wasn't hearing it go off.

She crawled forward, through the shattered headlight glass. A shard pierced her palm, shooting pain up her arm. Blood smeared the concrete under her hand leaving a grisly trail.

Two more thuds into the car ahead. He was still shooting.

"Police, throw down your weapon," the kid yelled and the shooting stopped. "Hurry!" he urged. The kid had fooled Brody.

Beth didn't need to be told twice. She sprang to her feet, ran between parked cars. He was on the ground, holding the door for her.

"Move it!" he said.

Beth dashed through the door. He jumped into the stairwell after her and a shot slammed into the door even as he was closing it.

"Up the stairs, my car's on the roof."

Beth took the steps two at a time, hand on the rail, legs pumping like pistons. At the first floor she heard the door open below.

"Lizzy!" Brody screamed. A piece of the wall ahead exploded, raining concrete. He was shooting from below. Two more floors. She pumped her legs faster.

"Hurry!" the hot dog kid shouted.

She was doing her best. More concrete blasted off the wall. A flying chip nicked her in the back of the hand. Now it was bleeding from both sides. The pain was huge, but she had no time for it. She passed the third floor, breath ragged now. One floor to go.

Two more shots. They weren't as quiet now, the silencer wasn't working as well as it had before. Another shot. But no blast of concrete.

"Run!" The kid shouted and Beth understood. Brody was shooting at the kid. He wanted her alive. He needed her to get to the diamonds.

She came to the top, burst through the door, the kid right behind.

"Other side of the lot." The kid charged ahead of her.

She stayed on his heels. The lot was so big. Brody would be on the roof long before they crossed it. She didn't see how they could make it. But seconds later the kid was fumbling a key into a beat up old Ford and they hadn't been shot at. Maybe Brody had given up.

"Get in." He pushed her behind the wheel. She slid over and he jumped in, keyed the ignition and the car rumbled to life. It sounded like a tank, but then he revved it up and it sounded like a hot rod. She laughed. A hot rod for the hot dog kid.

"What's so funny?" He squealed the tires as he backed out of the space.

"Nothing, everything. We made it."

"Not yet. He's most likely waiting below."

"You think?"

But the kid didn't answer. Instead, he shifted gears, gunned the Ford, popped the clutch and started for the down ramp with the wheels spinning, fishtailing between the park cars. Beth was sure he was going to crash into the wall, but he whipped the wheel around and entered the ramp at a speed way too fast to be safe.

"Oh shit!" she yelled as the rear bumper ricocheted off the wall. They corkscrewed down the ramp even faster then he'd accelerated toward it. The unmuffled Ford reverberated through the ramp like automatic gunfire. One floor, two, three, she was on a wild ride. She braced herself for a collision, because any second she expected they'd crash into a car going down ahead of them, but it didn't happen. They shot out of the ramp and into the airport traffic as if the way had been cleared for them.

"See him?" the kid said.

"No."

The kid stayed with the flow of traffic, slowed for the toll booth leaving the airport. Beth was apprehensive, she half expected Brody to jump in the car while the kid was paying the toll, but it didn't happen. Out of the airport the kid lost no time getting on the freeway, where she finally felt safe.

"That was one mean mother," the kid said.

"Yeah, he was." She leaned back, but she couldn't relax. "Who are you? Why'd you help me?"

"My name's Kevin, but I changed it to Flash on account of the Wolfman called me that when he bought a hot dog awhile back. I like the name. It's cool. So I figured I owe him one for sticking it on me. That's why I helped you. I'd a busted him away from the cops if I could, but that woulda been stupid. Why are they after him? And don't say it's 'cause he killed those folks. The Wolfman's no killer. He don't even carry a gun."

"How do you know that?"

"I can spot a guy with a gun a mile away. It's a talent I got. I spotted the gun the Ghostman had right off and made him for a cop. The Wolfman fooled me, though, 'cause he wasn't carrying. He's too cool for that."

"But how'd you know to help me?"

"I just told you. I can spot a gun. I followed you guys out of the terminal and I saw the cops take the Wolfman. You walked away, but this dude followed you. He had a gun and he wasn't no cop. So when he grabbed you, I knocked him down and here we are."

"I'm going to Long Beach."

"You got it." Then, "You wanna tell me what's going on?"

"How old are you?"

"Sixteen."

"You got a gun?"

"What kinda question is that? You think cuz I'm black that I carry?"

"I was hoping."

"Sheeet." He eased the Ford into the fast lane.

"I need to get to a phone."

"That, I got." He reached over, popped the glove box. "Just push the number an' hit send."

She punched Nick Nesbitt's phone number, but got no answer, not even a machine. She tried again, same result.

"Now I'm in trouble."

"What?"

"I was supposed to call a TV reporter. He was going to help me get Wolfe out of jail."

"Tell me. I'll help."

"It's about diamonds." She didn't know why, but she felt she could trust him, so as they tore up the miles in Kevin's hot rod Ford, she told him everything.

"So we're gonna break into the college in the middle of the night, find ten million dollars of diamonds an' take 'em to the police station so they'll let the Wolfman out of jail?"

"That's about the size of it."

"Cool." He took a deep breath, threw his shoulders back, sat up straight and stretched a hand toward her, palm upward.

She slapped it.

Chapter
Twenty-Five

"Stop the car!" Wolfe shouted as soon as he spotted the man following Beth.

"Not till we get where we're going," the cop riding shotgun said.

"There's a man following my wife!" Wolfe felt like he was going to explode.

"Right," the cop said.

"At least call Detective Norton."

"You can talk to him when we get to Long Beach," the cop said.

"My wife's in danger." They were past her now. He couldn't see her anymore. "The man's tried to hurt her before. She needs help."

"Why don't you sit back and pipe down? You can tell the detectives all about it later."

Wolfe wanted to scream, but he held it in. There was nothing he could say to persuade these men. They'd heard it all. He balled his fists, because he had too.

How Brody had survived the seas off Grenada, Wolfe couldn't fathom. But why he was in Los Angeles was obvious. The diamonds. There was nothing he could do right now, but maybe it wasn't that bad. The man wanted the diamonds. He'd follow Beth till she led him to them, he wouldn't hurt her till he had them in hand.

Beth had to rent a car, so she'd be in the airport a few more minutes. Then she had to call Nick, that would take more time. Once they arrived in Long Beach, he'd tell Norton. Norton would believe him. He had time. He prayed it was true.

* * *

Beth couldn't get Brody out of her mind. She'd known he was an excellent swimmer, but even so, to swim to shore through those seas was a superhuman feat. Then to come here. He must have known about the diamonds all along. He never was going to let her go once they'd gotten back to Trinidad. He was going to get her to sign the boat over to him, then he was going to use her to get the diamonds Frank had stolen. Brody wouldn't give up. He'd be more determined than ever, now that the bulk of the diamonds were at the bottom of the ocean.

She turned, looked out the back window as Kevin took the Bellflower off ramp in Long Beach. They were almost there.

"Ain't nobody following," Kevin said. "I been checking."

"You're real sure, Kevin?"

" 'Course I'm sure. And don't call me Kevin. I'm doing this cuz of my new name."

"Okay, Flash."

"More like it." Kevin stopped for a light. "Middle of the night." He looked both ways, ran it. "School's just up ahead."

"I know."

"We got a plan?"

"Get the diamonds, get away, go to the cops, get Wolfe out of jail. In that order."

"That's it? That's your plan?" Kevin turned left onto the campus road.

"Go straight, park behind the book store, we'll walk across the campus from there."

Kevin obeyed, parked between a new Ford pickup and a small red sports car. "What are all the cars doing here?"

"It's Friday night. The Forty Niner's open late."

"What's that?"

"A bar."

"You got a bar in the school?"

"Yeah."

"How you get any schoolwork done?"

"Some people don't." She looked over to the Forty Niner as they passed. Loud music came from inside. A band not a juke. Someone singing 'Honky Tonk Woman.' A young couple was making out at one of the picnic tables in front of the bar. Other than them, the place was deserted, save for the raucous sounds of the Stones copy band. There were no lights outside, the place was dark.

"Over there." She pointed to the Language Arts building on the other side of the quad. There were low hanging clouds, blocking out most of the moonlight. Trees swaying in the slight breeze appeared ghostly.

"This is spooky," Kevin said.

"Yeah."

"How we gonna get the diamonds?"

"I know where the locker is. I know the combination. It won't be hard."

"What if the building's locked up?"

"They have night classes. Afterward the night crew cleans them. They don't lock the doors till they're finished. And they always finish late on Fridays."

"How do you know?"

"The bar's open."

"You know a lot about this place."

"I used to live here."

"What do you mean?"

"In the dorms. I went to school here."

The band took a break and all of a sudden quiet ruled the campus. They started across the quad. Leaves rustling in the elm and eucalyptus trees now seemed loud. The quiet noise sent tingles chilling along her skin. It was as if she were walking in a cemetery after dark.

* * *

Wolfe wanted to strangle the two uniforms, but he was helpless in the back of the unit. He choked back a scream as they pulled up alongside Alvarez and Norton in the police parking lot.

"The girl at the airport," Wolfe said as Norton was getting out of the unmarked. "She's my wife."

"Congratulations," Norton said.

"I saw someone from the islands following her when we drove away from the airport. He's going to hurt her."

"Let's go." Norton slid back into the car as Alvarez pulled Mitchel out of the other side.

Wolfe ran around to the passenger side, met Alvarez leading Mitchel away from the car.

"Get out of here." Alvarez gave Mitchel a push. "I'll take care of things here."

"I owe you guys." Wolfe jumped in the car.

"Big time, Billy." Alvarez said something else, too, but Wolfe didn't hear, because Norton was spinning the wheels in reverse as he backed out of the parking space.

"Where we going?" Norton pulled the transmission into drive and shot between the parked cars toward the exit.

"Cal State Long Beach, the Language Arts building."

Norton squealed the tires out of the parking lot in a screeching left turn, burning rubber halfway down the block. He made another left on Ocean without taking his foot off the accelerator. The bullet in the leg may have slowed him down on foot, but it hadn't affected his driving. He was still the craziest driver on the force and right now, Wolfe was glad about his obsession with speed.

"Siren?" Wolfe said.

"This is Alvarez' car. Don't have one."

"And he let's you drive?" So Alvarez got the new Impala.

"Yeah."

Wolfe caught the albino's smile as approaching headlights reflected off his ghost-white face. His window was down, his hair, whiter than any diamond, whipped around his head. His upper lip was curled, not a sneer, something else. He looked maniacal.

"Car still has that new smell."

"Brand new . Alvarez loves this baby."

"And he let's you drive?" Wolfe said again.

"We're partners." Norton busted through a red light on Atlantic without looking. He really was crazy when he was behind the wheel.

"Jesus Christ!" Wolfe said as Norton cranked the wheel to avoid an old Volkswagen Beetle making a left onto Ocean. "You almost killed that guy."

"We had all the room in the world." Norton still had that skeleton grin on his ghostly face.

"Inches, if that."

"We made it."

"Yeah." Wolfe sighed. "We did." Now the only question in his mind was would they get to the college and Beth before she got the diamonds and Brody got her?

* * *

Halfway across the quad, Kevin jumped back. "What the heck was that?" He whispered loud.

"Cat, they're all over the campus. Come on." She quick walked across the rest of the quad, stopped at the entrance to the Language Arts building. She tried the door. It opened. "Told you."

"Let's get this over with." He was shaking.

"You don't have to be nervous. There's nobody here." Beth couldn't blame him, she was shaking too. Sweat dribbled from under her arms. Her hair was thick with it.

"Man, I don't even know what I'm doing here."

"It's upstairs." She took the stairway to the right.

"My momma always told me to mind my own business, but did I ever listen? Noooo." He couldn't be that scared if he could make a joke.

At the top of the stairs she was confronted with a dark corridor. She felt like the walls were closing in. Her palms were sweating now. She felt cold.

"It's too dark. We shoulda brought a flashlight." Vertigo seemed to overtake her. It was like when she was under the boat out in the middle of the ocean. She was so scared and there wasn't anything she could do about it. "We can't do anything tonight. We should go."

All of a sudden he had a flame in his hand. She gasped, calmed herself when she smelled the lighter fluid.

"No flashlight, but I got my Zippo."

"You scared me."

"It ain't me doing the scaring around here. Which locker?"

"Other end of the hall."

They took slow steps, moved side by side. She heard no sound, save for his breathing and her own panting heart.

"You're not really scared, are you?" He whispered.

"Terrified."

"Good," he said. "cuz I thought it was just me."

"Here." She stopped at a locker.

"Just like back in high school," he said.

"You're not old enough to have finished high school," Beth said.

"Sure I am. Got a high IQ, graduated last year."

"At sixteen?" She turned away from the locker. His face was dark, sweat glistening in the reflection of the Zippo's flame.

"Yeah. Straight A's, a four-point-oh average." He puffed out his chest.

"Really?" Beth looked into his black eyes. "So how come you're out at the airport selling hot dogs and not in college? Surely you must've been offered a scholarship."

"I was offered lots, but I gotta help my mom raise three little girls."

"Selling hot dogs?"

"See this shirt. The red and white strips mean you're buying a Flash Dog. That's the name of my business now, thanks to the Wolfman. I got eleven carts at the airport. I rent the space, supply the carts, find the dog men and split the profit. I'm like an entrepreneur."

"I'm impressed."

"And I'm still scared. Let's get those diamonds and get away from this place."

"Yeah." She turned back toward the locker. "Can you shine that fire on the lock?"

He did.

She felt the heat of the flame as she spun the lock. It opened on the first try. She took the combination lock off, held it tight in her right hand as she opened the locker. Books on the bottom, Frank's gym bag on top. She picked it up.

"How's it feel?" Kevin said.

"Heavy."

"Heavy is how it's supposed to feel." Victor Drake's voice rang out through the dark corridor. Then her face was bathed in light.

* * *

Wolfe tried to pull his seatbelt on as Norton took the corner from Second Street onto Studebaker Road, on two wheels, without downshifting, without slowing. The centrifugal force threw him against the door and for a moment, as he struggled with the belt, he was certain they were going over, but the car slammed down on all fours with a fishtailing lurch to the opposite side of the road.

"You're going to hit the truck!" Wolfe shouted.

Norton spun the wheel away from an oncoming tanker truck. Wolfe braced for an explosion as the tanker's front bumper ripped along the driver's side of Alvarez' Chevy. And then they were past it with Norton's foot still on the floor. Wolfe spun his head around. He didn't think Alverez would be selling him that Toyota, after all.

"It's a milk truck!"

Norton didn't seem to hear. Wolfe leaned over, looked at the speedometer. Ninety-five and climbing. It was as if Norton was the heart of the car, one with the machine. If anybody could get him to Beth in time, he could.

* * *

"Victor, what are you doing here?" But Beth knew as soon as the words left her lips. He'd been behind the sabotage on *Shogun*. He'd been using Noelle to get information and working with Brody all along. "Why?"

"The money. Why else?"

"That's not what I meant." She tightened her fist around the lock. Don't miss, she told herself. "I wanted to know why you drug it out so long. How come you just didn't throw us overboard and take the boat the first chance you got?"

"Ten million and one reasons." He sounded so smug. "I wanted to know what Frank did with the diamonds he stole."

"And the other reason." She could barely see his face above and to the left of the flashlight. He had a gun in his other hand.

"Noelle."

"Stay away from her."

"Or what?"

Kevin reached out to take her hand, felt the balled fist and the lock. "Oh, shit!" He started shaking, fell to the floor, dropped the Zippo and the flame flicked out. He was having a seizure.

"What?" Victor turned the gun on the kid.

Beth brought her arm back. It had been so many years since she'd played ball. Please, God, let me not miss.

She screamed as she threw it.

Victor's gun went off. The light fell, hit the floor, went out.

Kevin was up in an instant, the Zippo flaming again. "Faked him out good." He grabbed the bag from her, held the Zippo aloft with his other hand. "Let's go."

"Right behind you."

Kevin dashed down the hall with the lighter burning in his raised hand like the Olympic torch. Beth charged after him.

A shot rang out, thunder loud in the dark corridor.

"Down." Kevin snapped the lighter closed and all of a sudden the place was pitch dark.

Beth dropped to the floor, began crawling to the end of the corridor. She heard Kevin in front. He was on the ground too. Another shot. The bullet flew overhead, pounded into the wall at the end of the corridor.

"I'm at the stairs," Kevin said, a shouted whisper.

"You can't get away Beth." Victor's cultured British accent was gone now, his accent pure Trinidadian. "If you drop the diamonds, I won't come after you."

Beth was at the stairs. Still on her belly, she slithered around the stairwell. Another shot rang out.

Glass shattered. She grabbed the banister, pulled herself to her feet.

"I shoulda grabbed his gun!" Kevin said. She couldn't see him in the dark, but she caught the tension in his voice.

"Get going, you don't have to wait for me."

"Yeah I do. But we're going now. Stay with me."

"Go."

Kevin started down the stairs. She wished he'd move faster, but it was too dark to see. And she wondered why Victor hadn't come after them. Maybe he was too hurt to get up.

"We're almost there," Kevin said. "We're gonna make it."

Then they were on the first floor. Moonlight cascaded in the window on the double doors, illuminating the sheen of sweat that covered Kevin's face. He didn't look like a kid now, more a soldier about to face enemy fire.

"Okay," he said. "We bust outta here at a full out run and charge across that grassy space toward that bar. If anyone is after us, we go inside with all the people, cuz people mean protection. But if it's clear, we get in that car of mine and we ride."

"You're a born leader, Kevin."

"Call me Flash, cuz that's how fast I'm gonna be moving, once we get outside."

"Okay, Flash, let's do it."

They pushed through the double doors together.

"Hold it or I shoot him!" Brody grabbed Kevin as soon has he'd gone through the door. Beth stopped, turned toward his voice. He had a gun to Kevin's head. "Lizzy, Lizzy, Lizzy, did you really think you could get away from me?"

* * *

Norton, foot still on the floor, spun the car off Pacific Coast Highway and onto the campus. The road was dark. Giant trees lined the road, casting moon shadows—grotesque soldiers in the night, lit up for an instant as they flew by in Alvarez' brand new, battered Chevy Impala.

"Road ends!" Wolfe shouted.

"See it." Norton careened the Impala through a left turn, slamming the right wheels into the curb, the sound of rubber shrieking along concrete, echoing loud as Norton fought for control.

"Can you get it back?" Wolfe was frightened. They were so close, to wreck the car now was unthinkable.

"Trying." Norton spun the wheel to the left and the car screeched to the other side of the two lane street, jumped the curb and kept going.

"Tree!" Wolfe shouted.

"Yeah, yeah." Norton jerked the wheel back to the right, but not in time. The car ricocheted off it and was heading headlong for another.

"Do something!"

"Doing it!" Norton shouted back as he wrestled with the wheel. They missed the next tree, but Wolfe heard the pop as the side mirror was ripped from the car. Alvarez' Chevy was never going to be the same.

"Get it on the road!"

"I'm trying." Norton pulled the wheel to the right and the car jumped the curb. They were back on the road, but only for an instant as they jumped the curb opposite and all of a sudden they were speeding down the sidewalk between the campus bookstore and the Forty Niner pub.

"The Language Building is on the opposite side of the quad," Norton yelled.

"How do you know that?"

"I had a case here a while back. I know the whole place."

"There!" Wolfe shouted. The three people were lit up by the Chevy's lights. "He's got a gun."

"Hold on!" Norton hit the horn, clicked on the brights and aimed the car right for the group.

"You'll kill them."

"They'll jump out of the way."

The man pushed Beth away, pointed the gun toward the charging Chevy. Three bullets ripped through the windshield. Instantly they were blinded, the window full of spider web like cracks, but Norton kept his foot on the floor.

Wolfe felt the impact, a loud thud, as the Chevy took the man in the chest and rolled over him.

Finally Norton pulled his foot from the accelerator, jammed it on the brakes. "There's a throw down in the glove box!" He shouted.

Wolfe popped the box, took out a thirty-eight as Norton cranked the wheel, then he rolled out of the car as Norton fishtailed it to a stop.

"Beth!"

"There's another one." Beth pointed to the Language Building.

A man burst through the double doors. Wolfe recognized Victor Drake immediately, saw the gun in his hand as Victor trained it on Beth. Wolfe fired, missed with the first shot. Victor turned, bringing the gun around toward Wolfe. Wolfe fired again, Caught Drake in the chest. He pumped two more rounds into him.

Then it was quiet.

"You okay?" Wolfe asked Beth.

"Yeah, thanks to the Flash here."

"You?" Wolfe recognized the hot dog kid.

"So I guess we don't have to bring the diamonds to the police station to rescue you," the kid said.

"Guess not," Wolfe said.

"Ten million dollars," Kevin said. "I don't think you should give those diamonds to the cops. Lot's of brothers in Africa died for 'em. We should figure out a way to use the money to help them out."

"The kid has a point," Norton said. "You turn 'em in, they're just gonna get caught up in the system. Besides, you don't need them to get off the hook. Alvarez broke Mitchel on the Freeway. He told us everything."

"What?" Wolfe said.

"He cried like the baby he is."

"What did Jesse do?" Wolfe said.

"Let's just say that Mitchel has a low threshold for pain."

"What about Sterling? Is he going down?"

"No." Norton said. "Mitchel never had direct contact with Sterling. It was all done through Mark Skidmore. As far as Mitchel can prove, Skidmore was blowing smoke whenever he talked about Sterling."

"But he's guilty," Beth said. "He should go to jail."

"He's a United States Senator," Wolfe said. "They don't go to jail."

"They don't get the diamonds either," Kevin said. "Not if you don't turn 'em in."

"Keep 'em," Norton said. "Do what the kid wants."

"We could set up a non profit foundation," Kevin said. "We could even raise more money."

"Would you get a load of this kid?" Wolfe said.

"He's a business man," Beth said.

"I'm an entrepreneur," Kevin said.

Epilogue

"Hey, T-Bone, you seen my brother?" Arlie shouted out as he jumped out of the way of a runaway football. There were so many kids in the refuge camp now. It seemed everywhere he turned some kind of ball game was in progress.

"He's off somewhere with the doctor." T-Bone checked his watch. "Probably planning someplace for me to dig another latrine. She hasn't got it through her thick head that I'm supposed to be the supervisor. I'm telling you Arlie—"

"I know, don't ever get married." Arlie laughed. Dr. Noelle and T-Bone had only been in the camp for a couple of months and already they were running things. The soldiers in the blue helmets liked to think they were in charge, but when it came to getting anything done, it was T-Bone and his wife Dr. Noelle everybody turned to.

"Tomorrow's the big day," T-Bone said.

"Yeah." A shiver rippled through Arlie. Tomorrow, he, his brother Kennedy, his sisters and his mother, were getting on an airplane and going to California.

"My man!" Kevin shouted as he came out of the administration tent. Arlie had only met Kevin, who liked to be called Flash, yesterday, and liked him immediately. Kevin was going to be escorting them to America.

"Flashman." Arlie held out his hand and Kevin shook it. "Tell me again about the horses."

"Don't you ever get enough?" Kevin laughed.

"Not till my feet are on the ground in America," Arlie said. Kevin had spent most of last night telling him about the horse ranch that the ex-policeman and his wife owned. How they were going to make a home for him and his family. How they were going to be Americans along with three other girls in the camp that had no parents. To think, the policeman Wolfe might have bought that ranch with the very diamonds he and Kennedy had been forced to dig up from the river bottom. He smiled. "We earned this chance in America, me and Kennedy."

"Yes you did, boy," Kevin said. "You certainly did."

"Maybe there is a God after all." Arlie held his hand out, palm up the way Kevin had taught him.

"Who knows? Maybe there is." Kevin slapped his hand.

THE BOOTLEG PRESS CATALOG

RAGGED MAN by Jack Priest
BOOTLEG 001 — ISBN: 0974524603
   Unknown to Rick Gordon, he brought an ancient aboriginal horror home from the Australian desert. Now his friends are dying and Rick is getting the blame.

DESPERATION MOON by Ken Douglas
BOOTLEG 002 — ISBN: 0974524611
   Sara Hackett must save two little girls from dangerous kidnappers, but she doesn't have the money to pay the ransom.

SCORPION by Jack Stewart
BOOTLEG 003 — ISBN: 097452462x
   DEA agent Bill Broxton must protect the Prime Minister of Trinidad from an assassin, but he doesn't know the killer is his fiancée.

DEAD RINGER by Ken Douglas
BOOTLEG 004 — ISBN: 0974524638
   Maggie Nesbitt steps out of her dull life and into her dead twin's, and now the man that killed her sister is after Maggie.

GECKO by Jack Priest
BOOTLEG 005—ISBN: 0974524646
   Jim Monday must rescue his wife from an evil worse than death before the Gecko horror of Maori legend kills them both.

RUNNING SCARED by Ken Douglas
BOOTLEG 006 — ISBN: 0974524654
   Joey Sapphire's husband blackmailed and now is out to kill the president's daughter and only Joey can save the young woman.

NIGHT WITCH by Jack Priest
BOOTLEG 007 — ISBN: 0974524662
A vampire like creature followed Carolina's father back from the Caribbean and now it is terrorizing her. She and her friend Arty are only children, but they must fight this creature themselves or die.

HURRICANE BY JACK STEWART
BOOTLEG 008 — ISBN: 0974524670
Julie Tanaka flees Trinidad on her sailboat after the death of her husband, but the boat has a drug lord's money aboard and DEA agent Bill Broxton must get to her first or she is dead.

TANGERINE DREAM by Ken Douglas and Jack Stewart
BOOTLEG 009 — ISBN: 0974524689
Seagoing writer and gourmet chef Captain Katie Osborne said of this book, "Incest, death, tragedy, betrayal and teenage homosexual love, I don't know how, but somehow it all works. I was up all night reading."

DIAMOND SKY by Ken Douglas and Jack Stewart
BOOTLEG 012 — ISBN: 0974524697
The Russian Mafia is after Beth Shannon. Their diamonds have been stolen and they think she knows where they are. She does, only she doesn't know it.

BOOTLEG BOOKS ARE BETTER THAN T.V.

THE BOOTLEG PRESS STORY

We at Bootleg Press are a small group of writers who were brought together by pen and sea. We have all been members of either the St. Martin or Trinidad Cruising Writer's Groups in the Caribbean.

We share our thoughts, plot ideas, villains and heroes. That's why you'll see some borrowed characters, both minor and major, cross from one author's book to another's.

Also, you'll see a few similar scenes that seem to jump from one author's pages to another's. That's because both authors have collaborated on the scene and—both liking how it worked out—both decided to use it.

At what point does an author's idea truly become his own? That's a good question, but rest assured in the rare occasions where you may discover similar scenes in Bootleg Press Books, that it is not stealing. Writing is a solitary art, but sometimes it is possible to share the load.

Book writing is hard, but book selling is harder. We think our books are as good as any you'll find out there, but breaking into the New York publishing market is tough, especially if you live far away from the Big Apple.

So, we've all either sold or put our boats on the hard, pooled our money and started our own company. We bought cars and loaded our trunks with books. We call on small independent bookstores ourselves, as we are our own distributors. But the few of us cannot possibly reach the whole world, however we are trying, so if you don't see our books in your local bookstore yet, remember you can always order them from the big guys online.

Thank you from everyone at Bootleg Books for reading and please remember, Bootleg Books are better than T.V.

KEN DOUGLAS
& VESTA IRENE
WANGARAI, NEW ZEALAND

Printed in the United States
22766LVS00001B/38

9 780974 524696